THE PRESERVATION OF SPECIES

PART I

RULE OF EXTINCTION

PART II

STRUGGLE FOR EXISTENCE

PART III

BEASTS OF PREY

THE PRESERVATION OF SPECIES

As a civilization-ending comet approached Earth, several thousand mysterious pods landed in North America. Desperate to escape the end of the world, David Williams climbed into one with his children. The pod opened on an island inhabited by prehistoric creatures.

David found a handful of other survivors, including Sierra Preston, who helped him defeat a tyrannical madman and capture an alien creature that had been secretly observing the group.

The alien demanded to be released. It claimed the comet was deliberately sent by something called *gorgers* and revealed that the remaining people from Earth were being kept in storage ...

THE PRESERVATION OF SPECIES

PART II

STRUGGLE FOR EXISTENCE

GEOFF JONES

For Shannon

STRUGGLE FOR EXISTENCE

During the constantly-recurring struggle for existence,
we see a powerful and ever-acting form of selection.

– Charles Darwin

WATER FALL

Chapter One

"We just made first contact," Sierra Preston said. She looked at the nineteen people standing around the alien creature. Her heart raced. They'd been studying the alien's lifeless body, preparing to dissect it.

Then it began to speak.

The bloated creature reminded her of fat sea lions loafing along the harbor near Venice Beach, except the alien didn't have any fins or flippers. Its only real features were spidery appendages protruding from folds of skin at one end.

The alien's rumbles had come from somewhere in those flaps, and had been translated by its vehicle, which sat a few yards away. After a short exchange, the creature had grown silent.

"We should go over everything we learned," David said, standing with his kids, Kim and Barry. "Make sure we didn't miss anything." He spoke calmly and clinically.

Sierra wasn't sure if that was his doctor voice or his dad voice, but either way, she appreciated it. She trusted David more than anyone else in the group.

Several heads nodded in the small crowd.

"It claimed that the rest of the people who got into pods are in storage," Sierra said. "What does that mean? Are they in a holding pen somewhere?"

"I suspect they're in suspended animation," Priya said.

Priya was an astronomer and a bit of a nerd. Sierra loved her for it. Nobody could figure shit out as well as Priya.

"Like those of us from the other island," David said.

Priya nodded. "Bingo."

Sierra shivered. Everyone here had climbed into van-sized pods that showed up on Earth right before a comet wiped out the planet. The pods had brought them to a chain of islands in what turned out to be a giant wildlife preserve, but some pods had opened months earlier than others. Sierra's inability to account for the missing time unnerved her. "We have to find them," she said. "Wherever they are."

David's six-year-old son looked up, his eyes wide. "Is Mommy there?"

"I don't know, Barry," he answered. "Maybe."

Kim, Barry's twelve-year-old sister, shook her head. "Don't get your hopes up," she whispered, her lips trembling. "There were only a few thousand pods."

David pulled his daughter close.

Many people in the group held out hope that their loved ones had made it into pods. Sierra clenched her jaw. She had no such delusions. She'd seen her father's body at a suicide party. Or at least, she'd seen the body of the man she believed was her father.

She turned to Priya. "The alien said that the Ender was deliberately launched at Earth. I thought it was just a random comet. Was there any evidence that was an attack?"

Priya shrugged. "No, but I don't know how we could have known."

"Gorgers," David said. "The alien claimed the comet was sent by something called gorgers."

"What does that mean?" Kim asked. "Is it like a river gorge or something?"

"I assume it's a play on the verb, not the noun," Priya said. "A reference to feeding, gorging yourself."

"I'll tell you what it means," Cameron said from the other side of the alien. "It means there's something out there even worse than this sack of shit." She prodded the creature with the barrel of her gun. It didn't respond.

Cameron had been in the Army, but she came off more like a loose cannon than a trained soldier. Sierra didn't exactly trust her, but she was glad to have her in the group.

"Why would these gorger things want to destroy Earth?" Sierra asked.

"Maybe they saw humans as a threat," Reggie said. He and Sierra were two of the only three Black people in the group. He gave her a cold look. "Maybe they noticed how awful people were getting to be and decided a pre-emptive strike was in order."

Sierra had been raised by a rich white Hollywood executive and was the first to admit she'd had it easier than most. She wasn't blind to humanity's shortcomings. She'd seen plenty of terrible things over her twenty-three years, and plenty more in the past few weeks on the islands.

"They can't write off our species because of a few horrible people," she said. "And neither can we."

"Are you sure about that?" Reggie took off his baseball cap and rubbed his bald head. "I'm just saying, we got a decent group now. If we get those people out of storage, how do you know we won't end up with another Thad or another Joe?"

Murmurs came from the crowd.

"You're right," Sierra said. "We've got a good group and we've learned a lot. We need to build on that. We need to find more good people. If we end up with someone else who puts that at risk, we'll deal with him."

Reggie pressed his lips together and lowered his eyes. Like everyone else, he'd lost someone in recent days, but it seemed as if his trauma ran deeper.

Sierra looked around. "We're all that's left. Twenty people. If we don't get the other survivors out of storage, humanity is over."

Waldmire gestured at the alien. "This thing called itself a caretaker, which would imply some degree of benevolence. If it saved us from the gorgers, doesn't that make it an ally?"

Several people whispered in agreement. Waldmire was one of the oldest members of the group and everyone seemed to appreciate his measured opinions.

He'd been Sierra's neighbor in California and she'd known him all her life. He'd been like an uncle, always there, across the street. A few days earlier, one of the villagers had mistaken Waldmire for her father. Now she wondered if it might be true.

"I wouldn't trust this thing any farther than I could kick it," Cameron said.

"I think we should let it go," Priya said. "Put it back on its carriage and let it fly away."

"Yeah," one of the villagers called out.

"Fuck that," Cameron said. "We can't give up our only leverage."

"If we treat them like enemies, they'll only be enemies," Priya said.

"They did save us from extinction," Waldmire said. "That has to count for something."

"Not necessarily," David said. "They put us in a horrifying situation and then sat back and watched while people died."

David's comment brought a shameful quiet over the group. Many of them had also stood by and done nothing.

Sierra waited a moment before breaking the silence. "Figuring out how to operate the alien sled is our priority."

"Carriage," Priya corrected. "The caretaker called it a carriage."

"Whatever." Sierra turned to Morrie. "We have to learn how to fly that thing. It's our best bet for finding a way out of here."

Morrie nodded eagerly. Fresh-faced and red-headed, he was in his mid-twenties, though he barely looked seventeen. Morrie had been on the wrong side of everything that had gone down in the village, and now he was doing his best to make amends. He and Kim had been studying the alien's vehicle, which was about as big as a king-size bed. It could fly, turn invisible, and translate languages, but so far, they'd only managed to activate a light panel on the front console.

"Should we keep working on the raft?" Cameron asked. "If the rest of the people are off in storage somewhere, do we still need it?"

"Yes, absolutely," Sierra said. "We don't know how long it will take to figure out that sled. The raft is our next best way to search for answers. How big is this zoo? How do the aliens get in and out? What's on the other islands? There could even be another village somewhere."

She'd visited three islands, all of them populated with species from Earth, including dinosaurs and prehistoric mammals, but so far, this was the only one with any structures on it. An eight-foot perimeter wall circled a space the size of a baseball field, with a half-dozen simple buildings near the center.

"Don't forget about Randall," Cameron said. "He's still out there."

Randall had disappeared after Joe's reign of madness came to an end. Everyone believed he'd taken one of the canoes to a neighboring island.

"We can't waste time hunting him down," Sierra said. "We don't need to be vengeful."

"Speak for yourself," Cameron said. She patted her shoulder where Randall had shot her. "He needs to pay."

Sierra wanted to agree with her. Randall was responsible for what had happened to Josh, a teenage boy she'd saved from the Ender.

"Finding a way out of here needs to take priority," she said. "If you happen to run into Randall ..." She shrugged and let the sentence hang, unfinished.

Cameron nodded. "Well then, we should get to work while we still have light."

Roughly two thousand feet above them, some sort of ceiling or dome cast flat blue light in the daytime, then turned pitch black at night. They saw no sun, no clouds, no stars, or moon.

Reggie clapped. "All right, everyone without an assignment is on dinosaur detail." He'd overseen the disposal of the first Tyrannosaurus. The remains of the second one still needed to be hacked up and burned.

"Terrific," muttered one of the villagers.

"That thing's nasty," grumbled another.

"Come on," Reggie said. "Let's get it done before that ugly son-of-a-bitch stinks up the whole island."

Sierra wasn't looking forward to it any more than the rest of them, but she wanted to see it through. That Tyrannosaurus had killed Josh. The memory ripped her heart. She'd been right there when it happened.

Each night since then, she woke up soaked with sweat after reliving the moment, trying just a little harder to free him, and coming just a little closer, but it was never enough.

Each day, she tried to convince herself that she'd done everything she could.

David gestured at the alien. "Who's got watch duty this afternoon?"

Waldmire raised his hand.

The creature hadn't moved since it stopped talking. Sierra didn't think it could actually go anywhere, even if it wanted to. The appendages protruding from the end of its body weren't big enough to carry its bloated mass. They looked more like mouthparts or antennae than actual limbs. It might be able to flop around or something, but so far, it hadn't even tried.

"Give a whistle if it does anything," Sierra said. "Anything at all."

"What if its buddies come for it?" Waldmire asked.

"Let's not make it easy for them," Sierra said. "We should tie it down, like the sled." The alien's sled was anchored to nearby rocks and trees to prevent it from flying off.

"So your plan is to hold it captive in order to convince the aliens they shouldn't hold us captive?" Priya said. "That makes zero sense."

"They put us in cages," Sierra said. Scoffing, she added, "Cages filled with dinosaurs."

"They put us in a habitat with breathable air, clean water, and food. How do you know there's any place we could even live on their world?"

"How do you know there isn't?" Sierra asked.

Priya looked around and clomped her mouth shut. Everyone was watching, and Sierra knew she hated being the center of attention.

"We could have lived out our lives here without making contact, without even knowing they were watching us," Sierra said. "If we release that alien, there's nothing to stop that from happening." She squeezed the grip of her gun, holstered on her hip, hoping she sounded more confident than she felt. "I'm not willing to give up and accept our fate here. If they want their buddy back, they need to let us out and release everyone from storage."

Chapter Two

David Williams held a wooden spike onto the side of the raft while Cameron lashed it into place. Sharpened logs jutted everywhere, making the crude outrigger look like a giant wooden porcupine. Priya sat on the raised deck in the middle, weaving grass fronds to form the blade of a paddle.

The raft sat at the shoreline of the freshwater sea that surrounded the island. A hundred feet of powdery white sand stretched between the towering conifer forest and the calm turquoise water.

David told himself for the hundredth time that his kids were okay. He couldn't be with them every single moment and there were plenty of people watching out for them, especially now that they were the only children left.

Kim was helping Morrie study the alien carriage. David honestly thought she might be able to figure it out. She'd shown him a few tricks with the radios in his Cessna that his instructor hadn't known. Working on the carriage was good for her. It was helping her move on from what had happened.

Barry was playing with a little clique of women who seemed to use him as a coping mechanism, something to focus on other than the horrors of recent days. It gave David a break from the six-year-old's constant questions, not to mention his never-ending desire to count things.

As he worked on the raft, he caught himself staring more than once at the glistening skin on Cameron's long neck or the piercing sparkle in her eyes. He told himself it was nothing more than a harmless infatuation with an attractive woman, but then he would remember gazing at his wife like that and force himself to look away.

"We shouldn't be doing this," Priya said. "It's too dangerous. Not only that, it's a waste of time. The caretaker made it clear. The rest of the people are in storage."

Priya's jet-black hair was pulled tight in a knot, which made her seem even more serious than usual.

Cameron gave her a grim smile. "How do you know that alien was even telling the truth? The rest of the people might actually be on the other islands."

"There's no reason to think that," Priya said. "It stands to reason that the other islands are just habitats for more animals that will want to eat us."

"That's why we're using all the spikes," Cameron said.

David picked up another wooden stake and held it in place while Cameron fed him a vine rope. She smelled of salt and pine. Moving slowly to keep from torquing his bruised ribs, he wrapped the rope around the deck and handed it back to her.

She tapped his wedding ring. "You still wearing that, Ace? It's been months now." She held her head close to his, her lips partly open.

He raised an eyebrow. Cameron was many things, but she wasn't subtle. She really was beautiful, even with the scar running through her hair on one side. The fact that she was a little crazy somehow made her more attractive. Part of him wanted to run off in the woods with her.

David's wife, Lindsey, had been on the other side of town when the pods showed up and he hadn't been able to wait for her because a truck full of assholes had been shooting at him. Guilt soured his guts as he remembered climbing into the pod without her.

"I ... I still need time." For him, it didn't feel like months because his pod had only opened a few weeks ago. The time disparity made his head spin.

He wondered how long he should wait before he moved on. He wondered if he would ever be ready to move on. He wanted to believe his wife had found a pod, but it felt like too much to hope for.

He felt attracted to Cameron, and yet he missed Lindsey terribly. He missed her so much, even though they'd spent their final weeks arguing.

"Take whatever time you need, Ace," Cameron said. "I ain't going anywhere." She tilted her head seductively.

Priya chucked her paddle noisily onto the deck. "What else needs doing here?"

Cameron pointed to a pile of rocks they'd dragged to the beach on a woven mat. "Load those up for me."

"Really? Sticks and rocks? Against dinosaurs and aliens."

"You'd be surprised what you can do with sticks and rocks," Cameron said. "And sadly, we don't have much ammunition left."

Priya hefted the stones into a basket on the deck, two at a time. "This is pointless. We should just let the caretaker go before more of them come here and kill us."

"Those things are pretty reluctant to show themselves," David said. The aliens had only been spotted a handful of times, floating overhead and rendered nearly invisible by some sort of cloaking device. "For all we know, that could be the only one there is."

"We're playing with fire," Priya said. "They're way more advanced than us."

"Is that your scientific assessment?" Cameron asked with a mocking tone. "Why the hell didn't you tell us that thing was alive?"

Priya grabbed two larger rocks and threw them at the basket, hard enough to topple it and spill the rest onto the deck. "I'm sorry I don't have better answers for you. I was an astronomer. I studied the stars, not aliens."

David looked down, uncomfortable and embarrassed. The two women had known each other before arriving here and Cameron was pushing Priya's buttons the way Kim liked to push Barry's. After a moment of awkward silence, he said, "It's all right. Hell, I'm a doctor. I'm the closest thing to a biologist in the group, and I thought it was dead too."

"It isn't all right." Priya swung her arm back toward the village. "Everyone expects me to have all the answers. I don't. You sit here and mourn your wife back on Earth, but nobody seems to care that my boyfriend died less than ten days ago, gutted by a goddamn *Titanis* bird."

Cameron smiled wide. "How can you possibly know the name of the species?"

"Oh, fuck off."

Cameron crossed her arms. "I cared for Charlie too, you know."

"That was years ago," Priya spat. "Besides, you got to say goodbye." She dropped to the sand and sat against the side of the raft between two spikes, her face scrunched tight.

David turned to Cameron, unsure what to say. She rolled her eyes.

"How's everyone doing?" came a voice. Jasmine appeared at the end of the path. "Y'all been down here for hours," she said, her words sing-song-y, as usual.

Jasmine had been one of the first people to make David and his kids feel welcome in the village, and she was always doing her best to keep the peace.

She trudged across the sand, stopping beside a pair of dugout canoes. A third canoe had disappeared, presumably taken by Randall, the asshole who'd tried to execute David by shoving him from a cliff.

Jasmine stood with her hands on her hips. "That raft looks like a giant sea urchin."

"Anything new from the alien?" David asked, then added, "Are Kim and Barry okay?" He and Cameron maneuvered out of the crisscrossing spikes and met her on the beach.

"Our alien friend hasn't moved an inch. Kim and Morrie are still hunkered over that flying platform, and Barry is just fine, Shug. Dee and the others got him his supper and now he's helping build up the fire."

David relaxed slightly. "I hope Barry is behaving for them."

"Mostly." Jasmine smiled, a big, beautiful smile of perfect white teeth that shone bright against the dark skin of her face. Despite the smile, she looked sad. "He reminds me of my boys, back when they were small."

David swallowed. Everyone had left people behind on Earth. Everybody here had a story, all of them tragic.

He put a hand on Jasmine's shoulder. "Thank you."

She clasped his hand, squeezing it. "Is Miss Priya okay?"

Cameron smirked. "She'll be all right. She's just having a little pity party."

"Jesus, Cameron." David muttered.

Her hard-ass attitude sometimes crossed the line from sexy to obnoxious.

"Sorry." Cameron shrugged, not looking sorry at all. "I got no patience for emotional shit."

Jasmine patted David's hand. "Why don't you two head back to the village. Supper's over, but we saved you some." She lowered her voice. "I'll go talk to Miss Priya."

Cameron marched toward the trail. David followed her.

They stopped a quarter of a mile up the dirt path, right where Randall had shot Cameron. "I'm going to find that piece of shit," she said.

David turned and looked back. The island he and his kids had arrived on sat a few miles offshore, just visible beyond the end of the path. "Do you still think he's over there?"

She nodded. "It's the closest island, and he knows his way around."

In David's previous life, he'd never wished anyone dead. As an anesthesiologist, his business had been saving lives. But if Cameron took a side trip to kill Randall, this place would be just a little safer for Kim and Barry. In the end, that was all that mattered.

He couldn't wait to get back to his kids and hear about their day.

The smell of ash and charred meat permeated the forest. As they grew close to the village, hazy smoke wafted through the pines. Just outside the wall, the remains of the second Tyrannosaurus smoldered on a bonfire. Three villagers fed the flames with logs.

Cameron made a gun with her finger and fired off an imaginary shot at the dinosaur's burning corpse.

They passed through the opening in the eight-foot perimeter wall and continued up the path between uneven rows of crops. Numerous edible plants had been found on the islands. The villagers were growing corn, several types of squash, carrots, and a bunch of starchy tubers.

Unfortunately, it would be weeks or months before most of it was ready to harvest.

The common area sat beyond the fields, with benches, crude work tables, and several small campfires used for smoking meat. Reggie and Kevin stood at one of the tables, scrubbing plates and utensils from dinner. Reggie appeared to be doing most of the work, as always.

Jasmine had explained once that Reggie kept himself busy to try to forget about what had happened on Earth. When David asked what that meant, she'd clammed up.

Kevin was one of David's patients. His ulna had been fractured in the Tyrannosaurus attack and now his arm hung in a sling. Although he wasn't helping much with the dishes, he was still moving the arm around quite a bit, which was a good sign.

Other than those two, the village was quiet.

A pair of small sheds stood behind the common area, and beyond those, the four cabins. Now that they were down to only twenty people, there was room for everyone to sleep inside, though some, like Cameron, still preferred camping out under the trees just beyond the little creek. With a constant temperature of roughly seventy degrees and no real weather, it was easy enough to sleep outside.

"If you get lonely tonight, you know where to find me, Ace." Cameron grabbed a plate of food and peeled off toward the camping area.

His heartbeat raced as he imagined her body under him. The desire wasn't solely sexual. He felt completely alone and craved connection. He took a deep breath. It would be easy to slip away after Kim and Barry fell asleep.

He could do it. Part of him wanted to. Another part of him knew that he shouldn't. Not yet. He needed more time, if nothing else.

Feeling unsettled, he walked over to the main fire pit. The alien carriage sat just beyond, in the spot where David had been tied to a wooden frame a few days earlier.

Morrie's head drooped over the front of the carriage, his face hidden beneath his curly red hair. The poor guy needed to pace himself. He'd fallen asleep on the job.

David froze.

Kim lay sprawled on the ground a few feet beyond, her leg bent at the knee and one arm twisted awkwardly. David's stomach rose in his throat. She didn't look asleep.

She looked dead.

He raced over, dropped to the ground, and shook her. "Kimmie, wake up."

Her head lolled in his arms. He tilted her face back, lifting her chin to clear her airway and pressed trembling fingers against her neck. "Come on, baby." David's breath hitched. She had no pulse.

He bent close, pressing his cheek against her face. Her skin felt warm, but not warm enough. He listened for her breath, holding his own. Nothing. David's heart pounded.

He placed his hands on her chest and began compressions.

"Somebody help," he called out, his voice thin.

Kona, their golden retriever, wandered over and whimpered. The world closed in around him.

He bent and pinched Kim's nose, blowing twice into her lungs, then resumed compressions.

By the time the rest of the village crowded around, David had been at it for five minutes. He leaned over, convulsing with sobs, his mouth wide in a silent wail. His baby was gone.

Chapter Three

Randall Pond spent the day wandering around the beach and eating figs from trees at the jungle's edge. He didn't know what else to do.

He'd slept beneath the dugout canoe he'd taken from the other island, afraid a wolf-pig or one of those giant fucking birds would find him. The hilltop where he'd camped with Wayne and the others might be safer, and several times he'd started into the jungle toward it, but each time he stopped himself. The hike would take hours and that hilltop reminded him too much of Sierra and Dave and his goddamn kids.

There was plenty to eat down here, anyway, as long as he didn't need anything besides mother-fucking figs.

He sat on the overturned canoe and looked across the sea to the other island, with that fat plateau in the middle. Earlier, a column of inky smoke had risen up until it hit some sort of ceiling, proving this was all a big fancy enclosure.

Randall had been locked up plenty of times. He knew a prison when he saw one.

The thing that Dave had jumped on from the cliff had to be one of the wardens. It had been invisible until it crashed to the ground, and even then, it hadn't really looked like anything, just a big brown blob.

Randall chewed on another fig. They'd already given him the shits, but he was hungry. What he really wanted was some meat. He pulled out his Walther P22, popped the magazine, and opened the chamber. Sadly, no new rounds had magically appeared since the last time he checked.

Randall thought back to his early days on this island. Wayne had brought a goddamn arsenal. He should have demanded a gun back then, when he had the chance. Hell, he should have taken one from Wayne while he slept. The uppity son of a bitch had been eaten by a *T. rex* while carrying every last gun in his stupid rucksack.

A gurgle churned in Randall's belly. *Mother. Fucking. Figs.* He shuffled away from the canoe, dropped his pants, and squatted, spraying diarrhea onto the sand. What goes in must come out. If only that *T. rex* had lived long enough to shit out Wayne's guns before Dave killed it.

Randall froze as the final few drops of hot liquid dripped from his asshole.

The *T. rex* had fallen over a cliff on this very island. He had seen it splattered on the beach a thousand feet down. *This very same beach*, back where it curved around behind the big mountain. Randall pulled up his pants.

The guns should still be there. Wayne had even put them in plastic bags to keep them dry on the raft ride.

He started walking. If he got those guns, his options opened up considerably. He could hunt for wolf pigs. He could kill one of those claw birds and eat the whole thing himself.

He could shoot Dave.

Dave was everything Randall hated, a rich asshole doctor with two perfect kids.

After walking in the sand for an hour, Randall's legs were tired and his thighs were chafed. The side of the mountain crept closer to the sea, becoming a solid gray wall on his left, and leaving a strip of sand barely wider than a sidewalk.

Eventually the beach opened back up, revealing a hidden alcove dotted with palm trees. It might have been downright scenic if not for the splattered dinosaur carcass in the middle.

The *T. rex* lay sprawled on the pile of crumbled boulders that had broken free from the mountain above. Oklahoma roadkill never smelled so bad, not even the goddamn armadillos. Guts spilled from the dinosaur's mouth and from a slit under its tail, which had to be its asshole. Randall had never thought about it, but it made sense. Dinosaurs had assholes too.

He reached down to his belt and pulled out the one treasure he'd kept from the village, Josh's knife. Randall wondered what had happened to the kid. He'd left him tied up after smacking him around. The memory tasted sour. The sorry truth of the matter was that Josh had gotten in trouble while trying to impress him.

Randall shook his head and got to work. He'd done plenty of disgusting things in prison and far worse while running with The Piper. How bad could this be? At first, the knife wouldn't go through the dinosaur's scales, but he found a spot where its hide had split on impact. He widened the gash and sawed away.

The previous odor was nothing compared to the gut-punch that spewed from inside, so thick he could almost feel it.

After thirty minutes, Randall was covered with dark blood and a mound of organs lay piled on the beach. He didn't care. It wasn't all that different from cutting open a whitetail or skinning a neighborhood cat, just bigger. Cavernous, in fact. He sliced through a membrane that looked like the stomach. A hand spilled out.

Randall picked it up by the thumb, spotting Wayne's big U.S. Army ring on the middle finger. He chucked the hand onto the pile of guts without bothering to remove the ring. Jewelry had no value here.

He found a sturdy palm frond and propped open the cavity in the dinosaur's belly so he could crawl inside. He rolled Wayne's head and torso over and tugged the rucksack free, leaving the man's remains right where he found them.

Jackpot. Randall licked his lips, sticky with dinosaur blood. He placed the rucksack on dry sand and waded into the sea to rinse the gore from his clothes and hair, eventually stripping off everything until he was completely naked.

Life was starting to look pretty fucking good.

He opened Wayne's rucksack, carefully laying the contents on a palm frond to keep them off the sand. The guns all needed to be broken down, cleaned, and inspected. There were four pistols and three semi-automatic long guns. The M1911 was missing, along with the shotgun Wayne had been holding when he was eaten. Randall would go back into the guts and look for those later. The real score though, was seven boxes of ammo. Randall was a wealthy man.

He was also hungry. That *T. rex* had been lying there more than a week, but he decided to risk it. Josh's fancy knife even came with a flint.

An hour later, one of the dinosaur's stubby arms bubbled and smoked on a spit. Life was quite fucking good indeed.

Chapter Four

"Wake up!" Sierra pounded the side of the alien's massive body with her fist. It felt like hitting an overstuffed suitcase. "Wake up and tell us what happened."

The creature made no response.

David cradled Kim's head in his lap, tears flowing down his cheeks. Barry stood behind him, also crying.

"Somebody give me a knife," Sierra demanded. She took off her white leather jacket and tossed it aside.

The entire village crowded around. Cameron handed her a short blade. Sierra leaned over the front of the creature, where its appendages protruded from a series of flaps.

"What are you doing?" Priya asked, her voice iced with fear.

"I'm going to give it a fucking vivisection." She pressed the knife into the folds.

Cameron nodded. "Yes."

"What do you expect it to do?" Priya asked. "They're gone."

"I want answers. Why did it kill them? How did it kill them?"

"How do you know it did something?" Priya asked. "How do you know it wasn't the carriage?"

Sierra tightened her grip. "Whatever. I want an explanation. What happened?"

A shroud of darkness fell over the village. Sierra flinched, but it was only the night, dropping hard and fast the way it always did, as if someone turned a dimmer switch.

Empty blackness enveloped them in half a minute.

"Nighttime," Kevin said, never missing a chance to state the obvious.

"Shut up, Kevin," barked Cameron.

Embers glowed in the main fire pit, barely providing enough light to make out the faces of the people standing around. No one had bothered to prepare for night after they'd found Kim, Morrie, and Scott lying dead near the alien sled. Morrie had been working on the vehicle with Kim. Scott had been on watch duty, over by the alien.

"I'll get some torches," Jasmine said, her voice flat and dull for once.

David leaned over Kim, sobbing.

Sierra looked away, feeling the urge to offer some privacy.

Scott and Morrie had been placed on the ground side by side between the carriage and the fire pit. Someone had taken off Scott's navy blazer and draped it over his head and shoulders, covering his face.

Morrie's eyes were still open, staring lifelessly into the dark. His brother had been drowned in Thad's homicidal baptism. After that, Morrie had fallen in with Joe, only to realize later that he'd sided with a maniac. Since then, he'd been busting his ass to redeem himself.

Felicia knelt beside Morrie. Sierra didn't know much about her. She had the broad shoulders of a swimmer and a hard face. She closed Morrie's eyes with the palm of her hand.

When Felicia rose, Morrie's head rolled to one side, revealing a red glow in the dirt beneath his neck.

Sierra blinked. "What the hell is that?"

No one answered. Barry's cries grew louder. David didn't comfort him. He didn't seem to have anything left.

Sierra crouched next to Morrie and gently turned his head. The leather of her motorcycle pants cinched tight against the back of her knees.

"David," she said, waving him over. "You need to see this."

David's breaths lurched to a stop.

Jasmine walked up with a torch in each hand. The flickering firelight washed out the glow under Morrie's neck. "Get those out of here," Sierra snapped.

Jasmine looked dumbfounded as Cameron snatched the torches and flung them into the fire pit, where they sent a fountain of sparks into the night sky.

"David, get over here and look at this." Sierra pulled the blazer off Scott and shifted his head to the side. The skin glowed at the top of his neck as well. "There's something inside them."

David didn't move from his spot. Instead, he turned Kim's head in his lap and parted the short brown locks covering her neck. The same red ember glowed beneath her skin.

"Wh-what is it?" Barry asked, his voice hitching and hoarse.

"There's something under their skin," Kevin said, cradling his broken arm.

Barry wailed, producing a high-pitched shriek that made it impossible to concentrate.

"Dee, can you help with him?" Sierra asked. The blonde woman picked up Barry and carried him toward the huts. Three of her friends went with her.

Sierra turned to Priya. "What is it?"

"How the hell am I supposed to know?"

Several villagers started talking at once.

"Is something inside their heads?"

"How did it get there?"

"The alien put it there."

"Maybe it came from the carriage."

Sierra turned to the alien. "What did you do to them?" The creature lay motionless, as it had for two days after they'd first captured it. Back when they'd thought it was dead.

Just like Kim and Morrie and Scott.

A thin seedling of hope sprouted inside her. "What if they aren't dead?"

Everyone grew still and looked at her.

She tapped Scott's neck. "What if this thing under their skin is doing something to them?"

"You've got to cut it out of them, David," Cameron said.

He looked down at his daughter and opened his mouth, but nothing came out.

"How is cutting it out going to bring them back?" someone asked.

Sierra stood. "I don't know. It might not. But that light is on. It's doing something. We have to find out what."

Waldmire put his hand on David's shoulder. "It might be worth a try."

He looked up and spoke in a distant whisper. "I'm not going to autopsy my little girl."

Sierra pointed to the body of the caretaker. "That thing isn't moving, but it's still alive." She held David's gaze. "Priya, you think we were in suspended animation in the pods, right?"

Priya stammered, "Yes, I guess."

"You have to try."

"Why?" David whispered. "She's gone."

"Are you sure?" Sierra asked. "One hundred percent? You need to be Doctor Williams right now, not Kim's father. Give me a diagnosis."

"She isn't breathing." He sobbed. "There's no pulse. She's c-cold."

"Yeah. What else?"

David wiped his eyes and ran his hand along Kim's arm. "Rigor mortis hasn't set in, but sometimes that can take hours."

"What else?"

David opened his mouth, then swallowed audibly. "She didn't soil herself or lose bladder control. What about Morrie and Scott?"

Sierra shook her head. "No. David, you have to cut it out of them. It's doing something." She wasn't sure about any of this, but they had to try.

He looked down at Kim. "I can't slice into my daughter's neck. I can't."

"Then try Morrie first," Sierra said.

David looked up, fear and pain in his eyes, but maybe also his own seedling of hope. He took a deep breath. "Okay."

Chapter Five

Horror swelled in David's throat, like thick foam he couldn't swallow, making it difficult to talk or even breathe. Everything moved in slow motion. He unbuttoned his dark blue shirt and tossed it aside, sweating through the black t-shirt he wore underneath.

Spare clothing had been arranged to make pillows and cushions on the work tables where the villagers prepared their meals. David placed Kim onto one of the tables and kissed her cheek, just as he had so many times when she was sleeping.

Please let her be asleep.

He turned her head to study the red glow on the back of her neck. The aliens had violated her body somehow. It repulsed him, but it also gave him hope. The thing in her neck had done something to her he couldn't understand. It might still be doing something. If taking it out could bring her back, he had to try.

But he wasn't going to experiment on his daughter. He couldn't.

He kissed Kim again and moved to the table where Morrie lay on his stomach. Felicia, who had apparently been close to Morrie, had arranged a donut of clothing under his face so that his mouth and nose weren't obstructed. She placed torches around the tables.

"More," David said. "I need as much light as possible."

Scott still lay on the ground. Someone had folded his blazer to make a pillow beneath his head.

Felicia positioned a torch on a crude tripod and stepped up next to David. "Have you done anything like this before?" Thick dark eyebrows tightened on her face.

He gave her a flat look. "No."

"But you're a doctor?" she squinted, distrust in her eyes.

"Anesthesiologist. I've sat in on more surgeries than I can count." He paused. "I did cut up some cadavers in med school." He hoped to God this wasn't the same thing. He had so many doubts. Removing whatever was under their skin might wake them up, but it also might kill them, if they weren't actually dead.

Sierra touched his arm. "You've got this."

He took a deep breath. "Where's the boiled water?"

Felicia handed him a small wooden bowl filled with water and three hot stones from the fire.

David tested it to make sure it wasn't too hot. It sure as hell wasn't sterile, but it was all they had. He poured the clear water on the back of Morrie's neck. It was the only thing he could think of to prep the area.

"Knife?"

Cameron handed him a knife she'd honed against a rock and then sterilized over the flames. David took it, his hands shaking. They looked like someone else's hands. His hands never shook.

"You've got this," Sierra repeated.

He glared at her. "I'm not a surgeon."

"I know," she said. "Talk us through what you're doing."

He breathed in through his nose and touched the tip of the blade to Morrie's skin right at the base of his skull. "I'm going to part the muscle right here." It was the *Rectus Capital* muscle, or something like that. The blade trembled and he jerked it away, not wanting to shred the back of Morrie's neck.

"Ooooh, I can't handle this," Reggie said, wringing his baseball cap like a washcloth. "Blood makes me want to faint."

David glared at him. "Then why the hell are you watching?"

Sierra took Reggie by the arm and steered him away. "Go keep an eye on that thing," she said, pointing at the caretaker.

Reggie had helped, in his own way. David's anger steadied his nerves. He drew the knife down, right above the red glow, and split Morrie's pale skin. A few drops of blood pooled out. Felicia dabbed them away with a piece of white cloth.

David's training took over. As long as he kept clear of the cervical vertebrae, he wouldn't be anywhere near the spinal column. It wasn't like he was going to decapitate the man. "Give me the spoon." Cameron handed him a spoon from the collection of utensils they'd laid out on the table, also sterilized over flames. David used the spoon to hold the incision open so he could cut deeper. Morrie's skin parted, revealing pink tissue below.

"Why isn't there more blood?" Kevin asked, hissing through his teeth.

"His heart isn't pumping. We aren't likely to see more than a CC or two."

The knife hit something solid, producing a small *tink* that David felt more than heard.

He shifted the blade, digging under the object on one side. He wiggled the spoon deeper on the opposite side. Shiny metal gleamed at the bottom of the incision. Holding the utensils apart, he levered the object until it protruded from the wound. "Felicia, take it."

She plucked out the object using needle-nose pliers on the end of a multi-tool. It looked like a metal eyeball, with a two-inch optic nerve hanging from one end, its red glow the iris.

As Felicia pulled the object free, Morrie let out a blood-curdling scream.

Chapter Six

Two Days Before Impact

"Hey, come here," Morrie Vogel called to his brother from the cabin's front porch. "Austin, get out here, quick."

"What is it this time? More lions?" Austin didn't sound terribly interested.

Several days earlier, a pride of African lions had trotted across the cabin's backyard in the Colorado Rockies, undoubtedly freed from the zoo or an animal sanctuary.

"No. It's some kind of sound." The high-pitched whistling noise grew louder. Morrie shielded his eyes and scanned the sky.

"What's up, Rusty?" Austin asked as he joined him.

Austin never used his name. He always called him "Rusty," or "Carrot Top," or "Freckles." He thought it was hilarious, even though he was just as pale, freckled, and red-headed himself. Morrie couldn't quite see the humor.

He pointed to a glinting dot in the sky. "There."

"Is that from the Ender?" Austin asked. "Did a piece break off?"

"I don't think so. It's coming from a different direction."

The Ender had appeared in the northern sky two weeks earlier. Although everyone had known about the comet for more than a month, its first appearance sent much of the world straight to hell.

The pitch of the whistling changed to a heavy roar as the object disappeared behind a ridgeline five miles to the west.

Morrie tensed, expecting the sound of an impact, but none came. He watched for a plume of smoke. Nothing.

Austin walked inside the family cabin. At least some good had come from the end of the world. After years of estrangement, Morrie and Austin were back together. Mom and Dad would have been so pleased.

Morrie followed him in and turned on the television while Austin plopped on the couch and opened his laptop.

The national news showed a suburban park in Rapid City with two strange white shapes in the middle, one floating above the other. They looked like the halves of a sphere, or maybe a giant plastic Easter egg. A young man waved people forward and helped them climb into the bottom half. At least five people made it in, including the guy helping everyone, before the top half lowered back down on them.

When the shape closed, the whole thing lifted into the air.

"What in the world is going on?" Morrie asked.

Austin typed on his laptop. "Let me see what they're saying on the forums."

Morrie bit his lip, wary of starting another fight. Austin spent way too much time on religious forums these days. Their old arguments bubbled over. Morrie appreciated the messages in the Good Book but didn't see them as historical fact. Austin took it all at face value.

A tired-looking newscaster appeared onscreen. "Seven states across the Midwest and Central Mountain regions have reported these white capsules, from Wisconsin to Utah. Authorities from the Pentagon and the Federal Aviation Administration deny any knowledge of their origin. NASA has not responded to requests for a statement. Police in Colorado and Oregon have asked the public to avoid the pods, though we should note that no pods have been reported in Oregon at this time."

The screen cut to footage of a freeway map centered on the mid-Atlantic states. All of the east-west routes were bright red.

"The National Guard reports heavy westward traffic on Interstates 70, 76, and 90 as people depart the East Coast, presumably trying to reach these capsules. Smaller arteries are clogged as well."

The reporter touched his earpiece as a different map appeared, showing dots scattered across Colorado, South Dakota, Nebraska, Iowa, Minnesota, and Wisconsin. "We understand capsules have also been reported in Wyoming and Utah, but haven't updated our graphic yet."

Morrie took a deep breath. This had to be what he'd seen from the back porch.

Austin looked up from his laptop, flushed with excitement. "Hey Red, we need to find one of those capsules. It's the rapture. They're here to carry the virtuous off to Heaven."

On the television, cell phone footage showed a man shooting an elderly guy standing between him and a pod on a golf course. The shooter stepped past dozens of other bodies and climbed in.

Morrie grunted. "I'm not so sure about the virtuous part."

"Hey, I bet that's what we saw from the porch," Austin said.

"You really think so?" Morrie smiled. His brother didn't always put the pieces together as quickly as Morrie did.

Austin nodded, missing the sarcasm, which was probably for the best. He also didn't take ribbing very well. "Let's go. We need to find it before it's gone."

"Shouldn't we learn more about them first?" Morrie asked.

Austin pointed to the countdown clock in the corner of the television, which read 00:47:14:10 and ticked down every second. "Rusty, the apocalypse is in two days. We don't have time."

The television now showed footage from a Denver suburb, where a man stood before a pod, watching its top half rise. The screech of tires came from somewhere offscreen. The man dove out of the way as a cherry red sports car smashed into the pod. The front of the car crumbled against the capsule, which didn't budge from the impact.

Morrie's jaw hung open. The driver swatted the airbag out of his way and pulled himself through the side window. He was almost to his feet when the original man reappeared and tackled him. While they wrestled on the ground, a third man dove headfirst into the pod. The other two continued to fight as it floated away.

"They all would have fit," Morrie said, horrified. "I don't want to go anywhere near trouble like that. We came to the mountains to escape that sort of thing, remember?"

"The one we saw from the deck is in the middle of nowhere," Austin said. "We're the only people who know about it."

Morrie chewed on this for a moment. The area to the west was National Forest. The pod had to have landed a good eight or ten miles away, on the other side of a ridge running north to south. Austin was right. It was unlikely anyone else would see it. "If we find it, are we going to get in, just like that? Without knowing where it goes?"

"I told you where it goes. Besides, you know what happens if we stay here. We burn."

Morrie couldn't argue with that.

After collecting a few supplies, they took Austin's open-air Jeep down the gravel driveway. Morrie drove, to avoid getting carsick. They turned west on State Route Eleven, which would take them past the north end of the ridgeline. Once they got to the other side, they could head off-road and search for the pod.

Morrie had brought their grandfather's World War Two service rifle. Austin told him to leave it behind, but he refused. After what he'd seen on television, he wanted to be prepared.

When they reached the road, Morrie pushed the Jeep up to fifty. He looked over at his brother and saw something he hadn't seen in a long time. Austin was smiling. Morrie couldn't help but smile in return. If nothing else, the Vogel boys were back together again.

They rounded a wide curve with an oversized motorhome parked on the shoulder. Judging from the chairs, coolers, and other crap scattered about, it had been camped there for days.

Morrie pressed the pedal to the floor, hoping to avoid trouble. News reports had grown horrifying over the last few weeks, from the Baltic War to the Oklahoma scouring. The three-day shootout in Denver had been bad enough.

As they passed the motorhome, a woman appeared in one of the windows, mouth open and eyes wide. She pressed her hand against the glass.

Austin patted Morrie's shoulder. "Stop the car. We have to go back. Stop the car."

Morrie pressed the brake, a dark cloud rising in his heart. Everything about that motorhome screamed of danger.

Chapter Seven

Holy hell. Pain stabbed the back of Morrie's head. He tried to reach for his neck, but his arms wouldn't move. Someone was holding him down. He lay on his stomach, suffocating in a pile of nasty-smelling clothes.

It felt like the back of his head had been sliced open.

"Let me up." He spat the words through the clothes and flapped his hand, rapping his knuckles against something hard. "Who's doing this?" Tears welled in his eyes. "What's happening? Let me up." The pain was worse than anything he'd ever felt.

Someone took his elbows and raised him to a sitting position.

"Careful, slowly," came a voice.

Morrie blinked, trying to clear enough wet from his eyes to see. Memories flooded back. He was in the village. Thad was dead. Joe was dead. A wave of sadness hit him. Austin was dead.

He reached for the back of his neck, but his fingers closed on someone else's hand, which was holding a cloth against his head.

"Here, keep pressure on this." It was David, the tall guy who'd brought down the alien. Kim's dad. David slipped his hand free and Morrie clamped down on the cloth, pressing it tight against his neck.

Felicia appeared, dangling a bloody piece of metal in front of his face.

He tried to focus. "What's that?" It looked like a steel teardrop, covered in blood.

"This was in your neck. David cut it out."

Morrie felt dizzy. He wanted to close his eyes and sleep. He steadied himself on the surface below him. A table. He was on a table in the center of the village, with everyone watching him. He spotted Jasmine in the crowd and looked down. He hated for her to see him like this.

David leaned in close. "Are you okay?"

"No." Fresh tears fell. "Fucking hurts."

"I'm all out of lidocaine. Sorry." David studied his eyes. "What's your name?"

"Morrie."

The moment Morrie answered, David fired off another question. "How old are you?"

"Thirty-three."

"Where are you from?"

"Denver."

"What happened to Earth?"

"Huh? Oh." Morrie finally caught on. David was trying to make sure he was right in the head. "It got clobbered by the Ender."

"Start at fifty and subtract backwards by seven."

"Forty-three," Morrie said, then stopped and grimaced. "Screw that. Math isn't my strong point."

David squinted. "Sticks in a bundle are unbreakable. What might that mean?"

"It means you're asking me a bunch of stupid questions when my neck just got cut open."

"You were out for a long time," Felicia said. Her hard-ass expression softened. "He needs to make sure you're okay."

Morrie's heart hitched. "How long?"

"You weren't just out," David said. "You were lifeless. Not breathing. No pulse. Nothing. For at least an hour."

Morrie swallowed. "People are stronger when they work together than when they're alone."

David nodded, and a bit of the concern lifted from his face.

"Do you think I have brain damage?"

"That's what I'm trying to figure out. How's your vision? Balance? Taste and smell? Do you have a heightened sensitivity to pain?"

Morrie raised his free hand. "Sweet Jesus, yes. My neck hurts."

David shifted back and forth, studying him with narrowed eyes. "I think you're okay," he said finally. "I don't want to wait any more. I don't know how long it's safe to leave someone in that state." He turned to Sierra. "Get Kim ready."

"Why?" Morrie asked, confused. "Wait, is she out too?"

David nodded. "And Scott."

Morrie didn't know if he'd suffered brain damage or not, but being operated on without anesthesia hurt like hell. He didn't wish that on anyone, least of all, little Kim.

"Wait." He held up a shaky hand, trying to remember exactly what he and Kim had been doing. "You can't do this to her." It felt like an ice pick was lodged in the back of his head. A wet drop rolled down his spine, making him shiver. Blood. "I think there's another way."

"How?" David asked. That single word carried so much desperation Morrie forgot about his neck for a moment.

It all came back to him. "We were testing the controls on the carriage. Kim figured out that everything is paired, duplicated. You have to hit two controls at once to make it work."

Morrie scooted off the table but his legs wouldn't hold him and he collapsed to his knees. Hands grabbed him and lifted him. David and Felicia helped him stagger past the other tables. Kim lay on one of them, her eyes closed and her mouth open. Morrie led everyone over to the alien carriage, past Scott, who lay unconscious on the ground. He looked strange without his blazer on.

"Kim and I did something," Morrie said, shivering as another trickle of blood ran down his back. He sat at the end of the short console that wrapped around the front third of the carriage. Nearly everyone from the village moved close, watching.

Strange panels and shapes covered the inside of the little wall, like a computer console designed by Dr. Seuss. Clusters of creepy holes dotted the front. They reminded Morrie of the bottom of a wasp nest. The cluster in the middle even had shiny nubs inside, like larvae.

"Most of the controls have a counterpart on the opposite side," Morrie explained through gritted teeth. He touched a protruding knob with four buttons on the end. Kim had commented that it looked like a miniature cat paw. *Toebeans,* she'd called them.

Morrie took a deep breath, relaxing a little. If he could remember a word like "toebeans," his mind had to be okay.

"That's a control?" Sierra asked, sounding dubious. "It looks like a decoration."

Morrie started to nod, but stopped himself as the motion sent daggers through his head. "Go to the other side." He pointed across the carriage, to a matching control on the opposite wall, about eight feet away.

Sierra leaned in and found the little knob.

"We were testing them. The last thing we tried was the second button on each side."

Sierra pulled her hand away. "That's what knocked you out?"

"Yes." Morrie said, proud of himself for remembering not to nod. "But before that, we pressed the *first* one on each side. It made a long, whiney sound."

"Hey, I think we heard that," Reggie said, standing over by the alien. "Kevin and I. We were cleaning up dinner. I thought someone ripped something."

"That was it," Morrie said. "Kim and I both looked at each other 'cause we felt this big rush, like we just woke up, completely refreshed."

Sierra pointed back and forth between Reggie and Kevin. "Did either of you feel anything?"

"No, nothing," Kevin said. "We heard the sound twice though, remember?"

Reggie nodded.

Morrie rotated toward them, turning his whole body instead of his neck. "The second time had to be the one that knocked us out."

"Why didn't it knock us out?" Reggie asked.

"Why didn't it knock out the whole village?" Sierra added. Then she answered her own question. "It must have a limited range. That explains why it got Scott. He was close, standing guard by the alien."

"Wait," Felicia said. "Why would it knock out the whole village?"

"She believes we all have those things in our necks, Shug," Jasmine said.

Jasmine could always tell what other people were thinking. It was one of the reasons Morrie liked her so much.

"Bullshit," Felicia spat. "I ain't got one of those things in me."

"Enough talk," David said. He walked over, carrying Kim in his arms. "I want my daughter awake."

"Hold on," Sierra said. "Everyone else, get behind the work tables, and then take two more steps back."

The crowd moved away, most adding a few extra steps of their own.

David stood right at the front of the carriage, holding Kim. "Hurry."

Morrie reached in and nodded to Sierra on the other side. He pointed to the second toebean on the little cat paw. "That one knocked us out." He moved his finger to the first button. "And this one will wake her up." *Please, God,* he prayed.

The village was silent. The only sound came from the creaking leather of Sierra's white motorcycle pants as she shifted to reach the first button.

"On three," Morrie said, then he counted. They pressed the controls at the same time. The carriage made a loud zipping sound.

"Whoa." Sierra stood up, her eyes wide. "It's like a triple espresso."

Morrie had felt the same thing when he and Kim first triggered the controls, but now he felt nothing, other than the miserable hole in his neck.

"Dad, what are you doing?" Kim asked, cradled in her father's arms. "Put me down."

David let out a moaning cry of relief. Several gasps came from the crowd.

"What's going on?" Scott asked, still lying on the ground. "Ah, crap, did I fall asleep on the job?"

Kona walked over and licked Scott's face. The rest of the villagers crowded around, several wiping their eyes.

Morrie grinned wide. He'd gotten it right and the girl was okay. He stood, doing his best to ignore the pain in his neck, and wrapped his arms around David and Kim. The icing on the cake was the fact that they now had a good start on figuring out the controls.

"Seriously, Dad. What's going on?" Kim asked.

David kissed her forehead and lowered her to the ground. "Talk to me baby, how are you?"

"I'm fine." She winced, as only a tween could wince. "Why is everyone looking at me?"

"Time hasn't passed for her," Priya said. "This explains the people in storage."

"What are you saying?" Felicia asked.

"David, Sierra, and Waldmire all woke up months after us," Priya said. "But they didn't think any time had passed. The people in storage are undoubtedly also in suspended animation."

"That means everyone has these things in their necks," Morrie said, catching on. "Everyone here can be stunned."

Priya turned to face him. "Everyone except you."

Chapter Eight

Two Days Before Impact

Morrie pulled the Jeep onto the gravel shoulder a quarter mile past the motorhome. "Austin, we can't take the risk." Even as he said it, he saw the horrified face of the woman in the window, burned in his memory.

"We have to take the risk, Red." Austin gave him his best puppy-dog eyes. "Don't you see? We're about to be judged. This is our chance to be the good Samaritan, literally. A traveler in need, on the side of the road."

Morrie bit his lip. Helping strangers because you wanted eternal reward felt more transactional than virtuous.

"We don't know for sure that she's in need." He kept his voice low. In the open-air Jeep, it felt like anyone could be listening.

Austin gave him a side-eyed glare he'd seen many times from their mother. "The woman in that motorhome is going to die tomorrow if we don't take her with us. Don't tell me she isn't in need."

"What if she's dangerous? What if that's a trap and she's luring people in so she can rob them or—or cook them and eat them?" The question sounded preposterous, but they'd seen reports about exactly that scenario on the news.

Austin unbuckled his seat belt and put one foot on the gravel. "If you don't turn back, you can go on alone." This also sounded like something their mother would have said, God rest her soul.

Morrie cranked the wheel and started moving. "If this goes bad, you'll never hear the end of it."

He hoped he'd live long enough to make good on the threat.

They rolled slowly back around the bend in the road. The motorhome looked dead, like a beached whale. Morrie stopped a dozen yards away and killed the engine. He left the key in the ignition, just in case.

"Hello?" Austin called out.

No one answered. Birds chirped in the trees. Bugs buzzed in the grass. A faint wailing sound came from somewhere. It could have been inside the motorhome, but it also could have been miles away.

Austin climbed down from the Jeep. "Did you hear that?"

"Maybe." Morrie had heard it, all right, and it scared him. That pod he'd seen was so close, yet here they were, sticking their noses in something ugly.

Austin walked toward the motorhome and called out again. "Hello?"

"Austin, let's go." The hair on Morrie's neck stood on end. "We gave them a chance. They don't want our help."

The door swung open and a muscular man wearing nothing but white briefs and dark socks appeared. He leaned against the door frame with raised elbows and a silver pistol in one hand. Greek letters had been inked across his broad chest.

"Can I help you?" The guy had a thick neck and tousled two-tone hair. The lettering on his chest had to be some sort of fraternity, but he looked ten years past college. Twirls of hair sprung from his belly like broken coils on an old sofa.

Morrie crept toward his brother. He was going to get his *I told you so* moment after all, if they actually lived through this. And if they did, he would lay it on thick.

Austin stepped back. "We wanted to see if you need help."

The man blinked repeatedly. He was trashed. "I'm doin' just fine," he said in a syrupy voice. "Never better."

He was a grade-A douchebag if ever there was one.

Morrie grabbed Austin by the arm. "Oh, okay. Sorry to bother you."

He turned his brother around, steering him back to the Jeep, feeling a fraction of relief. Douchebag couldn't shoot them in the back, could he? They just had to climb in and drive around the bend. Forty seconds, tops.

"Help." The woman's voice was faint, but clear.

"Do not turn around," Morrie whispered. If they turned around, Douchebag would know they'd heard. If they kept going, he might assume they hadn't. They could call the police. They could come up with a plan. Or hell, they could just leave. The thought drove a spear of guilt through Morrie's heart, but the sad reality was that whatever was happening in that motorhome would come to an end after one more day.

Austin turned around.

Morrie reached for him, looking back, hoping the big asshole had already gone inside.

"Hold it right there, boys." Douchebag's gun pointed straight at them. His eyes kept blinking, like hazard lights. He stepped down, wincing when his socked feet touched the gravel. "This is going to be a whole new kind of fun."

Chapter Nine

Randall sat on a makeshift throne in front of the dinosaur carcass. Night had fallen, but the cliff walls around the little beach acted like a reflector, amplifying the light from his bonfire. The dinosaur's face lay a few feet behind the fire, almost like it was enjoying the warmth. Its body lay sprawled beyond, among the pile of boulders that had come down with it.

T. rex meat didn't have much flavor, but it was better than figs. The second three-foot-long arm now roasted over the blaze.

Randall's arsenal lay spread out beside him. He'd finally found the shotgun and the Colt M1911, deep in the dinosaur's bowels, which had necessitated a second bath in the sea. Now all the guns were disassembled on palm leaves next to Randall's seat. He'd rinsed them clean and wiped them down as best as possible and had been in the process of putting them back together when darkness hit. The Colt was the only one fully assembled. He'd have to finish the rest tomorrow, but for now, he felt safe. The site was secure, with open ocean on one side, a rock wall wrapping around most of the beach, and only a thin stretch of sand leading to the rest of the island. He had everything he needed.

"Bullshit." He needed a cold beer and Crystal. Every few minutes, he had to get up and rotate the dinosaur's arm. If she was here, she could do it for him. And plenty of other things.

Crystal was one of the few people Randall had ever met who actually liked him, but she'd gotten herself torn to shreds by another *T. rex*, thanks to Dave and Kim and Sierra and that whole fucking bunch.

Randall looked at the creepy blackness out over the water. The firelight illuminated only the first few yards of the sea. Beyond that, the world just ended. The island with the village was out there somewhere. He wondered if he should go back over and shoot them all. He'd be doing most of 'em a favor.

Randall got up, went to the fire, and shifted the stick holding the *T. rex* arm. The blackened skin bubbled with greasy fat and smelled like pork rinds. He couldn't eat it yet, though. He had cooked the shit out of the first arm and he was going to cook the shit out of this one, too. He couldn't risk getting sick from spoiled dinosaur meat.

The thought of hunting down Dave and the others gave Randall a charge. He'd be like a stalker in a horror movie, watching from the woods, waiting until someone went off alone, then *bang!* He could spare the ones he liked. If he kept hidden, they'd never even know it was him. They might think it was an alien or a demon or a ghost or some goddamn thing.

People thought all kinds of crazy shit. The Piper had thought it was his job to kill everyone before the comet hit. Wayne had thought it was his job to save everyone once they got here. Randall didn't believe any of that nonsense. He'd learned long ago that other people exist only to fuck you over. All you could do was endear yourself to the biggest asshole around and try to get yourself on the giving end instead of the receiving end. It was called "sycophancy," Randall's favorite word, and it had served him well over his thirty-seven years. He even liked the sound of it. *Sick-o, fancy.*

He stared at the empty blackness. Randall had never been top dog before. There'd always been someone to bully him. First his brother, then the gang leaders on the street, the gang leaders in prison, not to mention the guards, and then The Piper. But here, Randall was the biggest asshole around.

He smiled. Being top dog felt pretty goddamn good.

A snarl came from behind.

Randall grabbed the M1911, jumped up, and circled around the side of the dead *T. rex*. Shadows moved near the dinosaur's belly. Randall inched closer. Was something alive in all that mess?

The closest shadow backed away from the carcass. It was a wolf-pig, just like the one that killed Juliana. Dark blood glistened on its head. Behind it, another wolf-pig lifted its snout from the putrid pile of guts. The creatures were as big as prizewinning bulls and looked like warthog demons. The first one, the biggest, chuffed down a rotten piece of meat that looked like a human foot. Wayne's foot.

"Entelosaurs," Randall spat, knowing the word wasn't quite right. Juliana had called them something close to that, but Randall couldn't remember it. "Wolf-pig" was good enough. He raised the M1911.

The larger wolf-pig lurched closer, its lips pulled back from crooked teeth. They looked just like Crystal's teeth. Its ears rolled forward. It was going to tear him limb from limb.

Randall fired twice.

Both shots hit, but the tough fucker barely flinched. Randall wished he'd cleaned the shotgun.

He forced himself to stand his ground. Running might trigger a chase instinct. Besides, he was supposed to be the badass now. The smaller wolf-pig trotted toward the thin beach leading off to the rest of the island. "That's right, go on, scat." Randall exhaled, feeling relief, and turned back to the other one.

He aimed for the creature's eye and pulled the trigger again. A cloud of red mist burst on its cheek. It shook its head, as if clearing away flies, then took two steps closer.

Mother fuck. He really should have assembled the shotgun first.

Breathing hard, Randall tried to think of a way out. The sea was twenty feet behind him. Maybe thirty. He might be able to run and dive in. He couldn't swim for shit, but he didn't think wolf-pigs could either, not with those skinny little legs. He looked back to gauge the distance.

The one he'd believed was wandering off had actually circled around, flanking him.

Randall wasn't the biggest badass around. He was a sorry son of a bitch who was about to die. He swung his arm and fired at the one behind him, but couldn't tell if he hit it. He ran toward the bonfire.

The larger wolf-pig charged.

Randall swerved past the fire and jumped onto the *T. rex* carcass. It was the only place to go. He climbed up onto its nose, over its big glassy eyes, and up on top of its head.

The wolf-pig snapped at him, its jaws sideways. The end of its snout bumped Randall's boot.

He crawled further up, onto the dinosaur's shoulder.

Below, the smaller wolf-pig ran around the fire, trying to get at him from the other side. It stopped short, blocked by boulders as big as trash cans.

Randall aimed his gun at the larger wolf-pig, which moved away from the dinosaur's head and circled back toward the belly.

The gun trembled in his grip and his heart pounded. He didn't know how far those things could jump.

The wolf-pig kept coming, closer and closer, until it was out of sight below him. The dinosaur carcass wiggled.

Randall blew out his breath. It was feeding again. He was safe. It couldn't reach him, and it had plenty of food to keep it occupied.

Soon, the second wolf-pig circled back and entered the abdominal cavity as well.

Dig in, boys. Even between the two of them, they'd never eat the whole thing. He was safe for now. He could let them eat until they were stuffed. Maybe they'd wander off. Maybe they'd fall asleep. He might even be able to find a way up the cliff once daylight came and he could search for handholds.

The light from Randall's fire lasted another hour or so. In that time, seven more wolf-pigs joined the feast.

Chapter Ten

Two Days Before Impact

"Austin, we have to run." Morrie spoke without moving his lips. They had to get back to the Jeep. It was the only source of cover.

"We bring good news," Austin said, projecting his voice like a revival preacher. He held up both hands.

Douchebag closed one eye and aimed his pistol at Austin.

Morrie's heart lurched. His brother was about to die.

A woman flew out of the motorhome, crashing into the douchebag from behind. The gun went off, louder than any sound had a right to be.

Austin went down.

Morrie inhaled, desperate for air. His brother wasn't moving.

The woman and the man fell together, tangled. Douchebag screamed in rage. The woman wore tiny shorts and a halter top that barely covered her.

Morrie ran back to the Jeep, ashamed of himself but too scared to do anything else. He should have been running toward that poor woman, not away from her. He slid behind the wheel and hunched down, peering back over the dashboard.

The woman stood, her knees bloodied from the gravel. She spat in the man's face, then turned and ran barefoot across the highway shoulder. Douchebag raised his gun and fired at her, but he must have missed, because she kept going, disappearing into the woods.

"Austin!" Morrie shouted.

His brother didn't respond. He lay motionless on the ground halfway between the Jeep and the motorhome. Morrie's chest clenched. He reached into the back seat and grabbed the old hunting rifle. Douchebag, on his feet now, turned from side to side, as if he couldn't decide between pursuing the woman or coming after Morrie.

Morrie wasn't about to let him make the choice. He aimed down the barrel of the rifle.

"Wait, don't." Austin said, raising his head.

Austin was alive, thank God in Heaven, but this wasn't the time to turn the other cheek. The douchebag had shot at them, for Christ's sake.

Morrie pulled the trigger.

The shot went high, ripping through the side of the man's neck. Blood puffed in a tiny cloud. Morrie's ears rang, hollow and shrill.

The man dropped to his knees, revealing a second woman behind him who'd just stepped out of the motorhome.

Morrie's jaw dropped. "Oh God, no."

The woman placed her hand on her chest, like she was getting ready to sing the national anthem. Blood spilled between her fingers and she toppled face-first onto the gravel.

Morrie stumbled down from the Jeep, unable to catch his breath. He staggered toward the motorhome.

Douchebag hissed, holding his neck. He got one foot under him and started to stand when a third woman burst from the motorhome. It might have been humorous if it wasn't so horrifying. Women kept pouring out of there, like some kind of perverse clown car.

The third woman, whose wrists were handcuffed, ran up behind the man. She brought her hands down over his head and pulled tight.

Douchebag dropped his gun. Morrie raced forward and kicked it away, wincing at the 90-proof cloud surrounding the guy. The woman jerked her fists back and forth alongside the man's head, tearing into his already damaged neck with the chain between her wrists. Blood spurted everywhere.

Behind them, the woman Morrie had shot lay face down on the gravel, a red hole in her back the size of a saucer. Morrie felt dizzy. He wanted to stop everything, start all over, and remake every decision ever. Anything to avoid this.

Austin was on his feet now, creeping toward them.

The handcuff chain must have hit an artery, because the stream of blood erupted into a torrent, dousing Morrie. The man's eyes widened and he opened his mouth to say something, but the only thing that came out was more blood.

He slumped like a sack of dog food. The woman lifted her arms free, letting him collapse forward. She wore only underwear. Her skin was light brown and she had thick eyebrows. She picked up Douchebag's silver handgun from the gravel.

Morrie turned to his brother. "Are you okay? Are you shot?"

"I'm fine. I was faking it." Austin reached out to the woman. "Is anyone else inside?"

She shook her head, breathing hard and splattered with blood. For a moment, she looked like she might attack them, too.

Finally, she spoke, her words carrying a Hispanic accent. "Come help me get these fucking cuffs off."

She marched back to the motorhome, stepping over the woman Morrie had killed. Austin followed.

Morrie's legs felt tingly and numb, as if they'd fallen asleep. He dropped to his knees and cried in his hands. He'd killed someone. It had been an accident, but Holy Christ, he had killed someone.

Several minutes later, Austin returned, carrying a blanket. "This is Felicia," he said. "Felicia, that's my brother Morrie."

Felicia had dressed in oversized clothing. The handcuffs were gone and Douchebag's gun was tucked into the waistband of her jeans.

Austin placed the blanket over the dead woman's body, then walked along the shoulder, peering into the woods. "Any sign of the other woman?"

Morrie got to his feet, which felt like a monumental accomplishment, and shook his head.

"Fuck that bitch," Felicia said. Her dark curls were pulled into a tight ponytail above her thick eyebrows.

"We have to find her," Austin said.

"She was that *pendejo's* girlfriend," Felicia spat.

"Wait, I'm confused," Austin said. "She was his partner? I thought she was his victim."

Felicia rolled her eyes. "She was both."

The three of them stood in silence. Shiny blue flies with crimson eyes crawled on Douchebag's bare skin. One disappeared into his open mouth.

"Why don't you come with us?" Austin said.

Felicia's hand went to the gun grip in her waistband. Her lips twitched.

After a long moment, Morrie realized what was going on, and it tore into his aching heart. She was scared of them. Morrie and Austin were two of the nicest people around. Hell, they'd just rescued her, but she was afraid to go with them.

"I'll take my chances on my own." She backed away and started walking up the road.

"Hold on, we've got to get to the pod," Austin said. "We can all go."

"What are you talking about?" Felicia stopped and looked at them.

Austin grabbed Morrie's wrist and led him over to her. He explained what they'd seen on television.

"Where did these pods come from?" Felicia asked.

"God sent them," Austin said. "He sent them to save us."

The comment knocked Morrie out of his paralysis. He rolled his eyes. "We don't know where they came from."

Felicia squinted, undoubtedly wondering how she could possibly trust a pair of strangers, including one who had just killed an innocent woman.

Austin held his hands out at his sides. "I promise you, we don't want to hurt you in any way. We won't try anything. And don't forget, you've got a gun."

Finally, she gave a small nod. "Show me."

They all got in the Jeep and started west. After ten or fifteen minutes, they turned south across a meadow of tall grass.

Less than an hour later, they found the pod sitting in a creek that ran through the valley.

Felicia got out and walked around it. "Where does this thing take us?"

"They take you to heaven," Austin said. "I told you. They're salvation for the worthy."

She put her hands on her hips. "What if you ain't worthy?"

"Then it takes you to the other place." Austin sounded like he had it all figured out.

Felicia scrunched her lips and nose. "So what if both types of people get in the same pod? One saint and one sinner. What happens then?"

Austin looked confused. "I don't –"

Felicia held up her fists, showing pink scrapes around her wrists. "I just murdered a man with my hands."

"That—that was self-defense," Austin stammered.

She smirked. "Hardly. He was already shot when I did it." She gestured at Morrie with her chin. "Your brother killed an innocent woman."

The comment hit Morrie like a two-by-four. All the air rushed out of his chest.

Felicia got up in Austin's face. "Will you risk taking us with you? Maybe you should leave us here, just to be safe."

Austin looked back and forth between them. Was he actually thinking about it? Tears formed in Morrie's eyes.

"Here's the thing, though." Felicia jabbed her finger at Austin, as if she'd caught him cheating. "If you leave in that pod without us, you condemn us to die. You'd go straight to hell for that, wouldn't you? You can't win."

Austin's jaw dropped. Despite everything she'd been through, Felicia had the balls to call out his nonsense.

"She's got you, man," Morrie said.

Austin stared off into the distance.

"God didn't send that thing to help us," Felicia said. "If he really wanted to help people, he's been doing a shitty job of it." She turned back to the pod. "All we have to do is touch it?"

Without waiting for an answer, she slapped the pod's surface. A black line appeared around the middle and the top rose slowly upwards. She climbed inside.

Morrie's heart somersaulted in his chest. They were really going to do this. He started forward.

Austin grabbed his arm. "Wait. Maybe you should leave that behind." He gestured toward the rifle.

"If we're going to hell, I'll take a shot at the devil," Morrie said. He didn't know where they were going, and it terrified him. He wasn't about to leave the gun behind.

Austin seemed somehow okay with his answer. They climbed in.

Morrie eased onto the soft black surface next to Felicia, his heart pounding. The top half lowered back down, just like they'd seen on television, covering them in pure darkness.

Austin prayed. After a short while, Morrie and Felicia joined him. When they all grew silent, Morrie began to fear they might be trapped in the pod forever. He couldn't tell how much time passed and thought he might have dozed off at one point.

A perimeter of light startled him as the pod opened up again. Morrie squinted. He felt sore, like he'd been sleeping for a day and a half, and the back of his neck ached. He sat up, heart pounding.

Rock walls surrounded them, along with a bunch of other pods. "It isn't hot enough to be hell," Morrie said.

An imposing old bald man stood outside their pod. "Welcome."

"I got it, Red," Austin said, suddenly excited. "I figured it out. The pods don't take you to heaven or hell. They take you to purgatory. You get one last chance to prove yourself."

A broad smile formed on the old man's face as he helped them out. "Purgatory." He spoke the word as if it had been right on the tip of his tongue and he'd finally remembered it. "That's exactly right. My name is Thad. Welcome to purgatory."

Austin beamed as he climbed out. "I told you so, Red. I told you so."

Chapter Eleven

When Sierra woke, her mind was made up. If there was something inside her head, she wanted it gone. Kim, Morrie, and Scott had been switched off, like an electronic device, and she couldn't stand the thought of aliens controlling her body. She would ask David to operate on her, right after breakfast.

She pulled her leather riding jacket over her shirt, shoved the revolver into the holster on her hip, and headed to the center of the village.

Carol, the oldest survivor at seventy-eight, handed her a plate of mashed yellow tubers. "Here you go, Sweetie."

"Thank you."

"Do you really think we can find a way out of this place?" Carol asked.

"Yes. That alien has to have come from somewhere. I don't think it lives here in the islands."

"Please don't leave me behind." Carol wrung her hands together. "I know I haven't been much help."

Sierra touched her arm. "No, you're a big help here. Don't you worry. We're not leaving anyone behind."

The promise seemed to lift Carol's spirits. Sierra went to look for a seat. She spotted Waldmire sitting alone.

Shortly after Sierra turned nine, her mother had moved out. She'd grown up believing legendary Hollywood executive Rick Preston was her father. He'd been a good dad, when she saw him, at least, and she'd always been proud of the toughness she learned from him. Now there was the possibility Mom had been banging the older guy across the street. Had that caused the divorce? Sierra was biracial. Her mother was Black and both Waldmire and Rick Preston were white. She didn't know what to think.

Waldmire's face lit up as she walked over. "Good morning." He patted the rough-hewn bench next to him.

Sierra sat down. "Any news?"

Waldmire pointed across the main fire pit, where a small group had gathered around the sled. "Morrie didn't waste any time getting back to work this morning."

"Good. The sooner they figure it out, the better."

"After yesterday, some people are concerned they're playing with fire."

Sierra rolled her eyes. "We can't give up now. We have to keep trying. Don't you agree?"

He tilted his head. "There's a valid argument on both sides."

The non-committal answer irked her. Waldmire had been a judge before retirement, which probably explained why his responses were always so measured.

She studied his wrinkly face. Felicia had mistaken Waldmire for her father. She claimed they both had the same smile. So far, Sierra hadn't been able to muster the courage to ask. If Waldmire was her biological father, it would mean the determination, independence, and tenacity she'd inherited from Rick Preston were all a sham.

"Any update on our guest?" Sierra asked. She took a bite of the tuber mash, which tasted more or less like potatoes, but with a tart zing.

"It hasn't moved an inch."

She exhaled. "Priya was supposed to be studying it, but she's been avoiding the thing ever since it spoke."

"What are you going to do about that?" Waldmire asked.

It felt like he was challenging her, the way her father used to, so she gave him a Rick Preston answer. "I'm going to get someone else to study it. Cameron maybe."

"Do you really think Cameron would be good at that?"

"Of course not." Sierra raised her finger. "The point isn't to get Cameron to study the alien. The point is to make Priya jealous.

She knows Cameron could never do it right. That'll get her back on the job."

Waldmire laughed. "That's some world-class manipulation right there."

She tipped her head with a small bow.

"No, seriously, Rick would have been impressed." His eyes twinkled, and for an instant, she saw a resemblance to her own face.

Butterflies swirled in Sierra's stomach. Waldmire had opened the door to the subject. He'd said "Rick," not "your father." She licked her lips. She could ask him something vague about her parents to see where the discussion went. She just needed to form the right question.

"I'm not sure that's the best approach for Priya, though," Waldmire went on. "She just lost her boyfriend and from what I've seen, she's feeling scared and alone. She needs sympathy right now." He shrugged, his face peaceful and calm. "At least, that's my read on it."

Sierra pursed her lips, deflated. Rick Preston had always maintained that a touchy-feely approach was a waste of time.

"What's on your agenda for today?" Waldmire asked.

"I'm going to see if David will cut the device out of me, and anyone else who's willing." She touched the back of her head, probing.

"You'll need to get Morrie to knock you out first."

She chewed her lip, confused. "I don't want to be stunned. The whole point is to prevent that from happening."

"I understand, but how could David begin the operation if you're conscious? Do you really think you could hold still while he slices into your neck?"

Cold dread washed over her. "I hadn't considered that."

They sat side-by-side and ate their breakfast, staring off over the fields.

"How are we doing on food?" Waldmire asked.

"There's plenty of dinosaur meat for now. Some is still getting smoked and some is getting cut up for stew before it gets too tough. Jasmine and a few others are trying to improve irrigation so the crops will grow faster." Sierra let her shoulders drop. "Everybody's doing something but me."

Waldmire put his arm around her. "That's what being a leader feels like sometimes."

The hug felt comforting and she leaned in, the shoulder of his Henley warm against her cheek. "I don't really want to be in charge," she said, though it wasn't completely true. She didn't trust anyone else to make the right decisions.

"These people look up to you," he said. "You've had an impact here."

His compliment made her feel a little better. She decided to test the waters by asking what he remembered about her mother. But before she could open her mouth, a commotion came from beyond the main fire pit. People were cheering.

Sierra stood to get a better look.

Kim and Morrie sat on the alien device, floating two feet above the ground.

Chapter Twelve

David ran to the carriage. He'd told Kim to keep away from the thing. It had practically killed her, and now she was floating on it. He grabbed her under her arms and lifted her off. The carriage, which had been sliding forward at a steady crawl, stopped immediately, still hovering at waist-height.

"Dad!" Kim squirmed like a dog in a bathtub. "Put me down."

"Hey, come on," Morrie pleaded, still in the vehicle.

"Yeah, they were just getting somewhere," Cameron said, standing with Kevin off to one side.

David dropped Kim on her feet, suddenly aware of his audience. He clamped his mouth shut, calming himself before he said something he'd regret.

"I'm with David," Kevin said. "That thing is dangerous. No one should be anywhere near it."

David extended an open hand in Kevin's direction, nodding. At least someone here agreed with him.

"We're figuring it out," Morrie said. "We just made it move, for crying out loud."

"Fine," David said. "You can keep working on it, but not my daughter."

Morrie pointed at Kim. "*She* figured it out."

"Come on, Ace," Cameron said. "She isn't a baby. Don't coddle her."

He scowled, holding his tongue. Barely.

"It isn't safe," Kevin said. "What if they crash it?"

Kim rolled her eyes. "Dad, we're being careful." She turned to Sierra, who was walking up with Waldmire. "Would you *please* talk to my dad?"

"It's my decision, Kim," David said. "I don't want you anywhere near this thing."

"That's bullshit."

"Language," he said.

Disbelief fell across his daughter's face. "Really? After everything that's happened, you're concerned about bad words?"

David felt himself growing hot. "Kim, you were clinically dead for an hour. You had no heartbeat. We don't know what that thing might do. I'm trying to keep you safe."

"We aren't safe. We're prisoners. We have to fight back." She sounded exactly like Sierra.

"Your father is right," Kevin said. He gestured at the carriage with his broken arm, still in a sling. "You're risking all our lives, messing with that thing. Look what you did yesterday. I think we should dismantle it."

David held up his hand. "Now hold on." He didn't want Kim working on it, but he didn't think it should be destroyed.

"Dad, let me show you what we've learned." Kim started toward the carriage, reaching.

Kevin grabbed her arm with his good hand. "Don't you touch it."

"Hey, easy," David said. His hackles rose at the sight of Kevin laying hands on her.

Kim shook free. "Look, every control has a counterpart on the opposite side." She gestured at the little mushroom shapes with buttons on them. "But they aren't always the same. Some are completely different." She pointed to a curved structure. It looked like the lever used to dispense pop at a fast-food joint.

On the opposite side, Morrie ran his hand over a cluster of shallow holes that honeycombed the inner wall. "You have to activate the controls in unison," he explained, pressing his thumb in one of the holes. "That's why you need two people." He stretched his other hand across the carriage. "A human can't reach both sides."

"I'm impressed you got it moving," Sierra said.

Morrie shrugged. "Kim deserves the credit. She said we should think about how that creature's limbs work. We should mimic its movements."

"How many controls have you tried?" David asked. He couldn't help but be fascinated.

Morrie shrugged. "I dunno, maybe half. It's a lot of trial and error."

David clasped his hands together and forced himself to keep his voice steady and calm. "You're going about it wrong. You need to document everything. Every combination you try, even those that don't seem to do anything, they all need to be written down." He looked at Kevin. "That way, we can undo anything harmful."

Kevin squinted. "You hope."

"Paperwork," Waldmire chuckled.

"Yeah, one problem," Kim said. "There's hardly any paper here."

Waldmire put a hand on her shoulder. "We'll figure something out. I was a courthouse stenographer before you were even born. I'm an expert on paperwork. We can make scratches on wood or something like that."

Kim turned back to David, eager hope on her face. "So if he documents everything, can I keep working?"

"You can supervise and help document," David said. "From a distance."

The look she gave him cut to the bone. He wished Lindsey were here to back him up. He felt alone.

Kevin cradled his broken arm. "So they're just gonna to keep messing with it, even though they might blow us all up?"

Sierra stepped forward. "Until our prisoner starts talking again, that carriage is our best hope of getting out of here. We have to keep studying it."

"If anything happens, it'll be your fault," Kevin said. "I ain't going near it."

"Exactly." Sierra swiveled around. "Everyone should keep their distance any time Morrie is working on it."

Kevin looked like he wanted to argue further, but instead, he shook his head and wandered away.

"What about me?" Kim asked.

"Supervise and document," David said.

She looked furious.

Morrie scowled. "Who's going to help me? I need a new partner."

Before anyone could answer, Kevin shouted from the other side of the main bonfire, "Hey everyone, look. Something's coming."

Chapter Thirteen

Sierra swung around. A blurry shape floated over the fields and stopped just short of the main fire pit, where it hovered twenty feet in the air, like a shimmer of heat.

Morrie climbed off the captured carriage and threw ropes across it, securing it to nearby stumps and rocks. A few yards away, Reggie and four others stood guard over the alien prisoner, which was still tied down.

Sierra started toward the blurry cloud.

"Careful, Sweetie," Waldmire warned. He sure sounded like a dad.

The villagers clustered together. Most were standing among the benches that fanned out beside the fire pit. A few stood at the work tables.

Cameron drew her pistol.

Sierra leaned close to the tall woman and spoke quietly. "Don't point it at them unless they threaten us. Let's give them a chance to talk."

Cameron narrowed her eyes as if she didn't agree, but she kept the gun pointed down.

Sierra walked past the fire pit, stopping ten feet from the shimmering shape. Nervous sweat trickled down her back.

Power through, Rick Preston said, deep in the back of her mind. She balled her fists, resisting the urge to draw her own pistol.

"What do we do?" Dee asked, fear in her voice. She crowded close to her friends, three other twenty-something women who'd been in the village since the beginning.

"Everyone else keep back," Sierra said. "Stay out of its range." If it stunned her, Morrie and Kim could use the carriage to wake her back up.

Kevin pointed with his good arm. "It's uncloaking."

The shape solidified, a bubble popping in reverse, to reveal another alien on another sled. The new creature looked exactly like the one they had captured, a big brown lump with limbs and appendages wriggling at one end, like the mouthparts on an aquarium shrimp. From below, the sled reminded Sierra of a skiff. Its flat bottom had no visible means of propulsion, and was smooth and clean, except for a few rods protruding from the edges.

The sled descended until it was five feet above the ground, facing off with Sierra. The creature rumbled. A moment later, a mechanical translation came from its sled. "*The caretaker must be freed.*"

Sierra looked past the crowd at the alien they had captured. Its appendages twitched, the first sign of movement since yesterday.

"Let us out of this place and we'll free him," Sierra said, swallowing.

"Sierra," Kevin hissed. "Don't piss it off."

The alien rumbled. Its sled dipped forward slightly as it emitted a translation. "*You are free to go where you like.*"

She wasn't getting through to it. "How do we get out?" she asked. "How do we leave the islands? We want to visit your world, meet your people."

More rumbling, followed by fluttery whispers, like a flock of birds, all flapping their wings at the same time. "*There is no out.*"

"What the hell does that mean?"

The alien didn't answer. It merely floated there.

She tried a different approach. "Who are you?"

"*A caretaker.*"

"What do you want with us?"

"*To preserve you.*"

This was going nowhere. She switched gears. "Bring us the rest of the people in storage."

She looked over her shoulder while she waited for the translation. David had picked up Barry. Most of the villagers huddled together in a tight knot. Jasmine, Dee, and a few others were backing away. They were all at a safe distance, assuming her theory about the stunning range was correct. She scanned the crowd, looking for Priya, wondering if she might be able to come up with better questions, but she couldn't find her.

The alien's hisses and rumbles resulted in a single word. *"No."*

"Those are our people." She couldn't show fear. Rick Preston had taught her that much, so she showed anger. Her voice grew sharp. "You have no right to keep them prisoner."

"Are you sure you know what you're doing, Shug?" Jasmine asked. She was overcautious, someone who would never rock the boat. Sierra ignored her. This boat needed rocking.

"The other specimens are safe."

"Where are they?"

No answer.

Sierra's breathing grew rapid. "We aren't specimens. We won't remain in this cage. And we won't release your companion until you bring us the rest of our people."

"There's another one," Felicia called out. A blurry shape descended into the village near the side opening in the wall.

Sierra spun. A third shape floated in from the opposite direction. Time seemed to slow down. She reached for the pistol on her hip. "Get back," she shouted. "Everyone spread out."

It was too late.

A high-pitched whine enveloped her and everything went black.

Chapter Fourteen

The zipping sound came from all three carriages, positioned around the crowd. Everyone fell to the ground.

Everyone except Morrie.

That answered that. They *all* had devices in their necks. Morrie winced as Jasmine collided with a bench on her way down.

When the douchebag from the motorhome opened fire, Austin had dropped like a rock, playing possum. Morrie did the same thing, careful to land in a position that allowed him to watch. He clenched his jaw to keep from screaming when his head hit the dirt, jolting the wound on his neck.

The caretakers rumbled and hissed at each other for several minutes. Morrie had gone down two or three seconds after everyone else, but they didn't seem to notice.

Something new appeared in the air, shiny with yellow highlights. Morrie shifted slowly to get a better look. An oblong shape slightly bigger than a caretaker floated over the work tables. Metal arms hung in a cluster at the front, giving it the appearance of a bloated tick.

The flying metal tick approached the prisoner alien, which lay on the old gallows platform Morrie had helped construct. He'd wanted to tear that thing apart for firewood. It was a shameful reminder of his mistakes.

One of the mechanical arms unfolded from the cluster of limbs on the floating tick-thing and reached toward a vine rope tied across the caretaker. It almost seemed alive, but it had to be a robot, some kind of drone. There weren't any windows and the thing wasn't big enough to hold an alien inside.

A spark popped at the end of the mechanical arm, snapping the rope. The drone was cutting the prisoner free. Morrie didn't know what to do. If they took the alien away from here, it might be for the best. He could use the carriage to wake everyone up, and with any luck, they'd be left alone after that.

The drone's arm moved to the next rope. Spark, *snap*. Spark, *snap*.

In less than a minute, the prisoner was cut free. It flexed its appendages and made several of those strange rumbling sounds. One of the other three aliens flew down close to it and rumbled a response.

The silver and yellow drone turned around to face the prisoner's carriage, which was also secured by a spider-web of vine ropes. Its mechanical arm went to work. Spark, *snap*.

Oh shit. If they took the carriage, Morrie wouldn't be able to revive anyone. He gauged the distance to the shed containing his rifle. Maybe fifty feet. Too far. Plus, the Garand M1 was empty and the damn thing was a bitch to load. His thumb had the bruises to prove it.

The floating robot moved its arm to the next vine. Spark, *snap*. Only three ropes remained.

Cameron had been carrying and she was just a few yards away. Morrie took a deep breath, counted to three, and rolled to his feet. He bounded across several bodies, stumbling when he caught his foot on someone's arm. He hopscotched over Kevin and Felicia, then steadied himself on the rocks lining the fire pit.

One of the caretakers dropped directly in front of him and another high-pitched zipping sound ripped through the air. Morrie grinned. It was trying to stun him. The back of his head still throbbed, but he was free from their control.

He spotted Cameron and the grin faded. She lay directly below the alien's carriage. He couldn't reach her without crawling under it.

Another *BZZZZZTTTTT* came from behind as a second carriage closed in. The third one hovered over by the prisoner.

Morrie grabbed a stout branch from the fire and lobbed it at the closest alien. The burning log hit the bloated creature and slid down inside the front corner of its carriage, out of sight, but still smoking.

The alien rumbled loudly and shot up, flying away from the village. The other caretaker, the one that had snuck up behind him, turned on its cloaking device and disappeared as well.

Morrie cackled. These bastards had flying invisible cars but he was fighting them off with sticks.

Across the crowd, the tick-shaped alien drone moved sideways over the captured carriage and snapped another rope. Only one remained.

Morrie looked for Cameron's gun, but there was no sign of it. He huffed, grabbed another burning log, and charged.

The drone hovered four feet above the ground, a floating silver and yellow blob the size of an overturned refrigerator. Morrie gripped the burning stick like a baseball bat and swung as hard as he could, hitting the side of the machine dead-on.

Sparks exploded from the end of the log, showering him. Embers struck his face, one right on his eyelid. Gasping, he dropped the remains of the log and swatted his face until he was sure his eye hadn't burned out.

The drone wobbled from the impact but seemed unharmed. The damn thing was solid.

Another zipping sound blasted through the air as the remaining alien abandoned its buddy on the ground and floated toward him.

Morrie's confidence swelled. "Keep trying, asshole."

The drone flew toward him as well. A new arm stretched out of the cluster hanging from its front. Small round objects lined the arm behind a wicked blade. At first, Morrie thought the objects were some kind of ammunition, but then he recognized the shapes. David had removed one from his neck. The drone was trying to implant a new stunner.

"Oh, no you don't." Morrie snatched one of the ropes that had secured their prisoner's carriage. If he could capture this flying robot, it might give them even more leverage. As the drone floated close, he looped the rope over the blade arm and stepped sideways. "Gotcha." He tied a quick bowline and pulled it tight, then tumbled out of the way.

A broad smile swelled across Morrie's face. He'd done it. He had tethered the drone to a stump. It swung in the air, pivoting back and forth at the end of its line.

The remaining alien floated over and descended. Morrie sucked in a breath, horrified. It was about to crush him.

He rolled out of the way and scrambled to his feet, then darted around the drone, still straining at its leash. Morrie moved behind it, keeping it between him and the attacking carriage.

The rope holding the drone jerked upward, already near the top of the stump, then slipped free.

"Shit."

Untethered, the drone continued to rise. Morrie grabbed the rope with both hands and jerked, pulling the front end of the robot back down.

The alien on the carriage charged. One of the antenna-like stalks protruding from the front was aimed right at Morrie's heart.

He dodged sideways and looped the rope over the stalk. The snare pulled tight as the alien passed.

The drone and the alien carriage were now tied together. Morrie stumbled back.

The alien tried to pull away but the robot tugged in the opposite direction, crashing into a short tree. It swung its spark arm toward the rope connecting them, but the carriage bucked and pulled so much it couldn't make contact.

Morrie ran back to the fire pit and grabbed two more burning branches. If he torched this last alien, maybe it would fly off, dragging the robot with him.

It wasn't necessary. The robot and the alien both turned on cloaking devices and disappeared as they climbed into the sky. The vine rope was still visible between them, each end vanishing into a shapeless blur.

The alien prisoner, still lying on its spot but no longer tied down, produced a series of angry rumbles as the two blurry shapes disappeared over the forest canopy.

Morrie stood alone, surrounded by bodies and breathing hard. The back of his neck throbbed and one of his palms burned, either from a rope burn or maybe from holding a flaming log. It didn't matter. He'd protected the village. He'd saved everyone. He'd even managed to hold on to the alien hostage and its carriage.

The prisoner retracted its limbs between its folds of skin and grew still again.

Morrie ran to the woodpile, where he found a branch about the length of a broom handle, then hurried to the carriage. He climbed aboard and kneeled by the little toebean control, then reached across to the opposite side with his stick.

"Steady now," he muttered.

He pressed the stick against the correct control on the far side. Once he had it securely in place, he touched the corresponding button next to him.

VVVVVRRRRRREEEEEEEEEET!

Kevin sat up. "Something happened."

Several other people close by began to move. Felicia rolled over and pushed herself to her feet. About half the village remained motionless, but that made sense. They were all out of range.

"Kevin, Felicia, help me drag everyone over here." Morrie smiled. He'd done it. Finally, he had done the right thing.

Chapter Fifteen

Priya Rami sat on the raft by the shoreline, whittling spear points with a knife and watching the sea. The water was fresh and pure, which fit the zoo paradigm. It wasn't actually a sea full of islands, it was a moat separating a collection of habitats. In the eighty-five days she'd been here, no one had ever seen anything in the water.

Until today.

When she first came down to the beach, something had splashed a hundred meters out.

She'd crept to the shoreline as a series of expanding ripples slowly vanished, leaving the turquoise surface as still as ever. After waiting a while, she had returned to the raft, where she watched and whittled, occasionally wondering if she'd imagined the entire thing.

Priya's thoughts went to Charlie, as they so often did now, filling her with an intense longing she craved like a narcotic, despite how much it hurt. They'd been an odd couple, a white blue-collar trucker from rural California and an Indian American astronomer fifteen years younger, but they'd also been a hell of a team. Charlie had gotten shit done, and he'd been respected for it. People listened to him. To both of them. People came to them for advice. Priya and Charlie busted their butts to make this place work. They'd shared a cabin and they'd certainly enjoyed one another in bed. Priya's throat tightened.

She might have even started to love him.

With Charlie dead, Priya felt purposeless. Everyone expected her to be an expert on the alien, but she'd studied the goddamn thing for days without even realizing it was alive. Her whole life had been about learning the rules. The rules of physics. The rules of mathematics. The rules of chemistry. Alien biology didn't seem to follow any rules. That frightened her, and worse, it made her feel stupid.

"Whatcha doin'?"

Priya swung around and rose on one knee, holding the sharpened pike out in front of her.

Scott stood behind the raft, his slacks rolled up and his shoes and socks in one hand. He still wore that silly suit coat, of course.

Priya relaxed her grip on the spear. Scott might be tedious and annoying, but he was also harmless. "I'm carving spears and watching the water," she said.

That was only the tip of the iceberg, but she wasn't about to explain that she was sitting here grieving for Charlie, stressing over the way Sierra was making all sorts of decisions with incomplete information, and lamenting the fact that she no longer felt like she understood the very world around her.

Scott climbed onto the raft and stood there, holding his shoes way too close to her face, assaulting her with odors of sulfur and spoiled cheese.

"The water? I thought there wasn't anything out there."

"I saw a splash twenty minutes ago," she said, breathing through her mouth, which decreased the odor but somehow made things worse. She imagined microscopic particles of Scott-foot-smell landing on her tongue.

"Like another dinosaur?"

"I don't think so," Priya said. "I don't know what it was."

The answer was way too common these days. There was so much she didn't understand. She turned back to the sea, in case there was another splash, and resumed whittling.

"Huh," Scott offered, adding tremendous insight to the discussion. "Want some help?"

She didn't want his help, but if he started whittling, at least he'd have to put his shoes down. She glanced at his silly jacket. "Suit yourself."

He placed the loafers off to one side, oblivious to her pun, then grabbed a spare knife and a stick. The arms of his coat bunched up as he started whittling.

Priya took a tentative breath through her nostrils. The air smelled mostly fresh.

"What do you think caused the splash?" he asked after a few minutes.

"It might have been one of the caretakers," Priya said. "I'm wondering if they could be aquatic."

"Oh yeah?"

"They don't seem to be ambulatory on land. And their faces remind me of crustaceans, with all those moving parts."

Scott looked lost. "Crustaceans?"

How could anyone not know what a crustacean was? "Yeah. Crabs, lobsters, shrimp."

Her disdain must have come through in her tone, because he explained himself. "Oh. Gotcha. I'm from South Dakota. No crustaceans there, but if you wanna know about antelope, whitetail, or pheasants, I'm your man."

"Do you have woodlice?"

Scott scratched his hair. "I sure hope not."

Priya squeezed her eyes shut. "Are there pill bugs or roly-polies in South Dakota?"

"Oh, yeah. Lots of those."

"They're crustaceans." Priya knew she was being obnoxious. Most people just thought of them as "bugs" and didn't appreciate taxonomy lessons.

"Gotcha," Scott said. "You know, you're pretty smart."

She let out a long breath. "Anyway, if the aliens are aquatic, it might explain why there aren't any fish or other sea creatures. The water might actually be the aliens' home, and not part of the menagerie." Scott squinted at *menagerie*, but Priya moved on. "It might also explain why the aliens said we couldn't come into their world. We wouldn't be able to breathe."

She placed her sharpened stick on the growing pile and picked up another.

Scott smiled. "Were you this smart as a kid? What kind of hobbies were you into?"

The questions didn't make any sense, so she ignored them. "The morphology of the caretaker's bodies also seems aquatic. They're too big and blobby to move around on land without those sleds. They remind me of pinnipeds."

Scott stared.

"Seals and walruses."

"Gotcha." He finished his first spike and reached for another, but froze, staring at the water. "Is that whatcha saw before?"

Priya followed his gaze.

Offshore, the water spread apart as a blurry shape lowered itself through the sea. It matched the rectangular footprint of a carriage, but when the shape passed below the surface, the water sloshed over the outline of a dome-shaped bubble.

"Look," Scott pointed back over the beach, where a second hazy blur was passing overhead. It had to be another carriage, with its cloaking device activated. Wisps of smoke trailed this one. The second cloud submerged into the sea like the first, but with smoke bubbling up behind it.

"They both went to the exact same place," Scott said.

"They did?" Priya was angry with herself for not noticing.

"Absolutely."

They watched silently for a few minutes as the sea grew still. Just when Priya was about to suggest they go back to report their discovery, Scott grabbed her shoulder, his eyes wide.

"What the hell is that?" A new blurry shape floated toward the sea, but this one had some sort of solid tail.

As it drew closer, the tail turned out to be a vine rope running through the air. A few yards back, the rope ended at the edge of yet another blurry cloud.

"I don't get it," Priya whispered. "Why would two caretakers be tied together?"

The blurry shapes came to a stop out over the water. The first cloud moved down, pulling the rope vertical. The second cloud followed.

"One of 'em's towing the other, like a broken-down Dodge," Scott said.

"Crap. I wonder if they recovered the carriage we captured." The idea didn't ring true, though. Aliens wouldn't pull it along with a vine rope, would they?

"Those two also went to the exact same place," Scott said.

Priya picked up a pair of spears.

"Whatcha doin'?" Scott asked.

She walked to the shoreline and positioned the spears side-by-side in the sand, pointing out to sea in the direction the shapes had gone. "I'm marking the place they went in. If they all went to the same spot, there must be something special about that location."

Scott stood straight and looked her in the eyes. "I think there's something special about you."

Priya bit down on the insides of her cheeks to keep from laughing. *What a segue.* Reading other people had never been her strong point. She'd been too self-absorbed to notice that Scott had been flirting with her all this time.

He smiled.

"Scott, I appreciate the compliment, but I'm still mourning Charlie." The line came easily. It was true, and hopefully it would fend him off until he lost interest.

"I understand," he said. His lower eyelids trembled, and for a moment Priya thought he might cry. He offered her another smile, but this one looked lonely. "It's gettin' late. I guess I'll head back." He turned and walked across the beach without a word.

Priya watched him disappear into the forest. She felt terrible for how she'd treated him. He wasn't a bad guy. They just didn't have anything in common. Her shoulders fell. Actually, they did have something in common. They were both utterly alone.

Chapter Sixteen

Randall only had one shot left. The rest of the ammo lay down by the remains of his fire. Most of it had been scattered around in the sand when the fucking wolf-pigs ate the *T. rex* arm right off the spit he'd built.

Fourteen of the beasts were now feeding on the dinosaur's carcass, leaving a sagging mess barely able to hold Randall's weight. He sat on the ribs, which wobbled more and more each time the wolf-pigs tore at the guts from inside the cavity.

Randall licked his chapped lips. He hadn't had any water all day and night would fall soon. If the carcass collapsed in the dark, the wolf-pigs would tear him to shreds. He'd seen the damage just one of them could do. It would be a nasty death.

One of the larger wolf-pigs looked at him and huffed a throaty bellow, its muzzle black with dried blood.

Another wolf-pig appeared at the edge of the little beach, bringing the count to fifteen.

"Shit."

The new wolf-pig trotted toward him. Just before it reached the dinosaur carcass, a loud whine ripped through the air, like someone zipping up the world's biggest sleeping bag. The wolf-pig fell over on its side, its tongue hanging between crooked teeth onto the sand. *All* of the wolf-pigs dropped, as if their bones had turned to rubber.

"What the hell?" Randall crept forward on the dinosaur's ribs and peered down. At least five of the fuckers lay slumped in the cavity beneath him.

A rumble came from above, followed by an odd voice. *"Caretakers need assistance with human specimens."*

Two rectangular shapes materialized as they floated down alongside the rock wall. They hovered in front of him, each carrying a big brown mass on top.

Randall squeezed the pistol grip. There were two of them and he still only had one round left. "Who are you?"

One of the shapes made a deep, stuttering rumble, and then a voice came from somewhere on its vehicle. *"Caretakers."* The voice sounded like a robot on a bad television show.

Was this the same kind of thing Dave had jumped on? Randall had seen that one from the top of the canyon, eighty feet up. He hadn't been able to tell what he was looking at then, and he could barely tell now. The thing had the face of a lobster, where all the little mouthparts moved around. He'd seen a tank full of lobsters at a fancy restaurant once and always wondered why the fuck anyone would want to eat something like that.

Randall looked at the wolf-pigs scattered around the beach. "Is it safe for me to get down?"

"Yes."

He slid off the carcass, staggered to the shoreline, and bent to drink like an animal. No water ever tasted so good. The air was better here, too. He drank his fill, took an extra gulp, and stood.

"Caretakers need assistance with human specimens," the brown thing repeated.

Except for the moving parts, the creature looked like a big turd. It had to be some kind of alien. No way anything from Earth looked like that.

"What kind of assistance?"

"Caretaker in village must be released. Human specimens do not cooperate."

Randall laughed. "Of course they ain't cooperating. Most humans just wanna fuck you over."

He kicked one of the wolf-pigs, which lay motionless right where it had fallen.

The alien said nothing.

Randall pieced the story together. "The humans on that other island captured your buddy. Is that it?"

He took a few steps toward the guns, spread out near the fire. The wolf-pigs had really trampled them, and one had even collapsed right on top of the whole mess, but he spotted a magazine for the M1911 off by itself in the sand.

A hovercar dropped down in front of him and produced more farty rumbles. *"Free our companion and we will place human specimens in storage."* It hovered between him and the magazine.

"Storage?" That sounded pretty goddamn ominous. He wondered if it included him. "Which one of you is in charge?" He wanted to focus his attention on the leader.

"Caretakers are equals."

It figured. The aliens were goddamn communists. He looked at both of them. "If I help you, what do I get in return?"

The aliens rumbled back and forth at each other for a long time, until finally a translated message came from the hovercar. *"What do you want?"*

That was an easy question. He wanted Dave and Sierra and all of those other fuckers to drop dead. He wasn't sure he should say that, though.

He also wasn't sure he was setting his sights high enough. He could still be top dog. He could be in charge. People would have to do whatever he told them. "If I help you put the bad humans away, will you leave me in charge of the rest?"

After a moment of rumbles, the alien replied, *"Human specimens are too dangerous."*

"You've got dinosaurs and wolf-pigs, and you're flying around in hovercars. How the hell can humans be dangerous?"

"Human specimens interfere. Human specimens engage with caretakers."

This answer made a strange sort of sense. A *T. rex* was a bad motherfucker, but it would never jump off a cliff onto a hovercar. Still, these guys had advanced technology.

"Why can't you just take them out yourselves? Why do you need me?"

The alien replied with another bout of rumbles. *"One human specimen does not torpor."*

"What the hell is torpor?"

A whiney zipping sound came from the hovercar. The wolf-pig lying on Randall's guns staggered to its feet like a newborn calf. Randall glanced around. The one near the water shifted up on its knees. Within seconds, all fifteen were back on their feet.

Randall raised his gun. "I thought they were dead."

The zip-whine repeated and the wolf-pigs all collapsed again.

"Torpor."

"You can do that to humans?"

"Yes. Except one."

"Why not?"

"Unknown."

"Well, can't you do something else? Shoot 'em or something?"

"Specimens are controlled with torpor."

He let that sink in for a minute. These alien shitbags were in over their heads. "You ain't never had to deal with nothing like humans before, have you?" No dinosaur was smart enough to figure out torpor, but somehow, the assholes in the village had. "How does torpor work? How do you think they stopped it?"

The alien didn't answer.

Randall put a plan together, thinking fast. "What you need is someone in charge of the humans. Someone who won't interfere with your business. That's me." He tapped his chest with his gun. "Your buddy got captured because the wrong people were in charge. I can free him, and then I can make sure those humans don't interfere no more."

Randall stood back while the aliens rumbled at each other. It was a safe bet the dinosaurs and wolf-pigs hadn't ever tried to negotiate with them either.

Darkness fell, as thorough and complete as always. Randall couldn't even see the gun in his hand, much less the two aliens in their hovercars, but they were still there, rumbling away. He walked slowly in the direction of his campfire, where he found a few embers still glowing. If he could get the fire built up again, he could have wolf-pig for supper and maybe even start putting the guns back together.

The rumbling continued for a while, until finally something was translated into English. *"If you eliminate the interfering specimens, you may remain."*

Randall smiled in the dark. "My pleasure."

Chapter Seventeen

David hadn't seen Barry all morning, Kim was stewing, and Morrie, his number one patient, looked like hell. For the moment, however, none of that mattered. He couldn't stop grinning. He was doing something he never expected to do again after crashing the Cessna.

He was flying.

After the aliens' visit yesterday, everyone agreed it was more important than ever to learn how to operate the carriage, but David still wasn't comfortable with letting Kim work on it. As a compromise, he let her direct the experiments while he sat at the controls. She was furious, and he honestly couldn't blame her.

But he was flying.

Sorta.

The carriage couldn't rise more than three feet off the ground because of the rope tethers. Still, they'd been at it since daybreak and they'd made a ton of progress. It would change everything. They could explore other islands. They could collect fruit from treetops. They might even be able to fly out of the menagerie, to the aliens' world.

"Press C, D, and G next," Kim said, sitting on the rock wall of the fire pit, about fifteen feet away. She'd assigned a lettering system to the holes clustered on the dashboard. Beside her, Waldmire marked a flat piece of wood with the charred end of a stick.

"C, D, G," repeated Morrie. "Okay." He sat cross-legged in the front right corner of the carriage, while David sat on the left, which was the pilot-in-command's seat, at least on Earth.

"Three, two, one," David said, and they touched the controls simultaneously.

The carriage lurched sideways, slamming David against the short front wall as Morrie tumbled into him, groaning.

"Did you touch the right ones?" Kim asked. Judging from her tone, she was sure they hadn't.

"Third, fourth, and sixth," Morrie said, sliding back to his side.

"Third, fourth, and *seventh*," David said. "Are you okay?"

Morrie's skin looked sallow and his eyes were droopy. David had put off operating on anyone else's necks because he wanted to monitor Morrie's recovery, and the more he saw, the more he grew concerned.

"It's nothing," Morrie muttered. "I get motion sickness."

David felt a swell of relief, along with a pinch of embarrassment. He should have picked up on it earlier, but he'd been too excited about flying.

Cameron walked up. "Nice ride, Ace."

He turned at her voice, excited to show her what he'd learned. The thought struck him like a hammer to the heart. It was exactly the sort of sentiment that he'd always directed toward Lindsey.

"When are you going to take me for a ride?" she asked, flashing an enticing smile.

Scott followed her over, wearing his blazer, as always. He pressed his hand into the foamy black surface of the carriage. "It's the perfect ride for a date, Doc. It's even shaped like a bed."

David looked down, uncomfortable that his daughter was hearing this discussion. The way his emotions were swirling, he didn't trust himself to come up with a response.

"Can you please try the right controls now?" Kim asked, not bothering to hide her annoyance.

She'd figured out so much, only to be forced to sit and watch. He really ought to let her take a turn. After spending the last several hours trying out different controls, the carriage was beginning to feel reasonably safe, even when Morrie screwed things up.

"Hold on," Morrie said. "I need a minute."

Kim crossed her arms and scowled.

Waldmire gave her a sympathetic look, then turned back toward the others. "I understand you saw something at the beach yesterday, Scott."

Scott waved his hand dismissively. "Priya was the one who spotted it. She thinks the aliens come and go from the water." He leaned forward over the carriage. "How does this thing work?"

David gestured at the cluster of holes in the front wall, each one the size of a quarter and about an inch deep. "These holes control direction, but in combinations that don't make much sense."

Scott looked uncertain. "There's no logic to how they're placed?"

David shrugged. "We think maybe it's like a keyboard, you know, where the common letters aren't next to each other."

"Why holes?" Scott asked. "Why not a joystick and a yoke? That at least would make sense."

"Because it wasn't made for us." David pointed at the alien, once again tied down on the wooden platform a few yards away. "See that thing's knobby little limbs? The holes are a perfect fit."

"Gotcha. So how do you lift off?"

"These two." David touched two of the holes. "But when you combine them with others, it all changes."

"Wait, why aren't you moving?" Scott asked.

"You have to touch controls on both sides at the same time," Morrie said, pointing to a cluster on his side. "That's why one person can't fly this thing alone. It's too far to reach across."

Cameron walked around and leaned on the front of the carriage. "Where's the throttle?"

David tapped a half-cylinder that looked like a hockey puck embedded in the side wall.

"That looks more like a trim wheel," Scott said.

David made a double take. A comment like that could only have come from someone with experience in the cockpit.

Scott gestured for him to continue.

"You have to nudge this wheel forward or back to change velocity," David said. "But it won't hold its position the way a throttle does. You have to keep adjusting it. And for some reason, acceleration is managed separately from velocity."

"I'm impressed," Cameron said.

He raised his eyebrow and smiled, pleased with himself.

"Will you please try the correct sequence again?" Kim grumbled from the fire pit.

Scott and Cameron stepped back. David checked that Morrie placed his fingers on the correct controls, then counted down from three.

The carriage slid smoothly sideways, stopping when it reached the end of its tethers.

"Not bad, Ace," Cameron said.

"Let's try a landing," David said. "Back to center, then forward and down to the ground, nice and easy."

"Okay," Morrie said, without much confidence. They placed their hands on the controls and David counted down again.

The carriage bucked like a mechanical bull and slammed to the ground. Morrie grunted, holding the back of his head.

"Is your neck okay?" David asked.

"No," he blared. "It's sick of getting bounced around. I'm gonna go lie down. We've been working all morning. I need a break." He stood and stalked off toward the work tables.

"Stay where other people can see you," David called out. "Tell them to come get me if your condition changes."

"Whatever you say, Doc." Morrie didn't look back.

"My turn," Kim said, standing next to the carriage, her arms crossed.

David was ready to let her try. They never would have figured out the controls so quickly without her. He opened his mouth to say as much, but Kim kept talking.

"Or would you rather to take your slutty new girlfriend for a ride?"

Scott snorted. Cameron looked bemused.

David grew red. "That isn't appropriate, young lady."

She held his gaze. "Oh, like it's appropriate for a married man to flirt with someone other than his wife?"

The comment stung, especially because he couldn't dispute it. But he also couldn't let his twelve-year-old talk to him like that.

"You aren't flying anything until you learn some manners."

"Fine," Kim growled. "I don't want to be anywhere near you. You left Mom on Earth to die."

David's skin prickled. "Jesus, Kim, you know that isn't true."

"Oh yeah, then where is she?" She opened her eyes wide and made a show of looking around. "Don't see her." She stormed off toward the cabins.

No one said anything for a small eternity. Finally, David stood. "I should go talk to her."

Waldmire held up a hand. "I wouldn't, if I were you."

"I didn't leave Lindsey behind," David said, looking around at everyone. "People were shooting at us. We had to get in the pod. I didn't have a choice."

"I believe you," Waldmire said. "Kim is grieving. Give her time."

David exhaled. Lindsey had often complained that he didn't give Kim enough time to cool down when she needed it. He turned to Cameron. "I'm sorry she called you that."

She shrugged. "Don't sweat it, Ace. I've been called worse."

He offered her a nod, genuinely appreciative. If their roles had been reversed, he wouldn't have remained so calm. He turned to Scott, trying to shift his focus. "Were you a pilot?"

Scott gave a clumsy salute. "I was First Officer for a regional airline in South Dakota, several years back."

Cameron glared at him. "You told everyone you were a hotel manager."

Scott shrugged, which made the shoulders on his blazer bunch up around his ears. "I'm a renaissance man."

She snorted.

"I quit flying a couple of years back," he said, as if that explained everything.

David wondered why anyone would leave a job in aviation to become a hotel manager, but decided not to press the issue. Right now, he just wanted to fly. It would keep him from going after Kim and saying something that would only make things worse.

"Come on," he said, patting the seat next to him.

Scott climbed in and took Morrie's spot, spreading the tail of his jacket behind him.

Cameron and Waldmire watched while David gave Scott a full overview of the controls. He also showed Scott the controls they *hadn't* figured out yet, including a separate cluster of holes in the center of the console with beady lumps inside. Going over the controls gave David confidence. They really had figured out a lot.

"Where do we start?" Scott asked.

"Let's make a short lift-off." Scott's fingers went to the correct spots. David smiled. He'd been paying attention. "Okay, the hardest part is the timing. We have to do this in sync."

They wobbled on take-off and listed slightly to the right, but the carriage rose up to the end of the rope tether. They were flying.

David talked him through a series of movements. Scott quickly proved to be a solid co-pilot. Morrie may have helped figure out the controls, but he didn't have the situational awareness, balance, and timing needed for flying. Scott got better with each maneuver.

After an hour or so, Barry ran up with Dee and three weary-looking women trailing behind him. David knew the feeling. Barry could be exhausting.

The boy climbed onto the carriage and squeezed between him and Scott.

"Have any of you seen Kim?" David asked the women.

"She climbed one of the trees over in the camping area," Dee said, glancing at her friends. "You should probably steer clear of her for a while."

"What did she say?"

Dee crossed her arms. "I'll never tell. But she's pretty pissed."

One of the friends nodded. They all looked to be in their late twenties.

David sighed. He needed to cool it with Cameron, at least for now. He probably shouldn't even talk to her when the kids were around.

"Are you going to start operating on people soon?" Dee asked. She looked nervous at the prospect.

"Sierra insisted on going first," he said. "Where is she?"

"She went down to the beach looking for Priya," one of the other women said.

David nodded. As long as Sierra was busy, he could get in more flight training, which scratched an itch he hadn't realized needed scratching.

Dee plucked a rope anchoring the carriage to a tree stump. "You aren't going to get very far tied down like this."

Scott elbowed David. "Whatcha think? Time to take off the training wheels?"

He looked over at the vine rope. The carriage felt surprisingly safe. Some sort of stabilization mechanism kept it upright, like a self-balancing scooter. "You know, it is getting to be a hindrance."

The moment he said this, Cameron climbed aboard and sat down behind him. "Let's do it."

"Yeah," Barry said.

"No, no, no," David said. "It's too soon. We're just figuring it out. Besides, it's got a weird drift to the right." It was probably Scott's failure to keep up, but he didn't want to say so.

Scott huffed. "Oh, come on. You already pissed off one kid."

The comment made David bristle, even though Scott's tone was light and jaunty.

Barry wrapped his arms around his neck. "Please?"

Mud crusted the boy's hands, but David didn't care. He was glad one of his kids didn't currently hate him.

"He's all yours," Dee said. She and her friends turned and wandered off.

"Please, Daddy," Barry repeated.

David wasn't sure what to do. If Kim found out he let Barry sit on the carriage while they practiced, she'd be livid. She'd call him a hypocrite. He tried to convince himself that wasn't fair. She was only twelve, after all, while he was an experienced pilot. Besides, they really needed to move around more than a few feet to fully understand how this thing worked, and taking Barry along was the best way to keep an eye on him.

"Okay, okay," he said finally. "Here's what I'll agree to. We're not going far and we're not going high. We'll stay low and slow, just a few feet off the ground, out over the fields." He felt comfortable with the controls for that much, at least, and all they had to do was remove their hands to make the carriage stop and hover in place. They'd be safe. "Just over the fields," he repeated.

Barry and Cameron nodded.

Scott offered him a thumbs-up. "Roger, captain."

David gave him a series of instructions while Cameron untied the vine tethers and handed them down to Waldmire. A moment later, the carriage rose up to about ten feet. As they floated slowly toward the fields, David's cheeks pulled wide.

He was flying.

Just over the fields, he tried to tell himself. *Low and slow.*

In less than an hour, they were soaring over the treetops toward the canyon.

Chapter Eighteen

Sierra found Priya at the coast, staring out to sea. She seemed to have given up. She'd been keeping away from the alien prisoner ever since it started communicating, and in the last day or so, she'd practically disappeared.

Before that, Priya had been like a partner to Sierra. They'd figured things out together. Now, it felt like she was avoiding her, too.

She crossed the beach, hoping she could find a way to get the old Priya back.

Yesterday, while everyone else got stunned, Priya had been down here, where she claimed to have seen the aliens fly into the water. Sierra walked up and stood next to her, looking out at the flat blue surface. "So this is the spot?"

"Yes. Straight out from here." Priya used her foot to nudge a spear lying in the sand, its point right at the shoreline.

"And you're sure it was them?"

"Yes. I saw the rope that connected two of them together. If you don't believe me, I really don't care."

Sierra held up a hand. "I believe you. I just wish I'd seen it." Like everyone else in the village, she'd been stunned at the time. Turned off. Unplugged. "Any sign of them today?"

Priya shook her head.

"How far from the shore?" Sierra asked, wondering if she could wade out and search the area. As far as she knew, the seas here were completely empty. There weren't any fish, or crabs, or even seaweed.

"I'm not sure. A hundred meters, maybe. Right about there." Priya extended her finger. "I think." She sounded defensive.

The glassy water reflected the empty blue sky, making it difficult to tell where she was pointing. Sierra was a decent swimmer, but without knowing exactly how far to go, she would probably be wasting her time. She sighed.

"Sorry I can't be more precise," Priya snapped, clearly sensing her disappointment. "What difference does it make, anyway?"

Sierra shrugged. "I was thinking I might swim out to see if anything's there."

Priya took her arm and pulled her face-to-face. "What? You can't. What if they stun you? You'd sink to the bottom. They're dangerous. Can't you see that?"

Sierra shook free. "Yes. But I'm not going to let it stop me. Otherwise, what are we supposed to do? Just live out our lives here like zoo animals?"

Priya held her gaze, which wasn't easy for her, Sierra knew. She disliked eye contact. "Why not? Joe is dead. Randall is gone. We have food, shelter, clean water. What more do we need?"

The argument was so foreign, so *alien*, Sierra barely knew how to respond. Had the trauma they'd been through broken Priya? If so, losing her as a collaborator was the least of Sierra's concerns. She was worried about her as a friend. The poor woman was hurting.

"I don't think we can trust the aliens," Sierra said, keeping her tone measured.

"They said they only want to observe us."

"Yeah, but what if they get bored and drop a bunch of dinosaurs on our island, just to observe that?"

"What other options do we have?" Priya asked.

"We need to show them we're sentient beings, worthy of being treated as—"

"As equals?" Priya asked. "You can't be serious."

"Maybe not equals, but we aren't like the other creatures here. We've developed morality, self-reflection, art. That has to count for something."

"What do you expect them to do?"

"I expect them to let us out of here. We deserve to live with some autonomy and stability. We aren't fish in a tank."

"How do you know that's even possible? This might be the only safe place for us."

"We have no control over our lives here. I'm not willing to live like that. Hell, we can't even control our own reproduction."

None of the women in the group had menstruated, and no one had gotten pregnant. Sierra wondered if the neck devices manipulated their hormones, or if there were implants somewhere else in their bodies. For all she knew, the aliens had tampered with their organs. Her skin crawled at the thought.

"Holding one of them prisoner is doing exactly the same thing to them that they're doing to us. It will escalate. If we piss them off, what's to stop them from putting us all into storage? Or worse?" Priya blanched. "They're way more advanced than us. We have no idea what they could do."

Waldmire was right. Priya was definitely scared.

"You're terrified of them, aren't you?"

Priya puffed up. "Of course I'm terrified. We don't understand anything about them." She pointed in the general direction of the path. "I couldn't even tell that the one in the village was alive. It didn't breathe or move for days, and then it started talking. Everyone expects me to have all the answers. I was an astronomer. That doesn't make me an expert." She looked at the sky and snorted. "There aren't even any stars here."

Sierra summoned Rick Preston, even mimicking his intonations a bit. "You have to power through, Priya. You have way more scientific training than anyone else here. You know more than you think. The village needs you."

Priya tilted her head. "Why in the hell are you talking like that?"

Sierra smirked. "There's no bullshitting you, is there?"

"Nope," Priya said, with a smug smile.

"My father was a big-shot Hollywood executive, a take-charge kind of guy. I was channeling him." She let out a long gush of air. "At least I think he was my father. Now I'm not so sure."

Priya squinted. "Huh?"

"Forget it. My point is, you don't have to have all the answers. You just have to keep trying. We'll figure it out if we work together. That prisoner is the only leverage we have. It might be the only thing that's keeping them from stunning us all and packing us away." She looked around at the islands offshore. "The other animals in this place, the rhinos and dinosaurs, they go their whole lives without even seeing the caretakers. We captured one of them. We've learned how to cut out the stunner device. We've got this."

Priya looked down and nodded faintly. When she looked back up, it seemed as if a weight had lifted from her shoulders. "You don't give up, do you? Did you get that from your father?"

Sierra produced a bitter smile, remembering Rick Preston's body at the suicide party. "That's what I used to think."

Priya squared her shoulders. "I've been wondering if the creatures might be aquatic. They certainly aren't mobile on land."

Yes. This was the old Priya, thinking things through. "Have you thought about offering our prisoner food or water? Maybe we could get it talking again with a bribe."

"I can try," Priya said.

"All we can do is try." Sierra nodded toward the forest. "Come on. Let's get back."

Priya pointed at the sea. "Shouldn't someone keep watch here?"

Sierra was already thinking about that. "Let's put Waldmire on the job. He can whistle so loud we'd hear it in the village. Also, Morrie and David are making real progress with the sled. If we could get it out over the water, maybe we can see if there's anything down there."

Priya nodded. "Maybe we can figure out how to fly it *into* the water, like the aliens."

Sierra chuckled. She hadn't thought of that. This was the Priya she needed.

They were halfway across the beach when a slurping splash came from behind. They turned and froze.

A blurry shape rose from the sea, directly out from Priya's spear. Water spilled over the sides, marking its outline, the size of an alien sled, but with a dome over the top.

"We should run," Priya whispered.

"No. If we run, they'll know we spotted it. Try to look casual."

"There's another."

A second blurry cloud emerged from the sea, directly below the first, which was now flying straight toward them. Water dripped onto the spear at the shoreline. Priya tensed. Sierra took her arm and to her credit, Priya didn't flinch or pull away.

"They're coming," Priya whispered.

A third shape rose behind the second.

"It's okay. They're just flying over us," Sierra said, hoping she was right. If they got stunned here, it might be hours before anyone found them.

By the time the first caretaker passed overhead, most of the water had dripped off, leaving only a light trickle. Sierra held her breath as drops pattered on her head and shoulders. She kept her gaze fixed on the sea while the other two blurry clouds floated over. Several seconds after the third one passed, she asked, "Are they gone?"

Priya looked back. "The last one just disappeared over the treetops. They're headed to the village. We have to warn them."

Sierra kept her attention on the spreading ripples where the vehicles had first appeared, fixing the distance in her mind. "They'll get there way before we ever could. There isn't anything we can do."

"What if they stun everyone?"

"They can't stun Morrie. He'll fight them off like he did before and wake everyone up." Sierra walked toward the water. "I've got the spot in sight. I want to see where they came from. I'm going out there."

"You're crazy," Priya said, with a touch of admiration.

The ripples had vanished by the time Sierra reached the shore, but she kept her focus on the point where they'd been centered, maybe a hundred yards out. Now that she'd seen it herself, she knew exactly where to go.

"Hold on," Priya said.

Sierra pursed her lips, bracing for an argument.

"Give me a second and I'll drag a canoe over. We'll go out together. That way, I can keep you from doing anything reckless."

Sierra smiled. This was the old Priya. "We'll see," she said. "Depends on your definition of reckless."

Chapter Nineteen

The carriage flew thirty feet above a thundering herd of wooly rhinos. Alice Cameron liked them much better from the air. No risk of getting gored or trampled.

David, who sat cross-legged in the front left corner, glanced back at her, a goofy grin spread across his face. The edges of his eyes crinkled with crow's feet and his cheeks pulled wide, making him look older and younger at the same time. Next to him, Barry looked like he was on a ride at a theme park. Even Scott, sitting in the front right corner, had a glint in his eye.

Cameron couldn't help but smile too. She wanted to take the controls and see how fast this thing would go. David kept the speed low, around ten or fifteen miles an hour, but still, they were finally getting somewhere, both literally and figuratively. They could explore the other islands safely now. They would float above them, out of harm's way, and they could do it all without endless hours of paddling.

Barry leaned over the front console, counting the rhinos. David clenched the boy's shirt tail, keeping a tight grip on the kid.

While Barry was preoccupied, Cameron pressed against David's back, watching his hands on the controls. He looked over his shoulder again, their eyes only inches apart. She enjoyed the feel of his body. It had been way too long.

The canyon zig-zagged on their left, a lightning-bolt scar that ran almost all the way through the plateau. As they neared the end, with its little waterfall trickling from the back wall, David told Scott to turn left ten degrees. They each touched a pair of the creepy little holes and nudged the half-cylinders protruding from the inside wall.

The sled turned left, but it tilted slightly to the right at the same time.

"Keep that corner up," David said, his voice smooth and commanding. Scott had been a commercial pilot, while David only flew private planes, yet Scott deferred to everything he said. Cameron didn't handle authority all that well when it was directed at her, but when directed at someone else, it was pretty damn hot.

They adjusted the controls and the sled leveled out as they passed over the waterfall.

The herd of rhinos regrouped off to the right. "I bet we could hunt them from the air," she said.

"How you figure?" Scott asked. "I thought we couldn't spare the ammo."

The group had used a dozen rounds to bring down a single rhino on their ill-fated hunt.

"We'd drop a net on one of them." She pictured short logs tied to the edges of a woven vine net. The rhino would get tangled and the herd would leave it behind. It would be easy to spear after that.

"Hell, yeah." Scott said. "I love it."

They passed the back edge of the plateau, soaring out over the treetops. No one had explored this part of the island, but from above, it looked exactly like the side they lived on, with a forest of pine trees all the way to the beach.

Barry rose up on his knees again, holding on to the front of the carriage. "Can we go there, Daddy?" He pointed to a much smaller island a few miles away.

Tropical foliage rose in the middle of a long, white sand beach surrounded by turquoise water. Cameron felt a wistful pang. It reminded her of Hawai'i.

"It's too far," David said. "We need to get back. I should check on Kim."

"It'll only take a couple of minutes," Cameron said, reaching around and hugging his chest. She spoke into his ear. "Maybe we can grab some fruit."

She had talked him into flying up over the plateau and she felt confident she could get him across to the next island.

David smelled like dirt and sweat and wood smoke. She really wanted to spend time with him away from everyone else. Cameron didn't care what the kids thought, but David sure as hell did, and she had to respect that. His dedication to them was part of what made him so attractive. If they flew across to the other island, she could look for someplace that she and David could return to later, alone.

They raced above the forest, almost to the coast. The wind cooled her hair. For the first time in a long time, Cameron felt happy.

"It's your call," Scott said. "I'm game, though."

David looked over his shoulder at Cameron, his eyebrow raised. She tightened her grip on his chest just the tiniest bit. He sat up straighter, leaning into her.

The craft dipped to the right again.

"See, there's something wrong with this thing," David grumbled. He and Scott brought the front corner back up. "We need to figure it out."

"We've got it under control," Scott said. "You can take some fruit back as a peace offering for your girl."

David tensed under Cameron's arms as they passed the beach and floated out over open water, three hundred feet above the surface. "Come on, Ace," she whispered. "We should at least scout it out. Show me what you can do." She felt him relax slightly, and then she pulled away. If he wanted her arms around him again, he had to earn it.

He looked back at her, conflict clear on his face. He didn't want to take unnecessary risks, but he also really wanted to keep flying.

"What if we drop down to twenty feet or so above the water?" Cameron suggested. "If we do that and keep our speed low, we should be perfectly safe."

David's eyes twinkled. She'd given him just what he needed.

"Okay," he said finally. "Just a quick flyby. Then we head right back. We're not landing."

Cameron smiled and squeezed his shoulders as he turned forward.

"Slow descent," he said, touching two of the little holes. One lowered them vertically, like the collective on a helicopter, and another dropped the pitch of the nose. Cameron had begun flight training in the Army, focusing mainly on choppers, but the program ended when the comet showed up.

The front right corner fell suddenly.

"Don't drop so much," David barked.

"I'm not," Scott said.

"He wasn't," Cameron said. "I was watching."

David's hands danced across the controls "Bring it level." The carriage evened out, then just as before, the right front corner fell sharply. "Stop descending." They were more than halfway to the small island. "That's enough. We're going back."

No one argued with him.

David and Scott adjusted the controls, but the flying car continued its downward curve.

"What's happening?" Barry asked.

Cameron leaned over the side. Goosebumps pricked her arms. The surface was two hundred feet below, flat as glass. A fall from this height would be like hitting concrete.

"Trouble's coming," she said.

Chapter Twenty

For the first time in hours, Morrie didn't feel the need to puke. Between the pain in his head and nausea from riding that damn carriage, it was a wonder he hadn't blown chunks all over everyone.

He lay on a bench near the fire pit with his eyes closed. He'd nodded off for a short while, but now he needed to get up and make himself useful. He wanted to review Waldmire's notes to see if they gave him any idea how to activate the cloaking device.

He also wanted to make sure Kim got the credit she deserved. She'd figured out at least half the controls, maybe more. She'd earned a turn as test pilot, and she'd probably weather it better than he had. He was proud of her, and proud of himself, too. He was finally on the right side.

"Morrie, Shug, wake up," Jasmine said. "Something's coming."

He sat up on the bench. "Caretakers?" He was ready. They couldn't stun him, and if they stunned anyone else, he could use the carriage to wake them, just like yesterday.

Except the carriage was gone. His confidence shriveled. David and Scott had disappeared on a test flight right before Morrie's nap.

"It's something else," Jasmine said.

A pod floated in over the fields, exactly like the one Morrie had found with Austin and Felicia in that mountain stream all those months ago.

Jasmine glanced his way. "Be ready for anything."

Jasmine wasn't the sort of person Morrie would have been close to on Earth. She was big, boisterous, and Black, while he was just as small, quiet, and white as could be. She was also at least ten years older than him. But she was the warmest soul he'd ever met. To her, everyone was "Sugar" or, if she really liked you, "Shug," and she was always trying to take care of people, to help them out. What difference did any of that other stuff make?

"Hey everyone, come and see," Kevin shouted, pointing with his good arm. "They sent a pod."

The villagers crowded around. Kona barked.

Morrie hurried to the storage shed, grabbed his rifle, and carried it over to the stone fire pit, where the heat felt good against his back. He wouldn't be caught off guard this time.

The pod descended in the field just beyond the work tables and settled in the dirt, crushing some of the green shoots they'd planted.

"The caretakers gave in," said Kelly, a barista from Cheyenne. "They're bringing the other people."

Ever the optimist, that Kelly. Her comment brought several nods of agreement.

Her boyfriend, Nick, moved close and took her hand. "Why isn't it opening?" he asked.

"You have to touch it," Kevin said. "You touch it to make it open."

Jasmine rolled her eyes. Morrie smiled. Kevin never said anything that wasn't completely obvious.

"Where's Dad?" Kim asked, walking up beside Kona.

"They took a test flight," Morrie said. "They should be back any minute," he added, hoping it was true.

Kim's face darkened with an expression that could have melted steel.

Morrie wondered if they could tie down the pod somehow, to prevent it from flying away. The smooth, curved shape would make it challenging. The pod looked like an egg, except tapered on both ends instead of just one, and as big as a van.

Jasmine headed closer, probably intending to welcome whoever was inside.

Morrie decided right then and there that he would invite her to join him for a walk on the beach, just to talk and get to know her better. If she had the balls to approach that pod, he could man up and ask her out.

"Why just one?" Waldmire asked. "There should be thousands."

Kelly shrugged. "Maybe it's a demonstration, like an act of good faith. They're showing us they can do it."

Nick pulled Kelly back a few steps.

Kona ran up beside Jasmine, sniffing and wagging. Everyone else drew close to one another, as if seeking safety in numbers, but not Jasmine. She stood her ground. Her hand moved toward the pod. Just before she touched it, an equator appeared, along with a sharp hiss. Jasmine jerked her hand away and took a few steps back.

Whispers of anticipation came from the crowd.

Morrie brought the Garand up in front of him and loaded it. He kept the barrel skyward, ready to bring it down in a split second. Something wasn't right.

Kona's tail drooped between her legs.

"Come here, girl," Kim called. She snapped Kona's leash onto her collar and tugged her deeper into the crowd.

The pod separated and the top half floated upward.

"It's opening," Kevin said.

Jasmine turned and gave him the stink eye again.

The top of the pod stopped moving and hung three feet in the air. A dark shape sat in the middle. Half the crowd took several steps back.

Jasmine leaned forward. "Hello? Who's there?"

"Where's Dave?" came a familiar voice. "I got a message for him."

"Holy shit, that sounds like Randall," Kevin said.

Morrie brought the rifle down to a firing position, trying to get a bead on the asshole. He placed his thumb on the safety, ready to nudge it forward.

"Somebody do something," Kim said, her voice low and trembling.

"David isn't here," Jasmine said. "We don't need any trouble." She shifted sideways, moving directly into Morrie's line of fire.

He jerked the barrel skyward and took a shuddering breath. *Dear God.*

"How 'bout Sierra?" Randall asked, still sitting in the center of the pod.

"She isn't here either," Jasmine said.

Morrie climbed up onto the wall of the fire pit, which gave him a clear view into the pod. He positioned his feet carefully. The ground was only a few feet down in front of him, but if he fell backwards, he would land in a caldera of hot coals.

"God damn it, where are they?" Randall barked.

One of the rocks wobbled beneath Morrie's feet. He shifted, just managing to keep his balance, and brought the Garand's stock back to his shoulder. Looking down the barrel, he placed the front sight over Randall's dark shape. "Get out of there with your hands up," he called out, trying to sound authoritative. "Don't try anything."

Randall didn't move. "Morrie, don't you cause no trouble now."

The shimmer of a cloaked carriage floated directly over the pod. Everyone surged back.

"Get away from them, quick," someone shouted.

"There's more," yelled someone else.

Morrie glanced to both sides. Two other blurry shapes closed in, surrounding them. He held still, careful to keep his balance.

Several people gasped. Felicia darted toward the perimeter wall. One of the clouds dropped in front of her. She lurched to a stop.

"Here we go." Kevin sat on the ground and lay back, cradling his arm against his chest, obviously preparing to be stunned.

Over on the gallows platform, Reggie threw another rope across the alien prisoner.

Morrie's heart jackhammered in his chest. If the aliens stunned everyone, he wouldn't be able to revive them until David came back. He tightened his grip on the rifle.

He had to deal with Randall by himself.

Chapter Twenty-One

Priya dragged one of the dugout canoes next to Sierra, who stood frozen at the shore. The bow sloshed in the water. She didn't know what Sierra was up to, but she was fairly certain it would be right on the line between bold and downright *lōlō*.

"Can you grab a couple of rocks?" Sierra asked, keeping her gaze on the sea.

"Why? Haven't you got enough rattling around in your head?"

Sierra chuckled and held her hands about a foot apart. "Melon-sized." She pulled Joe's big pistol from the holster on her hip. "Wait. Take this. Hide it by the raft."

Priya took the gun, which was heavier than she expected, and walked over to the spikey raft, trying to convince herself it would be okay. All of her coworkers at Keck Observatory stayed in their little boxes, always doing what was expected, including her. Sierra wasn't like that. She thought of things other people wouldn't. Like dropping stones on an underwater alien city from a canoe, or whatever Sierra had in mind.

She found the basket of rocks on the raft and dumped them onto the deck. Her instincts screamed, *return to the village*. They could observe whatever was happening from the safety of the woods. Priya shook her head. Sierra would never go for that, and despite all of her misgivings, she thought maybe Sierra was right. Whatever was happening at the village was out of their control.

Priya selected two rocks, hid the gun in the bottom of the basket, and walked back to Sierra. She hadn't moved.

"Did I miss anything?"

"No. I'm keeping my focus on the spot they came from, to mark the distance. Did you find some rocks?"

"Yeah. Right here."

Sierra didn't bother to look at them. "Perfect. Put them in the canoe."

"Ballast?" The dugout made hollow sounds as Priya dropped each rock inside. "What's going on, Sierra? What are you planning?"

She didn't answer. Instead, she reached back and grabbed the prow. "Help me push it in the water." Without looking away from the spot, Sierra pulled the boat forward.

"Maybe I should stay here," Priya said, her fear competing with her curiosity. She still wasn't sure what Sierra intended to do, but she had the feeling it was something akin to throwing rocks at a hornet's nest.

"Your call," Sierra said. When she was thigh deep, she brought the canoe next to her and stepped inside. She reached back, slapping blindly for a paddle.

Priya sighed, her curiosity winning out. She climbed in the back and extended a paddle toward Sierra's grasping hand.

"All three of them surfaced at the exact same place," Sierra said as they paddled out. "I think their civilization is below us."

"And now you're going to bomb it?"

"Something like that." She sounded like she was trying to be coy. "Slow down. This is the spot. At least, I think it is. Stop paddling."

Priya looked over the side. The water was too deep to see anything but a murky blue-gray void. "If we had enough rope and a log, we could mark the location with a buoy."

"Why? So we can come back later?" Sierra placed her paddle in the canoe and sat up on the prow, facing Priya. "I want answers now." She fell backwards into the water. A moment later, she surfaced, took a deep breath, and then floated face-down.

Priya had never met anyone so impetuous. Sierra leaped without looking. And yet, Priya held her breath, barely able to contain her excitement about what they might discover.

Sierra came up for air.

"What did you see?"

"Nothing yet." Sierra took another big breath and dove below the surface with a froggy breaststroke. A sheen of bubbles marked her path away from the canoe.

Priya looked over to the forest, wondering how long it would be before the caretakers returned. Were they at the village? What if they came back while she and Sierra were blocking their route? Maybe this was a mistake. Maybe they should go try to help the others. What if everyone was stunned?

Sierra surfaced four or five meters away.

"Anything?"

She didn't answer. Instead, she took a deep breath and submerged again. This time the bubbles all came up at the same spot, which meant she was diving deeper, not swimming around. Without a sun overhead, the water didn't have any sparkle. It was like staring into nothingness.

A minute later, Sierra broke the surface and sucked in air. "Over here," she gasped.

Priya brought the canoe next to her. Sierra held onto the side, breathing hard.

"What is it? What did you find?"

"There's a ring," Sierra said. "A circle. Right below me. I swam halfway down to it."

"Is it a structure?" Priya wanted to see it herself.

Sierra pushed wet hair away from her face. "I think it might be the entrance into our menagerie. I think it's how they come and go. Like an airlock, maybe."

"How big?"

"Big. Way bigger than the sleds."

Priya looked around, certain the caretakers would be back any minute. "What should we do?"

"Give me one of the rocks," Sierra said. She blew in and out, taking deep breaths.

Priya sat still. "What if you piss them off? What if it springs a leak? You could drain the whole sea."

Sierra shrugged. "Then we'll be able to walk to the other islands."

"Yeah, and everything on the other islands can walk here."

Sierra made a curious face. "That would be interesting. But don't worry, I'm not going to bomb it." She held out an open hand.

Kneeling right at the edge, Priya lowered a rock to her. "What are you doing?"

Sierra cradled the rock against her side and gripped the edge of the canoe with her free hand. "I'm just going down to see what I can find out. Be right back."

Priya leaned away to keep the canoe from rolling over. "What? You can't go down there. How do you know it's safe?"

"Sometimes you just have to go with your gut." Sierra took one more slow, deep breath.

Before Priya could say anything else, Sierra let go of the canoe and disappeared.

Chapter Twenty-Two

"Bring that corner back up," David said, trying to keep the fear from his voice. The carriage listed thirty degrees to the right. If they flipped over, nothing would keep them from falling out. There were no seatbelts, nothing even to hang onto. The carriage was just a big floating platform. He touched the control that ought to roll them back level. "Bank left."

If they fell from this high, they'd be killed on impact.

Scott did as instructed, but nothing happened. He looked at David with wide eyes.

The sled continued to tip.

"Lower the left side."

They triggered the controls and the carriage leveled out somewhat, but the front also dipped forward. Everyone leaned back.

"Are we going to be okay?" Barry asked.

I don't know, we'll find out, won't we? The old phrase buzzed through David's head. "We need to get lower." He didn't know if the vehicle was damaged, out of fuel, or what, but it wasn't responding properly. A dark thought passed through his mind. What if the caretakers were controlling it? He brushed the possibility aside. If the aliens were controlling it, surely they would do more than cause the front corner to list downward. "How high are we?"

"About a hundred feet now," Cameron said.

"Straight descent for three seconds," David instructed.

"Three seconds," Scott repeated.

They touched the controls that caused the sled to drop, but it moved faster than before. If they hit the water at this speed, they'd be pancaked against the sled's surface.

"How far back is our island?" David asked, not daring to look around.

"More than a mile," Cameron said.

That settled it. There was no turning back. The island they had been flying toward lay less than a half mile in front of them. "Push closer," he said. "Try for the beach."

They lurched forward, but the front right corner dipped again.

"Enough," David said. "Roll back to the left." The carriage didn't respond. Instead, it spiraled, dropping steadily, now fifty feet above the water.

He never should have brought Barry. What the hell had he been thinking?

The end of the long beach reached toward them like a scythe. Stubby plants dotted the higher ground and dense vegetation covered the island's interior. They had to get closer.

The carriage listed farther to the right. "Compensate," David called out. He and Scott adjusted their controls simultaneously. The spiraling continued, but not so tightly. The craft leveled as it drifted downward in a wide, curving arc.

"What if we jump out?" Barry asked.

"No," David shouted. If they jumped, the carriage might come down on top of them. Even a minor bump could knock them out. Unconsciousness meant drowning. There wasn't time to explain all that. "Brace yourself, Bud. Curl in a ball."

Barry did exactly as instructed, thank God.

"When we hit water, get clear. Don't let it pull you down." He turned and barked at Scott, "Side slip to the right."

They both touched three different controls, which should have slid them right, but nothing happened. Scott pounded the control panel. "We're done."

"I'm not done," Cameron grunted. "Get us closer to that island."

"Let's try reverse," David said. "Maybe we can get closer by backing up. On my mark." He placed his hand on the controls and glanced over to make sure Scott was ready. They spiraled lower. Directly ahead, the island they'd come from swung into view, which meant the new island was behind them. *"Now."* The carriage jerked backwards so hard David felt like he might fall forward over the console. The spiraling continued, but they were also moving closer to the new island. When the turn started to take them back out to sea, he shouted, "Enough, stop."

They were still a hundred yards from dry land and losing altitude rapidly.

Scott rolled into a ball, face-down on the foamy surface of the carriage. He clasped one hand over his neck and put the other over Barry's back. David's heart stuttered. Scott was shielding his son.

Dropping fast, they spiraled around to face the little island again.

Cameron grabbed David by the shoulders and pressed him down, tucking him next to Barry. He placed his arm over the boy's head, hoping the foamy surface would absorb some of the impact.

The carriage lurched and shuddered. Barry wailed. David's stomach tumbled into his throat. He couldn't tell if they were still spiraling. It felt like they were moving sideways. If they hit the water with a high lateral velocity, they'd flip over. The carriage would knock them unconscious and crush them.

He held his breath.

The impact slammed him flat. A whooshing splash enveloped him, then the sound of cracking metal. David bit his lip and pain throbbed in his chin.

He flailed for Barry, who was no longer under his hand. Just as he opened his mouth to shout his son's name, the smothering weight of water spilled over and swallowed him.

Chapter Twenty-Three

Sierra plunged through the water, holding the rock against her side like a football, descending faster than she'd expected. Pain stabbed her ears. She pinched her nose and equalized her eardrums, repeating the action every few seconds. She knew this was crazy, but she didn't care. She had to do something. She wanted answers.

Her clothes clamped against her skin as the pressure increased and the temperature dropped. The circle on the seabed below grew larger. It had to be thirty feet down, maybe forty. She was heading straight for it, face first. As she went deeper, darkness closed in and she began to wonder if she'd made a mistake.

No one had seen anything in the water here, but that didn't mean some horrible monster wasn't lurking in the depths. Priya thought the aliens might be aquatic. Sierra tensed, imagining one of those brown blobs grabbing her with its spindly limbs.

The cold pressed in tighter and tighter as the artificial ring on the seabed drew closer. It was segmented into hundreds of little keystone-shaped wedges, with an empty gray circle in the center, at least twenty feet across.

If it was an airlock, she couldn't see any way to control it. Maybe something in the sleds opened it.

She was almost out of air and hadn't learned anything. She needed to swim for the surface and try again. Fear squeezed Sierra as tightly as the cold pressure. This was a mistake. She was too deep. She'd never get back up. Her ears felt like they were going to burst, but she couldn't equalize them any further.

She dropped the rock just as she was about to hit the flat surface in the center of the ring, then reached, bracing for impact so she could push off and swim back up.

Her fingers sunk into something soft, like gel. She kept moving, sinking to her elbows. A buzzing sensation ran through her arm, almost electrical. Her last bit of breath escaped.

Panicking, she kicked and tried to jerk her body backwards, but she continued to descend.

She squeezed her eyes shut as her head entered the goop. It felt like a plastic bag over her face. She flailed, desperate to breathe, as the gel tightened around her waist. Her kicking only propelled her deeper. The squishy goop pressed from every direction, and the prickly buzz surrounded her. She needed to breathe so badly, but she didn't dare open her mouth. She couldn't let the goop inside her. She brought both arms to her face and pulled her legs close, curling into a fetal ball, unable to tell if she was still moving. Maybe she'd stopped. She would die here, congealing in this jelly.

Sierra burst through into open air with a sickening squelch and continued to fall.

DOWNFALL

Chapter Twenty-Four

Randall sat in his pod, enjoying the show. The hovercars emitted those high-pitched whines and everyone collapsed, even the dog. Some of the bodies fell on top of each other. A few went down hard.

"Fuckin' awesome."

A lone figure remained standing, up on the rim of the big fire pit. Morrie. The one person the wardens couldn't torpor was that ginger son of a bitch? How the hell was that possible?

Morrie held the old Garand up against his shoulder, aiming right at him. He was a hundred feet away, well within the rifle's range.

Maybe he should cut a deal with him. Morrie knew his way around guns and might make a decent lieutenant.

"Get out of there," Morrie called out. "Or I'll shoot you dead."

Randall snorted. If that red-haired pussy was going to shoot him, he would have fired already.

A shot rang out. The bullet whizzed past, right between the two halves of the pod.

Randall dropped flat in the center of the bowl, his back pressed painfully against his own collection of guns.

"You missed," he muttered. His nuts pulled up tight the way they always did in a firefight.

"Hands where I can see them," Morrie shouted. "Or I swear to God, I'll put a bullet in you."

Still on his back, Randall stuck his hands above him.

The rifle barrel didn't move. Motherfucker had a steady hand. That meant that his first shot was a warning. He'd intended to miss.

"Keep your hands up and slide out, now," Morrie shouted.

Randall breathed in the metallic tang of his guns. They were all right there, lying beneath him, but that red-haired prick had a clear line of sight into the pod from his perch up on the rocks. He couldn't try for them.

"Now," Morrie shouted.

"Alright, alright," Randall called out.

Rocking on his shoulders and hips, he scooted sideways, keeping his hands up, where Morrie could see them. He stopped to rest when he was off the guns and lying on the foamy surface of the pod. Fortunately, the pistol in his waistband still pressed against the base of his spine.

"Keep moving," Morrie shouted.

"I'm going, goddamn it," Randall shouted back. He shifted sideways, moving slowly to prevent the M1911 from popping out of his waistband. When he reached the edge of the pod, he sat up, hands still in the air.

"Hop down and walk toward me," Morrie called.

Randall slid to the ground. A trickle of sweat ran down the inside of his leg.

"Hands up," Morrie yelled. The rifle's barrel was aimed right at Randall's heart. From this range, he couldn't miss, not with a rifle.

Randall had to get closer before he could make a sure shot with his pistol. He raised his hands, but only to shoulder height, and started weaving through the torpored villagers.

He doubted Morrie would shoot someone in cold blood, but he sure as hell didn't like the sight of that rifle barrel pointing at him. His nuts were clenched up so tight they might be gone.

"I don't think you know what it's like to shoot someone," Randall said, testing him.

"Actually, I do," Morrie said. He didn't sound like he was lying.

Randall slowed his pace. He was probably close enough to take him out with the pistol now. He just had to get that rifle pointed somewhere other than his goddamn chest. He wished the aliens would help, but didn't see any sign of them. He shook his head. "I don't believe it. You never killed anyone."

"I did," Morrie insisted. He didn't look proud of it, though. He looked downright distraught.

"Did he deserve it?"

"No," Morrie cried. "*She* didn't."

Randall kept a straight face, but inside, he was a barrel of laughs. Slowly, he lowered his hands. "I don't deserve it, either."

"You helped Joe," Morrie spat, his words full of venom.

"So did you," Randall said.

Morrie flinched.

"At least I ain't killed nobody," Randall said.

It was true, as far as Morrie knew. Randall hadn't killed anyone since he'd been on the islands. Not yet, anyway.

"Sounds to me like you're the bad guy here." Randall didn't really believe in good guys or bad guys, but he was pretty damn sure Morrie did.

The look on Morrie's face confirmed it. "I'm not. I'm just trying to do what's right."

"What's right?" Randall looked around at the villagers. "What's right would be for you to put that gun down and help me make sure everyone's okay. I promised the aliens I would take care of them."

"You did?" Uncertainty grew on Morrie's face, but the Garand didn't move.

Randall turned toward the pod behind him, careful not to turn too far. He didn't want Morrie to see the M1911 in the back of his waistband. "Of course I did. How do you think I flew here in that pod?"

"Why did they stun everyone?" Morrie asked.

Randall relaxed slightly. He had him. Morrie was asking questions about the aliens. He wasn't talking about shooting him anymore. Probably wasn't thinking about it, either.

"They wanna move everyone to a safe place, where there's plenty to eat, and nothing trying to kill us."

"They do?" The gun lowered slightly. It was still pointing at Randall, but not right at his heart.

Randall nodded, fighting hard to keep from grinning. When you promised someone exactly what they wanted, they tended to believe you.

"Wait, why didn't they offer to do that earlier?" Morrie asked. His eyes narrowed and the gun moved back up.

"'Cause I explained everything to 'em," Randall said. "I told 'em how Joe was the problem."

"And Thad," Morrie said.

"And Thad," Randall agreed. He'd all but forgotten about that business with Thad, but apparently Morrie was still bent out of shape over it.

Morrie looked like he desperately wanted to believe him.

"Tell you what," Randall said. "Hop down. You can come over here and tie me up, if that makes you feel better."

Morrie's face softened.

"Do that, and then you can stop pointing your gun at me, which would make me feel a whole lot better. We can talk this all through and I'll explain everything."

Morrie glanced at the two-foot drop in front of him.

"Just be careful jumping down," Randall said with a laugh. "Don't shoot me on accident."

Morrie shook his head. "No. Never."

Randall's hand trembled next to his hip, like a cowboy at high noon.

Morrie stepped sideways, positioning his foot on one of the larger rocks. His finger came out of the trigger guard. He looked at the ground and shifted his weight to hop down.

As he began to drop, he raised the barrel of the rifle, pointing it toward empty sky.

Randall reached back, grabbed the M1911, brought it out, and fired.

He knew he'd made the shot before the recoil registered in his hand. Blood puffed in the center of Morrie's chest and he slammed backwards into the rock wall as his ass hit the dirt.

The tang of gun smoke tickled Randall's nostrils. He licked his lips. The village was his.

Chapter Twenty-Five

Cameron tumbled underwater, desperate for air. Finally, she sensed light. *Up.* She kicked with her legs and pulled with her hands. Her boots and the heavy canvas of her pants weighed her down.

Something smacked her face, both firm and soft. It was an arm.

She grabbed, clutching, until she found a small hand at the end. Barry. The boy wasn't moving.

Squeezing his wrist, she kicked upwards, her long legs fighting the water's weight.

Air!

She broke the surface, sucked in delicious air, sputtered it out, and sucked in more. She kicked hard and pulled Barry up until his head cleared the surface too. The boy still wasn't moving. She started a sidestroke, using her weak arm to hold Barry's face above water.

The kid felt like a bag of wet laundry and the island was a good thirty or forty yards away. *That's barely more than one lap in a pool, you wuss.* She sped up her stroke.

The sea all around was empty, except for bubbles breaking the surface. Where the hell were David and Scott? She didn't want to leave them behind, but she couldn't dive down and look for them while carrying Barry. *Fuck.* Cameron kept swimming.

She wanted to reach around and check for the Beretta in her waistband. She thought she could feel it against her backside, but she wasn't sure. *You lose that gun and you're truly fucked.* She couldn't stop to check, though. She had to get Barry ashore.

The boy slipped, his face dipping below the surface. Cameron twisted and pulled him higher. "Wake up," she shouted in his ear. He didn't respond. She had to get him ashore, *now.*

Something grabbed her from behind. A million dark fears rocketed up her spine. Cameron released Barry, turning to fend off whatever was attacking her.

"It's me," David shouted. He caught Barry and helped prop up his face. "Kick harder."

"Announce yourself next time," she sputtered, but warm relief flooded her. Relief that she wasn't being attacked by another goddamn monster and relief that David had survived.

They swam together, faster now, pulling Barry between them, until Cameron felt sand beneath her boot. She brought both feet down, digging in with relief. Side-by-side, they dragged the boy onto the beach.

David dropped to his knees, twisted Barry's head to the side, and stuck his finger in his mouth. Water dribbled out. He turned the boy's head straight up, pinched his nose, and blew into his lips.

Cameron hugged her arms across her chest, unable to do anything but watch and wait.

Barry sputtered on the first rescue breath. He gasped and gagged, rolled onto his side, and coughed up a quart of water.

David bent over him, shaking with something that was half sob, half laugh, and a hundred percent joy. A big stupid grin spread across Cameron's face. They were okay. She reached around to her back and found more good news. The Beretta was still there. It would need to be stripped and dried, but at least she had it.

"Hey thanks for the help." Scott sloshed ashore and dropped to his knees a few yards up the beach, peeling off his sport coat.

"Are you okay?" she asked.

"Yeah, yeah, I'm good."

A week ago, Cameron might not have cared one way or another, but now she was glad he'd made it. David's altruistic nature might actually be rubbing off on her.

She drew the Beretta, pulled back the slide and released the magazine. Water dripped onto the sand. It definitely needed to be broken down.

Barry coughed incessantly, still clearing his pipes.

"Is the kid okay?" Scott asked.

David nodded, his face pulled tight, as if fighting back tears.

A nasty odor caught Cameron's attention. "What's that smell?" Something on the island gave off the mustardy tang of a poorly maintained pet store.

Scott smirked. "It's not me."

David shrugged and Barry kept coughing, a little more slowly now.

They were on a thin stretch of beach that curved into the sea like the bottom of a crescent moon. Further inland, waist-high plants grew here and there with sharp jagged leaves protruding from stubby barrel-shaped trunks. They looked like oversized pineapples half-buried in the sand. A thousand feet beyond, the vegetation grew thicker on the main body of the island.

Cameron noticed something new, something she hadn't heard in months. The sound of bugs. Clicks and chirrups came from the jungle covering the middle of the island. *Terrific.* The one thing she'd liked about this stupid wildlife preserve had been the lack of creepy crawlies.

Barry finally grew quiet.

David leaned over him. "Are you okay?" He held the boy's chin and leaned close, looking into his eyes.

"Uh-huh." Barry started crying and wrapped his arms around his father.

David helped him to his feet. "Cameron found you. She saved your life."

She waved the comment away, hoping Barry would keep his distance. Kid hugs were gross. Wet kid hugs could only be worse.

"What do we do now?" Scott asked. He shook his jacket in the air, sending water everywhere.

"We wait," David said. "They'll come for us on the raft once they realize we're in trouble."

"How will they know which way we went?" Barry asked.

No one answered the question. Cameron shivered as the relief she'd felt drained away, leaving an icy chill. They hadn't told anyone where they were going.

Chapter Twenty-Six

Sierra sucked air into her burning lungs and opened her eyes. She'd passed through the membrane at the bottom of the sea, but she hadn't stopped falling. She coughed and sputtered, desperately grateful for each breath. Somehow, she was no longer underwater. Wind chilled her skin as she plummeted through open air. Dim shapes filled the gloom around her.

Twisting, she tried to figure out what the hell was happening. A massive sphere rose up below her, almost as if she was falling toward another world.

Disorientation and confusion clenched her stomach. She inhaled deeply, trying to calm herself, trying to focus. The air tasted normal, no different from on the islands.

The sphere below wasn't another world, but it was as least as big as that giant Epcot ball at Disney World. Glowing lights dotted its surface, along with a smattering of antenna-like poles jutting out in every direction.

As she fell closer, she realized why it seemed so much larger at first. She was falling in slow motion.

Somehow, she fell through the air at the same speed she'd been falling underwater, maybe even slower. She grasped for an explanation. Had the aliens stunned her? Was she in a fugue state, hallucinating from lack of oxygen?

The strange sphere grew closer and she got her bearings enough to realize it was off to one side, not directly beneath her.

She would just miss it.

Maybe it was a water tower, a big ball on a column, like the ones used by cities without mountains nearby. The idea made no damn sense. An entire ocean was above her.

Sierra was falling slowly, but she was still falling. The thought of impact, even at this speed, terrified her.

Directly below, one of the antenna-like poles protruded horizontally from the side of the round structure. Sierra reached and caught it, her fingers wrapping around the end. *Gotcha.* Her momentum swung her beneath the pole. She tensed her arms, expecting them to be jerked from their sockets if the pole didn't snap, but neither happened. Her stomach lurched as she came to a stop, hanging from the end. Every movement felt unnaturally slow except her heart rate, which buzzed in her chest like a hummingbird.

Sierra closed her eyes, overwhelmed. Nothing made sense.

Assess the situation, came Rick Preston's steady voice. She opened her eyes. Large spheres hung motionless in the air all around her. The space felt like a vast cavern, but the ceiling and floor didn't look like rock. Both appeared artificial, flat and smooth. If this cavern had walls, they were too far away to see in the gloom. The only light came from little square panels dotting the spheres.

There didn't seem to be any caretakers here, unless they were cloaked, but why would they be cloaked? And if they were here, why weren't they coming after her for intruding into their space?

Like a kid on the monkey bars, she shimmied along the shaft toward the sphere. When she reached it, she let go with one hand, hanging effortlessly with the other, somehow buoyed, as if still underwater. Her stomach crept up her throat.

"It's the gravity," she whispered.

The gravity was somehow lower here, beneath the sea. She performed a one-armed pull-up, raising her chin easily to the pole. Somehow, the gravity was weaker in this chamber than on the islands. It was one more piece of alien technology she couldn't understand, like magic pods and invisible flying sleds.

She lowered herself back down. Hanging by one arm, she touched the gray wall of the sphere with her free hand. It felt like polished metal. She held her breath, listening. The chamber pulsed with the low thrum of machinery. She inhaled deeply through her nose and detected an acrid metallic scent.

A dozen other spheres loomed nearby, some as big as the one she was hanging on, some smaller, and none supported by columns like the water tower she'd imagined. They just hung in the air. They almost seemed like giant balloons, except they didn't drift or bob the way balloons would. Everything here was motionless. Everything felt *alien*.

Sierra looked up. A glowing purple circle ringed the portal she'd passed through, somehow holding back all that water above. She spotted three other purple circles on the ceiling, two similar in size, but a third that looked huge. None of them were close, and she couldn't even see the far edge of the big one.

Below her, the floor slanted away in the dark. The distance was difficult to judge because of the slope and the dim light, but she had to be at least ten stories up.

Unease and confusion threatened to overwhelm her, but she also felt a zing of elation. She was *out*. She'd escaped the menagerie. She'd found the exit. Hell, this was epic. She was the first human being in history to enter alien territory.

She wished David was here to compare notes and bounce ideas. Well, maybe not *here*. The height would have terrified him.

Hanging from the shaft required little effort, but she couldn't just hang there forever. Her arm would eventually tire and if a caretaker came along and stunned her, she'd fall. The only place to go was onto the sphere.

Small pastel light panels dotted the curved surface. The closest sat above the pole and off to one side. She performed another chin-up and reached for the panel with her free hand, grabbing its top edge easily.

The light panel was cool to the touch, with no markings or switches. It simply glowed. She tried to pry off the cover, but it wouldn't budge.

She spotted a rectangular opening a few feet above her.

Yes. A way in.

The opening was roughly the size of a door, but it ran horizontally across the sphere instead of vertically. Strange metal brackets protruded from its corners.

Using the shaft she'd been hanging from as a step, she climbed higher, reached, and caught hold of the opening.

Her elation faded when she pulled herself up. It was a cubby, not an entrance. Sierra climbed in, crouching in the small space. It was just big enough for her to lie down, like a bunk maybe. Or a crypt.

She turned around and sat down, surveying the vast chamber. The closest sphere was maybe two hundred yards away, and a little smaller than the one she was on. Beyond that, a dozen others floated in the gloom. It was too dark to see any walls, assuming they were out there.

Her initial excitement about making the history books began to fade away. She was trapped.

The portal she'd fallen through was a good five hundred feet up. She couldn't see any way back to it. She shivered. The air seemed colder than on the islands, though it was difficult to be sure with wet clothes and hair. The weight of the situation pressed on her shoulders, despite the low gravity. She wasn't just trapped, she was alone. Her fear added to the chill.

She couldn't think of any advice from Rick Preston. His life lessons hadn't covered getting stuck in an alien cavern beneath the sea.

She leaned out from her cubby and looked around to see if she could get any higher. Maybe she would find something at the top.

Just above her, a pair of indentations sat side-by-side on the sphere's surface. Each one was about the size of a shoebox and some sort of metal cylinder ran horizontally through them. She reached up and tapped one of the cylinders with her fingertip, testing that it wasn't hot, or freezing, or even electrified. Nothing. She grabbed the cylinder and pulled. It didn't move. She tried twisting it. Still nothing.

Her hand was growing slick with sweat, so she reached up to grab both cylinders at once. The moment she touched the second cylinder, a whooshing hiss blew into her face from above. Sierra tightened her grip on the bars and closed her eyes until the blast of air subsided. She opened one eye, confirmed there wasn't any danger, then opened the other.

A horizontal black line appeared two feet above her, splitting the sphere.

"Is this a different kind of pod?" she whispered.

The top half of the sphere floated upward. Holding onto the cylinders, Sierra rose up on her toes, trying to peer into the gap. If this was a pod, it was huge, way too big even for a dinosaur.

As the gap grew and light spilled inside, she stood there gripping the little handles and wondered if she'd lost her mind.

The sphere was filled with rocks.

She had to get closer for a better look. She released one of the pipes, then waited to see if the top of the sphere would close back down. It kept rising.

Stretching, she grabbed the rim where the sphere had split and pulled herself up, climbing onto a four-foot ledge where the two halves had been connected. She placed her hand on one of the rocks piled before her. It looked exactly like the boulders scattered throughout the islands.

Sierra's chest felt tight. She was on a giant floating ball filled with boulders. Nothing made sense.

Don't overthink things, Rick Preston always told her when she struggled with homework in high school. *The simplest explanation is usually correct.*

The simplest explanation was insane. She'd nearly drowned, she was trapped alone without any food or water, and her monumental discovery was a gigantic storage container filled with landscaping supplies.

She combed her fingers through her wet hair. She hadn't brought any food. She hadn't planned ahead. A pinch of panic tightened her windpipe. She couldn't stay here. The top of the container might close back down, flattening her. And she sure as hell couldn't climb inside on the rocks. If the sphere closed, she could be trapped in there forever. She would need to climb back down to the cubby. After that, she had no idea what to do.

The sound of moist squelches came from above. Sierra leaned out, peering beyond the floating top half of the sphere.

A pair of shoes protruded through the membrane in the purple ring on the ceiling, followed by legs.

"Yes." She recognized Priya's maroon pants.

Priya's torso emerged, along with her hands. The moment her arms came free, they flailed desperately. A stone dropped past, falling in slow motion. After several agonizing moments, Priya's head slipped through, and she fell, coughing and sputtering.

"Priya," Sierra shouted. "Priya, over here!" There was nothing she could do but watch as Priya fell. The stone hit the ground somewhere below, clattering and bouncing away.

Priya's eyes met hers for a moment, and then she tumbled past with a blood-curdling wail.

Chapter Twenty-Seven

"We have to make a fire," Cameron said as she led David, Barry, and Scott up the beach. "But first we need to get to high ground."

The island rose gradually as they moved from the curved spit of sand toward the tree-covered center. They wove between stumpy little plants and an alarming number of shit piles, which looked like the droppings of a giant bird. Fist-sized turds sat in the middle of dried white smears.

Cameron shivered, remembering the terror bird she'd wrestled at the end of a pike after it gutted Charlie.

"Why high ground?" Barry asked.

Cameron pointed to the closest pile of crap. "We need to find someplace safe from whatever produced that. After dark, we won't be able to see a thing. We'll be defenseless."

Barry reached for his father's hand. "Daddy will keep me safe."

David pulled Barry close, icy determination on his face.

Cameron clenched her throat and turned away, but she kept glancing back from the corners of her eyes. After her own wretched upbringing, David's concern for Barry and Kim made her heart ache. She'd never known that kind of love. She wasn't even sure she could handle it.

"Why don't we just make a fire here?" Scott asked. "That'll give us light and we can keep looking for shelter after dark."

"Do you have a lighter?" Cameron snapped. "Matches? Flint?"

"No. But can'tcha rub sticks together or something?" He had draped his wet coat over one shoulder. "Didn't they teach you that in the army?"

"It could take hours," she said. "It isn't as easy as everyone thinks." Once, during a week-long survival exercise, Cameron had tried to make fire without any tools. After three hours, she'd produced nothing but blisters on her palms. She looked up at the sky, or ceiling, or whatever was up there. Night was a lot less than three hours away.

"How long do we have to stay here?" Barry asked.

"They'll come find us," Cameron said.

"How do you know?"

"Because I'm here. They love me too much."

David laughed. Cameron allowed the edges of her mouth to curl.

As they worked their way inland, the chunky little plants gave way to wispy trees with weird feathery leaves, maybe twenty feet tall and spread out thinly. Stubby ferns also grew here and there in the hard-packed dirt, along with another kind of plant that was nothing but three-foot stalks, like oversized asparagus. Further in, the jungle grew denser. Hopefully they would find a rock pile or something they could climb onto up ahead.

Scott put his coat back on, though it was clearly still wet.

"Are you cold?" Barry asked, sounding dubious. "Why do you always wear that coat?"

The temperature on this island was exactly the same as on the one they'd left. The whole terrarium had perfect climate control.

"It's a long story," Scott said.

"What does that mean?" Barry asked.

"What is this, twenty questions? I like to look nice."

Cameron snorted. "You look silly in that sport coat."

"It's a blazer, not a sport coat," Scott insisted.

Cameron didn't know the difference, but his answer made one thing clear. Scott had a new nickname.

"I thought you worked at a hotel," Barry said. "But then you told us you were a pilot."

He scowled at the boy. "I was a pilot for a few years, then I *managed* a hotel after that."

"Why did you quit flying?" David asked.

Something rustled in the brush up ahead. None of the others seemed to notice. It sounded small. Hopefully.

"I didn't quit. Hey Cameron, why don'cha try to make that fire while we still have light?"

"I told you, Sportcoat. We need to find a place to spend the night first." She pushed forward, annoyed. "Starting a fire could take hours. If nightfall hits before we manage it, we're fucked." The trees around them were too spindly to climb, but some larger ones up ahead looked promising.

As they moved deeper into the jungle, they passed dead branches on the ground. At least there was plenty of kindling. Cameron picked up a stick that felt like a decent club. She hadn't cleaned out the Beretta yet and she hated feeling defenseless.

A sergeant had bragged to her once about modifying a nine-millimeter cartridge to start a fire during his survival training. He claimed to have pried the bullet from the casing and stuffed a tiny wad of cloth in its place. He'd fired the modified cartridge into a pile of twigs and bark, lighting it right up. She wasn't sure she believed him, but it was worth a try. First, though, she had to break down the gun and dry everything out. She couldn't risk a misfire.

Something twitched in the vegetation a few feet away. Cameron froze and raised her stick. She'd gotten too far ahead of the others.

A face filled with teeth burst through a wall of ferns. Cameron swung her club at the gaping maw. The jaws chomped, ripping the stick from her hands.

A great leathery bat wing flapped around the creature as it spun on her. Cameron dodged past, heart pounding, trying to get behind the thing. It looked like an oversized lizard with knives for teeth and a head that belonged on a lion.

David and Scott shouted something, but she ignored them. If the animal got its jaws on her, she'd be torn apart.

Outstretched lizard legs tore across the ground as the creature charged.

Cameron sidestepped and realized the leathery flap wasn't a wing. Instead, a curved three-foot fin grew on its back. The creature's torso was about the size of a person, but its tail more than doubled its length, extending six feet beyond its back legs.

She dodged past the creature and grabbed its tail, which felt like sandpaper. The animal shook with the strength of a horse, almost pulling free. It arced around toward her, hissing and snapping, but as long as she had it by the tail, it couldn't charge at her or the others. *This is fucking crazy.* She squeezed harder, wrapping both arms around the tail, holding it tight against her side.

Scott crept forward. "Tell me what to do."

David stood farther away, keeping Barry back.

"Fuck if I know," Cameron grunted. The creature swung her sideways. On Hawai'i, they'd been told to use shovels to bash in the brains of pet iguanas that got loose and threatened the wildlife. "Smash its head somehow."

Scott looked around on the ground.

The animal thrashed, whipping its tail, slamming her into a tree. Cameron clenched her fingers and pressed the tail against the trunk. She hefted the lizard's back legs off the ground so it could only use its front feet for traction.

It arced its head toward her, snapping. The head wasn't shaped like a lizard's head. It was shaped more like a hyena, with a blocky snout. Its teeth were huge, especially two big canines in the front. It had to be some kind of dinosaur.

The fin on its back resembled the fin of a sailfish, with long spikes every few inches. Flaming orange streaks ran up each side. It smelled of moldy leather. The creature clawed the ground with its front legs, hissing and twisting, trying to break free, but as long as she held its tail against the tree trunk, it couldn't get enough leverage.

Scott ran up, holding one of the barrel-shaped plants against his belly. Clumps of sandy roots hung from the trunk. Blood beaded on his chin where the sharp leaves jabbed him. Grunting, he hefted the stubby plant up over his head and heaved it at the dinosaur. The plant bounced off the creature's thick neck and rolled away.

The dinosaur flinched from the impact but kept writhing. Cameron rotated around the tree, holding the tail against the trunk to keep the bastard from coming at her.

When the creature twisted toward the tree, she held the tail in place. When it twisted away, she dragged the tail around, keeping it pinned. They'd already circled the tree once, shredding fibrous bark from the trunk.

Cameron's arms trembled with exertion. Sweat glued her shirt to her body and her knuckles were raw where they'd been battered by the trunk, but she couldn't let go or the creature would turn on her.

David darted in and grabbed the barrel-shaped plant Scott had thrown. He held it against his side, pointing the spiky top toward the dinosaur.

"Hurry," Cameron shouted. She couldn't hold on much longer. The creature pawed the ground, dragging her halfway around the tree. "Spear its face."

David shoved the sharp leaves at the dinosaur's eyes. He must have done something right because the fucker wriggled even more.

"Keep at it." Cameron tightened her grip.

David jabbed again, grunting. The sharp fronds came back wet and bloody. He'd punctured its eye, or maybe the skin around the socket. The creature opened its boxy jaws and hissed.

Scott appeared next to him with another stubby plant, even bigger than the first. He shoved the sharp end between the dinosaur's jaws.

It bit down, blood flowing from its gums. Scott kept shoving and David stabbed again. This time he definitely nailed it. Snotty goop spilled from the creature's eye and it jerked harder than before.

One of the dinosaur's rear legs landed on the tree trunk and it shoved forward. The leathery tail pulled free, burning Cameron's palms.

David jumped back, putting himself in front of Barry. "Here." He hefted his plant to Scott.

The creature bit down on the plant still wedged in its mouth, and shook its head, shredding it.

Scott reared back, holding the barrel-shaped trunk overhead, and chucked it at the five-foot sail. It ripped several slashes in the thin skin, then bounced away.

The creature spat out the remains of the plant in its mouth and ran off into the jungle, its claws smacking the ground.

Cameron pumped her fist. Her whole body swelled, surging with adrenaline. They'd done it. Hand-to-hand combat with a mother-fucking dinosaur. Her heartbeat pounded in her ears. Her arms felt like rubber and her hands felt like they'd been flayed, but she didn't care. They'd won.

David came close, looking her up and down with genuine concern. "Are you okay? Did it hurt you?" He put his hand on her arm and she felt a spark.

She grinned. "I'm fine."

"You're kinda crazy," he said. His eyebrow twitched like it wanted to go up. God, he looked so good right now.

Cameron grabbed the back of David's head and pulled his mouth to hers, biting at his lips. His hands landed on her lower back, fingers practically on her ass, and she pressed her lips harder, hungry for him.

"Hey, I helped too, don'cha you know," Scott said.

Barry ran up. "Daddy?" He sucked in a lungful of air and shouted, "That's not Mommy!"

David pulled away, babbling. "Barry. I'm sorry. It's okay. We were just scared and ..." He picked up his son and squeezed him without finishing the thought.

For a brief moment, his eyes met hers again, then he pushed forward through the jungle.

Chapter Twenty-Eight

Sierra looked down from the middle of the giant floating structure. "Priya? Are you okay? Where are you?" Except for a few panels glowing here and there, she saw nothing on the sloping floor below.

"Hello? Sierra?" Priya's voice sounded distant and frightened, but she was alive. "I slid down a slope and hurt my wrist."

Sierra leaned forward, peering into the darkness. "I can't see you. Can you find me? I'm in the middle of the big ball that split in half."

"I don't know. The gravity is low here. How is that even possible?"

All this shouting might draw attention from the aliens. But then again, if this was their civilization, why weren't they around?

"Can you find a way back up? Or a way for me to get down?"

Several long moments passed. When Priya finally responded, her voice came from a different direction, still below, but now off to the side. "I don't see any way I can reach you. What is this place?"

"I don't know." Sierra lowered her voice. The sound carried in the dim emptiness. "If it's where the caretakers live, I haven't seen them yet. I'm coming down."

They'd be better off together and there wasn't anything she could do up here on a container full of rocks.

Her heart rate picked up at the thought of jumping off, despite the fact that Priya had survived the fall all the way from the ceiling.

She lowered herself into the little crypt-sized cubby again. It would have been terrifying to climb around on something like this on Earth, but the low gravity made it so easy it felt safe. She could support her weight with very little effort. She dropped back onto the antenna-like shaft that she'd caught when she fell into the cavern. She crouched, grabbed the pole, and lowered herself to hang by one arm, just as she had when she first arrived.

Seven or eight feet lower, where the bottom half of the structure began to curve away from her, a trio of metal rings stuck out, like hula-hoops embedded in the sphere's surface. Kicking her legs, she swung her body and let go. She caught two rings, one in each hand, and dangled there.

Even though she knew she'd fall slowly in the low gravity, she felt a desperate urge to get as far down as possible before she dropped.

A grid of octagonal panels lined the surface near her knees, with foot-wide gaps between each one. She reached for the closest panel, finding just enough of an edge to grasp with her fingertips. The panels covered the bottom of the sphere and she swung along like a gibbon from one to the next until she was hanging from the lowest spot.

"I see you," Priya called out in a loud whisper, closer now. "Hurry. I want to show you something." Her dim shape passed over an orange light on the broad slope below. Sierra couldn't gauge the distance accurately, but it had to be more than fifty feet. This was a bad idea. She didn't want to be here. Her fingers cramped and her shoulders trembled.

"Bend your legs when you hit," Priya called out. "Let yourself roll downhill."

"Easy for you to say." Sierra tasted the terror David seemed to feel from even the slightest height. Looking down made her stomach tumble. She couldn't possibly let go.

Power through, came Rick Preston's voice. It was one of his favorite sayings, but it didn't help. She needed to know that she'd be okay if she dropped, but there wasn't any way to know for sure.

She closed her eyes and tried to calm herself.

Faith gives me strength when I need it most, Waldmire had told her. *I believe because believing helps me.*

She couldn't know for sure, but she could believe.

Sierra took a deep breath and let go.

"Shit, shit, shit." She pinwheeled her arms as she fell, tumbling and contorting. The ground rushed up at her in slow motion, hitting the side of her leg. She bounced sideways down the sloped floor. When she finally lay still, she kissed the smooth metal surface. She'd survived. She was back on solid ground again.

Priya ran down, breathing hard. "Are you alright? Did you break anything?"

Sierra's elbows, knees, and butt all felt sore. She patted herself gingerly, finding nothing worse than a scrape on her forearm. "I'm okay."

The low gravity, along with the slope, had kept the impact from causing any real damage. More importantly, she was no longer alone. She wanted to wrap her arms around Priya, but she knew she wasn't the touchy-feely sort, so she settled for grasping her hand. "You came after me."

Priya smiled. "Sometimes you just have to go with your gut." She pulled Sierra to her feet.

The slope was steep and the view downhill was jaw-dropping. The floor descended as far as she could see, with dozens more of those floating spheres overhead. "How far does this cavern go?"

"I'm going to turn your world upside down," Priya said. "This isn't a cavern."

Sierra squinted. "What is it?"

"Come on," she said, excitement in her voice. "I have to show you." Priya set off sideways across the slope.

Sierra scrambled after her. "What did you find?"

The floor was even steeper than she'd realized, and would have been awkward to traverse without the low gravity. To her left, the floor sloped up, disappearing in the dim light, and to the right, it sloped down. Every ten yards or so, they passed one of the glowing panels protruding from the floor.

Directly ahead, a wall materialized in the gloom. Priya led her to a dark octagonal opening at floor level, or slope-level, or whatever.

"Is that a passageway?"

"Not exactly," Priya answered. "It doesn't make sense. Nothing here makes sense."

"You can say that again. Where does it go?"

"Oh, you'll see." She seemed to be enjoying the build-up. "You're going to love it."

As they drew closer, tiny white lights became visible in the far end of a short hall.

"There's light in there," Sierra said.

"You sound like Kevin."

She didn't understand. "The guy with the broken arm?"

"Yeah. The guy who always states the obvious."

Sierra stopped. "Thanks a lot."

Priya's shoulders fell. "I'm sorry. Yes, those are lights. There's a window at the end of this little hallway," Priya said. "Those lights are on the other side."

"What are they?"

Priya's eyes twinkled, even in the gloom. "Come and see."

Chapter Twenty-Nine

Randall grabbed a fistful of Morrie's clown-orange hair and lifted his head so he could look him in the eyes. Morrie didn't look back. Randall had made a clean kill, right through the sternum. A length of cloth around Morrie's neck held a bloody bandage against the base of his skull. Randall dropped the head to the ground with a heavy thump and wiped his hand on his trousers.

According to the aliens, Morrie was the only one Randall needed to worry about, but he didn't want to be surprised by any fakers, so he checked to make sure everyone else was knocked out. Sure enough, they were all down for the count. He stopped at Elizabeth, the hottest chick in the village, and squeezed her boob. She stared lifelessly. He thought about pulling up her shirt for a peek, but decided that was gross. Randall was many things, but he wasn't a fucking necro.

One of the grub-like aliens lay on the platform where Morrie had been constructing a gallows so that Joe could hang Josh. It had to be the same alien Dave had jumped on from the cliff. Randall couldn't tell if the thing was torpored or not, but it sure wasn't goin' nowhere. Ropes ran across it, like that giant who got tied down by the little assholes on the beach.

He gathered his firearms from the pod and placed them on one of the work tables, keeping the M1911.

Next, he cleared each cabin, searching for Dave and Sierra. Dave's boy was missing too, along with Josh, the little Hindu bitch, and the asshole who always wore a suit. He would need to keep his guard up until he found them.

Back at the center of the village, something floated down from the sky that looked like a giant metal bumblebee, with a bunch of robot arms sticking out from the front. Randall put his hand on his gun. The bumblebee floated over to the alien on the gallows platform. It didn't make a sound, which seemed wrong. It ought to buzz.

Randall moved closer, looking for a window. Whoever was inside this new vehicle had to be a lot smaller than the wardens.

Rumbling farty sounds came from the alien on the ground. It wasn't torpored after all. Three hovercars appeared, floating right over it. The wardens onboard farted back.

The big bumblebee thing extended a mechanical arm. It touched one of the ropes, snapping it with a puff of smoke.

"Bad-ass," Randall said.

The bumblebee shifted to the next rope. Spark, *snap*. Its movements were perfect, mechanical. Maybe there wasn't anyone inside. It seemed like some sort of robot drone.

Randall stepped forward and used Josh's knife to help free the alien. When the last vine fell, three arms extended from the drone. Each one telescoped out like an old-school radio antenna. They grew to about twenty feet, then slithered under the alien's bloated body like metallic snakes.

The three little arms clicked and popped, solidifying. Although it seemed impossibly unbalanced, the drone lifted the alien from the wooden platform.

"Fuckin' A." Their technology was way beyond anything on Earth.

The drone carried the alien out over the fields, where an empty hovercar sat waiting. It hadn't been there earlier. Randall chewed his lip. He didn't like the way all this invisible flying shit just came and went. The drone placed the alien on the hovercar and the metallic arms retracted back to the front of its body, where they hung, curled like a witch's fingers.

The alien settled in for a moment, touching the controls with its own snaky arms. It rose from the ground and flew straight at Randall, stopping in front of him, where it rumbled again, but this time the sounds were translated by a speaker somewhere on the hovercar. *"Lie down. Torpor may cause injury upon collapse."*

Randall tensed, raising his left hand and reaching for the gun with his right. "You don't understand. We had a deal."

One of the other wardens dropped down next to him and rumbled. *"This specimen may remain."*

Randall backed away, careful not to make any sudden moves.

The newly-freed alien farted out a response. *"Human specimens are unsuitable for observation. Human specimens interfere."*

Randall tapped his chest with the gun. "This human doesn't make trouble."

The second warden, his advocate, rumbled again. *"This specimen will manage other humans and prevent interference."*

The alien he'd freed moved closer. *"Human specimens must be returned to storage."*

Randall rolled his shoulder, getting ready to blast a hole in the ungrateful cocksucker.

The warden arguing on his behalf made another series of noises. *"Observation of human specimens must continue. Caretakers may encounter other species capable of interfering."*

The first alien was silent for a long while before it responded. *"This specimen may still interfere."*

"Bullshit," Randall said. "If there's one thing you'll learn about me, it's that I know how to follow instructions." This approach had helped him rise above the fray in more than one ugly situation. He gestured at the other alien with his gun. "I did exactly what your buddy asked, didn't I?"

Randall listened while his advocate rumbled. Its response threw him for a loop. *"This specimen can be controlled. Torpor was verified in the storage container."*

They'd knocked him out while he was in the pod. He had to endear himself to these assholes before they zapped him for good. "Look, if you want to observe human specimens, you can't do it if we're all in storage. Leave me here, and I'll keep the others from causing trouble. I can make sure everyone's happy and no one gets too big for their britches."

The wardens rumbled at each other, but the conversation wasn't translated. Randall squeezed the grip on his gun. After another minute or two, the former prisoner floated up into the sky and disappeared.

The other one turned to face him. *"Remain here."*

Randall felt a tickle in his gut. They were going to let him stay after all.

"Your herd will be reactivated."

The warden's finger-like limbs moved toward the front corners of its hovercar.

It took a moment, but Randall realized that his "herd" was actually the crowd lying unconscious all around him. "Wait. These humans are no good. They've been spoiled. We need to start over. Things will go better with a new herd."

The alien said nothing.

Randall pointed to the dozen or so bodies lying in a mess by the fire pit. "What happens if they stay in torpor? Will they die?"

The alien rumbled. *"Specimens eventually deteriorate unless preserved in storage containers."*

Randall didn't give a shit if they deteriorated, but in order to make a convincing alpha, he ought to protect his species. "Let's preserve them, then," he said.

The long spindly appendages danced over the hovercar controls.

"Wait, can you wake the dog?" He'd always wanted a dog, and here was his chance.

The hovercar made that zippery sound and Kona jumped up. The golden retriever walked over to Kim and licked her face, whimpering.

"A few humans are missing from this herd." Randall said. "Bad people. The ones who interfered. I need to find Sierra and Dave."

Kona barked. That bitch knew her master's name.

The hovercar produced its robotic voice. *"Want David."*

"Yes, I want them. Do you know where they are?"

The alien's arms moved across the controls and lights flashed on its wrinkly hide. *"Four human specimens are on island seventy-one."*

"What the hell does that mean? Is that a different island?"

"Yes."

It had to be them. Randall didn't know how they'd gotten there, but at least he didn't need to worry about them for now. "You've got more humans in storage, though, right?" he asked.

Another *"Yes."*

He licked his lips, thinking. He needed people who would serve him, the way he had served Joe and the Piper and all the others before that. He'd be top dog, a real alpha, and he thought he could actually make it work if he laid out the ground rules up front. He'd learned from Joe's mistakes. Randall also wanted someone like Crystal, someone who liked him enough to fuck him without a ton of coercion.

"Can you bring new humans out of storage?"

Rumble rumble. *How many?*

Randall's jaw dropped. The warden was taking his order like the cashier at a drive-thru.

Before he could answer, thirteen white pods appeared over the trees just beyond the low end of the village. They settled in the fields, crushing several rows of crops. At first, Randall thought it was a delivery, a new herd for him, but when the pods opened, they were all empty. They were here for a pick-up.

The bumblebee drone floated over to Jasmine and extended its spindly arms beneath her. It carried her to the first pod, where it placed her inside, gentle as a momma putting her baby down for a nap. It flew back to pick up another body as the pod closed.

Randall wasn't sure how many people to ask for. What if they sent him a bunch of tedious fatties like Jasmine? He shuddered. What if they only sent men? He turned to the warden. "I need to pick out the right people. If you send me the wrong ones, they'll make more trouble. They'll interfere, just like these ones did."

The alien didn't respond. Maybe it didn't understand what he was asking.

The yellow drone kept picking up bodies and placing them in the pods.

Randall tried a different approach. "Take me to storage and let me choose."

"No."

"I did what you asked," Randall said. "I saved your buddy."

Over by the fire pit, the drone picked up Kim and carried her to one of the pods. The top half lowered, sealing her in.

Sucks to be you, Dave. He'd never see his little girl again. Randall hoped he could tell him that someday, and rub his face in it.

Hell, he could do more than that, if he wanted. "Wait," he held up a hand. "I need to keep that one." She might be useful.

"Which one?"

When the pods closed, they all looked exactly the same. Randall walked over to Morrie's body and dipped two fingers in the hole in his chest, then walked over and wrote "Kim" on the pod using Morrie's blood.

Kona whimpered and barked, her head down.

The alien vehicle said, *"Kim."*

Randall was impressed. These fuckers could read.

He took a few steps toward the dog. "It's okay, girl."

Kona's hackles rose and her tail tucked between her legs. A low growl came from deep in her chest.

The robotic voice on the hovercar said, *"Don't like. Keep away. Don't like. Keep away."*

Randall stared over at the alien. "Why are you telling me to keep away? That's my fucking dog now."

The alien hovercraft produced a series of dog barks.

Kona tilted her head.

Randall looked back and forth between the alien and the golden retriever. "Holy Shit. Were you translating the dog?"

"Yes."

Randall chuckled. From the sound of things, Kona needed to be broken in.

The robot drone carried Waldmire over and deposited him in a pod. Sierra and the old guy were close. He might make good leverage, too. Randall used Morrie's chest for a paint-can again and labeled Waldmire's pod with a big bloody "W." He walked back to the warden. "Will they be safe here, or do you need to take them off to storage?"

"Specimens are preserved by the containers."

"All right. Leave them here for now. How do I choose new people?"

"You cannot go to storage."

Randall pushed. "You already demonstrated that you have excellent judgment. You chose me to help you out, and I freed your buddy, exactly like you wanted." His fingers flexed near the pistol. If he pushed too hard, it might decide to torpor him after all. "You're experts at running this place, but I'm the expert on humans. Let me pick the right specimens. You won't regret it."

The warden didn't respond immediately. Randall's balls drew tight as he watched the creature's little arms. If they looked like they were about to trigger torpor, he would empty the whole magazine into the big fucker.

Finally, it rumbled a response. "*You may choose. A harvester will bring control.*"

Randall's nutsack relaxed. The only harvesters he knew about were grain combines churning up wheat fields in Oklahoma, but he liked the sound of "control." It sounded pretty fucking good, indeed.

Chapter Thirty

Priya's heart pounded as she stepped into the octagonal hallway. The window at the far end showed a vast starfield. She felt a renewed sense of purpose. She was an astronomer again.

Sierra stopped at the entrance, bracing her forehead against the top edge. Her mouth hung open. "I – I don't understand."

"We aren't on an alien world," Priya said. "We're on a gigantic alien ship." She walked slowly, careful to keep from bouncing in the low gravity and bumping her head, though she wanted to leap with joy. The stars at the end seemed impossibly bright.

Sierra, who was twenty centimeters taller, had to stoop over.

"We're in space," Priya said. She wasn't just an astronomer. She was an astronaut.

"Now who's stating the obvious?"

Priya chuckled. "I deserved that."

The window sloped forward. Priya leaned onto it and turned her neck from side to side, trying to see the outside of the ship, but the view showed only stars.

"Can you figure out where we are in space?" Sierra asked. "Do you recognize these stars?"

Priya pointed toward Canis Major. "There's Sirius, Adhara, Delta, Beta, Eta, and Omicron. They're lined up the same as they are when viewed from Earth, which means we're still close, astronomically speaking." Warm pride filled her.

"How close?"

Priya shrugged. "I'd have to watch for a while before I could hazard a guess."

"Are we moving?"

"Yes. Look." She placed her hand on the window and watched as Sirius slid slowly behind her fingers. "But I can't tell if we're moving or rotating. Again, I would need to observe for a while."

Sierra took a deep breath. "We have to tell the others."

"How do you propose we do that?"

Sierra pushed away from the window, stooping in the short tunnel. "I don't know. Come on."

Priya followed her back out to the main chamber, where the floor sloped down to the left and up to the right as far as they could see in both directions, with an array of giant spheres hanging overhead. She felt exposed. Out here, the aliens could be watching. They could come from any direction. She cradled her wrist against her chest. It still hurt from the fall, but she didn't think she'd done any serious damage. It felt like a mild sprain.

Sierra turned to her. "Which way should we go?"

It was nice to be included in the decision. "Up," Priya said, pointing right.

"Are you sure?"

The question annoyed her. Of course she wasn't sure. She shrugged. "Up gets us closer to the islands, and closer to the tops of those spheres. Plus, there's a known limit to how far it can go. We'll run into the ceiling eventually."

"Sold." Sierra started up.

Climbing the forty-five-degree slope was easy enough in the low gravity.

Priya pointed at the spheres overhead. "Do you have any idea what those things are? How do they just float there? Nothing here follows the laws of science." It unsettled her.

"The one I landed on was full of rocks."

"What?" Priya winced. "Your head is full of rocks. What are you talking about?"

Sierra smiled. "It's a big storage container filled with the same boulders that are scattered around the islands."

"What do you think the others contain? Dirt? Sand?" Priya took a deep breath. "Maybe the other people? Do you think they're in the spheres?"

Sierra scrunched her nose. "I hope not. The rocks were all piled in there together."

After fifteen minutes of climbing, a second octagonal opening appeared on the right, identical to the first, with another window to the stars. Priya longed to just sit and watch, but they pushed on.

A few hundred meters past the second corridor, the slope came to a dead-end. The wall before them was at least fifty meters tall and lined with cylindrical columns of various sizes.

"What the hell is all this?" Sierra asked.

"Pipes?" Priya put her hand on one of the columns and felt a thrum. "Water filtration maybe?"

Sierra looked at her, squinting. "Are you sure? How can you tell?"

Priya shook her head. "Of course I'm not sure. I wish you would quit asking me that. We're under the sea. They look like pipes. It feels like something is moving inside. Water needs to be filtered. It's merely a guess."

They turned left and walked along the top of the slope. Up here, they were higher than some of the spheres floating in the chamber, but too far away to get onto them. Priya searched for control panels or access hatches along the wall, but found nothing. Just hundreds of pipes or conduits, or whatever they were. She wondered if one of them fed the waterfall at the end of the canyon. It had to come from somewhere.

After more than half a kilometer, they came to another side wall and were forced to start back down the slope. There weren't any windows on this side. The wall was just a flat, featureless gray surface extending forward into the gloom.

"I want to see the stars again," Priya said after they'd hiked down roughly as far as they'd come up. "Let's go back over."

They started across. Out in the middle, Sierra stopped and pointed at a purple ring on the ceiling, about five hundred meters up, maybe more. "I think that one is our portal."

"Come on," Priya said. "We're completely exposed out here. I like it better by the walls. If someone comes along, we can duck into one of the little hallways." She felt like an interloper.

"Let 'em spot us," Sierra said.

She was far too brazen. "What if they stun us and throw us back in storage?"

Sierra shrugged and followed Priya across the slope. When they reached the wall, they turned right and started down, their footfalls barely registering in the vast chamber.

"I don't suppose you have any food?" Sierra asked. "I think we missed dinner."

"No, but we'll die of thirst long before we die of hunger." Their clothes were dry now. Priya realized with regret that they should have wrung the water from them into their mouths.

"Terrific."

Priya counted her steps and after about a kilometer, they came to another octagonal opening. She went inside for a quick look. The view had shifted slightly, but that didn't tell her much.

They kept descending and passed a corridor every kilometer.

"My feet hurt," Sierra said. How steep do you think this is, anyway?"

"Forty-five degrees," Priya answered. Her feet had been hurting for a good while now. Her toes jammed into the front of her shoes with every step.

"How do you know?"

"The slope aligns with the angled side wall in those octagonal corridors. That makes it forty-five degrees."

Sierra chuckled. "Impressive."

It was an incredibly basic calculation, but the praise felt nice and distracted her from the cramping pain in her feet and her growing weariness.

By the time they reached the fifth corridor, the spheres were too high to see in the gloom. Priya grew increasingly uncomfortable. She wished she was back on the islands. Everything there felt semi-normal, at least in comparison.

They continued down the slope.

"Why did you come after me?" Sierra asked.

Priya chuckled. "I was just asking myself the same thing." She had wanted to show that she could be brave and bold like Sierra, but that sounded lame. "I figured it would be better to face whatever was down here together instead of alone."

Sierra smiled. "You're right."

"I usually am," Priya said, mostly joking. "Also, I never heard the story about how your father is not your father."

Sierra took a deep breath. "I've been wondering if Waldmire might actually be my biological father. Felicia thinks there's a resemblance."

"I can see it. You two came here in the same pod, right? How did you know him?"

"He was my neighbor. He was always there, as far back as I can remember. Mom moved out when I was nine and I was raised by that Hollywood producer I told you about." She shrugged. "I always thought he was my dad."

"If he raised you, he was your dad," Priya said.

"I know," Sierra said. "I didn't mean it like that. I'm just annoyed with the idea that my parents might have deceived me my whole life. It's like my childhood was a lie."

"What does Waldmire say?" Priya asked. The discussion helped distract her from the growing suspicion they would never escape this place.

Sierra gave a guilty grunt. "I haven't asked."

Priya never could understand why anyone would be afraid to know the truth.

"You should ask him. If he isn't your father, he'll be flattered. And if he is, it would mean you're not alone here." She'd felt so alone since Charlie died. "And maybe he can explain why he kept it from you all these years."

Sierra didn't respond. Priya decided that when they got back, she would ask Waldmire for her.

They walked on for a while and when Sierra spoke again, she sounded equal parts weary and grumpy. "There has to be a way out of here. The caretakers obviously come and go through the ceiling portal. Where do they go after that?"

"Maybe there are more openings above us. The walls here are three and half kilometers high. There could be openings anywhere up there."

"How the hell do you know how high the walls are?"

"Geometry."

Sierra gave her a sideways glare, but didn't ask for a proof.

By the time they reached the seventh octagonal corridor, Priya's feet and shins were killing her, and she was hungry, thirsty, and exhausted. She walked into the little tunnel for another peek at the stars. She wished she could stay long enough to estimate the ship's movement. "What do you think about getting a few hours of sleep before we go further?"

Sierra scowled. "I don't want to give up. We have to find ... something."

"I'm not proposing we give up," Priya said. "I'm simply proposing we get some rest while we have the opportunity." She forced a yawn, which wasn't difficult considering how tired she felt.

Sierra yawned back, right on cue. "Let's keep going, at least a little longer." They started down again.

Priya didn't push, and she didn't need to. They only made it another four hundred steps before Sierra changed her tune. "Maybe we should get some rest. If we ever do find someone, I want to be ready for them."

Priya jumped on the idea. "We can take turns. One of us can keep watch while the other sleeps."

"Sold. Let's stop in the next tunnel."

Priya smiled. She would fall asleep watching the stars.

The light coming from within the eighth corridor seemed brighter than the others. Priya got there first and saw something she never thought she'd see again.

Earth.

She hurried down the passage and leaned forward on the sloping glass. Her heartbeat pulsed in her fingertips.

"We're in orbit," she said.

Earth drifted into view from the right side of the window, with the Indian subcontinent facing them. Her family's home.

Madagascar rotated toward them from the left. The east coast of Africa followed soon after.

Sierra crouched next to her, tears on her cheeks. "It's beautiful."

Priya froze. *Too* beautiful. "It shouldn't look like this. There should be a cloud of dust and smoke covering the entire planet. Some areas should still be burning."

"Maybe the Ender wasn't as bad as everyone thought," Sierra said.

"No. The science was solid. Unless …" Her stomach lurched. "What if the Ender never hit? What if we all got in those pods for nothing?"

Sierra didn't answer.

The interior of Africa rotated past. It didn't look nearly as green as Priya thought it should, though she wasn't a hundred percent certain.

"Lights," Sierra said. "We should look for lights, when nighttime passes by."

Priya nodded. "The terminator."

Sierra wrinkled her nose, obviously confused. "Great movie."

"It's the name for the shadow between day and night."

"When do we see this terminator thing?"

Priya tapped the window. "We may not. This could be a Lagrangian orbit."

"What?" Sierra sounded frustrated.

"It's an orbit between Earth and the sun. We'd only see the sunny side."

By the time North America rotated into view, the planet had moved far enough to fill the window. The Appalachian Mountains were brown and barren.

"The Ender must have hit," Sierra said. "That definitely doesn't look right."

Central and South America were also brown, with only a few tiny splotches of green here and there. The desiccated Earth broke Priya's heart.

They watched silently as the West Coast slowly came into view. An inland sea covered the Los Angeles basin and Baja California was now a string of islands.

Sierra sat down and exhaled. "We have to get down there."

The thought made Priya dizzy. "What? How?"

"I don't know. We have to find a way. We have to get everyone out of the village and out of storage and then we have to go back there. It's our home."

As the Pacific Ocean rotated past, Priya searched for Hawai'i. That was home.

The planet turned, but the islands were gone. The Ender had wiped them away.

Chapter Thirty-One

The trees didn't look like real trees to Cameron. They looked like weird paintings of trees in an art museum. Abstract or impressionistic or some damn thing. She wasn't sure. She'd never been much for art.

Thick branches jutted straight out from smooth trunks, then curved skyward, ending in clumps of tiny leaves that looked like squirrel nests. The largest clumps looked big enough to support a person.

Cameron chose a tree with plenty of room for all four of them, and lots of those right-angle branches. She didn't think they'd get much sleep, but at least they'd be safe.

David boosted Barry to the lowest limb. From there, the little monkey worked his way upward until he stood on a branch twenty feet up, one hand on the trunk. "Look at me!"

David's lips pulled back in a grimace. "Hold on with both hands, Barry."

"He's okay, Ace," Cameron said. "This is just what we need. The sailbacks can't reach us up there."

They'd seen two more as they moved inland. She'd instructed everyone to walk close together, hoping it made them more threatening. It seemed to work. The dinosaurs had kept their distance.

"Sailback? Is that what they're called?" Scott asked.

"How should I know, Sportcoat?"

He narrowed his eyes. "Blazer."

"Barry, you had a little plastic one that looked like them," David said. "What kind was it?"

Barry shrugged. "I don't remember."

"I'm sure Priya knows," Cameron said. "Come on, let's start climbing."

David looked up, his face pale and sweat on his brow. "Maybe we could use some vines to secure ourselves once we're up there."

"Good idea," she said. If they were anchored, they might actually be able to doze a little. "Let's hurry though." She had no idea when night would fall, but it couldn't be far off.

"How about this stuff?" Scott pulled a hairy strip of bark from a different kind of tree, one with thin wispy branches that only grew near the top.

She peeled off a sample. It tore easily up and down, but when she tried to pull it apart from the ends, she couldn't. "Nice work, Sportcoat."

Scott smiled and didn't correct her.

They stripped several yards of fibrous bark from that tree and a few others nearby. It would be even stronger once they braided the strands together.

"Come on, let's get up there." Cameron draped the fibers over her neck. The others simply didn't appreciate how fast night would come on.

Barry, who had remained in the tree, climbed even higher as Scott pulled himself up.

Cameron turned to David. "Give me a boost." Her left shoulder was still weak from the bullet wound.

She smiled as David's hands went to her butt, letting him do most of the work.

Scott found a branch on the opposite side of the trunk from Barry. Cameron settled on a spot below the boy.

"Did you get fired from being a pilot?" Barry asked.

Cameron had never much cared for kids, but she liked the way Barry blurted out whatever came to mind.

"Airlines have strict rules against drinking," Scott muttered.

"You shouldn't drink when you're flying," Barry said.

"Yeah, well, sometimes we do things we shouldn't, don't we?"

"My dad hardly ever drank until the Ender came," Barry said.

David pulled himself up to a branch opposite Cameron. He reached around the trunk and grasped her forearm, which felt nice. She leaned sideways to look at him, but his face was pressed against the smooth bark. "You okay, Ace?"

"I got a thing with heights," he said, breathing hard. "I could go for a drink right about now."

She rolled her eyes. They were less than thirty feet off the ground. "Come on, you pussy. This isn't high."

"Sorry, my mistake." He released her forearm and she regretted saying anything.

"It's okay, Daddy," Barry called from above.

"Thanks, Bud." He didn't look up.

"Tough luck," Scott said. "There's no booze at the end-of-the world zoo. That's how I knew this wasn't the afterlife."

Cameron missed having a stiff drink every now and then, too. She pulled a couple of bark fibers off her shoulder and started weaving them together. Maybe if she could tie David to the tree, he'd relax a little. Both of his arms were wrapped around the trunk in a bear hug.

"How did you get that big scar?" Barry asked. "Was it another dinosaur?"

Cameron touched the smooth skin running through the hair above her ear. The kid's habit of asking whatever came to mind wasn't quite so amusing now.

"Barry, that isn't polite," David said.

"I got this when Priya ran me off the road," she said dryly.

"It adds character," David whispered, so that only she could hear. He looked around the trunk at her, holding eye contact.

She offered him a thin smile. "Thanks."

Night came on suddenly, as always. The sky transitioned from the flat light of daytime to pitch black in about thirty seconds.

David sucked air through his teeth. "Shit."

"I've got a rope ready," Cameron said. She swung it around him on one side and caught it on the other, then pulled it snug and tied it tight. "That better?"

He breathed hard in the dark. "I can barely tell which way is up. Feels like I'm falling."

"Can you feel the branch under your butt? That's down. You're fine. You aren't going anywhere."

Barry's voice came from above, small and shaking. "I want to get down."

"Give me your hand, Barry." Scott said. "I gotcha."

The boy sniffed.

"Pass me some vines," Scott called down. "I'll secure Barry."

"I need to finish braiding them, Sportcoat."

"It's a blazer," Scott said. "Pass them up. I can braid them."

"How do you know how to make braids?" Barry asked.

"I had a little girl," Scott said, his voice thin. "I was an expert at braids."

Cameron waited for Barry to ask what happened to her, but for once the boy kept his mouth shut. Everyone here had a shit story to tell.

Another half hour passed before they finished braiding the vines. The work was probably sloppy, but it was better than nothing. Cameron used the last one to tie herself to the trunk and tried to relax.

She didn't think she'd actually be able to sleep. They'd all be saddle-sore tomorrow, and if anyone had to pee in the night, she had no idea how they'd do it.

Resting her head against the smooth trunk, she closed her eyes.

Sometime later, an itch on her back woke her.

The itch moved. Scratched. Cameron dismissed it, her thoughts groggy. A branch must be blowing against her.

Except there's no wind here.

She snapped awake, her eyes wide, but it made no difference. She couldn't see anything. She reached around with her hand, grasping for whatever was crawling up her back. Her fingers touched something hard and segmented. Some kind of huge bug.

She screamed, but she didn't have enough air, so only a pathetic squeal came out. She pulled her shoulder blades together and leaned her head back. Sharp claws clenched her skin through her shirt.

"What's wrong?" David's disembodied voice came from the darkness ahead of her.

She grabbed the creature. It was as thick around as a baseball bat. Hundreds, maybe thousands, of wriggling, grasping claws dug in, tightening on her flesh. She pulled hard, tugging the segmented thing.

Searing pain lanced into her shoulder blade, lighting her up like a flash-bang.

She squeezed and yanked, flinging the creature into the darkness. It landed on the ground below with a thud.

"Fuck fuck fuck." Her back burned with a pain even worse than what she'd felt when Randall shot her.

"What's the matter?" David demanded.

"Are you okay?" Barry cried out. "Wh-what is it?"

"There was a bug on me," Cameron said. The words came out in a shudder. She hissed as the pain swelled. Her stomach roiled and she was certain she would vomit.

"A bug?" David mocked. "Who's the pussy now?"

She wanted to rip off his balls and feed them to him.

"It was huge," she roared. "It bit me."

"Oh, fuck," Scott said. A flapping, smacking sound came from somewhere above. The whole tree shook.

Cameron pulled her head down and raised her shoulders, like a turtle retreating into its shell. If one of those bugs fell on her, she would die. Her heart would seize and stop.

It landed on David instead. "Gaaa-aah!" He shook and squirmed. A moment later, she heard it hit the ground.

Cameron clawed blindly for the rope holding her to the tree. Thank God she'd use a quick-release hitch. She found the knot and yanked it free.

"Daddy, there's one up here," Barry said, his voice high-pitched with terror. "I can hear it."

"It's okay, Bud," he said, breathing hard. "It's just a bug. Leave it alone and it won't hurt you."

"Bullshit," Cameron spat, barely able to speak. Pain blossomed across her back. She pulled her leg over the branch, grabbed the trunk like a bear cub, and slid down.

She'd gone down at least twenty feet when something long, hairy, and wriggling landed on her. She let go, fell the last several feet onto her back, and rolled across the jungle floor, screeching and writhing. The creature was tangled around her neck. Her hand found purchase and she flung it away, but it wasn't another bug. It was Barry's vine rope, or maybe Scott's.

"Fuck fuck fuck." She wanted to flee, but she had to wait for the others. "Get down here." It felt like a burning knife was embedded in her back. The pain made her dizzy. It had to be venomous. Had she gotten a fatal dose?

As she pushed up to her feet, her hand touched a hefty stick. She grabbed it and held it out in front of her, a sword in the dark.

Scott shouted orders, guiding Barry and David down. They made a lot of noise, including a fair bit of mewling from David, but somehow reached the ground without breaking anything.

"Listen," Scott hissed.

They all held their breath. The jungle was alive with the crackling, tingling, crunching sounds of bugs in every direction.

Cameron's skin crawled and the need to vomit returned. She bit it back. "Beach. Hold hands." She reached out, slapping David in the chest, groping until she found his hand, and started off, her other arm waving the stick back and forth so she wouldn't walk into a tree.

The sounds of bugs crinkled directly in front of her, so she steered away, hopefully still moving toward the goddamn beach.

"What if the dinosaurs are out?" Barry asked.

"Then we go in the sea," Cameron answered. They could swim out from the island and tread water until the sun came up. Assuming she lived that long. She pictured her organs breaking down from the venom.

"No way," Scott said. "Dinosaurs can swim. That's what you told us, right, David?"

"They can," Barry said. "They really can."

Something brushed Cameron's outstretched arm and she yelped, but it was only a branch. David squeezed her hand. She pulled onward until she felt sand under her boots, sweeping the stick back and forth in front of her like a minesweeper.

Homing in on tiny splashes from the rippling sea, she led them to the wet hard pack, then turned right and walked along the shore.

"Do you have a plan?" David asked.

"I'm heading back to the sand spit," she groaned through gritted teeth.

A hiss came from the right.

Barry screamed.

Cameron held the stick in the direction of the sound. If it charged them, there wasn't anything she could do but flail in the dark. She felt dizzy and short of breath. "Get in the water." She led them in until they were knee deep.

"What if something grabs us from below?" Scott asked.

"There's nothing in the water," Cameron snapped. "The dinosaurs can't see us any better than we can see them, and maybe the water will block our scent."

"What if they have night vision?"

Night vision required dim light. The real concern was thermal vision. Or maybe she had that backwards. Everything was fuzzy. Black dread clouded her mind. She couldn't die from a fucking bug bite. It wasn't fair.

Another shuffling sound came from the right, somewhere on the beach. Barry squealed and danced deeper into the water, pulling the others with him.

"Be still," David whispered. Something moved slowly across the sand only a few yards away.

"Keep going." Cameron pulled his hand. She wasn't sure how much longer she would last.

They marched single file, moving slowly to make as little noise as possible. Twice more, they heard shuffling in the sand, and once they heard branches breaking up near the tree line.

After a while, Scott whispered, "We're at the end of the island."

"How do you know?" David asked.

"I can hear water sloshing on the other side of that little strip."

Cameron listened, but couldn't focus. With a great deal of effort, she brought up a mental picture of the long finger of sand curving out into the water.

"Let's go ashore," Scott said. "If we hear anything, we'll come back in."

Cameron nodded, then remembered they couldn't see her. "Okay," she whispered.

They moved at a glacial pace, edging their feet forward a few inches at a time until they were out of the water and walking on hard, wet sand.

Cameron expected to kick one of those giant lizards at any moment. Barry breathed loudly and Scott sounded like he was sucking air between his teeth.

When they reached powdery dry sand, Scott stopped them. "This should be good."

"Are those things nearby?" Cameron asked, feeling the malaise that came on with a nasty fever. She dropped her stick. Holding it took too much effort.

"I don't think so," David said.

Cameron pulled him close and hooked her arm around his neck. Her legs weren't going to support her much longer.

He lowered her to the sand. "Let me check your back."

She inhaled sharply as he ran his hand under her shirt, past her bra strap. She'd imagined this moment going quite differently.

"Christ, there's a welt the size of a golf ball. You really were bit."

"No shit," Cameron breathed. She wanted to close her eyes and lie down. Stars sparkled in her vision. "I don't feel so good, Ace."

He cradled her head to the ground. "We need to slow your heart rate and get you some water. Barry, give me your shirt."

After a bit of commotion, she felt cloth on her lips. David squeezed, and water dripped onto her tongue. She knew she was in bad shape because she didn't even care that it was fouled with kid sweat. She sucked down the water and started to relax. Everything felt heavy.

"Cameron?"

David called her name, but he sounded far away.

"Cameron? Answer me. Cameron?" His voice grew softer and softer as the world faded to black.

Chapter Thirty-Two

Randall slept like a king. He'd pulled the makeshift bedding from the other huts into Joe's old cabin, the farthest one up the slope, and made himself a nest to sleep on. After years of shitty beds in prison, sleeping on the street, and more recently, camping out on the ground, it felt downright regal.

The aliens left him alone overnight. Kona peeked in the cabin once, but wouldn't come in. Other than the dog padding around, the village was dead silent.

He woke up hungry and wandered down to the cooking area, where he found a wooden bowl full of oatmeal-like sludge with a dried film on top. It tasted better than it looked, so he carried it to the benches and dug in. He needed more people here, especially some women who knew how to cook.

The pods containing the villagers sat out in the fields like eggs waiting to hatch. Randall had only wanted the wardens to leave Kim and Waldmire behind, but they'd left all thirteen pods. At times, it seemed that he confounded them as much as they confounded him. Too bad Crystal wasn't in one of those pods. Randall shoved the thought aside. There would be other Crystals.

After finishing the porridge, he found a big stash of dried meat in one of the storage sheds. It tasted exactly like the *T. rex* arms he'd cooked on the other island, gamy and chewy. Randall held out a piece for Kona. "Hey girl, want some dinosaur meat?"

The dog made a low rumble. Randall didn't need aliens to translate. It was obviously dog-talk for "*fuck off*." He flung the meat at her, meaning for it to smack her in the muzzle, but she snapped it out of the air and ran away with the prize.

He squinted. If he was gonna be alpha, he had to do better than that. The dog wouldn't get another bite till she learned some obedience.

While he sat digesting his breakfast, the yellow drone from yesterday floated in over the fields, with some sort of orange ball clasped between four of its mechanical arms. The object was about the size of a beach ball, but looked like it was made of metal. The drone stopped directly in front of him and lowered the sphere.

"For me?" The wardens had promised to bring him something called *control*, and this must be it. Randall reached up, like Moses accepting the Ten Commandments from God. He cradled the ball against his chest. It weighed at least thirty pounds.

Grunting, he hauled it to one of the wooden tables where the villagers prepared meals. A warden materialized overhead. He flinched and dropped his hand to his gun. "You shouldn't sneak up on a guy like that," Randall muttered.

The warden rumbled at him. *"Use control device to select human specimens."*

"How does it work?"

"Touch the sides."

Randall clapped the ball on both sides, then stepped back as the sphere rotated in place and split apart. The top half flipped up, revealing a circular surface covered with little knobs protruding from shallow holes. A pinprick of light glowed in the center of each knob. The surface of the bottom half was smooth, flat, and gun-metal gray.

The two halves of the sphere touched in the back, but they weren't connected. The top half just floated there and the bottom half was balanced on an edge so that its surface faced him.

The alien rumbled. *"Tap the control panel."*

Randall reached for the little nubs on the top half. Each one had a smooth ball inside. He tried to roll one of the balls, but it didn't move.

"Tap the control panel," repeated the alien.

Annoyed, Randall tapped the flat surface of the bottom half. Nothing happened. Which made sense, because there was nothing there. This was stupid.

"Two touches."

He tapped it twice. Still nothing. He unfolded his fuck-you finger and tapped the empty grey surface with both fingers at once.

A bunch of weird-ass shapes appeared, floating in the air between the object and Randall. They looked like hieroglyphics. He stepped back. "What the hell is all this?" He turned to the warden floating nearby and the shapes vanished. When he faced the device again, they reappeared.

"That's a hologram, ain't it?" The shapes looked solid, but when he reached for them, they flickered. "Shitty holograms." In the movies, you could pass your hand right through a hologram without screwing it up.

The warden rumbled. *"Choose storage."* It tapped something inside its hovercar and a moment later, two grid shapes flashed on either side of the holograms.

Randall reached for them, but again, his hands went right through them. He gritted his teeth, annoyed.

Below, the surface of the bottom half-sphere was no longer plain and empty. A smaller set of holograms covered it. Two shapes on the sides flashed off and on. Randall leaned in close and they vanished.

He stood straight and the shapes reappeared. Apparently, his eyes had to face all those little flashlight nubs in order to see any of this nonsense.

The two shapes on the panel were flashing in sequence with the two that were floating in the air. "They're related, ain't they?"

He tapped one of the shapes on the flat surface. Nothing happened.

The alien's rumble sounded annoyed. *"Two touches."*

Randall scowled and touched both shapes at the same time.

The floating holograms expanded to fill a space about three feet wide in front of him. Each one displayed the shape of an animal, except for the sixth, which showed the outline of a man.

"Choose human specimens."

The surface of the half-sphere below was now covered with similar squares. Randall used two fingers to tap the one with a human shape.

A man with a scar on his lip appeared, floating right in front of him.

"Is that man in storage?"

"Yes."

The man looked like a hard-ass. Randall didn't want anyone who might try to take over. He spotted the arm of another person at the edge of the hologram.

On the surface below, the edge of a second box appeared beside the first. Randall touched it, but nothing happened. He tried two fingers. The box shifted slightly. He dragged sideways, and the next box slid into place.

The hologram changed to a stern-looking woman with wrinkles around her mouth. *Hell no.* He scrolled again. A small map of North America hovered above and to the right, with a red dot on it. Each time Randall called up a new person, the dot jumped around. "That's where they came from, ain't it?"

The dots were concentrated in a range that ran from the Great Lakes down toward southern California. There weren't many as far south as Oklahoma City. Randall had been damn lucky to find a pod.

"Why'd you pick these spots?" Randall stuck his finger into North America. "Why not Russia or Africa or some other place?"

He got a lengthy rumbling answer and waited for the translation. *"Insufficient time was available to specify storage container landing locations."*

"Are you trying to say it was random?"

"Yes."

He rolled his eyes. "You could have just said so." He started to scroll through the holograms of people again, then stopped himself. "Wait. How the fuck did you collect dinosaurs? They didn't climb into any goddamn pods, did they?"

"Harvesters collect sleeping specimens."

"Why didn't you collect people the same way?"

"Insufficient time was available before the impact of the comet. Storage containers were sent to allow human specimens to self-collect."

Randall had to take a minute to translate the translation. "The comet was coming and you didn't have time to abduct everyone, so you sent a bunch of pods at the last minute, hoping people would get in on their own."

The alien didn't answer, but then again, it wasn't really a question.

Randall shrugged. "Well, it worked." He went back to his scrolling. A blonde in a tank-top captured his attention. Her bare belly looked tight and taut, at least in the hologram. "Now we're cooking. How do I bring her here?"

"Select the storage container."

"Which one is that?"

The alien tapped something inside its hovercar and an oval hologram floating in front of Randall began to flash.

He reached for the oval, then stopped himself, remembering that he had to find the corresponding shape on the touchpad below.

This whole thing was just a fancy-ass computer. He hated computers. As soon as he learned how to use one, they changed everything and made him feel stupid. Computers were just another way for limp-dick geeks to make themselves look smart.

He tapped the shape with two fingers. The hologram of the woman shrank out of the way and the oval grew larger, becoming a pod, with a new set of hieroglyphics around it.

The alien rumbled right behind Randall's head, vibrating his whole body. *"Touch the map."* A moment later, a shape like a guitar pick flashed in the air.

Randall found a little matching guitar pick on the side of the pad and tapped it with two fingers.

The pod shifted out of the way and now a blue ocean filled with green islands floated in front of him. Randall loved maps. They made a hell of a lot more sense than computers.

"Touch island seventy-four."

He didn't see any numbers, but the alien did something inside the hovercar and one of the islands flashed near the bottom left. Randall used two fingers to activate the corresponding shape on the touchpad.

The hologram zoomed in and he recognized the island he was on, with the plateau in the middle covered by clusters of red dots. "Those are the giant rhinos, ain't they?" The canyon zig-zagged right up the center of the plateau, with a little blue line running through the middle, which had to be the creek. Randall followed the line down to the village, which was only a small circle from this far out.

The surface of the control pad showed a simplified diagram of the island. He used two fingers to expand a dot where the village should be and the view zoomed in, both on the touchpad and on the hologram floating in front of him. The little circle became the perimeter wall around the village, with its three openings, one at the bottom where the path led down to the beach, a smaller one on the right where the outhouses were, and a tiny one at the top where the creek came in from the canyon. Two red dots glowed near the middle, just below the cabins. One was stationary and the other moved slowly toward the blue line.

"Kona, come," Randall shouted. Over by the cabins, the dog looked his way, then stopped and lapped water from the creek.

On the hologram, the moving dot stopped by the blue line. Randall grinned. "That's us."

The hovercar was a yellow rectangle right below him. Thirteen white circles sat about an inch further down. Randall looked over his shoulder at the pods.

"So all I have to do is choose a spot on the map and it will bring that woman here?"

"Correct."

Randall licked his lips, but he wasn't ready to pull the trigger yet. He touched the oval shape off to the side, which brought the pod back into focus. From there, he worked his way back to the grid of people again. Browsing was good enough for now. He smiled. This control device was like the menu at a Chinese restaurant, filled with pictures of things he could order.

"Humans must be managed for observation."

"Yeah, yeah," Randall said. That was a job he could handle. "I'm gonna manage the shit out of these humans."

As he continued to scroll, he found plenty of smoking hot women. He could bring them all to his island. He grew a boner just thinking about it. He also spotted a few men who looked like they might work out. Tough guys, but not too tough. The power to pick and choose stiffened him even more. This was what alpha felt like.

The alien began to float away.

"Hey, what else can I do with this thing?" Randall asked.

"Additional functionality has been disabled," the caretaker rumbled. *"Humans must not interfere with caretakers."*

"Yeah, yeah. Fine."

The alien continued to float off, turning invisible as it went.

Randall turned back to the holograms, trying to remember everything they'd shown him. Fucking computers.

Down in the fields, Kona curled up next to the pod containing Kim. Somehow the dog knew she was in there.

"What am I going to do with you, Kimmie?" Randall said, tapping his fingers against his lips. She was insurance against anything Dave might try if he ever came back, just as Waldmire was leverage over Sierra. But leverage would only work if he saw 'em coming. He didn't like the thought of having to constantly be on the lookout.

Randall turned back to the control device. The solution might be right in front of him. He touched the guitar pick shape that brought up the map of the islands.

He tried the triangular island on the right, which was where he'd gotten the guns from the *T. rex*. Maybe Dave and Sierra had gone looking for him there. Red dots crawled all over the place, like ants on an anthill. He touched several, but each one brought up an image of a wolf-pig, a terror bird, or one of those little blue monkeys. That island had a shitload of monkeys.

Randall zoomed back out. The next closest island was to the north, above the plateau. How the fuck could Dave and Sierra have gone there? Randall selected the island, a long curving arc shaped like a toenail clipping. He saw something unusual right away. A yellow rectangle drifted back and forth near one end, close to a cluster of red dots.

The rectangle had to be another hovercar. He tapped it, but nothing happened. "Additional functionality has been disabled," he said, repeating what the caretaker had told him. They'd turned off anything that would allow him to fuck with them.

Randall touched one of the red dots next, and the hologram showed that suit-wearing asshole from the village. "Looky who I found." The second dot was Dave and the third was his little nose-picker. The hovercar had to be observing them.

The last dot caught him off guard. "Cameron? How the fuck is that bitch still alive?"

The four of them were bunched together on a thin stretch of sand with a ton of other red dots blocking their access to the rest of the island. Randall selected one and a lizard dinosaur with a half-circle fin on its back appeared. He tapped several others. They were all fin-lizards.

He wished there was a way to watch Dave and his pals get eaten by those dinosaurs, but watching dots on a map was about as fun as watching piss dry. At least he didn't need to worry about them.

He had to find that Chinese menu again and pick out his new villagers. It took him twenty minutes just to get back to the right spot. Fucking computers.

Chapter Thirty-Three

Priya took one last look at the stars. Earth had slid from view while she slept. She wanted to stay and watch, to verify the ship's rotation and orbit, but that wouldn't give them the answers they really needed. Why had they been brought here? Where were the people in storage? What had happened on Earth? She turned and walked out of the octagonal corridor.

"I think I see something," Sierra said, waiting for her about ten meters down. "There's a wall ahead."

Priya squinted in the gloom. "What do we do if it's a dead end?" They could walk across the bottom of the sloped chamber and climb back up the other side, but if they didn't find anything new before they reached the top again, they were truly trapped.

Sierra didn't answer. She didn't need to. They would die here.

After descending a little further, however, they saw that the wall didn't extend all the way down. It stopped about a hundred meters up, leaving an opening directly across from the bottom of the slope. Inside the opening, a horizontal floor disappeared into a wide, dark passageway.

"What do you think is in there?" Priya asked, keeping her voice low.

"Only one way to find out." Sierra continued down the slope.

Priya followed, nervous, but eager to be walking on a flat surface for a change. She hoped to see something new when they reached the bottom. Instead, she saw only darkness. Sierra gave her a nervous glance before starting forward.

Even though the ceiling was a hundred meters above them, the space felt small after the vastness of the slope room. The only light came from behind, stretching their shadows out ahead of them.

"What are those?" Sierra pointed off to the right, where two small round shapes lay close together in the middle of the floor.

"Baby spheres," Priya said. "They aren't big enough to float yet." She snorted. Silly jokes helped keep her fear at bay.

Sierra walked over and picked one up. "Our diving weights."

Priya had forgotten all about them. She should have been searching for them.

They started forward again, each carrying a stone. It wasn't much, but it gave Priya comfort to hold something she might be able to use as a weapon.

Between the low gravity and the growing darkness, she found it increasingly difficult to keep her bearings.

"What if there's a drop-off?" she whispered. It felt like they were walking into nothingness.

Sierra didn't answer, but they both slowed, testing their steps with their toes, as if approaching a staircase in the dark.

"There," Sierra whispered a few minutes later. "The light at the end of the tunnel."

A faint glow appeared ahead. As they grew close, it expanded, revealing another vast chamber, even dimmer than the slope room behind them. The floor continued into the new space as far as they could see, barren and lifeless.

Above, giant silver objects were suspended at roughly the same height as the passage they'd just walked through. Unlike the spheres in the slope room, these were arranged in an orderly grid.

"It's a hangar," Priya said.

"Hangar?" Sierra repeated. "Do you think those are some kind of planes? Or spaceships?"

"Who knows?" Priya said, creeping closer. "But they're definitely *hanging*."

Sierra groaned. She also let out a tiny snicker.

The objects hanging overhead were bulbous at one end with long, tapering points at the other. It was difficult to judge their size because they were a hundred meters up, but they looked about as big as the regional jets Priya sometimes took between Hawai'i and O'ahu.

She stepped out from the tunnel for a better look. A second layer of the objects floated above the lowest layer and at least two more above that. There had to be thousands. Maybe tens of thousands.

Sierra craned her neck. "Do you think they're some kind of pods? Could this be storage?"

"These are different," Priya said. "They're much larger and they aren't shaped the same."

"Yeah, but there had to be different sizes," Sierra said. "The dinos and rhinos would've needed bigger pods."

Priya shrugged. "Good point."

"They're definitely different, though," Sierra said. "These look like giant silver teardrops."

"Lachrymiforms," Priya said, showing off.

"What?" Sierra sounded both impressed and annoyed.

"Shaped like teardrops."

"You're such a dork," Sierra said, though her comment carried a light, friendly tone.

Priya grinned, still studying the objects overhead. "I always won at trivia night."

Sierra chuckled.

Two long thin structures curved out from the bulbous ends of the objects, one on each side. They looked like wings, but they were far too thin. Priya squinted, wishing she could get close enough to study them.

Sierra tossed her stone a few feet in the air, light as a tennis ball in the low gravity. She caught it and reared back, ready to throw. "What do you think will happen if I hit one?"

"Hold on." Priya raised her hand. "What if they're munitions? Those things are lined up like missiles."

"At least we'd get some attention."

"Yeah, why don't we explore a little further before you blow up the place?"

Sierra uncocked her arm. "Fair enough."

They started forward, more or less following the wall on their left, which seemed to be a continuation of the wall from the slope room, but without any of those octagonal hallways.

The pastel lights in the previous chamber had given the slope a pink hue, but here everything was gray. The dim light didn't seem to have a source. Everything was just gloomy. Maybe this was some long-deserted crypt.

Priya was about to tell Sierra to throw her rock at one of the objects and be done with it when she spotted a circular hole in the floor ahead, about as wide as a backyard swimming pool.

They slowed as they drew close, then kneeled at the edge.

Five meters below, a pair of empty carriages were parked nose-in against the curved wall.

Sierra lowered her legs over the edge of the pit and dropped down, landing gently in the low gravity.

"You don't ever stop to think," Priya hissed. "You just act. It's going to get you killed."

Sierra looked up at her. "Sometimes you just have to go for it."

"Are you sure you can get back out?" Priya asked.

Sierra jumped, caught the edge of the pit, and pulled herself unnecessarily close to Priya's face. "Piece of cake. Come on."

Priya looked around, expecting a security squad to swoop in, but the ship remained as lifeless as ever. Leaving her stone near the rim, she lowered herself over the side.

Seven orange spheres sat along the wall between the two carriages, each one sixty or seventy centimeters in diameter. They looked like the buoys used by fishermen to mark crab pots. Priya placed her hand on one and rolled it toward her, studying it.

"You found your baby spheres," Sierra said.

The surface of the sphere was smooth and empty, without anything to indicate its purpose. She rolled it back into place.

The carriages were attached to the wall by some sort of brackets. A docking mechanism for a third carriage sat empty on the wall equidistant from the other two, with a rectangular alcove where the vehicle's nose would go.

Sierra bent and peered into the little cubby. "There was something just like this on the giant sphere I was climbing on," she said. Her mouth twisted the way it did when she was thinking. "I suppose that means it was also a place for sleds to dock."

A cluster of holes dotted the wall above the docking port. Priya stood on her toes to study them. Each hole was about three centimeters in diameter, with a little knobby protrusion inside.

"Those are just gross," Sierra said. "They give me the creeps."

"Trypophobia," Priya said. "Fear of freaky-looking holes."

Sierra shook her head and chuckled. "Nerd."

"We've seen those before, too," Priya said, walking over to one of the carriages. She pointed at a group of holes on the dashboard.

Sierra wrinkled her nose. "Do you think this is where they control the ship?"

"If so, there's no one at the helm. Of course, that could be because we're parked in orbit."

Sierra poked at the controls on the carriage. "If we knew how to operate this sled, we could take one up for a better look at those teardrop things. We could also fly back to the slope room and see what's in the rest of those giant spheres."

"Even better, we could go back to get the others," Priya said. "And breakfast."

She leaned over the vehicle, studying the dashboard. She knew the controls on each side had to be operated in tandem, but that was about it.

A shape passed overhead, a whisper in the air.

Priya pressed herself against the wall of the pit.

Sierra jumped up to hang from the rim.

"What are you doing?" Priya whispered.

"Watching to see where it goes."

"What is it?"

"A sled," Sierra said. "It disappeared in the same direction we've been going." She pulled herself the rest of the way up. "Come on. Let's see where it went."

Priya remained in the pit. "No way. These carriages are too valuable to leave behind. We should try to figure out how to fly them."

Sierra shook her head. "That could take forever. We have to keep looking."

"For what?" Priya said. "We already found something."

"Answers," Sierra said, with steel in her eyes.

She was determined to confront the caretakers. Priya wished she knew how to muster that much bravery. She stood firm, frowning, trying to come up with a better plan.

"Here's a compromise," Sierra said. "If we don't find anything by the time we're ready to sleep, we'll come back here for the night."

"Are you *lōlō?* We can't sleep here. They might spot us."

She shrugged. "One of them flew right over without even noticing us."

"Yes, but the next one might fly in here."

Sierra scowled. "How about one hour? We keep going for another hour, and if we don't find anything new, we'll come back and try to figure out the sleds."

"Carriages," Priya corrected.

"Whatever," Sierra said.

Priya took one last look around the pit, then decided that Sierra's plan was reasonable, given the circumstances. "Okay." She reached for the edge to pull herself up.

Sierra grasped her forearm and lifted her out. The gesture somehow made Priya feel strong, even though Sierra was the one doing all the work.

They collected their rocks and started walking again. Priya ticked off the seconds, ready to call it when they reached an hour.

After twenty-one minutes, they came to a second hole, more than twenty times as wide as the first. It seemed to go down forever, disappearing in black shadow.

"Are you going to jump into this one, too?"

Sierra tilted her head. "There's bold, and then there's crazy."

They split up and circled the outer edge, searching for anything noteworthy. At the antipodal points, halfway around from each other, Priya could barely see Sierra. She hurried on, meeting up with her on the far side.

"See anything?" Sierra asked. "Handholds? Anything?"

"No," Priya said. "But I bet that carriage flew down there." The hole was big enough for the teardrop missiles to fit through, even with those long skinny wings.

"Are you sure?"

"Of course not. I told you to stop asking me that."

Sierra sighed. "Maybe we've gone far enough. Maybe we should go back and try to figure out the sled."

"Finally," Priya said. "You've seen the—" She froze without finishing her thought.

Several hundred meters beyond the giant hole, a faint glow rose from yet another pit in the floor. She clutched Sierra's arm, turning her to face it.

"Light." Sierra grinned.

They started toward the pit, which was small, the same size as the first one they'd encountered. Lights flashed and flickered from inside.

Priya's chest tightened as they drew close. "Do you think it's them?" she whispered.

"I hope so," Sierra said quietly. "It's time we got some answers."

"They could stun us." Priya made a snapping motion with her fingers, but without any sound. "Just like that."

"All we can do is keep trying," Sierra said. "Come on. Let's watch the watchers."

They inched toward the pit on hands and knees, sliding their stones in front of them, careful not to let them scrape the floor.

"Power through," Sierra whispered. Priya couldn't tell if she was talking to her, or herself. Maybe both.

Several clusters of holes dotted the walls, just like in the first pit, but here, bright lights shone from them, moving around like miniature searchlights.

As they approached the rim, they saw that a caretaker sat on a carriage docked beneath a set of dancing lights. The beams adjusted constantly, keeping their focus on several of the spindly appendages rising from the folds at the end of its body.

As with the first pit, there were two other docking stations. Both were vacant, though the light beams above them were active.

Priya swallowed, her throat dry. If another caretaker came along to dock at one of those empty stations, it would spot them easily.

Sierra scooted forward the last half meter, sliding her stone in front of her. When she got right up to the edge, she froze. Lights above the vacant station on the opposite wall shifted and aimed directly onto her face.

Priya squeezed her eyes shut. They'd been spotted. She wanted to get up and run, but she didn't know where to go.

Sierra grasped her wrist and pulled her forward. Priya opened her eyes, one degree at a time. A hazy blur floated in front of her. Three or four beams shifted, snapping to her face. The image solidified.

The lights weren't a security device, they were some sort of projection technology. Priya shifted a few centimeters closer, almost to the rim, flat on her stomach.

The view was hazy and faded at the edges, like looking through a frosted window. It was also amazing. The lights showed her a landscape covered with dinosaurs.

A pair of sauropods, possibly titanosaurs, reared up on their hind legs and slapped their necks against each other like bull giraffes competing for a herd.

Priya stared, eyes wide.

The image changed to show a troop of paleolithic hunters stalking a mammoth across grassy plains.

The holes on the wall used some sort of retinal projection, beaming images directly into Priya's eyes. If the lights knew she was there, it was only a matter of time before the alien would notice, too. They ought to flee, but she couldn't tear herself away.

The view switched to a giant sloth as tall as a house. It mounted a smaller companion leaning against a tree-trunk and pumped her like a jackhammer.

Were these creatures on the islands? If so, the menagerie was even more diverse than she'd imagined.

An allosaurus fed on a carcass that might have once been a stegosaur, while her babies ran between the bones, stealing bites and then darting away.

Priya wanted to watch everything, to study all the different animals, to learn about them. A bittersweet thought moistened her eyes. Charlie would have loved this.

The image flickered and switched to a village. *The* village. Priya leaned forward, looking for her friends.

Beside her, Sierra tensed.

A lone man stood at one of the work tables, tapping an orange sphere that had split open. The top half angled toward his face, shining similar beams of light into his eyes.

It was Randall.

Chapter Thirty-Four

David and Scott dragged Cameron's unconscious body further out on the spit. Her boot heels dug double furrows in the sand. A cluster of twenty-six sailbacks followed them. Barry was keeping count. Movement came from the jungle and another five or six marched onto the beach. A few were bigger than crocodiles, but most were the size of Komodo dragons.

One of the smaller ones charged toward Cameron's feet, its mouth open. Barry raised the stick high like an ax and brought it down on the animal's head. It squawked and fled, crawling over a larger one, which snapped off the last few inches of its tail. The wall of dinosaurs stopped advancing.

"Good job," David said, though it horrified him to see his six-year-old that close to the creatures.

They lowered Cameron gently onto the strip of beach, which was only about fifteen feet wide this far out. The phalanx of sailbacks facing them stood shoulder-to-shoulder.

David had done his best to keep Cameron comfortable overnight, shoving sand under her head for a pillow and draping Scott's blazer over her core when her temperature dropped. Her pulse and breathing remained steady but her lymph nodes felt swollen and she exhibited body tremors off and on. He felt powerless. There wasn't anything he could do but hope her system would fight off the toxin.

"We're running out of room," Scott said. "If we keep this up, we'll be swimming soon."

The sand spit curved out behind them for another hundred feet before narrowing down to nothing. They'd retreated a few yards every hour or so since daylight had revealed the creatures, which had apparently wandered toward them in the night.

Scott took the stick from Barry and stepped up between Cameron and the dinosaurs.

David rubbed his eyes, weary with fatigue. "Give me your shirt again, Barry." He dipped the tail in the water and squeezed a few drops onto Cameron's lips.

"Ugghhh," Cameron groaned. "Got any whiskey?" Her voice was thick and groggy.

"Hey, look who's awake." David knelt next to her and stroked her hair from her temples.

She pulled herself onto one elbow, wincing.

"Take it slowly," he said. "How are you feeling?"

"Hazy."

He smirked. He felt the same, only from lack of sleep.

"What bit you?" Barry asked.

Scott glanced back, but kept his position between them and the dinosaurs, swatting any that nudged close.

Cameron swung her arm in a circle, testing it. "I think it was a giant centipede. It had a lot of fucking legs."

"Let me have a look at your bite," David said. He helped her sit and pulled her shirt up in the back. A few minor scratches ran along her spine. Above that, two large edema plaques covered her shoulder blade, with reddened injection points at the center of each one.

"How does it look?"

He chuffed. "To be honest, pretty awful."

She pulled her shirt back down. "Great."

"But there's no sign of tissue necrosis. Hopefully, you're over the worst of it. The fact that you're awake tells me you're producing antibodies to neutralize the venom."

"Yay me." She turned toward the sailbacks. "What's our plan?"

"I think we should dig a channel," Scott said. "A moat. They don't seem to like the water." The wall of sailbacks ran from one shoreline to the other, but the individuals on the sides kept clear of the sea.

"Why don't they like the water?" Barry asked.

"Look at 'em," Scott said. "Their heads are low and those fins probably weigh them down. If they went in the water, they'd drown, don'tcha think?"

He dragged his foot through the sand, making a little trench.

"That's going to be a lot of work," David said. "Any moat would have to be several feet deep and eight or ten feet wide to keep them from crossing."

"Plus, it would leave us stranded on a tiny island with nothing to eat but sand," Cameron said.

"I'm hungry," Barry said.

"I know, Bud," David said. "Me, too."

Scott frowned. "Well, I'm going to give it a go." He dropped to his knees and started digging with his hands.

The moment he went down, one of the larger sailbacks darted toward him.

Scott yelped and scurried backwards on his elbows. David snatched the stick and helped him up.

The big lizard stopped, lowered its body to the ground, and hissed. Glistening saliva dripped from three-inch fangs. Its fin was torn and tattered, with several missing spines.

"We gotta stay on our feet," David said. "The moment you got down to dig, it saw you as something small enough to attack."

"Go away!" Barry shook his fist at the animal.

The lizard inched backwards, pushing against the sand with its front legs. Its tail bumped one of the creatures behind it, earning a snarl.

"It's scared of us," Barry said.

"He's right," David said. The animals seemed threatened when the three of them stood together. "Cameron, can you stand?"

She got up and stood beside him, clutching his shoulder. The large lizard spun around and crawled over two smaller ones behind it. The whole line of them pushed back a few inches.

"Let's get 'em," Scott said.

"Wait," David said, but Scott stomped forward. David followed, gripping Barry's arm. Cameron's hand remained on his shoulder.

The cluster of giant lizards parted, but only to a point. Scott kept going. One of the smaller ones lunged at his foot. He danced backwards.

"Enough," David said. "Get back." They retreated to their original position.

"What do we do now?" Barry asked, his voice small and scared.

No one answered. Three new sailbacks wandered down from the jungle.

Chapter Thirty-Five

Every muscle in Sierra's body tensed as she looked down into the alien bunker. "We have to stop him," she whispered.

Randall was back in the village.

He was at one of the work tables, doing something with a strange orange object that appeared to be made from two halves of a sphere.

The view pulled away and rose twenty feet in the air, which meant the camera must be on a caretaker sled, probably cloaked, because Randall didn't seem to realize he was being filmed. As the camera panned, several pods came into view, sitting in the fields. Sierra closed her eyes, exhaling. The villagers were all safe in those pods. They had to be.

She opened her eyes and realized she was wrong.

Randall walked past the fire pit, where Morrie lay on his back, a gaping hole in his chest. Sierra pressed a hand to her mouth, grief tightening her throat. Beside her, Priya's breathing hitched.

She wished Cameron had killed that piece of shit. She wished she could kill him herself. Poor sweet Morrie. He'd been trying so hard.

Priya clasped her arm, eyes wide. "Let's sneak away." Her voice was nearly inaudible. "We need a plan."

Sierra shook her head, rage burning hot in her blood. There wasn't time to come up with a plan. Not while Randall was in the village. He'd killed Morrie. Nothing would stop him from killing the others, if he hadn't already.

Rising to one knee, she grabbed her stone and jumped into the pit, floating across half the space. She landed behind the alien.

Several lights above the creature flickered onto Sierra's face and the village reappeared in front of her, becoming almost three dimensional, right there in the pit. Randall looked close enough to touch.

The alien rumbled, loud and angry.

Sierra shielded her eyes from the light beams with one hand, which broke Randall's image into slivers.

"That man is dangerous. He will harm you. Tell them to knock him out right now."

The alien unfolded two of its spider-like limbs and reached for the opposite sides of its carriage, toward the stun controls. Sierra's heart skipped. It was going to knock her out instead.

A clawed brown finger unfurled at the end of each limb. Sierra lunged forward and brought her stone down on the little cat's paw control, breaking off the mechanism with a snap. A wisp of smoke floated up, carrying the chemical smell of burning plastic.

The alien produced a deep rumbling sound like a semi passing on the freeway.

"You have to hear me out," Sierra said. "We aren't the same as your other specimens."

"Human specimens interfere."

"That's right. That's because we're intelligent, like you. We developed culture and technology. We need to be in control of our own destiny. We don't belong in your wildlife preserve."

"Agreed."

Sierra took a deep breath. Finally, she was getting somewhere.

Chapter Thirty-Six

Randall browsed through the people in storage, skipping past any pods that contained more than one person, which turned out to be most of them. He didn't want to deal with pre-existing relationships. He searched for men first, rejecting anyone who seemed too soft or too hard, as well as anyone dressed fancy. The last thing he needed was a businessman who thought he knew better than everyone else. He picked out three, marking each face in his memory so he could find them again when he was ready to place his order. He needed one more, a guy he could use in some sort of demonstration, to keep the others in line. A flash of inspiration struck. A Black guy would be perfect.

His boner returned when he started focusing on the women. It was like browsing through a catalog. He wondered how many he should get. He considered eight, which would be two girls for every guy, just like in the old beach song, but the more he thought about it, the more the idea made him uncomfortable. He couldn't risk filling the village with a bunch of yammering chatterboxes. He decided on four, one for each man, counting himself. He didn't count the scapegoat. That guy wouldn't be around long. He settled on two blondes, a brunette, and a redhead. He could always order more later.

A gurgle came from his stomach. He popped a sliver of dried *T. rex* meat into his mouth, longing for something different. The rhino meat was better, nice and greasy. He switched away from storage and called up the map. After a minute of searching, he found a group of red dots on the plateau. Randall selected one and a hologram of a wooly rhinoceros appeared, with weird little shapes all around it. He hummed, long and low. If he could figure out how to torpor the rhinos, he'd have something good to eat.

Kona wandered close, sniffing, probably interested in the jerky. He smiled. "You want some?" He'd show her who was boss. The dog had refused to eat from his hands yesterday. She could go hungry for a while and see how that suited her.

He turned back to the device and studied the shapes floating alongside the rhino hologram. On the icon for Earth, a dot glowed somewhere in Asia, showing where the rhino had come from, probably back in caveman days. None of the other shapes meant anything to Randall, except for a grid just like the grid shape that allowed him to browse for people in storage.

Randall narrowed his eyes. Maybe he could bring a rhino straight to the village from storage. He just needed to come up with a way to kill it.

He found the corresponding shape on the pad and touched it. Nothing happened, even though he used two fingers. He spotted a matching shape on the opposite side and tapped them both at the same time. This double-touch bullshit was annoying. Sometimes he had to touch one spot with two fingers and sometimes he had to touch two different spots simultaneously.

The rhino hologram shrank and new shapes appeared above and below. Sure enough, he was right back in storage, but in a different section, browsing through animals instead of people.

Randall spotted a hairy elephant with the biggest goddamn tusks he'd ever seen. His mouth fell open. "That's a mammoth." He scrolled. At least scrolling always worked the same on this stupid machine.

"Holy shit." There were horses of all sizes, a weird-ass camel, and a long-necked thing that looked like a giant badger. He could order up all sorts of animals. He wanted a nice Angus heifer. He found some big-ass buffalos, but no ordinary cows. He kept scrolling. "Yeah, baby." There were several kinds of oversized deer. *Venison.* He also saw numerous beasts of prey, including wolf-pigs, bears, giant crocodile-monsters, and a saber-toothed tiger.

Randall grinned. He would love to see a saber-toothed tiger in action. Maybe he could get one to kill a rhino for him.

When it came down to it, none of these animals were anything like human beings. All they did was eat and sleep and fuck. They were animals, after all. That might explain why the aliens had such a hard time dealing with people. Randall smiled. Once he got his village in order, all they'd do was eat and sleep and fuck. It would be a win-win for everyone.

A rumbling sound blasted him from behind. Randall spun, crouched low, and drew his handgun, heart pounding.

One of the wardens floated close in a hovercar. *"Human specimen is causing problems."*

Chapter Thirty-Seven

"You have to release us," Sierra said. "Send us back to Earth. All of us, including the ones in storage. We won't interfere any further." It felt like a reasonable request, and the sooner she got the caretaker on her side, the sooner she could convince it to do something about Randall. "We'll be happy to share our knowledge with you. We can work together and help each other solve problems."

The caretaker rumbled. *"Earth was destroyed by gorgers."*

"No. Earth wasn't destroyed. I've seen it. It's still there."

"Observe."

"Observe what?" Did the caretakers have cameras flying around on Earth the way they did on the islands?

The alien reached out with two shorter appendages.

Sierra raised the stone. "Careful."

"Observe," the alien repeated.

She nodded. She had to give it a chance if there was any hope of finding common ground, and she really wanted to see whatever it wanted to show her.

The appendages tapped a control on the front of the sled.

Lights flickered on the wall above and dozens of beams projected onto Sierra's face. She took a step back. Earth floated in front of her, the Earth she'd always known, with dense greens and deep blues. The lights of cities sparkled on the eastern seaboard, under the shadow of night.

Intense longing filled her. She reached out to touch it, but her hand passed through, disrupting the image.

A bright, burning shape appeared above the planet, so real, it looked like it was falling into the pit. The Ender. It drew close, a smear of yellow with blue streaks near its edges. Mountains in Alaska glowed under its sallow light.

Sierra gasped. The caretaker wasn't showing her Earth as it was now. It was showing her the impact.

As the Ender closed on the Pacific, the upper atmosphere grew hazy. Clouds vanished. The comet punched into the ocean with an explosion of light. A glowing dome of fire spread from the impact, moving impossibly fast.

The destruction horrified her, but she couldn't tear her eyes away.

The comet sunk into the planet. Black rock vomited out to space. At ground level, a ring of flame burst outward, growing taller as it moved. Hawaii disappeared. The furious wall of fire raced toward Japan, the Philippines, Australia. When it struck Asia, the ground glowed hot as the blast passed over. A wretched spray of crust erupted and fanned out overhead, only to crash back down, hitting the land like massive bombs.

Sierra swallowed, her mouth as dry as dust. She was watching billions of people die. The projection ended as a roil of clouds spread across the planet, exactly the way Priya had described.

She still didn't understand. The Earth they'd seen out the window looked calm. It didn't exactly look healthy, but the fires had all burned out and the skies had cleared.

A terrible explanation came to her. "When did the comet hit?" she asked. "How long ago?" The sled translated her words.

"One hundred and fifty-two years."

Goosebumps rose on her arms. She'd been in her pod for more than a hundred and fifty years, switched off.

"Wait. That means Earth has had time to heal. We could start over. We could rebuild."

A swell of hope rose in her chest. If the caretakers returned everyone, there'd be enough people to keep the human race going. There might even be people left down there. She'd heard about underground bunkers. "Did anyone survive? Any people?"

"If humans survived, gorgers have consumed them."

"What?" Sierra's legs weakened. "Gorgers are on Earth?"

"Yes."

"Who the hell are the gorgers? What do they want?"

"Gorgers consume organic material."

Sierra tightened her grip on the rock. "Help us fight them. Do you have weapons?"

"Caretakers do not fight gorgers."

Of course not. Sierra exhaled, angry and exasperated. "You have to help us. Can you communicate with the gorgers? You could negotiate a truce."

"No."

"That's our planet. It's our home. We have to take it back. There has to be a way."

"Earth belongs to the gorgers."

"How many?" Sierra asked. "How many gorgers are on Earth?"

"Billions."

Chapter Thirty-Eight

"I'm not causing any goddamn problems," Randall said, his heart galloping from the warden's surprise appearance. Christ, he really needed some kind of warning system. "I didn't do nothing." He backed away, holding the pistol to the side with both hands, keeping it ready, but trying not to be threatening.

The warden floated closer. Kona followed, sniffing. She barked once and the machine translated. *"Hungry."*

Randall tossed her a piece of jerky to shut her up. Kona carried the meat away.

On the work table, lights flickered and flashed from the top half of his device. The warden seemed to be controlling it again. The saber-toothed tiger vanished and a new image appeared, but it looked more like a floating movie than a hologram. In the movie, Sierra was threatening an alien with a rock in some kind of high-tech room.

"Human specimen must be stopped," rumbled the alien.

Randall snorted. He wasn't the one causing problems, she was. "Why don't you torpor her?"

The alien rumbled and blurted, faster and louder than usual. *"Human specimen disabled torpor control."*

This news tickled Randall. The aliens weren't so all-powerful as they liked to think they were. "Why don't you have someone else torpor her?"

"No other caretakers are close."

"Where the hell are they?"

"Additional caretakers are returning from the preserve as quickly as possible." The alien rumbled a bit more. *"Command human specimen. Caretakers cannot be harmed."*

"What, you want me to talk to her?" Randall chuckled. He knew exactly what to do. "I'll stop her, alright. You just have to promise to show me how to use torpor."

The alien rumbled a lengthy response, but the translation was only one word. *"Agreed."*

Randall tapped the control pad on the bottom half of his device, pulled up the map of the village, and zoomed in until it showed the thirteen pods sitting in the fields. He glanced over his shoulder to see which one had the big rust-red "W" on it and tapped the corresponding pod on his device. A pod hologram appeared, with a shape floating off to one side that looked like two half circles, the way the pods looked when they were open. Randall tapped the corresponding shapes on the touchpad and sure enough, Waldmire's pod split apart.

He'd saved the old geezer for just such an occasion.

Chapter Thirty-Nine

David's heart ached. He never should have brought Barry. He should have left the boy in the village, safe and sound with Kim. The thought made him feel even worse. Kim had accused him of flying off and abandoning Lindsey, and then he'd done the exact same thing to her. He squeezed Barry's hand.

"We can't stay here," Scott said. "Why don't I make a run for it? I can lure some of them away."

"No," David said. "We have to stay together."

"What do we do tonight when it gets dark?" Scott asked. "We won't even be able to see them."

"Fire." David said. "Your idea of creating a barrier was good. If we could build a bonfire here where the beach is narrow, it would keep them away from us."

Scott yanked the stick out of his hand and held it in the air. "That's great, except this is our only firewood. Other than that, it's a perfect plan."

"Maybe one of us could swim around, grab some wood, and swim back with it," David said. He turned to Cameron. "If we did that, could you start a fire?"

She nodded, biting her lower lip. "I need to clean my gun first."

"If you're up to it, why don't you do it now?"

She grinned. "I'm always up for cleaning my gun." She pulled out the pistol and turned to Scott. "I need your sport coat, Sportcoat."

He glowered but handed it over.

"You guys keep them off me." She moved further behind them and spread out the blazer like a picnic blanket, then sat down and began to disassemble her pistol.

One of the smaller dinosaurs crawled toward Cameron. Its body was roughly the same size as Barry, though the fin and tail made it seem larger.

David stepped in front of it, waving Scott closer. He reached for Barry's hand. "You too, Bud."

The small sailback turned and darted away, bumping into another one, which snapped at it.

Barry breathed hard.

"It's okay. We got this." The words felt hollow. He wasn't sure they'd make it through the day.

While Cameron worked, the sailbacks watched and waited. Many of them were scarred with wounds that appeared to have come from other sailbacks. Most of their sails were streaked with fiery red and orange bands, though a few smaller ones were tinged with iridescent yellows and greens.

The sound of ripping cloth came from behind. Cameron had torn out a pocket from the inside of Scott's jacket. She ripped the cloth in half.

"Hey," Scott shouted. "What the hell?"

She thumbed a round from the pistol's magazine and pried off the end with her pocketknife. "I'm replacing the bullet with a piece of cloth. If I shoot this cartridge into a pile of kindling, it should light right up." Cameron wadded the cloth into a tiny ball and stuffed it in the opening. "Hopefully, anyway. I've never tried this before."

"Will it work on wet kindling?" Scott asked.

She shrugged. "I doubt it."

"Well, then, David's idea about one of us swimming to get wood isn't going to work. It would get wet on the way back."

"What if we all go?" David proposed. "We could walk along the shore and stay close together. I bet we could get past them. We grab some firewood up in the jungle and then carry it back here."

One of the larger sailbacks took a few steps closer. David and Scott stomped toward it, kicking sand. It backed away. David's heartbeat surged. Scaring them off was both terrifying and exhilarating.

"Carry it back?" Scott frowned. "Why not just build the fire up there?"

"On this little strip, we can use the fire as a barrier wall," David said. "Anywhere else, we'd need a ring of fire big enough to circle us. That would require way more firewood."

"There's plenty of wood up in the trees," Scott said.

"And also giant centipedes," Cameron said. She stopped working and glared at him. "I'm not spending any more time near those trees, Scott."

He grimaced and turned away. "Fine."

The more David thought about it, the more he liked the plan. "If this works, we can get some sleep, in shifts. And a fire out here will be easy to spot. It'll help the others find us."

"Can we shoot one of these bastards and cook it?" Scott asked.

David's mouth watered at the thought. It had been more than a day since he'd had anything to eat. "Yes. And then we'll burn the guts."

If the sailback burned like the Tyrannosaurus had, it would produce a column of oily smoke that could be seen for miles. They'd have food, protection, and a way to signal the others for help.

Cameron stood and pulled back on the top half of her pistol, producing a loud *ka-chink*.

"Get close," David said. "Let's do this."

Chapter Forty

The lights on the wall above the caretaker flashed on again. Sierra shielded her face, then peeked through her fingers. Randall reappeared, still in the village, leaning close. Sierra turned away, disgusted by those repulsive bloated eyes. She resisted the urge to look up to the ledge where she'd left Priya, afraid to give away her location.

"I hear you're causing trouble." Randall's voice filled her with cold hate. "Your old buddy wants to talk to you."

She faced the lights again as Randall stepped away from the camera. Waldmire sat on a wooden bench with his hands behind his back. Sierra's throat closed. She couldn't breathe.

Waldmire looked into the camera, which meant a caretaker must be floating in front of him. "My name is Waldmire Bock, and I'm glad to meet you. I hope our people can work together."

"Shut up," Randall said, pointing a gun at him. "I'm in charge of negotiations."

Sierra pleaded to the alien on the sled next to her. "Tell them to stun that man right now. He will hurt my friends and he will hurt you."

"I ain't done nothing but help them," Randall said, his voice buttery.

Fuck, he can hear me, Sierra thought. He could probably see her, too.

"These guys have learned they can trust me," Randall said. "We're helping each other out."

Cold hopelessness enveloped her. "No."

Randall squinted at the camera. "Sierra, you better stop whatever you're doin' before somebody else gets hurt."

Waldmire looked back and forth between Randall and the camera. "What are you—? A flicker of realization flashed across his face. "Sierra, you have to get away from there, right now." She'd never heard him sound so desperate. "You have to leave."

Randall swung his pistol. She couldn't see what happened, but the sound made it clear. When Randall stepped out of the way, Waldmire hefted himself back to a sitting position, shaking. Blood covered his mouth and he poked his tongue through a hole where one of his front teeth had been. His hands remained behind his back.

Sierra's throat shriveled.

Randall leaned close, his hideous face filling her view. "I'm going to torture your geezer friend till you stop interfering."

"I'm not interfering," Sierra yelled. She looked at the alien. "I'm trying to find a way for us to work together. What do you want me to do?"

The alien rumbled. *"Human specimen must be placed in storage."*

She trembled uncontrollably. "Then what?"

"Human specimen must remain in storage."

"Sweetie, please get away from there," Waldmire said.

Randall hit him again. This time she saw it happen.

"No," she screamed, her voice brittle and weak. "Stop." She turned to the caretaker. "You have to stop that man. He's evil. He will destroy you."

The alien rumbled. *"Randall specimen is assisting caretakers. Randall specimen prevents human interference."*

Randall snorted. "That's right, bitch. Your time's up."

Sierra brought the rock to her chest. These aliens weren't ever going to help humanity. They didn't see humans as anything but specimens. They would put her in storage and leave her there for all eternity. "Never."

Randall looked happy. "I's hoping you'd say that." He pulled a log from the fire pit. "I wonder how much skin I can burn off without killing him." Randall brought the glowing end toward Waldmire's face.

Sierra felt helpless. *"Stop."*

Waldmire looked down. "Sweetie, I can't let them use me to hurt you. Please understand. Please forgive me."

She didn't know what that meant, but it wasn't good.

Randall leered at the camera, but when he turned back, Waldmire was on his feet, blood dripping down his chin.

"You're a failure," Waldmire said. "You couldn't save Crystal. Wayne hated you."

Randall rocked back on his heels.

Waldmire stepped forward, his arms still tied behind him. "The aliens hate you. Your mother hated you. Your father. You're weak."

The alien floated higher, keeping them in view. Randall tried to bring up the burning log, but Waldmire advanced on him, getting right in his face.

"No," Sierra cried, suddenly understanding. Waldmire was a bargaining chip, and he was trying to take himself out of play, the only way he could. She reached for him, her fingers passing through his chest.

"You belong in prison," Waldmire growled. "You should be locked up for life."

Randall dropped the log, shaking.

"Please stop," Sierra sobbed. She swung around to the alien. "I'll do what you want. Just make him stop."

Randall shoved Waldmire back.

He tottered, but remained standing and kept baiting him. "You're going to lose everything. You're going to die here." Frothy blood turned Waldmire's goatee red.

"Shut up," Randall roared. He pulled out a gun.

Tears ran down Sierra's face. *Please stop.*

"You're a worthless turd. A shit-stain on the back of the bowl. You're a brown-nosed suck-up."

Randall punched Waldmire in the gut. He doubled over, but he looked up, still talking. "You're a bootlicker, a leech, a sycophant."

Randall fired. A red hole appeared in the center of Waldmire's forehead and he fell away, disappearing from the projection.

Sierra screamed. She slammed the stone into the alien. It felt like pounding a pile of dirt.

She turned to its limbs at the front of the carriage and raised the stone again. She would smash the fucking thing into a pulp, and then she would go find Randall and do the same to him.

Motion caught her eye. Another sled descended toward her.
A high-pitched whine filled the air and everything turned black.

Chapter Forty-One

Randall spun toward the warden, not sure how it would react to what he'd done. "I had to kill him. He was a threat." The gun shook in his hand. He hoped the alien wouldn't be pissed.

"The distraction provided an adequate delay." Randall looked at his control device, but the hologram showing Sierra was gone.

"Oh yeah? What happened?"

"The human specimen is in torpor."

Hot damn. Randall looked down at the old man. Waldmire had served his purpose after all. Blood oozed from the crater in his forehead and pooled in his eye sockets.

The hovercar drifted upward.

"Hold on, now," Randall said. "We had a deal. I did my part. You promised to teach me how to torpor."

The warden stopped, but didn't respond.

"I won't torpor you. I promise."

"Caretakers cannot be torpored."

"Then what's the harm? You already fixed this device so I can't mess with your shit. My job is to keep humans from interfering, and torpor will help me do that. It's exactly what you want. All you have to do is sit back and observe."

The alien tapped something inside its hovercar and the control device lit up again, showing an image of Randall himself, with several shapes on each side.

The alien rumbled. *"Select a specimen and touch torpor. Control must be close."*

A pale blue zig-zag shape flashed near Randall's neck.

He pointed. "That's it?"

The warden didn't answer.

He scowled. If he touched it, he would torpor himself. The alien might be trying to trick him into doing just that. Randall pulled his finger away.

The warden rose from the village, disappearing as it went.

Chapter Forty-Two

Cameron tucked the firestarter round into her chest pocket and held her Beretta at the ready. It was fully loaded with fifteen nine-millimeter rounds. Not nearly enough. The dinosaurs covered the beach, their sails a land-locked regatta.

Her back throbbed and her shoulder felt tight, but the dizziness had passed. She almost felt like herself again. Cleaning a gun always made her feel better.

She walked with David, Barry, and Scott along the water's edge. They moved slowly and steadily, like a recon squad, working their way past the sailbacks. She wasn't excited about carrying firewood all the way back out to the spit, but she sure as hell didn't want to spend any more time near those trees than she had to.

So far, the plan was working. As they walked, the closest sailbacks turned and scampered out of their way. Most were small, maybe ten feet long, with their tails making up half their length.

"Why don'cha shoot a couple?" Scott said. "Show 'em who's boss."

"No," Cameron said. "Every round is precious."

"They won't be very precious if we're dead. I bet one shot would clear the whole beach, just from the sound." He stomped his foot, which made the closest dinosaur dart away. "Plus we'd have fresh meat."

"We'd have to defend fresh meat while we tried to start a fire," Cameron said.

"How many rounds do you have, anyway?" Scott asked.

Normally, Cameron never answered that question, but Scott and David had both earned her trust. "Not nearly enough. A magazine and a half."

"So, what, twenty rounds?"

"Just over," Cameron said, impressed. Scott knew his firearms.

One of the sailbacks closest to the water took a step toward them. Scott lunged at it, roaring and waving his arms. His jacket flared wide like Dracula's cape. The dinosaur turned and scrambled up the beach.

"We're almost halfway," David said. As they moved along, the dinosaurs closed in behind them, maintaining a constant perimeter around the group. A smaller one scampered close. David smacked it on the nose with the stick.

"Look at that one," Barry pointed. "It's huge."

Several yards ahead, an absolute beast waited by the shoreline, blocking their path. Its fin had to be seven feet tall.

Scott picked up a handful of wet sand and flung it at the lizard's head. It hissed, baring jagged teeth inside boxy jaws.

The group halted ten feet from the big bastard. Scott stomped and yelled, but the creature stood its ground.

Cameron aimed at the dinosaur's face. The one that ambushed her yesterday in the jungle had charged with surprising speed. This one could be on them in seconds if it wanted.

"I'm scared." Barry reached for his father. "Up."

David gave the stick to Scott and hoisted Barry onto his shoulders.

The large dinosaur pushed itself backwards several feet.

"Look! It's scared of me now." Barry made fists in the air like a bodybuilder. "I'm bigger than you are!"

The little keiki was right.

"Everybody step forward and yell on a count of three," Cameron said. "One, two, three."

They screamed and moved together as one.

The large sailback flipped around and scrambled away. Its tail smacked the water, spraying them. Scott lunged and stomped on the tip, which made the animal hiss and wriggle-run all the way to the jungle. Several smaller individuals scattered out of its path.

They continued forward with Barry on David's shoulders. The sailbacks ahead of them all scurried off as they drew close.

When they finally reached an empty stretch of sand, Scott pumped his fist. "We're clear."

"We still have to get the firewood," Cameron said, looking up toward the trees.

Dinosaurs covered the beach to her left. Most lay motionless on the sand, but every single one of them faced in their direction.

David put a hand on her lower back, below the bite. "How are you holding up?"

She batted her eyes. "I'll be better once we're snuggled up beside a roaring fire." She knew she needed to be more discreet, but she couldn't help it. The comment just slipped out.

"Eeew," Barry said. "Stop."

David pulled his arm away.

Scott rolled his eyes and walked toward the jungle. "Let's hurry, then." He glanced back. "Or do you two need a moment alone?"

"Hey Sportcoat," Cameron called out. "Get back down here. We should go farther before we turn inland."

Higher up on the beach, several sailbacks inched his way.

"We're far enough," Scott spat. "There's plenty of firewood right there." He muttered something under his breath about being a third wheel and continued toward the jungle.

"Wait till we get farther," Barry called out. "Please, Scott."

"Get back here," Cameron said.

"She's right," David said. "We have to stay together so we look big."

Scott stopped halfway up the beach and turned around, hands on his hips.

One of the larger dinosaurs charged, covering half the distance before Scott could even react.

The sailback hit him open-mouthed, its head sideways, grabbing his upper thigh and jerking him to the ground. Scott screamed.

Cameron ran toward him, her gun ready. A few other dinosaurs scrambled away, but the big one attacking Scott held tight. The creature had to weigh four hundred pounds.

Scott pounded the animal's snout, clamped tight around his leg. "Shoot it," he hissed.

The creature shoved sand with its feet, dragging him backwards. Two other sailbacks crawled closer.

Cameron got up next to Scott and aimed the pistol, trying to get a bead on the animal's head, but it wouldn't hold still and she didn't want to risk hitting his leg. She aimed at the monster's thick neck instead and pulled the trigger.

BLAM!

A hole exploded behind the dinosaur's jaw. Blood gushed onto Scott's already-glistening slacks.

The approaching lizards turned tail and scurried into the jungle, clearing the beach for at least fifty yards.

David appeared next to her and grabbed Scott by the arms. He pulled, but the animal's mouth was still clamped around his thigh.

Scott wailed, clutching the top of his leg, his lips pulled back from his teeth and his eyes pinched shut.

Cameron touched the creature's eyeball with the hot muzzle of her Beretta. It didn't blink. Dead.

She stepped over Scott and dug the toes of her boot into the dinosaur's lower jaw. Grabbing the top of its mouth with both hands, she pulled, prying it open like a bear trap. Four-inch fangs slid from Scott's thigh. Oily blood pooled in the holes.

He made a long, drawn-out whine as he took in the wound. "Jesus, help me."

A gurgling sound came from the creature's gullet. Cameron flinched for her gun, but it was only air sputtering from the wet hole in the side of its neck. David dragged Scott down to the water.

Barry, who had kept out of the way, grabbed the stick and one of Scott's loafers, which had flown off in the attack. He ran behind his father.

Cameron kicked the corpse in the eye and followed them, cursing silently. They'd been so goddamn close.

Chapter Forty-Three

Priya huddled against the side wall of the vast chamber, a hundred meters from the pit where Sierra confronted the caretaker. She didn't know what to do. There was no place to hide. She could see maybe a half kilometer to the left, right, and straight ahead. Beyond that, the empty gray floor faded away to darkness. Row after row of those huge, streamlined objects hung high overhead. She was completely alone and any minute now, the caretakers would come for her.

When Sierra jumped into the pit, Priya had fled to the wall, where she'd collapsed, fuming.

I had a plan, dammit. She'd recognized the orange device Randall was using in the village. Seven of those things had been sitting right there in the first bunker, the bunker *without* any aliens in it. And if that *betichod* could operate this technology, she could sure as hell figure it out.

But Sierra just acted without thinking. Priya wanted to smack her silly for being so stupidly impulsive and leaving her all alone. She cowered against the flat wall, trying to make herself as small as possible.

If only Charlie was here. He always wanted to hear what Priya thought. He would have bounced ideas back and forth with her until they had a plan. Her chest ached. They'd been such a great team.

She considered running back to the other pit to experiment with the orange ball devices, but that would mean leaving Sierra. A second caretaker had just flown in, and for all Priya knew, they were giving her a lobotomy.

If it was harming her, she had to do something. Chomping the inside of her cheeks, she crept back toward the pit, slithering on her belly the last few meters until she was close enough to peer over the edge. She carried her stone with her, even though she didn't think it would do much good against two aliens.

Sierra lay sprawled on the ground like an old ragdoll. There wasn't any way to tell if she was dead or stunned.

The caretaker that had just arrived floated to one of the empty docking stations. When it got close, a pair of brackets clamped onto the front of its carriage and pulled it in with a solid clunk. The light beams on the wall above targeted the alien's tentacles.

Moving as slowly as a glacier, Priya slid along the side of the pit until she was across from the only set of lights that remained unoccupied. When she got close enough, a few of them shifted up, beaming three-dimensional images onto her retinas.

Priya froze, waiting for one of the aliens to notice, but they remained focused on whatever they were doing.

She shielded her eyes with her hand and looked over at the alien that had just arrived. It tapped the controls at the front of its carriage with a pair of long, phallic digits.

Priya removed her hand and the holograms reappeared. A bizarre oblong shape floated in front of her, like a giant metal shallot, roots included. After a moment, it slid aside and a second, familiar object moved into focus. It was a pod, just like the ones that had landed on Earth.

The pod hologram moved next to the oblong shape, then a rounded triangle flashed beside them. The triangle transformed into an elaborate schematic.

Down in the bunker, the alien tapped again and the schematic expanded.

Priya's lips parted with excitement. She was looking at a map of the ship. She recognized the slope room with all the spheres floating overhead, as well as the vast chamber she was in, with cylindrical pits in the floor.

The caretakers rumbled at each other and a dotted line appeared, running through the chamber to one of the pits.

Priya had seen enough. She needed to get away before they found her. She couldn't get any closer to Sierra as long as those two caretakers were down there. Still on her belly, she backed slowly from the pit.

Something floated toward her.

Every muscle tightened. She prepared to push up and run, cursing herself for not watching her surroundings, for letting her fascination with the technology distract her.

A metallic yellow machine descended into the pit. It was the shallot-shaped object the caretaker had selected a few moments earlier. But it wasn't really shaped like a shallot, she realized. It was shaped like one of the aliens themselves, a textbook example of biomimicry. Its body was an elongated orb and the structures she'd originally thought of as roots were actually arms telescoping from the front. It had to be some sort of mechanical drone.

Something thumped onto the floor beside Priya, stopping her heart.

One degree at a time, she rotated her head.

A pod sat two meters away, its top half rising slowly in the gloom. Of course. It was the second object the caretaker had selected. The dotted lines she'd seen on the map must have been a path for these objects to follow.

The silver and yellow drone-thing rose, carrying Sierra with those serpentine arms. It placed her in the pod. *Yes.* That meant she was only stunned. They wouldn't bother putting her in storage if she was dead.

Priya trembled. She was so close, she could almost reach out and touch Sierra. The top of the pod lowered.

She started backing up again, centimeter by centimeter, until she was far enough away to get to her feet without being seen by the caretakers down in the pit.

The pod hummed and rose in the air, moving in the direction of the slope-room. Priya's breathing picked up. Were they sending Sierra back to the village? Randall would kill her, or worse.

Gripping her stone, she tiptoed away from the pit, following the pod. It floated along, about four meters up, accelerating.

When she felt like she was far enough from the aliens, Priya broke into a bounding run. She moved swiftly in the low gravity, but the pod kept pulling away. Just when she thought it was going to disappear from view, it slowed and began to lower.

Yes. Priya pumped harder. She would open it up, get Sierra out, and smack her right in the face.

The pod appeared to sink through the floor.

By the time Priya realized what was actually happening, it was too late. The pod wasn't dropping into the floor, it was lowering into that giant bottomless pit, and Priya was careening straight toward it.

She tried to slow down, but the low gravity worked against her. Momentum propelled her forward.

Making a split-second decision, just like Sierra would, she leaned to the side and turned. She dropped her stone and pumped her arms, running as fast as she could toward the pit, but no longer straight on. She angled toward the side instead.

At the last moment, she jumped, hurtling through the air. Her heartbeat pounded in her ears. She flew like a superhero in the low gravity, soaring ten meters or more. She grinned, wanting to let out a whoop, but mindful not to make any noise.

She floated across the side of the pit and landed in a rolling tumble. Even though she knew she had to be quiet, she giggled. She'd done it. She got to her feet and pumped both fists, then hurried over to the rim.

The pod descended in the center of the pit, well out of reach, until it vanished in the darkness below.

Breathing hard, Priya looked around. She was truly alone now, but she knew where to go.

The run back to the first command pit took ten minutes. She dropped in and went straight to the orange spheres, desperately hoping they were the same thing Randall had been using, because if they weren't, she was all out of ideas.

Chapter Forty-Four

Randall was almost ready to repopulate his village, and if the new people gave him any trouble, he now knew how to torpor their asses.

First, though, he had to take care of the corpses. He couldn't leave Waldmire and Morrie there, rotting. It would invite too many questions.

Kona sniffed Morrie's body. Randall walked over and grimaced. The bastard stank to high heaven.

The last thing Randall wanted to do was dig a grave. He'd done enough of that when he first got to the village.

"Eat him, girl."

Kona just stared. It would take her ages to eat two full grown men. Randall had to deal with them himself. He played around with the control device for a while, hoping to order one of those flying bumblebee drones to carry them off, but he couldn't figure out how. The device wouldn't even let him select Morrie or Waldmire now that they were dead. He decided to drag them to the beach and dump them in the sea, where they'd float away. Hopefully something would eat them.

Morrie had to go first because of the smell. Randall tugged off the bandana wrapped around Morrie's neck and rolled him over, revealing a scabby scar on the back of the man's head. "What have we here?" It was in the same spot as the zig-zag torpor button the warden had shown him on the control screen.

Randall snickered. Morrie might have figured out how to keep from getting torpored, but he hadn't figured out how to keep from getting shot.

He grabbed Morrie's feet and pulled him through the village. By the time he reached the perimeter wall, his shoulders were aching. It would take forever to drag both bodies to the beach.

Just outside the village, a burned spot in the woods caught his eye. Randall dropped Morrie's feet and walked over to investigate, happy to take a break. A gray patch covered the ground, maybe twenty feet in diameter, with charred bits of wood scattered about. Randall knelt and touched the dirt. The gray stuff was ash. In the middle of the burn scar, he found bone fragments that were too thick to be human. They must have cremated the remains of the *T. rex* here. A flash of inspiration struck Randall, his best idea all day. He wouldn't need to drag the bodies to the beach after all.

Thirty minutes later, a pile of firewood sat in the middle of the ash circle. Randall hefted Morrie and Waldmire right on top, lit the bonfire with a torch, and watched the flames work their way up the sides. Waldmire's shirt caught first.

"Shit. I should'a stripped their clothes." Randall frowned. He needed to get better at planning ahead.

He turned and swiped away the ash footprints he'd made on the path, hiding any evidence that might raise questions from his new villagers. It was going to be hard enough to explain this whole situation as it was.

While the bodies roasted, Randall detoured to the storage shed for some jerky. Hard work made a man hungry. Next, it was time to secure his prized possession.

He carried the control device up to Joe's cabin, where he'd already stored his firearms. He intended to make that cabin strictly off limits to everyone else. He placed the device in the corner on a sturdy log that functioned as a little table and looked around to see if someone could spy on him while he used the thing. The window on the opposite wall was eight feet up, too high for anyone to look in. Looking out, all he could see was some trees over in the camping area.

The doorway was the problem. The villagers had hung reed curtains over the openings, which offered a little privacy, but no actual security.

Kona nosed her way inside, proving his point. Anyone could just barge in while he was away, and he'd never know it.

"What do you want, girl? You still hungry?" She'd been in the creek and stank of wet fur. He wagged a piece of jerky in the air. "Come on. Come on, girl."

Kona darted forward, snatched the dried meat, and disappeared out the doorway.

Randall smiled. The bitch was coming to respect him. He'd make a good master after all. Hell, he might even become a caring person for once in his life, now that he was finally getting the chance.

The smile disappeared when he noticed muddy footprints on the cabin's dirt floor. Randall scowled at the mess, but then he had his second great idea of the day. "Footprints."

He walked down to the fire pit, scooped up a bowl full of ash, and carried it back to his cabin, where he threw the powder in a swath across the floor. "Perfect." It wouldn't stop anyone from coming in, but at least he'd know about it. He'd need to keep some ash on hand to cover his own tracks, but it would be worth the effort. If anyone found out about his little toy, he wanted to know.

He felt like God, sitting back on the seventh day. Nothing could stop him now.

Randall turned on the device. He had to send the old pods away before he brought in new people, but he didn't want to get rid of Kim until he was sure Dave was no longer a threat.

He used two fingers to call up island seventy-one. After a little hunting, he found four red dots clustered together by the water, further up the beach than before.

He double-tapped one of the corresponding dots on the touchpad below and a hologram of Dave's boy appeared, with a little zig-zag shape near his neck. Randall tapped the shape with two fingers and waited. Nothing happened, as far as he could tell. Then he remembered what the warden had said. *"Control must be close."*

Damn. There had to be something else he could do.

He noticed the grid shape he'd used to scroll through all those different animals from Earth.

Randall smiled. He'd just had his third great idea of the day.

Chapter Forty-Five

Back in the first command pit, Priya picked up one of the orange balls and placed it on the surface of a docked carriage. The device immediately split in two. At first, she thought she'd broken it, but then the whole thing rotated, standing itself up somehow, just like the one Randall had been using.

The two halves remained touching at one edge. She patted the lower surface, where Randall had been tapping. The top half glowed, shining lights in her face. A series of shapes appeared to float in the space between her eyes and the device. She reached out to touch one, but her fingers passed through it, disrupting the signal. *Silly.* The shapes didn't exist. They weren't even really holograms, but merely tricks of the eye. She snorted. The images from this device looked incredibly sharp, probably because an entire cluster of lights focused on her eyes. At the top of the other bunker, the images had been blurry and distorted around the edges.

The most exciting thing was that the bottom half of the sphere now appeared to be covered with brightly lit icons. *Of course.* The projections turned the lower surface into a touchpad interface.

A shape flew over the pit.

Priya ducked, but it had already passed by. She stepped up onto the carriage to watch. It was a pod, twice as big as the one that had carried Sierra away. It flew toward the slope room, undoubtedly going to the islands.

She returned to the device. After studying it for a moment, she came to understand that most of the shapes in front of her were replicated in simplified forms on the surface of the pad below. Once that made sense, it was simply a matter of identifying each shape.

She found the little curved triangle that the caretaker had used to bring up a map. Tapping it did nothing, but maybe that was because alien controls always required duplication. She tapped the triangle twice. Nothing happened. She tapped it with two fingers.

A map appeared.

"Bingo."

Priya tried eight different motions before she figured out how to make the map zoom in and out, but it only took three before she learned how to scroll. She found the dotted line of the pod that had just passed overhead and followed it to the islands.

The menagerie map tempted her curiosity. She wanted to look at every island, to study them, to see what lived on each one. But now was not the time. She had to find Sierra.

The dotted line ended on a crescent-shaped island north of the village island. Whatever was in the pod was being sent there.

Priya let out a gasp as she connected the dots, literally. She could trace the line back and find out where the pod was coming *from*. She had to hurry before the pod reached its destination and the path disappeared.

She followed the line back into the ship. It came from the deep pit she'd jumped over. A smile pushed up the corners of her mouth. Sailing over the edge of that pit had been exhilarating, but figuring out how to use this device was even better.

The dotted line ended in a chamber at least as large as the one above her.

Storage.

Priya took a deep breath. She'd found storage.

Row after row of oval shapes floated in the chamber, some small, some large, and a few that looked big enough to hold a blue whale. There had to be hundreds of thousands of pods. The touchpad displayed a grid of corresponding objects. She tapped one with two fingers. An image of a salamander appeared, floating in front of her. She tapped the next pod. Another salamander.

She scrolled away and chose a pod from a different area. It showed a spindly crab. She scrolled again and found a bird that looked like a cross between a dodo and an eagle.

Priya's heart sank. She'd never find Sierra. She zoomed out so she could estimate the number of pods and calculate how long it would take to inspect them all.

A new dotted line appeared, coming down through the opening just like the previous one. She scrolled the map back out and followed the line to the slope room, where thirteen ghosted ovals descended from the sea. Priya looked at the touchpad to see if she could select one, but there weren't any corresponding shapes.

"Those must show pods coming back into storage," she whispered. Her heart skipped. She'd seen a dozen or so pods in the village behind Randall. If these were the same ones, they might contain the villagers. And more importantly, they would lead her straight to the human section in storage.

Something whooshed by overhead. Several somethings.

Priya dropped to her hands and knees, ready to crawl under the empty carriage. Then she stopped and chuckled at herself.

It was the same thirteen pods, flying right over her. She climbed onto the carriage and watched them disappear in the dark, heading toward the giant pit.

She returned to the device and followed the line to storage, where it ended with thirteen ghosted ovals. She touched the first pod that wasn't ghosted, hoping it would contain a human.

An image of Sierra floated in front of her.

This time, Priya actually laughed. She wouldn't be alone much longer.

She selected Sierra's pod, then used the map to navigate back to the bunker she was in, where a single red dot glowed, undoubtedly representing her. She touched a spot next to the bunker and a new dotted line appeared. Sierra was on her way.

Priya was getting the hang of it. While she waited, she navigated back to the storage chamber. The thirteen pods had come to a stop and she was able to select them now. An image of Jasmine appeared when she touched the first one. She touched several more, bringing up Felicia, then Nick and Kelly, the only real couple left in the village. Seeing them reminded her of Charlie. She shoved the aching emptiness down as far as she could.

She selected all thirteen pods and wondered if she should bring them here as well. If everyone stayed spread out, they could avoid getting stunned all at once. She was about to scroll out of storage when she noticed something else. A small sphere rotated in the corner of her view, with the familiar outlines of continents on it.

Earth.

Priya's heart somersaulted with excitement.

She found the corresponding circle on the panel below, not much more than a dot, and touched it with two fingers. A globe swelled until it filled the air in front of her, rotating slowly.

She waited for North America to come into view and then tapped the panel to zoom in on the eastern seaboard. She thought about zooming in on New York, but decided D.C. was a better choice. If anyone was alive there, they would have left messages in Washington. She kept zooming until she saw the remains of the Capitol building.

"Oof." Seeing the ruins of the iconic landmark hit her hard. She scrolled sideways, searching for the White House. A short wall lay in the center of the National Mall. "That wasn't there before." She tapped on it twice, trying to get a better look, then realized it was the Washington Monument, lying on its side.

The instant she tapped the Monument's ruins, thirteen ghosted ovals appeared, with a dotted line leading to them.

Priya's guts sank to her feet. "Oh ... shit."

She was pretty sure she'd just sent the pods to Earth.

Chapter Forty-Six

Blackness surrounded Sierra. She flailed, touching soft foam. She was in a pod. Her stomach clenched. Was she back in the pod with Waldmire and Josh? *Please let that be the case. Please let it all be a bad dream.*

A thin ring of dull light appeared around her. Sierra spun, looking, hoping, but no one else was in the pod. Josh was dead. Waldmire was dead. She'd lost them both. She'd used Josh as bait and abandoned Waldmire. The weight of her failure made it difficult to breathe.

She would never know if he was her father.

The top half of the pod continued to rise. A few feet away, Priya stood waiting for her.

Sierra crawled toward her, tears on her cheeks.

Priya raised her hand, and for a moment, Sierra got the strange impression that she was about to get slapped. Then Priya leaned in and embraced her.

"Waldmire," Sierra sobbed. "He's dead. Randall killed him."

"*Auwe.*" Priya squeezed her. "I'm so, so sorry."

Sierra held onto her. She didn't want to let go, even though she knew this was outside Priya's comfort zone. She forced herself to pull away.

"We have to kill that piece of shit. And the caretakers, too." She looked around and spotted the circular pit a few feet away. Her breath caught in her throat. "Are they still in there?"

"We're back at the first bunker, the empty one." Priya helped her climb down from the pod. Together, they dropped into the pit.

Sierra's legs felt wobbly. "What happened? How did I get here?"

"Let me show you," Priya said. "I've figured out a few things." She led her to one of the empty sleds, where two orange half-spheres balanced magically on their edges, one on top of the other. "Climb aboard. Let's see if we can get out of here."

Sierra sat cross-legged beside Priya, dimly aware she should be crying. She wished she could let out the horrible ache in her chest. "You—you can fly it?" She pointed at the controls in the opposite corners, too far apart for one person to reach. "I thought it takes two people?"

Priya tapped one of the strange half-spheres. "I can't fly it, but I think I can move it. I can send things from one point to another. That's how I got you here."

The top half-sphere lit up, shining lights in their faces. A diagram appeared, floating in the air before them.

"How?" Sierra rubbed the back of her neck, overwhelmed by confusion and grief. "What happened?"

Priya took a deep breath. "They stunned you and put you in a pod. I ran back here and got this device. It's the same thing Randall was using. I watched him and I watched the aliens and I figured out some of it on my own." She tilted her head. "I'm still learning."

"Okay." Sierra swallowed, trying to concentrate, trying to keep the sadness from overtaking her. She wanted so much to talk to Waldmire, to hug him.

Priya touched the circular panel on the bottom half-sphere with two fingers. "I've been waiting to try this."

The sled lurched free from the wall. Sierra yelped and clutched the dashboard.

Priya stuck her finger through a holographic rectangle with two red dots on it hovering in front of her face. "That's us." She touched something on the panel below and the image changed. "Elevation view. I discovered this on my own. Let's find a hiding spot." She tapped again and a dashed line appeared.

"Where?"

Priya pointed straight up as the sled started rising.

The acceleration pressed Sierra into the foamy black surface. She looked up, expecting to smash into the silver teardrop shapes above, but instead, the sled swooped between them.

They decelerated and jerked to a stop between two of the giant objects. "These are definitely not pods," Sierra said, trying to make sense of them. "Do you still think they're missiles?"

Whisker-like rods protruded here and there from the shapes, and two fins stuck out on each side, one long and horizontal, like a wing, and a short stubby one that angled downward.

Priya kept her nose buried in the device. "Hang on. I'm sending your pod back to storage. Don't want anyone to spot it down there."

Sierra looked over the edge of the sled. Thirty stories below, the pod floated away.

"I don't understand. How can you just move their stuff around without them noticing?"

Priya puffed out her cheeks and shrugged. "There don't seem to be many of them. I've only been able to identify four caretakers in the whole ship, and it's huge. They're all spread out." Her eyes darted back and forth. "There's something else I need to tell you."

"What?" Her reluctance made Sierra nervous. She was already struggling to get her head around everything. She felt a burning impulse to ask Waldmire about all of this. Every time she thought about him, she felt a crushing weight in her heart.

"After they stunned you, they sent your pod to storage." Priya pointed at the floating diagram. "See, it's below that big dark pit." Sierra couldn't tell what she was looking at, but she trusted her. Priya scrolled, stopping on an endless grid of round shapes.

"You found the other pods? That's fantastic." She couldn't understand why Priya wasn't more excited. She pointed, her fingers passing through the closest ovals. "Are those the rest of the people from Earth?"

"Some contain people. Some contain animals." Priya was definitely hiding something.

"So what's wrong?"

"Randall stunned the villagers and packed them up in pods. Then he sent them off to storage. Or maybe the aliens did. I don't know."

"Are you sure it was them?"

"There were thirteen pods. When you select them, you can see who's inside. It was definitely them. I saw Jasmine, Felicia, Nick, and Kelly."

"That's great. So, how do we get them here?"

Priya looked down. "I accidentally sent them to Earth."

Sierra felt the ground drop away from her. "What? How? You can't send them to Earth. You have to bring them back."

Priya scowled. "It was an accident, but it's what you wanted. I sent them home. I took action. Sometimes you just have to go for it, right?"

Hearing her own words again made Sierra feel worse.

"It isn't safe."

"Sure it is." Priya's brows furrowed. "These are the same pods that brought us here. It's what they're made to do."

Sierra shook her head slowly, fighting despair. "No. It isn't safe on Earth. The gorgers are there. After the Ender hit, they took over the planet."

Chapter Forty-Seven

David ripped away the tatters of Scott's slacks with both hands. Eight large puncture wounds circled his thigh on the front, two of them torn laterally from the animal's shaking. Glistening saliva covered the injuries.

"Barry, we need to clean it off. Cup water in your hands and splash his leg." The thought of his little boy helping triage these horrible lacerations made David sick, but he had no choice.

Barry crouched in the water and lifted a tiny handful.

"I'll be okay," Scott insisted through gritted teeth.

He was wrong. The trauma to his leg was severe and he was losing too much blood.

Cameron stood guard, holding her gun at the ready. David called her over. "Help me take off his coat and shirt. I need the shirt." Cameron pulled off Scott's blazer by the sleeves. He hissed as the motion jostled his leg. His collared polo came next, revealing a stark white potbelly.

David helped Barry cup more water onto the wounds. Every time they splashed clear, dark blood pooled up again. That was good, to a point. The bleeding would help clean out foreign material, and maybe even bacteria or venom. *Christ, what if these dinosaurs were venomous?*

"That's plenty for now," David said, rolling Scott on his side. Four additional punctures dotted the back of his thigh. *Shit.* The sand under the leg had turned an oily brown. "More water," he muttered.

Barry dumped another handful on the back of Scott's thigh, washing out most of the sand. Blood seeped from the wounds.

"Enough." David took Scott's shirt and folded it over lengthwise. "Lift up his foot, Bud."

Scott moaned as Barry raised his leg.

"You're doing great," David said, wrapping the shirt under Scott's thigh, trying to cover all the wounds. He pulled it around and knotted the ends together on the inside of the leg, the only place free of injuries.

"Hurts," Scott groaned, tears rolling down his cheeks. Blood blossomed through the makeshift bandage.

Barry grimaced and backed away. The boy had seen too many horrible things.

Lindsey's voice popped into David's mind, loud and brash. *Quit worrying about his psyche and figure out how to keep him alive.* They were still stranded on an island filled with dinosaurs.

"Get over here, Bud. Stay right beside me."

"We need a plan, Ace," Cameron said. A few sailbacks crawled closer, forming a quarter-circle around them. Higher up on the beach, one of them licked the bloody corpse of the big bastard that mauled Scott.

"Can we go in the water?" Barry asked.

"He's bleeding too much. If he gets in the water, the wounds won't clot and he'll bleed out." David was pretty sure that was going to happen anyway, but he kept it to himself.

One of the smaller sailbacks crept close, following the blood trail. Cameron ran at it, screaming. It turned and fled.

Scott started shaking. "God, I need a drink."

David propped him up to a sitting position and pulled his blazer back over his naked torso to keep him warm.

Cameron leaned in close. "What do we do?"

"We have to stop the bleeding," David said. "If we can find some moss or something, I can try to make a poultice."

"What about strips of that bark we used to make vines? Would that work?"

"Maybe." He shrugged, helpless and desperate. The vines had been fibrous. It was worth a shot.

"Okay," Cameron said. "Let's try it."

Scott nodded with more enthusiasm than the idea warranted. "Yes, hurry."

David took his arm. "We have to stay together and you have to get up."

Cameron grabbed the opposite arm.

Scott pulled his good leg under him and bounced on it. "I can make it."

Barry picked up the stick and held it out in front of him with both hands.

Cameron glanced over, her eyes uncertain. "Are you sure about this?"

David nodded. "Adrenaline is keeping him going right now. Let's take advantage of it."

They walked across the beach as a unit. Scott hopped, holding his bad leg off the ground. The closest dinosaurs backed away.

"What's that noise?" Barry asked.

David tilted his head. It sounded like air leaking from a balloon.

"Daddy, it's a pod." Barry pointed with the stick.

About fifty feet up the beach, a white pod descended toward the island.

"It's about time," Scott said. "They'll fix me." He took a wobbling hop toward the pod, forcing David and Cameron with him.

David stopped and tried to hold him back. "Wait."

Scott shook free. "It's my only hope, and you know it." He held David's eyes. "Suspended animation. You can get me out later and patch me up." He snatched the stick from Barry and used it as a cane, hopping another few steps.

Scott was right. Maybe after they'd gotten everyone out of storage, they'd be able to assemble a surgical team. At the very least, they could open his pod and attempt to treat him in a controlled environment, instead of on a beach covered with dinosaurs.

One of the sailbacks shuffled closer. David, Cameron, and Barry moved to intercept, blocking its path, while Scott hobbled on behind them.

"That pod's bigger," Cameron said, looking over her shoulder.

The pod kept descending, now only ten feet above the beach.

"Is it one of the aliens?" Barry asked, pressing against David's side.

"Maybe it's a medical pod," David said, grasping at straws. They were long overdue for a miracle.

Cameron grunted. "They never sent a medical pod for Charlie."

David didn't have a good response, but he held onto hope. It was all he had left. They hadn't known about the caretakers back then. Maybe something changed after they made contact.

Scott hissed and hobbled on, now twenty feet away from them. Blood covered his calf. He stumbled once but caught himself with the stick and managed to stay upright. He looked back. "Promise me you'll find me and get me out, okay?"

"Yes," Barry shouted. "We promise."

The pod settled in the sand another twenty feet beyond him.

"Come on," David said. "Let's go help him get in."

A black equator appeared and the top half lifted straight up.

"Wait." Scott raised his free hand and teetered against his cane.

"What is it?" Barry asked.

Cameron grabbed David's arm and pulled in the opposite direction. "Trouble's coming."

Something large moved inside the pod. Chills ran up David's back.

A roar blasted across the beach.

"That's a goddamn lion," Cameron whispered.

David shook his head. "Bigger."

Chapter Forty-Eight

Sierra locked eyes with Priya. "We have to do something. You sent those people to their deaths." She'd already lost Josh and Waldmire. Now she was going to lose David and Kim and everyone else.

"It was an accident." Priya held her gaze. "I don't need a lecture from someone who is constantly acting without thinking."

The comment stung. She deserved it.

"Fine. Whatever. We still have to do something. How did you do it?"

Priya pointed at the device. "You select a pod and give it a destination. The pods do the rest."

"And the aliens just let you?"

She shrugged. "I don't understand it either, but what else is new? They seem oblivious."

"That's insane. Don't they have checkpoints or locks or something?"

"They aren't human. It's arrogant to expect them to think like us."

Sierra gnashed her molars together. "Don't lecture me. You sent our friends to Earth. The gorgers will kill them."

"How do you even know the gorgers are real? And if they are, how do you know they're really dangerous?"

Sierra held up her hands. "Yeah, I'm sure it's all a big ruse, to keep us from trying to get home, since their stupid ship doesn't actually have any security measures. *Please.*" She pointed at the device. "Can you send down empty pods to bring them back?"

Priya reached, then pulled her hand away. "Even if I sent down more pods, I can't make anyone get in them."

"Then we have to go after them," Sierra said. "We have to go down in a pod."

Priya crossed her arms. "I don't know if I can operate this thing from inside a pod. We could be trapped forever if we tried that."

Sierra pointed at one of the objects floating beside them. "What about the missiles? Could we disarm one and use it to fly down?"

Priya didn't answer right away. Instead, she swiveled around, studying the objects. "Why would a wildlife preserve be equipped with weaponry?"

"I don't know," Sierra snapped. "You're the one who said they were missiles."

"I said they *looked like* missiles." Priya crouched, peering straight down the end of one of the wings. "That's definitely an airfoil." She sat back and leaned over her device. "Let me try to select one. Tell me if anything happens."

Moments later, a hole spiraled open on the tube in front of them. Sierra pointed. "The nose on that one just opened."

Priya looked up. "That isn't the nose, it's the tail." She seemed to be onto something.

"How the hell do you know that?"

"The camber of the wings tells you which direction is forward." Priya stood and peered into the opening. "This isn't a missile. It's some sort of ship." She snorted. "I was right all along. This really is a hangar."

"Are you sure?"

"I told you not to ask me that."

"Why would the caretakers have thousands of ships? You said you only spotted four of them."

"I don't know." Priya sat back down and waved for Sierra to do the same. "I want to try something."

A moment later, the sled rose upward, then stopped directly behind the opening. The tail was hollow, a giant straw leading into darkness.

"What are you doing?" Sierra asked, uncomfortable with how fast Priya was trying things. She bit her tongue. The shoe was on the other foot.

Priya shrugged. "I set that ship as the destination for this carriage."

The sled jerked forward into the tube. It felt tight around them, with only a few feet of clearance on each side.

"I don't like this," Sierra said as darkness swallowed them. "Maybe you should send us back out."

Priya's breathing grew loud. "I can't. It won't let me select the carriage again until it stops. Once you send something, you have to wait until it reaches the destination."

They huddled together in the dark as the hole behind them grew smaller. The only other light came from Priya's device.

Sierra hated the dark. Anything could be lurking there, just out of sight. She picked up the alien device by the bottom half-sphere and turned it around. The top half remained connected somehow. Its lights shone forward, making a weak spotlight.

She turned the device left and right, but it wasn't bright enough to illuminate anything on either side.

"No, aim it forward," Priya said, leaning over the carriage's front console. "There."

They flew toward a rectangular shape directly ahead. It looked like another set of docking brackets for a sled. Behind them, the opening they'd entered through shrunk into a distant circle.

They hit the brackets with a clunk. Something whirred and clicked, and then a hum filled the air as pastel panels lit up all around them. It felt like being inside a Christmas tree. The lights looked like the same panels they'd seen in the sloped room beneath the sea, which made sense, in a way. If Priya was right, this was simply the inside of another ship.

Ten or twelve feet in front of them, a vast wall curved around the front of the cabin. Thousands of creepy little holes honeycombed its surface. Just looking at them made Sierra's skin crawl.

"I think that wall is supposed to project an interface," Priya said. "Those look like more retinal projectors."

The brackets they'd docked with were on the end of a metal beam protruding from the front wall, holding the sled out in the center of the room.

Sierra's heart skipped as she peered over the edge. They were seventy feet up. The shell surrounding them was perfectly round, without any sense of floor or ceiling or walls.

"It's like being inside a flower," Priya said. "A morning glory that's closed for the night."

Sierra tilted her head. "I never knew you could be so poetical."

Shrugging, Priya pointed at the pole connecting the sled to the front wall. "That's like a giant pistil."

"Pistol? Like a gun?"

"No, the pistil. The structure in the middle of a flower that bees land on to pollinate."

Sierra smiled. "You're such a dork. I love you for it." She paused for a moment, then put her hand on Priya's forearm. "Now, you need to fly us to Earth." The magnitude of the statement sent a chill up her spine.

Priya tapped on her device. "I told you, I can't fly. I just send things."

"Whatever. Send us. Those thirteen people are in danger. We have to—" She stopped herself.

"What is it?" Priya looked up.

"There were twenty of us in the village. Take away you, me, Waldmire, and Morrie, and that leaves sixteen. Why were there only thirteen pods?"

Priya looked down. "Maybe some were doubled up. More than one person can fit in a pod, you know."

"Did you look inside all of them? Did you actually see everyone?"

Priya didn't answer. Clearly, she hadn't.

"Did Randall send any pods anywhere else?"

"Not that I've seen," Priya said. "The only other pod that's gone anywhere was larger, and it went to a different island."

Sierra scooted closer to the device. Several lights shifted to her eyes. "Show me."

Chapter Forty-Nine

"Get to the trees," David whispered, pulling Barry toward the jungle. Whatever was in the pod was bigger than any of the sailbacks. The dinosaurs seemed to recognize that as well. Most had already scurried away.

Scott looked back. "Go, run." His voice broke. "I'll keep it—" The creature roared again, interrupting him.

A giant lion jumped down on the sand, with the shoulders of an ox and the brindle coat of a pit bull.

"Saber tooth," Cameron breathed.

Two enormous canines jutted from the front of the monster's mouth. It looked at Scott, only twenty feet away, then turned toward David, Cameron, and Barry, a much larger meal.

"Here!" Scott cried. He dropped the stick and lifted both arms, flaring his jacket wide.

Guilt speared David's heart, but he turned and fled.

The remaining sailbacks on the beach disappeared into the jungle, flapping their legs like mad lizard clowns.

David glanced back as he ran. The saber-toothed cat flew through the air and landed on Scott, knocking him to the ground. He didn't even have time to scream. It sank knife-like canines in the top of his skull with a splintering crack. Wrenching sideways, it pulled Scott's head off and tossed it away. Blood jetted everywhere.

David shoved Barry forward, unable to process what he'd witnessed, unable to think of anything except *getting away*.

"Stay together," Cameron shouted. She remained close, even though she could easily outrun him and Barry.

The sound of crunching bone came from the beach.

"Daddy," Barry cried.

"Trees," David said. "Get to the trees."

"What about the bugs?" Cameron asked.

David didn't answer. The bugs didn't matter.

They sped up as they moved from sand to packed dirt, weaving between the scrubby barrel-shaped plants. A small sailback scrambled out of their way.

"Cats climb trees," Cameron said.

If they got high enough, maybe they could kick and stomp from above. Maybe Cameron could shoot it in the face.

Barry stumbled over a knot of foliage. David jerked him to his feet, nearly hard enough to dislocate his shoulder.

A big sailback snapped at Cameron as she jumped over its head. David and Barry dodged around it.

The saber-tooth roared, an angry blast that sounded way too close. David's heart surged in his throat.

Finally, they found the same kind of smooth-barked trees they'd climbed the day before. Barry reached for one of them.

David pushed him forward. "Bigger. We need a bigger one."

Another roar came from behind, as loud as a jet taking off.

Chills ran up David's back. "That one, there." He steered Barry to a tree that was three feet around at the base, grabbed his waist, and hoisted him to the first branch. Barry took off, scrambling higher.

Cameron moved close, her eyes tight on his. He'd seen that look before, when a Tyrannosaurus was coming after them.

"Your gun. Can you kill it?"

She grimaced. "Maybe? I don't know. Might just piss it off."

David cupped his hands under her feet and boosted her up. As soon as she was out of the way, he jumped, grabbed the branch, and pulled himself off the ground.

The saber-toothed cat roared again. *Please, just let that be a warning call, claiming its territory.* Maybe it wouldn't come after them.

Please, God.

He climbed up opposite Cameron. Her face trembled with pain, either from her gunshot wound or the centipede bite. Probably both.

The ground looked fifty feet away, though it was probably more like fifteen. The saber-tooth padded under them, its shoulder blades cycling up and down as it walked.

"Higher," David gasped. "Keep climbing."

Above, Barry had his arms and legs wrapped around the narrowing trunk like a fireman's pole. Further up, thin branches fanned out, each ending in clusters of leaves. Barry grabbed one of those branches and pulled himself up, jostling the foliage. An eighteen-inch centipede fell from the clumps, bounced off a branch next to Cameron, and tumbled to the jungle floor. Cameron squealed.

Ignoring the centipede, the saber-tooth jumped onto the base of the trunk and clawed its way up. Two yellow teeth as long as daggers bracketed its gore-covered chin. The cat moved in a spiral, curving past the lowest branch, then charging higher until it was just beneath David. Its stench wafted up, a mix of urine and something foul and bitter, like spoiled beer.

David kicked at its paw with his heel. The saber-tooth reached and swiped. Claws scraped his shoe, nearly stripping it from his foot.

"Daddy!"

David didn't respond. He was too busy scrambling higher, which horrified him almost as much as the beast chasing them. If they went too high, the branches would break and they would plummet to their deaths.

The saber-toothed cat shimmied ninety degrees around the trunk, passing the branch David had been on. Its claws sank in the bark like Styrofoam.

"Get higher," David shouted. He shoved Cameron's foot out of the way so he could grab the branch she was standing on.

"I can't go any higher," Cameron shouted, just below Barry. The thinning trunk bent over in a slow arc.

The cat reached for David. He kicked again, mashing its paw with his heel. The monster snarled and slid down several inches, its claws furrowing the bark. The sweet odor of sap merged with the animal's rotten musk.

The jungle floor wavered below, sickeningly far.

David used a branch above to pull himself higher and wrapped his legs around the trunk. There was no other place to put them.

The top section of the tree bent further. Ten degrees, then fifteen. David's weight pulled him around to the lower side, accelerating the bending motion.

The tree shuddered and shook. David squeezed tight. He knew he ought to climb back down, to remove his weight from the falling trunk, but he couldn't make himself go lower. The saber-toothed cat was right below him.

The trunk broke.

David bear-hugged the tree as the world upended.

Barry screamed.

Cameron shouted, "Shit, shit, shit!"

The treetop slammed into the upper branches of its neighbor, nearly yanking David loose. A dozen centipedes shook free from the foliage and pattered to the ground like hail.

The broken section of the tree remained attached to the rest of the trunk by a sliver of bark. The top twenty feet of the tree's crown extended horizontally across to the neighboring tree, where their branches intertwined.

David hung with his arms wrapped around the trunk, right next to the ninety-degree break. Further out, Cameron dangled over the void, hanging by one hand. Beyond her, Barry gripped the trunk with his arms and legs, hanging like a sloth.

David pulled himself up and sat on the horizontal section, his feet braced against the part that was still vertical.

Cameron pulled herself halfway up, reaching with her left arm, the one that had been weakened by the gunshot wound. Her fingers touched the trunk, then she fell back, swinging forty feet in the air by her other arm, the one weakened by the centipede bite.

Barry wailed, his eyes closed. He appeared to have a tight grip, thank God.

"It's okay, Barry. Just hang on."

The saber-toothed cat had slipped a dozen feet lower when the top of the tree snapped. Its eyes tracked Cameron's dangling legs.

"Hang on, both of you," David shouted. "Just hang on."

A twelve-inch centipede crawled out of the foliage toward Barry's hands.

David whimpered. "Listen to me, Buddy," he said, forcing his voice to remain steady. There's a bug coming toward you. A big one."

Barry squealed.

"It won't hurt you if you stay still," David said. "You have to let it crawl over your hands."

"Daaaddyyyy."

"Don't move, Barry. Don't you move. If you flinch, it will hurt you." He didn't know if it was true, but if Barry let go, the fall would kill him or cripple him. Either way, the cat would finish him off.

The front half of the centipede reached Barry's arms. It tested the pink flesh, then climbed onto him. Barry wailed but didn't move. God bless him, he did not move. Dozens of legs, each an inch long, poked into his skin, pressing deep for traction.

"That's it, Buddy," David called, tears rolling down his cheeks. "You're doing great."

Barry blew air in and out of his mouth, his face bright red.

Below, the saber-toothed cat waggled its head up and down as Cameron's legs swung. It reached out and swiped with one paw, just missing her foot. The jungle floor spun beneath them, a thousand miles down.

The centipede came to the end of Barry's arms and reached across to his knees.

"I can't, I can't," Barry cried as the creature bridged the gap.

"Yes, you can," David said.

The head of the centipede, as big as a baseball, reached Barry's shoes, then continued onto the tree.

"You're doing great," David said again. "It's almost off." Sweat rolled down his forehead.

Two-by-two, the remaining legs left Barry as the centipede crept across the trunk, straight toward Cameron's hand.

"I can't do it," she said.

The saber-tooth inched upward, captivated by her swinging legs.

"It's just crawling." David leaned over, trying to make eye contact. She didn't look up. "You've got to hang on. Barry did it."

She shook her head. "I can't."

David scooted along the top of the branch. If he could get to the centipede before it reached her hand, he could knock it off. It was a foot away from her. The jungle floor was miles below. Dizziness swept over him. He never should have looked down.

The trunk ripped and dropped a few inches, tearing against the portion that was still connected. David clenched his thighs, trying to keep his balance.

The centipede's head was six inches from Cameron's hand. Shiny black fangs curved from each side.

Below, the cat swiped again, this time making contact with the heel of Cameron's boot. She swung, screaming.

"You have to hang on," David ordered. "You're badass. You can do this."

Still holding on with only one hand, Cameron swung herself away from the cat. At the end of her swing, her legs started back.

The centipede's head was an inch away.

Cameron swung toward the cat.

The saber-tooth turned, letting go of the trunk with its front paws. It leapt, arms wide, grabbing for its prey.

"No!"

A high-pitched buzz blasted through the jungle.

The saber-toothed cat went limp as it flew through the air. It flopped lifelessly against Cameron's legs, then fell and hit the jungle floor with a wet, crunching thud.

The centipede touched Cameron's fingers. She released her grip, falling toward the cat.

David reached out, unable to breathe, unable to save her.

"You're okay. We got you," came Sierra's voice.

An alien carriage flew in under Cameron, catching her a few feet down.

David sucked in air and let out a long cheering laugh.

Cameron flopped onto her back. Sierra and Priya rode the carriage, which plunged fifteen feet under her momentum, then stabilized and remained airborne.

David shuddered with relief. "Get under Barry, quick." He waved them closer.

Priya shook her head. "I don't exactly fly. We need you for that."

Barry shimmied closer, still hanging from the bottom of the tree, while the centipede crept along the top, ahead of him. David broke off a small branch and smacked it, sending it sideways to the jungle below. When Barry reached him, he grabbed the boy by his arm and helped him down onto the part of the trunk that remained vertical.

Cameron looked around, still flat on her back, her eyes wide. She looked confused, lost, out of control.

David grinned, filled with warm joy. Adrenaline coursed through him, amping his emotions. She was okay. Thank God, she was okay.

He and Barry climbed down until they were low enough to hop over to the carriage. They were safe. And even more importantly, they had a carriage. They could get back to Kim.

Sierra grabbed David's arms, looking at him with rage in her eyes. "Waldmire is dead. Morrie too. Randall took over the village."

A hollow pit filled his chest. All the relief and joy drained away. "What about Kim? Is she okay?"

"No," Priya said. "Maybe. I don't know." She seemed to shrink as she spoke.

David's breathing increased. "What happened?" The light hadn't changed, but everything felt dark.

"Priya was trying to help," Sierra said. "She sent the villagers away. We have to go get them."

"Where the hell is she?" David demanded. "Where are we going?"

"Earth."

LANDFALL

Chapter Fifty

Two Days Before Impact

Airman Tyrell Carpenter drove the combination bulldozer-backhoe from the police impound yard onto the empty streets of Colorado Springs. He tried to focus on his driving, but it wasn't easy.

The unexpected orders had given him a tiny splinter of hope.

Tyrell had joined the Air Force seven weeks earlier at his momma's suggestion when rumors about the Ender began to circulate. In Colorado Springs, the Air Force and the Space Force ran the Cheyenne Mountain Complex, and for many people, including Tyrell's momma, Cheyenne Mountain meant survival.

He pushed the backhoe to its top speed of twenty miles per hour, heading toward the address he'd been given. He had no idea what he was supposed to do when he arrived, only that his ability to operate the tractor had gotten him called up. The address wasn't close enough to the bunker to raise his hopes much, but that didn't stop the splinter from needling him.

The underground bunker at the Cheyenne Mountain Complex was designed to withstand World War III. Over the past month, the population of Colorado Springs had ballooned to almost four million as desperate people poured in from across the country, all hoping to get in.

From what Tyrell understood, no one from the general public had been granted access, and in the armed forces, no one below the rank of colonel had gotten in. Certainly not any brand-new enlistees like him. According to the rumor mill, politicians had eaten up all the available slots.

He rounded a turn and spotted two uniformed airmen sitting on motorcycles in the intersection ahead.

Tyrell parked in the middle of the street, climbed down, and walked over to the men, both wearing full battle gear and both white, which was unsurprising. The Air Force Academy, like Colorado Springs, had a Black population of less than seven percent. As Tyrell's Momma liked to remind him, he wasn't in Alabama anymore.

He felt awkward in his cargo pants and black t-shirt, but he'd been out at the ranch when the orders came, and they'd specifically instructed him not to take time to change. The only gear he carried was his sidearm.

He saluted the Major General, thankful he'd learned to recognize basic rank insignia before they'd shut down the training program and sent him home. "Airman Tyrell Carpenter, sir."

"Major General Dodge." Dodge returned the salute and gestured at the other airman. "He's Staff Sergeant Landon."

Landon, a barrel-shaped man with a mustache only a white guy could pull off, handed Tyrell a spare motorcycle helmet. "Use this for communication."

Dodge held steady eye contact as he briefed Tyrell. "Three days ago, NORAD detected more than a thousand extraterrestrial targets headed for the American heartland. The first one made landfall in Minnesota twenty minutes ago."

Tyrell didn't know what was going on here. He thought he'd heard the word *extraterrestrial*. This felt like another initiation prank, which didn't make sense, because the Air Force training ops had long since closed down. He wanted to bail and head back to his dogs, his only source of happiness in these awful days.

Dodge kept going. "Analysts thought the targets were a first contact scenario, but it turns out they're empty. They appear to be some sort of lifeboats."

Tyrell's confusion must have shown on his face, because Landon jumped in. "You hadn't looked online today, have you?"

Tyrell shook his head.

"This shit is real." Landon pointed at the bulldozer. "Brass wants us to scoop up a UFO with that thing." He grinned. "Crazy, huh?"

Dodge glanced sideways at his Staff Sergeant. "Our orders are to procure one of the objects and deliver it to Cheyenne Mountain for further analysis."

Tyrell's little splinter of hope teased a nerve ending. The underground bunker at Cheyenne Mountain lay beneath two thousand feet of solid granite, with blast doors designed to deflect a thirty-megaton nuke. According to rumors, the supplies inside could sustain a thousand people for decades.

"If I carry this thing to the compound, can I stay there?" Tyrell knew he was out of line as the words left his mouth. He glanced at the Ender in the sky and let the question stand. At this point, what difference did it make?

Dodge narrowed his eyes. "I'm not authorized to make promises, airman, but once someone gets inside, it isn't easy to send them back out."

The little splinter of hope sang out as if someone had run a current through it.

He wanted to ask more questions. He wanted to know if this was bullshit or a prank or a mistake, or if there really was some cause for hope. But before he could figure out where to start, something fell from the sky, slamming into the parking lot of a strip mall three blocks up the street.

"Right on schedule," Landon chuckled. "That's some Air Force precision right there."

"Space Force gets the credit for tracking these bogies," Dodge said.

Landon scowled.

Dodge held up his hand and swung it forward. "Let's move. Double-time."

Tyrell returned to the idling tractor. He still didn't know what to think, but something was sure as hell going on. The throaty roar of the engine filled the cab as he shifted into gear, followed by a haze of sulfur exhaust. He put on the helmet and followed the motorcycles to the parking lot of a sushi restaurant he'd been partial to before the end of the world. *Inland Ocean.* Stupid name, decent Nigiri.

A squashed white sphere the size of a minivan sat on the asphalt. Tyrell doubted that it was from outer space, but if it got him into that bunker, he didn't care. He drove past the object, shifted into reverse, and backed into position.

"Tyrell, what are you doing?" Dodge barked over the helmet radio.

"I'm gonna grab it with the backhoe," Tyrell said. "If I try to pick it up with the blade, it'll just roll away."

"Good thinking," Dodge replied after a moment.

Tyrell grinned. He barely knew jack shit about the Air Force, but after three years in construction, he knew how to operate this tractor.

"We got company," Landon said.

Four men wandered into the parking lot, including a shirtless guy with a confederate flag tattooed across his back. Tyrell locked the door to the cab while Landon maneuvered his motorcycle between the civilians and the object.

"Hey," shouted a man with a bushy beard. "You can't do this." He pointed at the Ender in the sky. "That thing's gonna hit in two days."

Tyrell found the lever that swung his seat around to face the backhoe controls. He hooked the bucket over the object on his first attempt and then pulled the boom stick toward him to draw the arm closed.

The object didn't budge. Tyrell pulled the stick all the way down. Vibrations shook him as the bucket arm tightened, but instead of pulling the object to him, the tractor jerked across the asphalt toward it. *Holy shit, that thing must be heavy.* He should have lowered the stabilizer legs. The shaking stopped once the arm folded three-quarters of the way around the object, holding it in a snug hug.

"This is horse shit," yelled a civilian. "You cocksuckers have your bunker."

The crowd had grown to a dozen now. Most of the streets in Colorado Springs were barricaded, but people could still get around on foot.

"Let's go," Dodge ordered. "We got what we came for."

Tyrell reached for the knob to swing his chair back to the driving position.

Below, a guy wearing a Denver Broncos jersey ran around the other side of the tractor and slapped the capsule. The moment his hand made contact, a horizontal split appeared, right in the middle. The top half rose, uncurling the tractor arm with the shriek of protesting metal. Once the gap grew wide enough, the Bronco fan disappeared inside.

"Let us in," shouted someone in the crowd. "There's room for all of us."

The inside of the pod looked like it would max out at six or eight and the crowd had swelled past thirty.

A silver-haired man in a green shirt walked in from the street with a black semi-automatic long gun in his hands.

"Gun," Tyrell said. "Behind you, Landon."

Landon swung around, reaching for his sidearm, but he was too late. The man shot him from twenty feet away. Landon fell off his bike, howling, his hands on his chest.

Dodge appeared out of nowhere and dropped the shooter with a quick double-tap, spraying the people around him with blood.

The crowd parted, screaming. Some lowered themselves to the ground, hands raised, while others fled, and at least one or two climbed inside the pod.

Dodge ran over to Landon. "Goddammit, Tyrell, get moving," he ordered over the radio.

Tyrell spun his seat to the driving position. The top half of the pod stopped rising, but the backhoe's arm was still curled around it. He shifted to first gear and released the clutch. The tractor trembled as the tires ground into asphalt.

Dodge dragged Landon to his feet. "You're gonna be okay. Hang in there, airman."

The top half of the pod lowered, allowing the arm of the backhoe to curl closed again. The shirtless man with the confederate flag tattoo ran forward and squeezed through the foot-high gap.

The pod kept closing.

"Jesus, get him in, get him in," someone shouted.

The edges of the pod bit into the man's thighs as the top half closed, pinching them down to four inches, then three, then two.

Tyrell heard the screams inside the tractor cab, even over the rumbling diesel engine.

The man's legs dropped to the asphalt as the pod sealed shut. Bright blood streamed down the white sides, beading like water on a freshly waxed car.

Shrieks came from the crowd. Tyrell froze, picturing the scene inside the pod.

"Why aren't you moving?" Dodge demanded. The tractor's wheels whined on asphalt and the cab shook like a son of a bitch, but he hadn't moved an inch. Tyrell goosed the gas.

The tractor lurched, but instead of moving forward, it tilted as the pod lifted from the ground, pulling the backhoe arm with it.

"Oh, shit."

Tyrell clawed at the door handle, unable to turn it. The tractor tilted past forty-five-degrees. *The lock.* He hugged the seat with one arm to keep from falling onto the dashboard and fumbled for the lock.

The door swung open as the tractor left the ground, now hanging from the pod by the curled bucket arm. Tyrell threw himself out the opening.

He hit the asphalt and tucked into a roll. A woman in the crowd holding a baby stared at him, eyes wide, backing away. She looked up and mouthed a word, unable to find her voice. *Run.*

Tyrell scrambled forward. The ground shook as the twelve-ton backhoe landed right where he'd been only seconds earlier. Nuggets of asphalt pelted him.

A thousand feet above, the pod kept rising.

Chapter Fifty-One

David pushed the carriage as fast as it would go, somewhere around twenty knots, flying back across the sea, just above the surface. They'd wasted enough time, and were finally returning to the spaceship, a strange silver shape on the beach ahead of them.

"We'll get her, David," Sierra said from behind.

He didn't reply. The detour pissed him off, even though he knew they needed the food. None of them had eaten in more than a day. Cameron had wanted to roast the saber-tooth, which would have taken hours. Priya suggested searching the sailback island for fruit, which might have turned up nothing. It was Barry who came up with the idea of returning to their first island, which meant traversing open water twice, there and back again. At least it had gone quickly.

They'd flown the carriage to the narrow point at the end of the island, where Randall, Wayne, and Juliana had supposedly arrived. They collected konapples, fireballs, and some knobby yellow berries that tasted like avocado. The carriage was now loaded with all kinds of fruit, none of which would do Kim any fucking good if she was dead.

David glared over his shoulder at Priya. "Is there any chance you're wrong? Is it possible they didn't go to Earth?"

Priya looked up at him, pain on her face. "I'm sure."

David turned forward, biting his tongue. She'd sent his daughter away from him.

To his left, the island with the village drifted slowly past, the plateau rising up in the middle. Randall was there somewhere.

"Is that really a spaceship?" Barry asked from behind, his hands on David's shoulders.

David turned his head and forced a smile. "I sure hope so." It didn't look like a spaceship. It wasn't really shaped like anything.

The ship was spherical on one end and at least twenty stories tall, with two thin wings jutting out from the sides. At the other end, the sphere tapered down to a long horizontal stem that ran twice as long as the ship was tall.

No, it actually was shaped like something, David realized. It was shaped like one of those rubber aspirators they used in pediatrics to suck fluid from a newborn's nose.

"Take us to the end of the tail," Priya said.

"That's a tail? I thought it was the front." David shook his head and muttered to Cameron, "Steady climb." She moved in sync with him and they drifted higher. This new carriage handled much better than the other one, confirming his theory that it had been damaged.

Sailbacks scattered as they flew over the beach.

"Dimetrodons," Priya said.

Cameron snorted. "I told you she'd know what those dinosaurs were called."

"Everyone thinks they're dinosaurs," Priya said. "They're actually protomammals."

David didn't give a damn what they were. He focused on the ship, trying to make sense of the design. Two thin wings extended from the front of the bulb in long, graceful curves, like oversized canards. Further back, stubby winglets angled down from the middle of the hull, like the pectoral fins on a shark. A dozen or more rods and stalks protruded from the surface. He didn't know if they were antennae, pitot tubes, or warp thrusters. How could they possibly expect him to fly it?

The ship didn't even have landing gear. It floated four feet above the sand.

David and Cameron brought the carriage to a halt near the end of the tail, which turned out to be hollow, with a channel running straight down the middle, a dozen feet in diameter. He looked back at Priya. "You want us to fly in there?"

"Yes."

David gave Cameron a few brief instructions and they drifted slowly into the opening. Inside, the tunnel widened into a spherical chamber about half as big as the outer hull. Square pastel panels dotted every surface, some of them glowing dimly like disco decorations from the 1970s.

"What kind of spaceship is this?" Barry asked.

"Alien," Priya quipped. "Keep going, straight ahead."

The chamber surrounding them was seventy or eighty feet away in every direction, including down, more than enough to trigger David's fear of heights.

Priya rose up on her knees and pointed to a rectangular shape in the center of the room. "You have to dock us. Nudge into those brackets."

David and Cameron eased the carriage forward until they made contact. The brackets clasped the front corners, pulled them closer, and clamped the carriage in place. The interior darkened as the opening in the tail spiraled shut, but a second later, more pastel panels blinked on, brightening the chamber enough for David to make out the faces around him.

At the same time, his stomach rose in his throat as if he was falling. He clutched the short front wall of the carriage.

"What's happening?" Barry asked.

"The gravity is lower," Priya said. "It's the same everywhere else in the alien ship. The mothership, or whatever."

From what Priya and Sierra had told them, the island menagerie was actually a chamber inside a vast spaceship, which meant *this* ship was really more like a shuttle.

David released his grip on the console. He took slow deep breaths, trying to calm his stomach.

"Nice flying, Ace," Cameron said.

"You, too." She was almost as good as Scott, despite having virtually no practice. He turned around. "How do we get to Earth?"

"Give me a minute," Priya said, tapping on her strange device.

"We don't have a minute. You sent my daughter away."

Sierra touched his arm. "She didn't mean to. Yelling at her won't help."

"Just tell me how to fly this thing."

Priya kept tapping. "You don't fly it. I send it."

Next to her, Barry jumped in place, floating four feet straight up and pinwheeling his arms as he came back down. "Look, Daddy."

David wanted to smile at his son's exuberance, but he couldn't. All he could think of was Kim. She was on a devastated Earth that was supposedly inhabited by alien invaders. Assuming she was even still alive.

"What does it look like?" Cameron asked. "Inside the mothership?"

Sierra pointed at the curved walls around them. "Kinda like this, but much, much bigger. Most of it's pretty dark."

"When do we get moving?" David asked, impatient with the small talk.

"We already are." Priya shifted close to him and rotated the device in her lap so that bright lights shone in his eyes, creating a hologram that appeared to float out in front of him. "We're flying over the sea right now. This is a map." She reached out and stuck her finger through a circle. "It's routing us to one of these portals." A tiny nasal aspirator hologram approached the circle.

"Are you sure?" David asked. "It doesn't feel like we're moving."

"You can't feel anything once the low gravity kicks in," Sierra said.

"We're in the superstructure now." Priya said. She switched to a schematic that didn't make any sense.

"How do we get out of the Mothership?" Sierra asked.

Priya pointed at a much larger circle. "That's an airlock. At least, I think it is."

"Is that the giant pit we saw?" Sierra asked.

"No, that was storage. This one is even bigger. It's further back."

David shook his head. "I don't believe they're just going to let us fly right out."

Priya shrugged. "So far, they haven't stopped us."

"In a way, it makes sense," Sierra said. "I don't think they ever gave it any thought."

"Why not?" Barry asked. Apparently tired of jumping, he now sat at the back of the carriage, organizing fruit into little piles.

"You wouldn't worry about zoo animals driving off in your car," she answered. "And you wouldn't bother to lock the door on a room with a fish tank. You wouldn't even think about the fish leaving."

Priya exhaled and looked up from her device. "We're in space."

"Bullshit," Cameron said. "How do we know we're not still sitting on the beach?"

"I'm telling you, we're in space." Priya said. "You do your job and quit worrying about mine."

Cameron's nose flared. "What exactly is my job?"

"You were in the Army. You should have protected Scott. Hell, you should have stayed in the village instead of going off joyriding."

Hollow guilt sank in David's guts. The joyriding had been his fault.

"Or maybe," Priya continued. "You could have gone after Randall back when you had the chance."

Cameron jabbed her finger at Sierra. "I was ready to kill Randall, but she told me not to. This is her fault as much as anyone's."

"You think I don't know that?" Sierra snapped. Her grimace tightened into an angry sneer. "If you guys hadn't flown off, you would have been there when Randall showed up. You could have stopped him then."

Cameron chortled. "You're one to talk. You abandoned everyone, including your buddy Waldmire."

Sierra turned red. "I know."

Priya held up her hand before Cameron could say anything else. "She believes Waldmire might have been her biological father."

Cameron looked away, her jaw clenched.

"I thought your dad was that Spielberg guy," David said quietly. She'd told him stories about growing up with a Hollywood executive for a father.

"I did, too," Sierra said. "Until recently. Now I'll never know."

David wasn't sure what to say. He recognized the guilt and pain in her face. He knew exactly how it felt. He'd abandoned his daughter for a joyride on an alien hovercraft. He'd let his excitement about flying get the better of him. Hell, he'd been showing off too, flirting with Cameron. If Kim wasn't okay, he'd never forgive himself.

They sat in silence.

"What do we know about the invaders?" Cameron asked after a while, her tone neutral and measured. "The gorgers."

"The caretakers said they would kill anyone they encountered," Sierra said. "They told me they consume organic material."

"What else?" David asked. He had no idea what to prepare for. "How many are there? What kind of weapons do they have?"

"They said there are billions." Sierra shook her head. "They didn't tell me anything else."

"Wait, how can Earth even be habitable?" Cameron asked. "Shouldn't everything be on fire?"

"Oh yeah." Sierra gave a bitter laugh. "We were all asleep a little longer than we thought. The Ender hit a hundred and fifty-two years ago."

"What does that mean?" Barry asked.

David didn't know what it meant. Fatigue was starting to cloud his mind and each new piece of information felt overwhelming. "It means you're a hundred and fifty-eight years old, Bud."

"Cool."

"How long will it take us to get to Earth?" Cameron asked.

"Good question." Sierra gestured at Priya's device. "Can you find out?"

"I'll try."

"Anything else you can figure out would be great," Sierra said.

"Can you turn on the carriage's cloaking device?" Cameron asked. "That would give us a tactical advantage."

"I'll do my best," Priya said. "This thing didn't exactly come with a manual."

David closed his eyes while they talked, grateful someone was lucid enough to ask intelligent questions. He needed sleep. The carriage was roughly as big as a king-size bed, with a foamy surface. He lay down on the inside front corner and Barry joined him, snuggling in his arms. *We're coming, Kim.* He prayed that his daughter was still alive. Holding Barry made him feel slightly better. He fell asleep cuddling the boy against his chest.

Sometime later, he woke to Cameron shaking his shoulder. "You're going to love this, Ace," she whispered.

David untangled himself from Barry, who was out cold. The interior of the ship was much brighter. He pulled himself up to look over the carriage's dashboard and gasped.

The front wall of the chamber was gone and he was looking at Earth, which floated in front of him, surrounded by a sea of stars.

"We really are in space," he said, feeling numb.

Earth looked dried out and the coastlines seemed different, but even so, it was beautiful. It was home.

Cameron leaned into him. "Priya got this working and then promptly went to sleep."

He reached out and his fingers sunk into the Atlantic Ocean. The front wall wasn't gone, of course. Hundreds of little projectors were sending images into his eyes.

Sierra, Priya, and Barry all lay asleep behind them on the carriage. David put his arm around Cameron and they watched the planet grow until it filled the front wall of the ship. Eventually, the others woke and joined them.

"I sent the pods to D.C.," Priya said. "I was looking for signs of life, and I touched the spot where the Washington Monument used to be. I didn't realize I had the pods selected at the time." She looked down. "Anyway, I've sent this shuttle to the exact same spot."

They all settled into the back half of the carriage and watched. Most of the land looked brown and dead, but bits of green ran along the shorelines of lakes and rivers.

"How fast are we going?" Barry asked.

David shook his head. "Faster than any re-entry vehicle ever built on Earth."

The alien technology seemed to handle it without issue.

A large storm loomed over the Ohio River Basin. "Weather," Priya said. "It's nice to see weather again."

The rubble of towns came into focus as they descended. Roads looked like the incomplete lines of a child's crayon drawing. Skeletal columns remained where bridges had been, like ghostly afterimages. Smudges of green gave hints of plant life along the waterways.

"Look for signs of the gorgers," Cameron said.

"Like what?" Barry asked.

She shrugged. "New structures. I don't know. Landing craft?"

David looked, but didn't see anything. "Where's Washington?"

Priya pointed at an area where the ruins looked thicker. "That's D.C., there along the Potomac."

Everything looked yellowish-brown. David looked for the Washington Monument, the Capital, the Reflecting Pool, anything recognizable. Bright sunlight washed it all out.

"The pods," Cameron said. "I see them."

He searched, holding his breath. Her eyes were a damn sight better than his. He pointed at a mound of beige rubble. "You aren't talking about that, are you?"

"That was the Lincoln Memorial," Cameron said. She took his arm and moved it to the right, lining it up. "There." David spotted the white specks.

"Are they sitting in sand?" Barry asked. "There isn't supposed to be sand in Washington."

"There is now," Sierra said.

The ground came up fast, but the artificial gravity kept them from feeling anything. When they were about five hundred feet above the surface, the image shifted to a side view instead of straight down.

They descended for another thirty seconds and then the panorama grew still, showing a landscape of sand and ruins.

David turned to Priya. "What now?"

"Undock the carriage."

He nodded and sat down next to Cameron. The docking mechanism released them the moment they started to back away and the projection lights vanished, leaving behind the expansive grid of dark holes. Normal gravity returned, making David feel sluggish and heavy. Behind them, the circular door at the end of the tail spiraled open, filling the cabin with harsh white light.

They turned the carriage around and flew slowly into the tail.

"Let's park here and scout it out," Cameron said.

They stopped the carriage halfway down the tunnel, which was plain gray and unmarked, like a giant water pipe. Everyone jumped down.

David pushed past the others to the end. He shielded his eyes from the glaring sunlight, so much brighter than inside the shuttle or back on the islands. The air flooding the ship smelled rich and humid, with a hint of salt.

Thirteen pods sat near a jagged wall of weathered blocks. He scanned the area for movement, searching for Kim.

Everything looked dead.

One of the pods had "KIM" scrawled on the side in the rusty brown color of dried blood. David's heart tumbled. Another pod had a "W" on it, but the rest appeared unmarked.

"What are those blocks?" Barry asked. They looked like a section of wall that had long ago fallen to ruin.

"That was the Washington Monument," Cameron said. There was no sign of the tidal basin or the reflecting pool, just endless sand.

The ruins of the Capitol Building sat in the distance, stark white against the blue sky. What remained looked like the Greek Parthenon, rows of dead columns no longer supporting anything.

"The pods are closed," Priya said. "Maybe everyone is still inside them."

David held his breath, holding onto it like hope. If Priya was correct, Kim was right there in front of him, a few hundred yards away, safe and asleep.

"No." Cameron pointed. "They went north. The tracks go off in that direction." David followed her arm toward the dark ruins of the city.

Chapter Fifty-Two

Two Days Before Impact

Tyrell, Dodge, and Landon dismounted their bikes on a high curving overpass that had been closed to traffic. Tyrell helped Landon pull off his body armor and then his shirt while Dodge made a radio call.

"Motherfucker, that hurts," Landon hissed.

"Pipe down," Dodge said, covering the microphone on his helmet. "You'll be fine." He stepped away.

Landon's ballistic vest had stopped the bullet, but a hand-sized welt covered his chest, with all the crazy-ass colors of a Caucasian bruise, red in the center, blurring to purple and then bright yellow at the edges. Landon's nipple was navy blue.

"Grab my first aid kit," Landon hissed. "Motherfucker."

"Where?" Tyrell asked, overwhelmed by all of his pouches and pockets.

"Here." He slapped a bulge on the side of his thigh. "Christ, what's the matter with you?"

"I hadn't completed basic yet," Tyrell said, fumbling open the pouch. "Sorry." He pulled out a medical kit.

"Wait, what? You're a trainee?"

Tyrell let Landon's words hang in the air. He'd been chosen for this mission because he could operate the backhoe. Since that was no longer an option, he felt useless.

"You don't understand, sir," Dodge said into his radio. "We can't bring a pod to you. The target object lifted our backhoe into the air like it was nothing."

They'd ridden the motorcycles onto the closed freeway and stopped on an overpass ramp that arced above a tent city of refugees. The smell of urine and malaise wafted up.

"Who's he talking to?" Tyrell asked.

"That's the General," Landon said. "Give me the instant ice pack."

Tyrell found it and handed it over.

Landon twisted it, cracking a tube inside, then held it against his bruise. "Motherfucker," he hissed. He reached up and plucked at Tyrell's plain black t-shirt. "Good thing it wasn't you, huh?"

Tyrell pulled away. This whole mission was a waste of time. He wanted to get back to the ranch and his dogs.

"Morphine."

Tyrell dug into the pack. "Shouldn't we get you to the bunker?" Maybe if he helped transport Landon to Cheyenne Mountain, they'd let him stay. He found a syrette and handed it over, then shoved the first aid pack into one of the pockets on his own cargo pants.

Landon gave him a shit-eating grin. "I ain't going in that bunker. I ain't on the list." He squeezed the morphine into his arm. "Dodge is in, though. His wife and kids are already there. Half a mile underground."

"Roger," Dodge said into his radio. "We will." He turned away from the other men and added. "Tell Michelle and the boys I love them, sir."

Landon grew quiet.

Dodge walked over. "New orders."

Tyrell helped Landon to his feet. He hissed like a snake, but kept his *motherfuckers* to himself.

"We're no longer supposed to collect a pod. Now they want us to get in one."

"Hell, yeah." Landon curled his bicep and rubbed the injection site.

"What?" Tyrell asked. "Where does it go?"

"Nobody knows." Dodge held his face rock-solid.

Tyrell pointed at Cheyenne Mountain, a massive granite edifice looming to the west. "What about the bunker? What about your family?"

"Listen to me, airman. Our mission is to fly, fight, and win. We will go wherever these pods take us and we will protect Americans when we get there. Do you understand?"

Tyrell stood straight. "Yes, sir." Somehow, he was still part of the team.

"Let's get moving," Dodge said. "A drone pilot just spotted a pod on the eighth hole of the Silver Springs Golf Course."

They rode north, Tyrell driving Landon's bike, while Landon clung to him and shouted "motherfucker" every time his chest bounced against Tyrell's back.

"You got any family?" Landon asked once the road smoothed out.

"Nah. I had a girlfriend, but she bailed when the shit hit the fan."

"Mom and dad?"

"My momma's in Alabama." Tyrell said. He needed to call her, to tell her what was happening. His father had died during the last respiratory pandemic, alone and quarantined in the hospital, unable to speak because of a tube running down his throat. He didn't like to talk about it.

Fortunately, Landon didn't ask any more questions, though he did utter one final "motherfucker" when they arrived at the golf course and rode up onto the fairway.

Someone had gotten there before them, judging from the bodies around the eighth hole, but strangely, the pod was still there.

"Wha' th' hell happen?" Landon muttered, his words syrupy from the morphine.

Dodge slowed down and signaled for them to split up. At least ten bodies lay around the pod, which sat at the edge of a sand trap. A wall of six or eight piñon pines grew on the side of the fairway, presumably to protect nearby mansions from sliced golf balls.

"Why would they kill everyone but leave the pod?" Tyrell asked as he came to a stop. It didn't make any sense, but then again, neither did anything else that had happened today.

Landon slid off the bike and moved to a flanking position near the trees. "Mebbe they got inside and just dinn take off yet," he said with a yawn.

"Jesus, Landon, you need a nap?" Dodge quipped. He parked and approached the pod along the edge of the sand trap. "Check the bodies. See if any of these people—" Shots rang out before he could finish.

A mist of blood puffed from Landon's face and he arced over backwards.

Tyrell dropped to a firing position behind the motorcycle. "Trees!"

He'd seen a flash in the pines. "Get down."

Dodge fell out of sight in the sand trap as three more shots rang out.

Tyrell zeroed in on a flash at the base of the trees and opened fire with his handgun. The shooter stumbled forward onto his face. Or maybe *her* face. It looked like a woman. "Target down. Dodge, do you copy?"

No response. Tyrell shook. Holy Christ, he'd just killed someone. What the fuck was he supposed to do now? He took off his helmet and flung it away.

Sucking in a deep breath, he got to his feet. Most of Landon's face was missing. Tyrell shoved the horror aside and tried to let his paltry three weeks of training kick in. He crept to the sand trap, where Dodge lay on his back.

"Take papers," Dodge whispered. "Belt pocket." Except for his lips, he didn't move.

Tyrell fumbled open the pouch on Dodge's belt and pulled out a leather satchel.

"This? Is this it?"

Dodge didn't answer. Thick blood darkened the sand under his head. He was gone. Tyrell couldn't even think now. Everything was insane.

The pod sat twenty feet away. He fumbled open the satchel and found a letter signed by the president ordering *acquisition by any means necessary of an unidentified oblong object arriving in the United States.*

Could that pod really be a ticket out of here? He shoved the satchel in one of his other pockets and stood up. Tyrell had sworn to protect the Constitution. He would finish the mission. He'd go where the pod took him and protect Americans when he got there.

"You need to leave, son," came a thin voice somewhere above him.

Tyrell scrambled out of the sand pit. An old bald white guy in a brown work jacket stood in front of the pod. Blood covered half the man's jacket and a good portion of his pants.

"Pops, you okay?" Tyrell asked. "Where are you hurt?"

Gray stubble peppered the man's gaunt face, but no hair grew above his ears. He barely even had eyebrows.

The old man ignored him, probably in shock. *Join the club,* Tyrell thought. He just stood there with his back to the pod, looking off into the distance, arms at his sides.

Tyrell wondered if anyone else might have survived. He scanned the bodies.

A woman in a red camisole and pink pajama pants lay close by. The toenails on her bare feet were painted a matching red. Long slices ran across her arms.

The next victim was a stout man wearing a blood-matted coat. His cheek had been split open all the way to his skull.

Tyrell puffed air, trying not to let the gore overwhelm him.

Another body showed similar cuts, this one lying slumped at the edge of the sand trap, wearing the blue coveralls of a groundskeeper.

Tyrell called over to the old man. "These people weren't shot. Did someone cut you?"

"My boys are coming. If you ain't gone, they'll shoot you dead."

A chill ran up Tyrell's neck. "What boys?"

The old guy raised one bony finger and pointed. "Here they come."

A half mile away, a van tore across the grass, heading in their direction.

The man's right hand remained at his side. Tyrell caught a glimpse of a black handle. He drew his handgun. "What are you holding? Christ, what the hell's going on here? Drop your weapon."

The man shifted and Tyrell glimpsed a blade.

He felt like he was falling, out of control. He looked around. "Holy shit. You did this."

The engine was close enough to hear now. Tyrell stole a glance. A blue van bounded up the fairway.

The man stood in front of the pod and stuck out his whiskered chin. "I killed most of 'em. Evelyn got some, 'fore you shot her." Spittle flew from his mouth. "When my boys get here, they gonna fuck you up."

Disgust rose in the back of Tyrell's throat. This man and his wife had been killing anyone who came around, defending the pod until the rest of their clan arrived.

He made a tunnel in his mind, blocking out everything that didn't matter. The pod sat at the end of that tunnel. His orders were to go where it took him and protect Americans.

This man had just confessed to mass murder. He and his sons would kill him.

The van stopped somewhere behind him. A door slammed.

Tyrell was out of time. He didn't have a choice.

He marched forward, raised his pistol and shot the man twice in the heart. A two-foot machete dropped to the ground as the man collapsed.

Tyrell slapped the top of the pod.

"Daddy?" shouted a man's voice behind him.

Tyrell darted around the pod, jitters in his chest. Four men spilled from the van, looking around at the carnage. Three held guns. The fourth held a mobile phone.

As soon as the pod opened wide enough, Tyrell slipped inside. It smelled like wax and felt like lying on a dentist's chair.

"Daddy!" cried one of the other men.

"Where's Momma?" called out another.

The top half of the pod lowered, only a few inches left. Right before it closed, Tyrell realized that the guy holding the mobile phone had been filming him.

Chapter Fifty-Three

Earth was a devastated wasteland, but it was still Earth. It felt more real to Sierra than the islands ever had. She kneeled on the sled behind David and Cameron as they floated ten feet above what had once been the south lawn of the White House, following the tracks from the pods.

They would find the others. Sierra was sure of it. Being on Earth gave her hope. The warm sunshine on her arms reminded her of Venice Beach. So far, they hadn't seen any signs of an alien invasion. No gorger occupation. Just sand and ruins.

The tracks had led northwest toward the remains of the White House, and then turned away before getting too close. It was easy to guess why. Other than a few chunks of wall rising from the sand like old bones, nothing was left of the building.

"Where are the gorgers?" Barry asked.

"Maybe they're made up," Priya said. "To scare us away."

"It's a little early to jump to conclusions," Cameron said. "It's a big planet. Maybe they're colonizing some other part."

"Like another state?" Barry asked.

"Maybe another continent."

"Let's hope you're right," David muttered. He and Cameron moved in sync, operating the sled as a team.

They continued west, following the tracks toward the remains of larger buildings, which were more intact than the White House, but not by much. Mangled husks of cars littered the streets.

As they left the barren grounds of the Ellipse, the sand below grew messy, making it difficult to tell footprints from ripples.

"Hold on," David said. He and Cameron brought them to a stop, hovering ten feet up. Everyone leaned over the sides of the sled, studying the ground. "It looks like they wandered around." Tracks crisscrossed in every direction. "Which way should we go?" he asked, sounding angry and frustrated.

"North," Cameron said. "They probably went deeper into the city. It's what I would have done."

"No. We should go west," Priya said. "Toward the river. There's more green that way and they'll need water." A few tufts of grass grew here and there, but they hadn't seen any actual trees since they landed.

"What do you think, David?" Sierra asked. "Which way would Kim have gone?"

He looked at her with an expression of guilt and despair and shook his head.

Sierra mulled it over. The tracks were all just divots in the sand, not actual footprints, so it was impossible to tell if they were coming or going. Several blocks away, a road angled off diagonally toward the northwest. She pointed. "Let's split the difference and follow that street."

"That was Pennsylvania Avenue," Cameron said, reaching for the controls. They started moving again. A moment later she called for them to stop. "Hold on. I see something."

Sierra rose up on her knees. "What? Where?" She only saw ruins, desolation, and sand.

Cameron pointed. "That's Reggie's hat."

A blue lump sat at the edge of what had once been a sidewalk.

Cameron glanced over her shoulder. "Let's land and check it out."

Sierra nodded, eager to set foot on Earth again.

David held Cameron's gaze for a moment, then he nodded too. Together, they lowered the sled in the middle of the road, where nothing could sneak up on them. A wall of ruins ran along the street to the west, but empty sand surrounded them in every other direction, all the way to the remains of the White House.

Cameron drew her gun and hopped down. "Stay close together."

Sierra climbed out and twisted her feet in the sand. Even with everything in ruins, this was home. She belonged here, not in some artificial menagerie. Heat from the sun tingled her skin and the breeze jostled her hair. The wind had picked up since they arrived, blowing the storm their way.

David stepped out next and Barry started to follow, but David spun around. "You stay on the carriage," he said with a tone that left no room for discussion.

Sierra approved. The boy had a tendency to run off.

Priya took Barry's hand. "I'll stay here with him."

Sierra, David, and Cameron walked a few yards to the object. It was Reggie's cap, all right. Cameron stood guard with her gun raised, scanning the wall of ruins.

Sierra held the cap so Priya could see it. "They were here."

"Kimmie!" Barry shouted. "Where are you?"

"Shush!" Sierra snapped. She had wanted to leave Barry behind in the shuttle, but of course David never would have gone for that. The way things were going, he might not ever let the boy out of his sight again.

Barry glared at her.

"Maybe the kid's onto something," Cameron said. "Our voices will carry a lot farther than we can see."

"Kim!" David roared.

"Kimmie!" Barry yelled. "Jasmine! Dee!"

David raised his hand, silencing everyone. They stood frozen for several seconds, listening.

They heard only the far-off rumble of the approaching storm.

"Shit," David muttered. "They're nowhere near here."

Sierra touched his arm. "It's okay. They made it this far. They're still out there somewhere. We'll find them."

"Come on," Cameron said. "Let's keep looking."

As Sierra turned back to the carriage, she spotted a line of tracks running alongside the building that looked different. She shielded the afternoon sun from her eyes. Wind had blown drifts against the wall and the tracks cutting through looked fresher than the tracks out in the open.

"Hold on a second." The sun shining over the top of the roof made it difficult to see. She stepped closer until she passed into the shadow of the building, a crumbling hodge-podge of red and white masonry with jagged holes throughout.

"Was this them?" David asked. He passed her and knelt beside the tracks. Someone had walked right along the building. David stood and went left. "I'll see what's this way."

Sierra kept moving to the right. The tracks turned into a wide opening that might have been a garage. "I think they went in here."

The garage sloped down and the floor above had collapsed, partially blocking the entrance, but the tracks definitely went inside. "Come have a look," she called to the others.

Something moved in the shadows. Sierra squinted. "Kim?"

A creature charged out on a mass of clacking legs, crashing into her and knocking her into deep sand at the edge of the shadow.

Barry screamed.

The creature was roughly the same size as Sierra, but seemed bigger because of all the legs. Her first thought was, *giant spider*, but its body arched up in the back, like a scorpion.

"Shoot it, Cameron," Priya shouted.

The monster's low-slung head was all mouth, surrounded by wriggling, reaching mandibles, with foot-long pincers on the sides.

Sierra scrambled backwards, her wrists sinking in the sand until she passed into the glaring light. Blinded, she raised one hand to block the sun.

The monster skittered forward and stopped. A pouch under its tube-like head bulged and it vomited a stream of yellow bile. Most of the goop splattered just shy of Sierra's feet, but several drops landed on her motorcycle pants.

Smoke rose from her legs and burning pain stabbed her shins. Sierra's muscles began to seize.

The pincers on the side of the creature's gaping maw twitched wide as it crept closer.

Chapter Fifty-Four

Tyrell turned on his phone, but the signal was dead and the light didn't help much. The inside of the pod was black and featureless. The ceiling felt just like the firm, yet cushy surface underneath him.

Dear Jesus, he'd killed two people. He never thought he would kill anyone. He'd only joined the Air Force because his mother thought it might get him into Cheyenne Mountain.

Think about the ranch. Think about the ranch.

When basic training shut down and they told the new enlistees to go home, Tyrell had adopted fifteen dogs from a local animal shelter, every last one in the place, and took them to an abandoned ranch on the east side of the city. His girlfriend bitched that he cared more about the dogs than her, and maybe it was true. Tyrell had never felt as much love as when those dogs crowded around.

He plundered the stores for pet food and began driving farther and farther to different shelters, carrying bolt cutters after he discovered some of them had been abandoned. Within days, he had nearly two hundred puppers. All those wagging tails gave him peace and joy in a time when both were in short supply.

Mealtimes became contentious, but Tyrell found if he scattered food in the yard, the way his momma used to throw seed for chickens, the dogs would spread out and wouldn't fight so much. Tyrell tossed extra kibble off to the side for a few timid individuals, including a beagle named Darwin and a poodle named Noodle.

He pounded the inside of the pod with his fist. Those men had watched him shoot their father. It had been his only option, but dear

Jesus, it filled him with empty despair.

He closed his eyes and pictured the dogs chasing each other. A tireless Weimaraner named Scout always instigated, leading a pack through a figure-eight pattern around the trees. Tyrell relaxed his fist and slowed his breathing. He thought about the dogs running up to him, wagging their tails, licking his face. He lay in the pod for a long time, focusing on the memory, trying to remain calm. He might have dozed off.

Light spilled onto him as the pod split open.

A forest surrounded him, with seven other pods nearby and people standing around, dazed, just like him. He climbed out.

No one seemed threatening, so he kept his sidearm holstered, but he unsnapped the safety strap, just in case, remembering the old man with the machete.

"Where are we?" asked a woman in a black yoga outfit. "Are we still on Earth? It looks just like Earth."

"We're alive," laughed a skinny guy in baggy pants. "That's all that matters. We made it."

"It can't be Earth," said a woman with broad shoulders poking through designer holes in a green sweater. "Why would the pods take us somewhere else on Earth?" Her brown hair was cut with bangs every bit as out-of-date as her sweater.

"It has to be Earth," said a man with salt and pepper hair wearing a brown leather jacket. "We weren't in the pods long enough to go anywhere else."

"Where's Judith?" asked a tall woman with striking red hair. She went from pod to pod, leaning inside each one. "She was right behind me."

"Holy fuck, I've gone to heaven," cackled a chubby man, the last person to climb out of the pods. "It's all babes here."

"Aw, go to hell," said a woman with frizzy blond hair. She wore dozens of bracelets on her arms.

The chubby guy was onto something, though. All of the women were stunning. And everyone but Tyrell was white. Four women and four men, counting himself. He focused on the three other men. They were more likely to cause trouble. One old, one skinny, and one chubby.

The tall red-haired woman began to tremble. "Judith?" She hugged herself and looked off into the woods, tears running down her cheeks. "Where are you?"

Tyrell raised his arms, waving everyone closer. "Hey, gather around. It's okay. I'm with the Air Force. I was sent to protect you." He tried to sound like Major General Dodge. Most of the group looked confused, which wasn't surprising. He felt pretty damn baffled himself. "Let's get everyone's names." A simple meet-and-greet might give them a sense of stability. He made eye contact with the redhead. "If Judith is here, we'll find her."

The blonde in the yoga outfit pointed at him. "Oh shit, that guy's got a gun."

Tyrell kept his hands out, away from his sidearm, and turned slowly so they could see he didn't mean any harm.

The woman in the yoga outfit stepped forward, squinting. "Wait a second. I know you."

Tyrell had never seen her before. It had to be a case of mistaken identity.

She jabbed her finger in his direction. "He's the guy from the news. He shot that old man on the golf course." She looked around at the others. "Shot him dead and took his pod."

Tyrell's shoulders dropped and his legs felt like rubber. *Shit.*

Something bumped Tyrell's hip and he reached for the gun. Too late. The holster was empty. He spun around.

The woman with bare shoulders held Tyrell's pistol. He felt a heavy weight on his chest. The first thing they told him when they issued his firearm was that he must maintain control of it at all times, at all costs. He imagined his momma clucking at him for only paying attention to the men. The thought shriveled his heart. He would never see his momma again.

Everyone eyed Tyrell with distrust. The feeling was familiar, but that didn't make it any less uncomfortable.

The guy in the bomber jacket circled him, keeping his distance, until he came to the brunette. "Nice work, sweetie." He reached for the gun. "I'll take that."

"The hell you will." She glared from the sides of her eyes.

He didn't back down. "Why should you get to keep it? Do you know anything about guns, Miss?"

The woman didn't back down either. "It's *Detective*, thank you."

Tyrell tensed. "I'm with the Air Force," he said again. "I swear."

"What's your name, airman?"

"Tyrell. You?"

"Jordan." She had a square jaw and perfect teeth. She popped the magazine from his gun and emptied the chamber. "Let's try to keep the temperature down." She handed him the empty firearm. The magazine disappeared into the pocket of her jeans.

The overweight guy who thought he was in heaven shoved past them both. "Hey, look, there's a trail." Stale body odor followed in his wake.

"Wait," Tyrell said, trying to show concern for everyone's safety. "We should stay together."

The tall redhead craned her neck. "Judith?"

"Hey babe, who's Judith?" asked the skinny kid with a buzzcut. He looked only a year or two out of his teens.

"My daughter," she whispered, her eyes glazed over. "She was right behind me."

The guy stroked her back, obviously taking advantage of her distress.

The chubby guy waved them over from the trail. "Holy fuck, everybody come here."

"Let's go check it out," Jordan said, addressing the group.

The old guy in the bomber jacket sneered at Tyrell before starting toward the trail. "Don't you try anything," he barked. His eyes narrowed, exaggerating his crow's feet so much they looked like crow's wings.

Tyrell waited a moment, then followed him.

Several yards up the path, a thin white man stood at an opening in an eight-foot wall. He looked as if he was waiting for them. A clearing lay inside the wall, with a few small buildings beyond.

The man raised his hand in greeting. His eyes bulged under bushy eyebrows. "Hi. I'm Randall. I'm in charge here. Welcome to the rest of your lives."

Chapter Fifty-Five

Cameron charged toward the bug monster attacking Sierra. It wasn't a giant centipede, but it was definitely some kind of fucking bug. A blur of legs carried a curved, segmented body. The only thing resembling a head was a low-slung tube at the front, which ended in a gaping mouth with pincers on the sides.

Sierra squealed, grasping her thigh and shaking her foot. Tendrils of smoke rose from her shins.

Cameron fired twice, putting two rounds in the side of the creature's head-tube. Mustardy fluid burst from the impacts. The monster lurched to a stop and turned in her direction.

"Get up." She grabbed Sierra's forearm and pulled her to her feet, wincing at the stench of burned flesh.

The creature sidestepped like some kind of crab, wobbling along on segmented legs that sprouted from nodules under its body. Her shots seemed to have hurt it, but only a little.

Cameron shoved Sierra behind her and raised the gun again, squinting from the sun's glare. She didn't know where to aim. Keeping herself between the creature and Sierra, she backed up, trying to draw the thing out of the shadows, so she could see it better and figure out where to shoot.

The creature lurched forward, but the moment its front legs passed into the sun, it retreated.

"It doesn't like the light," Cameron said.

A sack under the monster's mouth bulged and gurgled. "Don't let it puke on you," Sierra hissed.

They scrambled further back as the creature spewed pus-colored vomit into the sand where they'd been standing. Sharp odors of ammonia and vinegar stung Cameron's nostrils.

"Daddy!" Barry screamed.

David stood against the side of the building, ankle-deep in drifts of sand. The monster saw him, or sensed him somehow, because it didn't seem to have any goddamn eyes, and turned toward him.

He looked at the carriage, which sat maybe thirty yards away. A chill ran up Cameron's spine. He'd never make it. The bug monster would be on him in seconds.

"Wait!" Cameron shouted. "Run straight here." She jabbed her finger at the ground in front of her. "Trust me, David."

If he did what she said, he'd be moving closer to the creature instead of away from it, but ten steps would put him in bright sunlight. She hoped he would trust her. She hoped she was right.

David looked at the carriage, where his son sat with Priya, then pushed off the wall and ran straight out.

The bug-thing darted toward him. He swerved past it. The creature skidded, turned, and followed, but it stopped when it reached the sunlight. David kept going.

"Come on, let's get out of here," Cameron said. She and David helped Sierra limp to the carriage, keeping to the middle of the street.

The creature moved parallel to them, staying in the building's shadow, its pointed feet stabbing the sand. Every few seconds, it reached toward them with one of those long-ass legs, then flinched back, like someone testing a bath that was too hot.

Cameron kept her gun aimed at the thing, ready to empty the magazine if it decided to charge.

"Get in, get in." Priya pulled Sierra aboard.

The muscles in Cameron's neck tightened with disgust. This bug was even worse than the giant centipedes. She broke away from the others and took a few steps closer, trying to make sense of it.

The creature's pale body was segmented, like something that lived under a log. Coarse hairs sprouted from its legs. Thick yellow goop oozed from the holes where she'd shot it. The creature's tail curved over its head, with slimy green growths wriggling at the end.

It crept toward her. When the glaring sunlight hit the top of its head, the skin turned red and appeared to tighten. It backed away. Pincers stretched wide at the sides of its mouth, where a dozen small mandibles wiggled around a maw full of teeth.

She knew she should save her ammo, but the thing was so fucking hideous, she couldn't stop herself. She pointed the Beretta at the top of its head, right in the center, about a foot behind its mouth, and pulled the trigger.

The shot tore open a hole right where she'd aimed and yellow fluid coated its back. The creature flopped to the ground.

Cameron sneered, satisfied, and returned to the carriage.

Sierra had unzipped her riding pants at the ankle and pulled the white leather up to her knee. Red blisters dotted her skin. Barry clung to David while he examined her injuries. It looked like she had been spattered with cooking oil.

"I'm okay," she hissed.

Cameron nudged David with her elbow. "The others aren't anywhere nearby. They would have heard us and shown themselves. Let's take off."

He didn't respond. He stared into the distance, his face ashen.

"What's the matter, Ace?"

David trembled. "If they ran into one of those things ..."

Cameron glanced over at the monster. It looked like a dead spider now, with all its legs bent up around its body.

"It's okay," she said. "I killed that one easily enough. If they ran into one, I'm sure they handled it."

David looked pale. "What if they ran into more than one?"

How the hell was she supposed to answer that? *You're right. They're probably dead. We should look for someplace safe. Maybe a tropical island somewhere.* She bit her tongue.

The despair on David's face gutted her. She grabbed his hand. "Hey. We can't give up. Come on, Ace. They've only been here a few hours. I'm sure they're fine." The words felt like bullshit, but Cameron was never much for giving pep-talks.

"That thing kept to the shadows," Sierra said. "It seemed like direct sunlight hurt it."

"It definitely had some kind of light sensitivity," Priya said.

David nodded slowly. "Sunlight. We have to find them before dark."

"We don't have that long," Priya said, pointing west. "We have to find them before that storm gets here."

Chapter Fifty-Six

Tyrell listened while the others bombarded Randall with questions, glad to no longer be the center of attention.

"Where are we?"

"Who sent the pods?"

"Who are you?"

"Where is everyone else?"

"What's in those buildings?"

Randall patted the air, shushing them. "I'm gonna answer all your questions. This place was made for us, to keep us alive after the Earth was destroyed." He spoke with a drawl. Not quite deep south, but somewhere nearby.

"Who made it?" Jordan asked.

Randall smiled. "Alien guard-keepers. They put me in charge."

"Give me a break," said the old guy in the bomber jacket. "Why would they pick you?"

The guy had a point. Randall gave off the vibes of a weasel.

Randall squinted. "There was another group here, before y'all. They fought and argued and half of 'em killed each other, so the aliens took 'em away." His words came out smooth, almost rehearsed. "They nearly gave up on humans altogether, but I convinced them to give us one last chance."

"How could that happen already?" asked the woman with all the bracelets. She wore a tight, low-cut shirt over billowing harem pants. "We just got here."

Several others nodded.

Tyrell watched Jordan through all of this. Her expression remained neutral, but her eyes were alive, taking everything in.

"You were in your pods longer than you think," Randall said, looking at the shirt instead of the woman. "You were hibernating, like a bear."

This brought another round of chatter, most of it sounding dubious.

Tyrell scanned the area. "Where are these aliens? What do they look like?"

"They don't wanna be seen. Y'all might not never see one."

The guy in the bomber jacket stepped forward. "How do we know you aren't making this up? You still didn't answer my question. Why'd they put you in charge?"

Randall set his jaw. "They don't think like us. They don't know how to handle humans. They said we were too hard to take care of. I told them I could keep people from hurting each other."

"Good luck with that." The man hitched his thumb at Tyrell. "This guy shot somebody and stole his pod."

Tyrell clenched his arms, fighting the urge to make fists. "It wasn't what it looked like," he said, keeping his voice as steady as possible.

Randall looked him over but didn't say anything.

The woman with all the bracelets pointed into the village. "What's in here?"

"It's the home they built for us. You're free to use the cabins, except the one farthest up the hill." Randall paused. "You're not allowed anywhere near it."

"Why not?" she asked.

"It's where they talk to me sometimes," Randall said.

The old guy rolled his eyes. "Give me a break."

"Yeah, I agree with grandpa here," bracelets said. "I don't buy your story."

"Dean," said the guy in the bomber jacket. "My name is Dean."

"Oh, sorry," she said. "I agree with Grandpa Dean."

Dean rolled his eyes again.

Randall walked up to him. "Tell you what, Dean. If you give me a chance, you'll find I'm on the level." He looked at the others. "Why don't y'all come in and let me show you around?"

The woman in the yoga outfit pointed at Tyrell. "What about this guy? He's dangerous."

Tyrell breathed slowly, forcing himself to remain still.

Randall looked him up and down. "Did you do it?"

He held his head high. "The man I shot helped kill two Air Force officers and a bunch of civilians." He left out the fact that he'd also shot the man's wife.

"That's not what it looked like on the video," said the woman.

Tyrell spun toward her. He'd had enough. "You think I don't know that? The man I shot butchered a dozen people with a machete."

Ms. Yoga Pants slid behind Randall, touching his arm.

Randall turned to the others. "It don't matter what he did. What any of you did. Everybody gets a fresh start here."

Tyrell winced. Randall's absolution made him sound guilty. He looked at all the glaring faces and felt completely alone.

Randall clapped him on the back. "Everyone come on in." He faced into the village and spoke loudly, projecting. "There's somebody here I want y'all to meet."

Chapter Fifty-Seven

Cold sweat trickled down David's sides. Sunset was still four or five hours off, but judging from the clouds to the west, it would be dark in half that time. He tried to focus on flying the carriage.

"What the hell was that thing?" Cameron asked.

"It had to be a gorger," Sierra said from the back.

"No way," Cameron said. "It was a giant bug. That thing didn't fly through space, and it sure as hell didn't send the comet."

"It didn't even look sentient," Priya said.

David didn't care what it was. All that mattered right now was finding Kim. They flew three hundred feet up, so they could see farther. He wished he was in a plane instead of this stupid flying platform. Behind him, Priya, Sierra, and Barry all leaned over the sides, scanning the ground. Each time he glanced their way, it sliced his nerves to see them hanging over the void.

"Maybe it's something that mutated after the comet hit," Cameron said. "I mean, is there anything like it?"

"Its mouth looked like a sand striker," Priya said. "But species don't evolve so drastically in such a short time."

"Maybe the caretakers lied about how much time has really passed," Cameron said.

"For that kind of evolution to occur, these buildings would all be dust by now." Priya said.

"What's a sand striker?" Barry asked.

"It's a worm that buries itself on the ocean floor and snatches fish when they swim by."

"Worms don't have legs," Barry said. "I think it's a giant spider."

Lightning flashed in the clouds to the west. They reached the Potomac and turned around for another pass over the city, following a grid pattern.

"How many legs did it have?" Priya asked.

"Ten," Barry said. "I counted them."

"The only animals with ten legs are crustaceans," Priya said.

"Why did sunlight stop it?" Barry asked.

"Sunlight didn't completely stop it," David said through gritted teeth. The creature had tested the light several times. He prayed to God that Kim hadn't encountered one of those things.

"Why would they come to a planet where daylight hurts them?" Cameron asked.

"Earth has equal hours of day and night, and plenty of cloud cover," Priya said. "Maybe more than before, thanks to the Ender."

"And ruins to hide in during the day," David muttered.

"What did it spit on me?" Sierra asked.

David had smeared her burns with mashed flesh from a konapple, hoping the alkaline fruit would neutralize any remaining acid. It seemed to have helped.

"Some insects vomit enzymes onto their food to dissolve it before they slurp it up," Priya explained. "But I've never heard of a crustacean doing anything like that."

"Wasn't there a movie about that once?" Sierra asked.

"Please stop," David said. "Christ."

"We're just trying to figure this out," Priya said. "The more we know about them—"

"I don't want to think about one of those things puking on my daughter so it can eat her," he growled. He didn't want his son thinking about it either. He glanced back.

Barry wasn't paying attention to the discussion. Instead, he was leaning over the edge of the carriage, like they were only three feet off the ground and not three hundred. Probably counting the damn buildings. Sierra had a firm grip on Barry's ankles.

David shuddered and turned forward, forcing himself to trust her.

"Wait, Daddy," Barry said. "I saw something."

"Steady stop," David instructed. Together, he and Cameron slowed the carriage until it hung in the air. His heart walloped in his chest as the wind buffeted them. They really needed some goddamn seatbelts. He turned around slowly.

"It was in that building over there." Barry pointed behind them, to a massive stone edifice with a square hole in the middle, just north of the National Mall.

Their ship sat a mile beyond the building, still parked where they'd left it, in the empty sand by the pods.

"What did you see?" David asked, daring to hope.

"A flash of light."

He exhaled. It was probably lightning reflecting off something.

Pryia kneeled over the edge of the carriage, making it dip slightly. David's chest fluttered just from watching her.

"That building is pretty close to the pods," she said. "It's worth a look."

"That's Main State," Cameron said. "It was the state department building. I think I see movement. Let's get closer."

Cameron had the best vision of any of them. If she'd spotted something, there was hope.

David whispered a prayer as they turned in a wide arc toward the south. "Please, please, please."

The building was shaped like a giant square, enclosing an open courtyard. A large chunk of the northern section had collapsed, leaving a wedge of rubble that spilled into the center.

Cameron pointed. "There."

"What?" David squinted. "What do you see?"

"A flash of light on the inside wall. The one in the shade."

"Something's moving," Priya said.

"*Ugh,*" Cameron groaned. "The wall is crawling with those things."

"Yeah, but look," Sierra said, her voice rising. "There are people down there."

David leaned over the front of the carriage, ignoring his fear of heights, searching desperately. He spotted a cluster of movement in the middle of the courtyard, away from the shadows. "It's them." He shuddered with relief. "Thank God. It's them."

A tight knot of people crowded together, most facing outward. One of them held a mirror overhead, reflecting sunlight.

David swelled. "Down, down, down." He and Cameron descended into the courtyard in a tight turning spiral.

Cheers greeted them.

"Praise Jesus," Jasmine sang.

"About goddamn time," growled Reggie.

"Kim," David shouted, still descending. "Where's Kim?" Everyone was moving around too much. He looked for Kona but couldn't spot her either.

"Hurry." Kevin waved. "We're in trouble."

They brought the carriage to a stop on the ground next to the crowd. David jumped out and ran from person to person, shoving each one out of the way. "Where's Kim? Where is she?"

Several people pushed past, trying to get onto the carriage.

"She ain't here," Felicia said.

His knees weakened. "No, God, no." The monsters had eaten his daughter.

"What happened?" Sierra asked.

A faint cry came from David's mouth. He didn't want to hear about it. He couldn't.

Jasmine grabbed him by the shoulders. "She was never here."

David shook his head. "What? Where is she?"

Chapter Fifty-Eight

Kim Williams looped the end of Kona's leash over a stubby knob on her tree and hurried to the center of the village. She didn't have much time.

Randall was at the far end of the fields, greeting the new people on the path to the beach. He'd ordered her to come down in five minutes so he could introduce her.

She glanced at his cabin, determined to find out what he was hiding in there. He'd threatened to kill Kona if Kim went anywhere near the little hut. She didn't think he was bluffing.

But he never said anything about looking in through the window.

Kim had picked a tree straight out from the side of his cabin. Unfortunately, it was too far for her to see anything but a strange glow that reminded her of looking down on the city with Dad in the Cessna at night.

She swallowed, fighting tightness in her throat. Dad and Barry were still out there somewhere. As long as Randall kept her prisoner, she knew they were okay. He muttered the word "insurance" to himself when she didn't do exactly what he wanted. Kim was the insurance. Randall wanted to use her against Dad somehow.

She wasn't about to let that happen.

She darted between the empty cabins and ran down to the little sheds by the work tables. Randall was still down at the opening in the wall with his back to the village. A bunch of new people were just outside, listening to him.

Kim slipped past the food shed and ducked into the one containing supplies. She found what she wanted immediately. The binoculars. She snatched them, then spared three seconds to look for Josh's knife. It wasn't there, which was probably for the best. Randall had guns, and there was some kind of rule that you couldn't bring a knife to a gunfight. Still, she felt the bite of disappointment. The knife might have given her more options.

She stepped outside, darted out of sight behind the sheds, and ran past the three empty huts that Randall had made her clean for the new people.

"There's somebody here I want y'all to meet." Randall's voice carried loud and clear. That was her cue. She kept running, clutching the binoculars extra tight so she wouldn't drop them. She leaped over the little creek and ran to the trees.

Kona lowered her head to her front paws, tail wagging. The sight of her gave Kim an extra boost. Kona was all she had left.

She reached her tree, pulled herself up, and wedged the binoculars into a junction between two branches. With the binoculars, she would finally be able to see what Randall was up to in his cabin.

She dropped to the ground, removed Kona's leash from the little hitch, and jogged back to the low end of the village.

The eight new people were asking questions. They looked lost. The women were really pretty, which was kind of strange, like maybe they were all going to be on a TV show.

Kim swallowed. The best way to avoid saying the wrong thing was to say as little as possible. Mom had said that to Dad a million times. Kona pulled on the leash, eager to sniff the strangers.

The group spotted her and froze. Kim held her breath. She hated being the center of attention. She dropped the leash so that Kona could bound over to the newcomers, which divided the group's focus, at least a little.

A Black man kneeled and held out his palm. "What's your dog's name? Can I pet her?" Kona licked his face and extended her paw for a handshake.

"Kona," Kim said. *Say as little as possible, as little as possible.*

Earlier, she'd heard Randall use the n-word while mumbling to himself about his plans for the village. At the time, she didn't know what to make of it, other than the fact that he was a racist buttwipe. Now she figured it must have had something to do with this man.

"Good to meet you, Kona. I'm Tyrell." He scratched vigorously on both sides of Kona's head.

Randall moved closer. "This is Kim. The aliens wanted to take her away with all the rest. But I saved her. I convinced them to let her stay. I promised to take care of her, just like I promised to take care of y'all."

A tall red-haired woman gaped at Kim and broke into an ugly cry, which was extremely creepy. One of the other women tried to console her, but it only seemed to make things worse.

Randall ignored them. "Kim is one of the lucky ones. The people that was here before killed each other. They even killed children. Ain't that right, Kim?"

She twirled a curl of hair with one finger. "Yes." *As little as possible.*

A big man pushed forward between a couple of women. "Hey, you're David Williams' girl. You made it. Where's your dad?"

Kim froze. "Mr. Vaughn?" It was the jerkface who'd taken the pod that landed across the street. She glanced at Randall, wondering what she was supposed to say. Was it okay that she knew Mitchell's name, or would he be pissed?

Randall teetered forward. "You two know each other?" His hand slid into his jacket pocket. He had a gun in there. She was sure of it.

Kim nodded. "That's Mitchell Vaughn. He lives across the street from us. I mean, *lived*." She stood perfectly still, except for her eyes, which flicked to Randall every few seconds, checking to see if she'd said too much.

The new people stared with confused expressions. There were two other men besides Mr. Vaughn and Tyrell, one old and one young. She scanned the faces of the four women, double-checking that none of them was Mom, which was dumb, of course, because if Mom was here, she would have run right to her, but Kim couldn't help herself. She missed her so much.

Mitchell walked over and looked down at her, hands on his hips. He stank of body odor. "This Randall guy says there's aliens around. Is that right? What happened to your old man?"

She played furiously with her hair. "I don't like to talk about it." This was a good answer. It didn't actually say anything, and it was also true.

Randall still looked tense, but he always looked tense, so it was hard to tell how angry he was. She wanted to just grab Kona's leash and run away, but where could she go?

"Well, I want to hear about it," Mitchell said. "Where's your brother?" He looked around. "Bobby?"

"Barry," Kim whispered.

Randall started closer, his hand still in his pocket. Kim wondered if she should run, and if so, which way.

Randall put his hand on Mitchell's shoulder and steered him into the village. "Come on, now. I got more to show you."

Mitchell looked back as Randall walked everyone up the path through the fields. "Good to see you, kid. I can't wait to hear what happened to your old man."

Chapter Fifty-Nine

Sierra pushed through the group, trying to reach two people lying on the ground. Carol stopped her, grasping her hands with an impressive grip. "Bless your heart. You came for us." Fresh blood glistened on the woman's arm and sweat plastered her white hair to her scalp, making her head look like a skull.

Sierra squeezed back. "Of course. Go get in the sled. We don't have much time."

Carol released her.

Sierra dropped to a crouch beside Kelly, who leaned on one elbow, her legs burned and blistered, worse than Sierra's. Nick lay beside her, unconscious and flat on his back, with someone's undershirt wrapped around his head. Kelly held his hand.

"David, get over here," Sierra called.

The courtyard felt like a cage, its four walls towering eight stories around them, the one to the west crawling with the creatures. Late day sunlight lit the wall to the east. Sierra wondered why everyone didn't just flee through the building in that direction. All the doors and windows were long gone. She looked closely and shuddered when she spotted movement inside. The whole building was infested.

David joined her. "You said Randall killed Waldmire and Morrie. Are you sure you didn't see any sign of Kim?"

"I never saw her," Sierra said. She started to add that even Randall couldn't kill a child, but then stopped herself. "We'll find her."

Felicia stormed over, a horrible grimace on her face. "Morrie's dead?"

"I'm so sorry, Felicia," Sierra said.

"I'm going to kill that motherfucker," she growled.

"Get in line," Cameron called over.

"Great," Sierra said. "The sooner we get out of here the sooner we all can go kill Randall."

"She has to be back on the mothership," David said. He had a faraway look.

Sierra stood, grabbed his shoulders, and shook him. "We'll find Kim, but first we have to help these people."

Behind him, the villagers were crowding onto the sled. Priya took Carol's hand and helped her aboard.

David nodded slowly. "Okay. Right." He kneeled and lifted the bandage from the side of Nick's face. The eye was a mushy mess.

"You have to help him," Kelly pleaded. "Do something."

David's expression froze, as if he was trying not to reveal what he really thought. Sierra wasn't a doctor, but it was obvious that nothing could be done for Nick's eye.

"We need to keep him stable," David said. "You've done a good job with that. When we get somewhere safe, we need to clean out his wounds."

Tears ran down Kelly's face and she sobbed quietly.

Sierra pulled her to her feet. "Come on, let's get you onto the sled."

"Where's Lauren?" Cameron asked.

Sierra looked around. She hadn't realized anyone else was missing.

"Dead," Reggie grunted. He held a metal trash can lid.

"How?" Sierra asked.

Reggie pointed at the building. "We came inside, hoping to find shelter, and maybe even supplies. Those things jumped us. They hide in the ruins during daylight. We couldn't get back out the way we came in, so we ran to this courtyard."

Sierra had barely known Lauren, but the human population was getting damn near extinct. They were down to fifteen people. "We can't lose anyone else."

Across the courtyard, the shadowed west wall bristled with movement as the creatures skittered up and down. They wandered in and out of openings that used to be windows. Most were roughly the size of a person. Another dozen or so waited down on the ground, just yards away, lined up at the edge of the shadow. Several were larger, as big as bears.

To the north, a large portion of the building had collapsed, leaving a sloping pile of rubble that peaked around the fifth floor and fanned out below. The rest of the courtyard was empty, except for a few concrete planters with the trunks of dead trees protruding from them.

Sierra and David walked Kelly to the sled. "How many people will this thing hold?" Sierra asked. "We have to get everyone out of here, right now." The crack of distant thunder punctuated her comment.

"Eight," David said. "Maybe ten."

There were already six or seven people on the sled and it looked full. "We have fifteen," Sierra said. "We have to fit everyone." They started back for Nick.

A cloud passed overhead, creating a brief moment of darkness, followed by sunshine. Thunder cracked, then a bigger cloud scrubbed the light completely.

"Here we go, here we go," Reggie said, holding the trash can lid like a shield. He moved between the sled and the line of monsters. "Felicia, get over here."

The creatures at the edge of the shadow surged like a wave at the beach. One of the larger ones broke from the pack and charged forward, its legs cycling, carrying its low-slung body like a battering ram armed with teeth.

Felicia cocked her arm and hurled a chunk of rubble at the charging monster. The creature's head swung sideways from the impact and brown goop splattered the concrete rubble.

David grabbed Nick under his arms and Sierra picked up his feet.

Bright sunshine returned as the cloud passed. The wave of monsters scrambled back to the shadows, hissing. The one Felicia had nailed staggered on wobbly legs.

Cameron offered her another chunk of concrete. "You've got a hell of an arm."

Felicia took it. "Thanks."

Reggie turned the trash can lid toward the sun, bouncing light onto the wounded creature. It emitted a mournful wail as it retreated to the shadows. He was using the metal as a mirror. It had to be the glinting light Barry had spotted from the air.

Felicia threw the second stone, hitting the wounded creature in the tail, which didn't seem to do as much damage. Another one, much smaller, skittered forward, braving the sunlight, and spewed yellow vomit at them. The spray fell short by several yards.

"Fuck that's nasty," Cameron said, holding her elbows tight at her side.

Felicia glared. "Yeah, welcome to our afternoon."

"They don't like the sunlight," Kevin said. "We have to get out of here before that storm blows in."

"Let's just go," Dee shouted from the front of the sled. "Somebody take off. You can come back for the others."

"No," Sierra yelled. That would be a death sentence. "We can't leave anyone behind."

"Then hurry," Dee said.

Sierra glared down at her as she passed the front of the sled, still carrying Nick. "You have to move."

"I got here first," she spat. "Let's just go."

Sierra wanted to smack her. "David and Cameron have to sit there to fly this thing. Out." She turned to four other people. "All of you, make room. We aren't leaving anyone behind."

This earned angry looks, but the others squeezed together, making room for Nick's unconscious body. Dee got up, stomped around to the back, and sat down again.

David squeezed into the front seat. "This isn't going to work." He was pressed up against the controls, barely able to touch them because his knees were in his face, and there still wasn't room for Cameron.

"How are the rest of us supposed to fit?" Felicia asked. "Come on Jasmine, make some room."

"Where you expect me to go, Shug?"

The sled was nearly full, everyone crammed together, but Sierra, Felicia, and Cameron still weren't onboard.

"Squeeze closer," Sierra said.

"I can't fly without Cameron," David growled. "And I still can't reach the controls. I need room."

Several people shifted and Cameron got into the co-pilot's seat. She and David pretzeled their arms around their legs to reach the front console.

Sierra squeezed onto the back. "That's all of us," she called out.

"Take off on three," David said. "Smooth ascent, straight up. One, Two, Three."

Nothing happened.

"We aren't moving," Kevin said.

"Try forward," David said. "Ten degrees up."

Still nothing.

"Shit." Cameron pounded the front wall of the sled.

"We're too heavy," David said. "That alien weighed eight hundred pounds. Fifteen people are three times that much. We need to offload half the group, take the rest to the shuttle, and then come back."

"No," Sierra snapped. "We have to stay together." Any discussion about who should stay and who should go would turn ugly fast.

"There's a shuttle?" Reggie asked.

"It's cool," Barry said. "You should see it." He produced the cap they'd found near the ruins of the White House and handed it to him.

Reggie pulled it on. "I wish I could."

"You will," Sierra said loudly.

Another cloud passed in front of the sun. One of the smaller creatures charged. Cameron swung her arm, taking aim with her pistol.

Felicia stood and threw a rock at the creature. The cloud passed and the monster squealed, retreating to the shadows. "The next cloud looks bigger," she said, sitting back down.

The wall of legs and mouths stood watching, ready.

"We're gonna have to make some hard choices," Reggie growled. "We have to leave someone behind."

Sierra shook her head. "There has to be another way."

"Oh, shit," Kevin said, looking up.

The first real band from the storm drifted above the courtyard. This wasn't going to be a cloud passing over. This was going to bring several minutes of darkness.

"We have to sacrifice someone," Reggie said.

"No," Sierra yelled.

He grimaced. "Then we're going to lose everyone."

Chapter Sixty

Sweat from Randall's hand greased the gun in his jacket pocket. That fat-ass and Kim somehow knew each other. Jesus Christ on a camel. The last thing Randall needed was someone asking more questions and poking holes in his story. He had to do something before those two got talking. He escorted the new people to the empty cabins, where they inspected each one even though they were all exactly the same. Kim stayed at the back of the crowd, watching and listening, but at least she wasn't talking. She knew better.

Randall stopped the group a good forty feet from his cabin and waited for them to gather around.

The plan had to change. Randall would make Mitchell the subject of his little demonstration instead of Tyrell. His grip on the gun relaxed. Mitchell would never get the chance to pry any information from Kim. He would see to that.

Tyrell stood with his arms crossed, watching him. Randall smiled. *It's your lucky day, boy,* he thought. *You get to stay.*

Tyrell didn't smile back.

"That's my cabin there." Randall pointed. "None of you should get any closer than this."

Dean snorted. "Oh, come on. You gotta be kidding me."

Randall stood tall. He'd expected this, and he was ready with an answer. "That kind of talk gets people killed," he said, planting a seed for his demonstration.

The redhead stepped forward, leaning, like she was trying to see inside. "Judith?"

A hippy wearing all kinds of bracelets pulled her back, which was a good sign. They were keeping their distance.

"She's looking for her daughter," explained the hippy.

"She's only three," the redhead said.

"What's your name?" Randall asked.

She looked around, shaking. "W-Wanda."

Randall covered his mouth with his hand so they couldn't see his grimace. How in the holy hell had he chosen someone named *Wanda*? He composed himself before he spoke. "She ain't in there. Sorry."

Wanda's face cinched up and she started sobbing.

He looked away, swallowing the urge to tell Wanda to shut the fuck up. That wasn't the sort of thing a leader could say. The skinny guy walked over and put his arm around her. Finally, someone here was doing something helpful. And clever, too. A girl in duress was a girl to undress.

Randall turned to the others. "Listen up. You're gonna be okay here. You'll see. It's a good life." This drew lots of blank stares. "Everyone just needs to be cool. And stay away from my cabin."

A few nodded. Most looked doubtful, but it was enough for now. Once he torpored Mitchell, they'd believe him. "Come on. Let's go sit down and get to know each other." He started toward the benches by the fire pit.

The skinny kid broke away from Wanda and hustled up next to him. "Hey, thanks for bringing me here. I'm Jerry."

He stuck out his hand and Randall shook. Shaking hands always made him feel queer, but he had to get over shit like that if he was going to be in charge.

The blond in the skin-tight yoga pants moved up on the other side. Randall enjoyed the sight of her bare belly.

"What is this place, really?" she asked.

The rest of the group followed close behind, listening.

"I told you," Randall said. "It's an alien planet."

"Oh, yeah? What's it called?"

"They ain't told me," he said. He knew she didn't believe his story. He wouldn't have, either. For the time being, it didn't matter. "How 'bout you?" he asked. "What are you called?"

"Gale." She smiled as she said it, showing teeth a million times nicer than Crystal's. She must have been a smoker once, judging from her sexy sandpaper voice.

"How many people were here before?" Jerry asked. He had a buzz cut and his pants hung low from his hips. He reminded Randall of himself, a few years back.

"Couple dozen," Randall said, keeping the answer vague.

"Where's everyone else?" Jerry asked. "From all them other pods? Weren't there thousands?"

"The aliens keep 'em safe. If things work out with y'all, they might give us more. We have to prove we can get along first."

Jerry nodded, but he looked unsure, just like the others. That would all change soon enough.

They reached the common area between the two little sheds and the main bonfire. Randall sat on one of the wooden benches. Gale and Jerry sat next to him and everyone else crowded around. Randall loved being the center of attention.

A woman in a green sweater with silly looking holes in the shoulders wandered toward the side entrance in the wall. She tilted her head, looking at the three crude buildings out by the edge of the woods.

"Those are the outhouses," Randall called out.

She turned back, scrunching her nose. "I sorta figured."

She was hot, but in a domineering sorta way. Randall licked his lips.

The hippy rubbed her hands together over the bonfire, which made her bracelets tinkle and clank. Randall wished he'd studied her more closely before he selected her. He'd never liked hippies.

Mitchell picked up a strip of jerky from a table in front of the sheds, where Randall had set it out for them. "What kind of meat is this?"

"Tyrannosaurus," Randall said. "Try some."

Everyone grew silent. Some stared. Others rolled their eyes or smirked. Not one of them believed him.

"Give me a break," Dean spat. His gray hair, leather jacket, and flannel shirt made him look like he belonged in a commercial for erection meds.

Randall walked over, grabbed a piece, and chewed on it to show it wasn't dangerous. The demonstration seemed to work, because Mitchell and several others tried the jerky.

Gale put her hand on Randall's forearm as he sat back down. "What is it, really?"

He smiled, enjoying the feel of her fingers on his skin. "I told you. Tyrannosaurus. I shot it up in the canyon."

"Okay. Whatever you say."

He could tell from her tone that she didn't believe him, but it was also obvious she wanted to stay on his good side. With her at least, Randall had chosen well. The tank-top hugged her tits and her leggings left little to the imagination. He was pretty sure she wasn't wearing panties. Gale had to be in her late thirties, but she was still a hottie.

She never would have given him the time of day on Earth. Here, though, she seemed quite interested. Randall sat back in a moment of sudden realization. Gale was a sycophant, working to endear herself, just like he used to. But now he was on the receiving end.

"Tell us more about the aliens," she said. "What are they like?"

Randall intended to keep the details secret. The less these people knew, the more power he had.

She put her hand on his knee. "Please?"

"They're just big brown blobs," he said. "Lots of claws and antennas at one end. No real faces." He shrugged. "I don't know, they're alien."

"What do we have to do to see one?" Dean asked, his tone demanding.

Randall glared at him. "If you go up to my cabin, you might meet one sooner than you like." It was a bluff, but he judged he could get away with it, for now. All he needed was a minute alone with Mitchell to set things in motion.

Dean held up his hands. "Do you really expect us to believe any of this? Give me a break."

"Would you just chill for a minute, Dean," Gale said. "We should be celebrating here. We survived the end of the world."

A few people nodded.

"We should be mourning," said the frizzy-haired hippy, looking down. "Everybody on Earth is dead."

Randall tried not to scowl. Hippies were such a fucking buzzkill. She sucked all the air out of the whole damn group.

Maybe it was for the best. He needed to break them up if he was gonna talk to Mitchell alone. "Why don't y'all go pick out your cabins? See if any of the spare clothes fit you. Get settled in. Maybe even take a few minutes to grieve." He was proud of himself for this last comment. It showed he cared. "Let's give it an hour, then I'll take you up to the canyon and show you some giant rhinos."

Dean shook his head, but kept his mouth shut for once. He rounded up the other three men and headed off. The women followed him, chattering quietly with each other.

Kim broke from the group, walking Kona toward the camping area on the other side of the creek.

"What's really going on here?" came a voice from behind.

Randall spun around, startled. It was the woman in the green sweater with the holes in the shoulders. She squinted, like she was assessing him. It gave him the creeps.

"I'm trying to give everyone a new life," Randall said. "That's what's really going on here."

"You've got a little girl prisoner and you've been lying ever since we arrived."

He wasn't about to take that kind of talk from a chick. "Listen, honey, I don't know who you think you are—"

"Detective Jordan Howarth, Wichita P. D."

Randall's heart jittered, but he couldn't let it show. "Listen, *Jordan*, I don't much like being called a liar, and that little girl is free to come and go whenever she wants." Sweet Christ in a sidecar, he'd somehow selected a cop. "I ain't touched her," he added, certain that Jordan was thinking the opposite. "Feel free to interrogate her if you like. She hangs out over in them trees." He pointed past the cabins.

Jordan didn't move. She was even worse than Dean. Randall's neck grew hot.

Mitchell, of all people, came to his rescue. The tubby guy walked past, heading off toward the outhouses.

It was the perfect opportunity. "I gotta take a piss," Randall said. He stood and walked away.

"I'll be watching you," she called after him.

"Wanna come watch me piss?" He knew it wasn't the sort of thing a leader should say, but he couldn't help it.

When Randall passed through the gap in the wall, he bent and pretended to tie his boots, which allowed him a sideways glance back inside.

Jordan left for the cabins. He exhaled. *I'll be watching you, too, detective.* He straightened and leaned against the wall, waiting on Mitchell.

A cop, a hippy, a negro, and a motherfucking *Wanda*. What kind of village was this? Gale was hot at least, and Jerry, the skinny kid, showed some promise.

Mitchell came out of the outhouse wiping his hands on his pants.

"Hey, I want to talk to you."

The tubby guy jumped like he'd been goosed. "Holy fuck, don't scare me like that."

"I need a right-hand-man," Randall said. Winging it, he added, "Kim tells me you're a straight shooter."

Mitchell tilted his head back. "Her dad and I didn't always see eye-to-eye."

"I believe it," Randall said. "Dave thought he knew better than everyone else."

Mitchell nodded and seemed to relax slightly.

Randall made a show of looking into the village, checking that no one was nearby. "Here's the thing. I need you to come up to my cabin."

"You said it wasn't safe." Mitchell shot him a sideways glare.

Randall swelled. The dumbass believed him. "It's okay. I'll take care of it. Wait right outside the door until I call you in. I'll show you how the aliens talk to me. You can see one of 'em."

The big guy took a deep breath and leaned back. "Holy fuck, for real?"

"You up for it?"

Mitchell nodded, shaking his jowls.

"You can't tell anyone. I need to trust you."

Mitchell leaned close and said, "Cross my heart," which was just about the dumbest thing an adult could say.

"Good. Give me fifteen minutes or so." Randall exhaled.

Once his demonstration was complete, every last cocksucker here would have to believe him. He slapped Mitchell on the back and they walked into the village.

Chapter Sixty-One

Priya felt like she was drowning. Everyone was going to die, and it was all her fault. She'd brought them here.

She sat on the carriage, stuffed against other people. The stink of their sweat choked her. Male sweat smelled different from female sweat somehow, and she couldn't decide which was worse. She also smelled someone's feet, which was definitely worse.

Sierra swung around. "Priya, can you control the shuttle? Can you bring it here?"

She swallowed. "I don't know. I can try." She propped the alien device against Jasmine's back and positioned it so the lights shone in her face. Several of the others watched with puzzled expressions.

Priya tapped the panel, diving through submenus she couldn't interpret, trying to make sense of it, hoping she wouldn't make things worse. Maybe she would accidentally stun them all. Maybe she should. At least then they'd be unconscious when they were killed and eaten.

The band of clouds passed over and the sun disappeared, dropping the temperature.

"Here they come," Kevin said.

It was too late. Even if she brought the shuttle now, it wouldn't arrive in time. The creatures raced toward them, their crab-like legs clacking across broken concrete.

Cameron stood and took aim.

Priya slid a sub-menu aside and gasped. *Bingo.* She spotted a shape she'd been hoping to find ever since she got her hands on the device. A half-bubble covered the top of a carriage icon. Invisibility. At least, she hoped so. The shape seemed correct, and so much of the aliens' iconography was based on shapes.

Ten or fifteen of the monsters picked up speed, charging straight at them.

"They're in spittin' range," Reggie said.

Someone screamed. David told Barry he loved him.

Priya found the corresponding icon on the panel below and tapped it with two fingers.

Cameron was sliced in half. A curved line ran diagonally through her midsection. Inside her torso, the pink and brown squiggles of her intestines hung in her belly. Her spine was a stark white star against the darker gore.

Dee shrieked.

"Pull her down," Priya yelled. "Pull her down!"

Felicia grabbed Cameron and yanked her down. The line slicing through her moved up her body as she descended, until she was whole again. She fell in a heap across David and Felicia.

The bisecting line hadn't actually cut through her, it had merely *shown* through her, right where her body had passed through the invisibility bubble.

"Everyone squeeze in," Priya said. "Quickly."

They were already crammed on top of each other like sardines, but they jostled closer. Someone's head connected with Priya's jaw, rocketing sparks through her vision.

"What the hell?" Reggie said.

"Shh-shh! Quiet," Priya said. "Shhhh!"

The creatures running toward the carriage stopped, one right next to them. Its legs bumped against the side. Polyp-like appendages flexed around its mouth.

Cameron raised her gun. Priya held up her hand, fingers splayed, not breathing. *Wait,* she mouthed. Cameron looked at her, confused. Priya nodded, trying to reassure her.

The moment stretched out interminably, then Cameron nodded back and lowered the gun.

No one moved while the creature stalked alongside the carriage. Its mouth opened and closed on the end of its flexible tube-head, with a gullet nearly a foot wide and sharp mandibles on either side. The pulsating sack underneath stretched and swelled. It bent to the ground, where smaller appendages danced across the dirt, feeding small bits of debris into the pink, tooth-lined orifice. A segmented, bulbous tail curled up and over the creature's back, like the body of a hermit crab when it came out of its shell, but not nearly so delicate. Finger-like knobs writhed at the end.

Finally, the creature wandered away.

"We're cloaked," Kevin said.

"Sh-sh-sh," Priya shushed, quietly as she could. She didn't know how much sound passed through the cloaking bubble.

Two other creatures, both smaller, scrambled closer.

One of the creatures stopped at the carriage. Its mouth and mandibles passed through the invisible barrier. The large pincers stretched wide, then scissored shut, inches from Dee's head. She leaned away from it, trembling.

No one breathed. The pincers twitched. They looked like the lower half of a lobster claw, the thin part, only much sharper. The creature turned and walked away.

Priya looked back at her device. She'd bought herself some time. They were safe, at least for now. She had to figure out how to remotely operate the shuttle.

"I can't do this," Dee whispered.

"Yes, you can," Sierra said.

The creature wandered to a planter near the center of the courtyard. It vomited onto the base of a blackened tree trunk, which began smoking. The creature's mouth extended forward, gnawing on the stump.

"Gorgers consume organic material," Sierra whispered.

"What are you talking about?" Reggie hissed.

"It's something the caretakers said." She pointed. "Those things are the gorgers. They have to be."

"That's bullshit," Reggie spat. "They're animals. How could those things send the Ender?"

Sierra shrugged. "I don't know."

"Maybe they have different variations," Priya said without looking up. "Maybe these are just workers or something." She didn't believe these creatures had sent the comet either, but Sierra's conclusion felt sound. The caretakers had told them gorgers took over Earth, and these creatures had done that, at least here in D.C. For now, they needed a name, and it fit.

She brought up the map of Earth and navigated to the shuttle. She still couldn't select it, no matter what she tried, probably because the carriage wasn't docked inside.

Lightning flashed overhead, followed by a boom only seconds later. Dee squealed.

"We should make a run for it," Felicia whispered. She pointed toward the south wall. "Back through the building."

"I ain't going back in there," Reggie said. "That's where Nick and Kelly got jumped. That's where Lauren was killed."

"If half of us run, that leaves room for the other half to fly out," Felicia said.

"Which half?" Carol asked.

"No," Jasmine said. "We just need to wait."

Thunder rumbled and the sky opened up. Raindrops pattered on the invisible bubble over them, rolling down the sides, giving it shape. The gorgers seem unaffected by the water. As they milled about the courtyard, a few more joined the one feeding at the planter, attacking the dead tree like pigs at a trough. Every few minutes, one vomited to soften the wood, then chomped on the steaming mess.

Barry gaped at the shape of the dome over them. "Can they see us now, because of the rain?"

Priya looked up. "Even if they can, I don't think they know we're here. I don't think they have object permanence."

"What does that mean?" Barry asked.

"Once something disappears, you forget it was there," Carol said. "If you can't see it, it doesn't exist."

The explanation seemed surprising coming from Carol, who didn't always have a mastery of object permanence herself.

"How the hell can something travel through space if it doesn't even have object permanence?" Reggie barked.

"I don't know," Carol said, even though his question had obviously been rhetorical.

Rain fell in sheets now, punctuated by flashes and thunder.

"We're going to die here," Dee said, her voice pitching higher. "One of those things is going to find us. I can't do this." She stood. The cloaking device showed a two-inch gap across her torso, right through her ribs.

"No, wait," Sierra cried.

Dee jumped out of the carriage and ran toward the south wall of the courtyard.

"Get back here," Sierra shouted.

Several gorgers turned toward the ruckus.

"Look, she's gonna make it," Felicia said, rising slightly.

Dee ran in a wide arc, avoiding the half-dozen gorgers on that side of the courtyard.

"No, she isn't," Reggie said.

Dee was almost to the wall, which was wide open, the glass windows long gone. Priya held her breath. If Dee could get through the building, she might make it. The pods were that way, and the sun was still shining off to the south.

Inside the building, a gorger dropped from the floor above and landed in front of Dee.

She slid to a stop, turned back to the courtyard, and sprinted. Her eyes were so wide they seemed to glow.

The gorger vomited, hitting Dee in the back. Momentum kept her running for three steps, then she fell on her face.

"Look away," David whispered. "All of you, look away."

Barry clasped his hands over his eyes. A few people turned their heads. Most continued to watch. Priya couldn't help herself. She reached reflexively in Dee's direction. Her fingers passed through the cloaking bubble and the ends disappeared. Water dripped from her fingertips when she drew them back in.

Smoke rose from Dee's body, swirling in the rain. The gorger's pincers clamped on her calves and it dragged her, screaming, toward the building. She dug at the ground, her fingers clawing furrows in the dirt.

A dozen other gorgers scrambled over, surrounding her.

The carriage shook with sobs.

Cold sweat dripped from Priya's nose. She trembled. She could smell everyone's stress and fear, trapped in their invisible bubble.

"Anybody else want to make a run for it?" Cameron asked quietly. "If enough of you go, we'll have room to fly this thing."

"Shut up, Cameron," Sierra hissed.

Reggie jabbed his finger at Priya. "Where the hell is that shuttle?"

Priya had tried everything she could think of to select the shuttle. She needed help. She wanted to bounce ideas off someone. There was so much she still didn't understand.

"It's no good," Sierra said. "Even if she brings the shuttle to us, we can't get inside." She looked from Priya to Cameron to David. "The entrance is a hundred feet off the ground, remember?"

"Goddamn it," Reggie said. "We never should have gotten out of those pods. We should'a stayed in them, asleep."

"That's it," Priya said. "I can bring the pods to us. That's easy." She selected all thirteen, and then scrolled across the map to an icon representing the carriage, where she double-tapped the closest spot available on the interface. "Done."

"How long will it take?" Barry asked.

The white circles moved along a dotted line a few inches from her nose. "Just a couple of minutes."

A break appeared in the clouds and the gorgers cleared the courtyard, retreating to the shadows.

Down by the south wall, Dee was gone.

"Everyone listen," Sierra said. "We need to be smart about this and we need to work together. When those pods get here, nobody runs off."

Several people nodded.

"Here they come," Kevin said, pointing up with his good hand.

All thirteen pods descended into the courtyard. They landed in an evenly-spaced pattern to the west of them. The nearest one was five meters away, in the shadow cast by the wall.

Priya felt as if the wind had been knocked out of her. The pods were *all* in the shadows. A few gorgers wandered among them without any real interest.

"Move 'em closer," Reggie growled.

"I can't," Priya growled back. "That's the only destination it will let me choose." The controls simply weren't precise enough.

"Quiet," Sierra whispered. "Here's what we need to do. The strongest people will run to the pods. Reggie, Felicia, Elizabeth, and Grace."

Elizabeth and Grace looked lost without Dee and Lauren. The four women had been inseparable.

Sierra gestured at the sling holding Kevin's arm. "Can you make it?"

He tilted his head. "I don't run with my arms."

"What about Priya?" Felicia asked. Priya froze, hating to feel the spotlight on her, and hating Felicia for putting it there.

Sierra shook her head. "We need her to operate the device."

Priya exhaled. She was valuable. She wouldn't have to leave the carriage. But most importantly, Sierra was making the right decisions. Decisions that would get them through this.

"I'll go too," Jasmine said.

"Are you sure?" Sierra asked.

Jasmine's face grew solemn. "I may be big, Shug, but I can haul this ass when I need to."

Sierra smiled.

Felicia glared at her. "So you get to stay here where it's safe and tell the rest of us what to do?"

"It doesn't matter," Reggie said. "The pods are all in the shadows. Those things will kill us."

More than a dozen gorgers wandered between the pods now.

Sierra took a deep breath. "I'm going to lure them away." She pointed to the right of the pods. "Up there."

Everyone turned to look. A large chunk of the building along the north end of the courtyard had collapsed, leaving a pile of rubble sloping up to the fifth floor. Hollow shells of rooms were visible beyond the pile, with jagged edges where their floors and walls had been. Water vapor rose from the concrete slope, creating the impression it was smoldering.

"That's suicide," Reggie said.

Sierra pressed her lips together, then continued. "Not while the sun is out. If I run up there, I can draw them along the side of the slope, in the shadows. If you all clear out fast enough, David and Cameron can fly up and get me before the clouds return." She looked at David. "Can you do it?"

He nodded. "Yeah."

"*Estás loca,*" Felicia muttered.

Priya's heart rose in her throat. She fought to swallow. "Cameron, hand her your gun."

Cameron made a bitter face. "I never hand over my gun."

"Give it to her," Priya said, in a tone she'd never known she could produce. "Now."

Cameron extended the gun to Sierra, grip-first, while glaring at Priya. Normally, she would have looked away, but she held her gaze. Sierra deserved that much, at least.

Chapter Sixty-Two

Kim sat in her tree, thirty feet above the ground. It was the only place she felt safe. Nobody could see her from directly below, and if someone tried to climb up after her, she could go another twenty feet higher. She wished there was some way to get Kona up there, too.

The binoculars were amazing. She looked into the window on the side of Randall's cabin, where she had a perfect view of the secret thing, though she couldn't figure out what it was. It just looked like an orange beach ball.

Below, Kona let out a friendly, *"Wooof."*

Kim opened her mouth to respond, but stopped at the sound of footsteps. Someone was down there. Whoever it was couldn't see her through all the leaves, but she couldn't see him or her either.

She swung the binoculars to look for Randall and found him walking back from the outhouses with Mr. Vaughn. Randall slapped him on the back and then headed toward his cabin while Mr. Vaughn headed toward one of the others.

A calm voice came from directly below. "Hey there, girl."

Kim relaxed slightly. It was Tyrell. She should have known. After all, Kona's greeting had been friendly.

Kim liked Tyrell, but she couldn't let him know she was up here. She didn't want to give away her hiding spot, and more importantly, Randall had told her if she talked to the new people without him, Kona would pay.

Lights flickered in Randall's window. Kim raised the binoculars. He'd split the orange ball in two. The top half sorta looked like one of those machines at a salon where old ladies stuck their heads in to dry their hair. Instead of sticking his head in it, though, Randall just stood in front of it. He seemed to be doing something to the bottom half with his hands, but his back blocked her view.

"What is this place?" Tyrell asked.

Kim froze. Did he know she was up here? She lowered the binoculars and inched along the branch until she found a tiny gap in the leaves where she could see all the way to the ground.

Kona lay on her back, legs spread out, while Tyrell scratched her belly. "Your girl Kim is scared to death, isn't she?"

Kim smiled. Tyrell was still talking to the dog. He obviously knew how to read people. Yes, she was awfully scared, but she wasn't going to let that stop her.

She raised the binoculars again. A bright blue octagon flew toward her face. She flinched, squeezing the branch with her free hand.

Nothing struck her. She brought the binoculars back and the object was still there, some kind of optical illusion. It looked like the octagon was floating inside the binoculars, even though it was way too big to fit. She turned the binoculars away from Randall's window and the shape disappeared. When she turned back, it was there again. Somehow, the floating octagon came from Randall's device, like a hologram, maybe. It was the weirdest thing.

"I wish you could tell me what's going on," Tyrell said. "It's hard to know what to believe."

Kona made the *woo-woo* sound she often made when someone stopped petting her. *More please.*

Tyrell laughed. "It's okay, girl. I'm one of the good guys. You can take that to the bank."

Kim's heart flip-flopped. She wanted to tell Tyrell everything she knew, everything that had happened, but at the same time, she wanted him to go away so she could concentrate on figuring out what Randall was doing.

"Now what are you up to?" Tyrell said.

Kim held her breath. That didn't sound like something he would say to Kona.

"I don't trust that guy one bit," Tyrell said. "Him or Randall." The sound of movement came from below.

She peeked between the leaves. Tyrell was gone. Kona whimpered.

Out near the buildings, Mr. Vaughn crept toward Randall's cabin, alone.

Kim looked around, wondering if she should do something, then spotted Tyrell again, through the branches on her left. He stayed on this side of the creek, moving parallel to the jerkface.

Mr. Vaughn paused thirty feet from Randall's cabin, then started up again, crossing the open ground. Randall was bad enough. If Mr. Vaughn teamed up with him, things would be worse.

He slowed as he got close to the entrance, then reached for the woven mat hanging over the doorway. His hand never made contact. A distant whine ripped through the air and Mr. Vaughn dropped to the ground.

Kim touched the back of her neck. Apparently, the orange ball thing could stun people just like the carriages. That was bad, but it wasn't terrible. As long as she kept her distance, she'd be safe.

Up the hill from her, Tyrell froze behind a tree trunk, keeping it between him and Randall's cabin. Kim focused her binoculars on him. Tyrell breathed hard, his eyes darting back and forth. She wished she could tell him it was okay. Randall didn't have any magic powers. He just had a weird alien device.

"Tyrell," Randall shouted.

Tyrell's eyes grew wide. Somehow, Randall knew he was there, even though he was standing behind a tree trunk.

Kim swung the binoculars back to the hut.

Randall stood at the entrance, looking in Tyrell's direction. "Go get the others," he shouted, his voice loud but calm. "They all need to see what happened here."

"You too, Kim," Randall said. "I know you're over there."

A sharp chill ran along her spine. Randall turned and stared in her direction.

She thumbed the focus knob and studied his face. He wasn't looking up at her, he was looking down below her. He couldn't see her, but he knew she was there. Somehow, he knew. She touched the back of her neck again.

The device. Randall's device must have an indicator that pointed out where everyone was. It was the only explanation that made sense.

"I seen you two talking," Randall called out. "That's a problem, Kim. You know the consequences."

The chill grew cold enough to stop her breath. When Tyrell was below her, it must have looked like they were together, talking, even though she was thirty feet above him.

She swung the binoculars over to Tyrell, who looked even more confused.

Kim began to tremble. If she tried to explain that she'd been up in a tree, Randall would figure out she'd been spying on him. She let the binoculars hang from her neck and clung to the branch with both hands. Or maybe he just wouldn't believe her. She was in trouble. Kona was in trouble. She had to do something.

Chapter Sixty-Three

David forced himself to breathe, slow and steady. They'd come all the way to Earth and Kim wasn't even here. Randall must have kept her in the village. He clung to the theory like a rope dangling over an abyss. The thought horrified him, but he had to stay focused. They had to get out of here so they could go back.

The clouds thinned, brightening the courtyard enough to send the creatures skittering back to the shadows. The rain stopped as well, at least for the moment.

"This is our chance," Sierra said. She looked around at others, packed tight in the carriage. "As soon as it's clear, get to the pods." Her eyes locked on his. "You gotta come for me." Her lips twitched.

He nodded. "We will."

As Sierra stood, the cloaking bubble bisected her for a moment, then she stepped down from the carriage. She stuck Cameron's gun into her waistband, grabbed the battered trash can lid, and took off.

"Get ready," David said, looking over his shoulder. Everyone knew the risk Sierra was taking. They damned sure better do their parts.

Sierra sprinted toward the pods first, where several of the creatures jostled one another. One puckered and puked in her direction, but she blocked the spray with the trash can lid. She turned and ran past the closest pods, keeping in the sunlight.

"Hurry," David whispered, urging her on.

Sierra ran along the building's shadow toward the rubble slope. The mass of creatures followed her, keeping on the shadow side. One ventured out, almost close enough to touch her, then scampered back.

The pods were clear. They still sat in the shadows of the western wall, but without any gorgers nearby.

"Out," David spat. "Everyone out."

Elizabeth shook her head. "I can't."

Sierra reached the mound of rubble spilling down from the north wall. She flung the trash can lid like a frisbee at the nearest gorger and started to climb, using her hands to pull herself onto one of the larger chunks.

Felicia touched Elizabeth's arm. "Yes you can. You got this."

Elizabeth nodded.

Felicia jumped out and led the way. Kevin followed, cradling his broken arm against his chest. Elizabeth and Grace went next, holding hands. They ran clumsily, but each time one of them stumbled, the other one caught her.

David scooted back, now that he had some room, and reached for the controls on the inside wall of the carriage.

Reggie helped Jasmine to her feet and they both climbed out. "Come on, let's do this."

Carol slid slowly out of Cameron's way. Barry scooted over to make room for her.

"Is that everyone?" David asked, praying they were light enough to take off.

"Yes," Priya said. "Let's go."

Out in the courtyard, Felicia passed into shadow and reached the first pod. She curved around it, slapping it as she went, opening it for someone else. She passed two more, slapping them as well. They split apart.

Gunshots barked, the echoes ricocheting around the courtyard. Sierra stood a quarter of the way up the rockfall, her legs wide, balancing on the rubble. In front of her, a gorger emerged from under a piece of concrete like a trap-door spider. Its legs clutched either side of the hole as it thrust its tube-like mouth toward her.

She fired again, and must have hit something vital, because it retreated into the crack.

"Hurry, Daddy." Barry gripped his shoulder.

"Lift off," David said as he touched the controls. He realized they hadn't discussed what they would do if the carriage still couldn't fly.

They rose from the ground. "Thank God," David said.

Barry hugged him from behind, holding on.

The six people who'd run to the pods had reached them, but the openings weren't wide enough to climb in yet. Felicia had slapped seven or eight pods and circled back, waiting as the tops rose.

A few gorgers noticed them and turned. The biggest one galloped straight for Jasmine.

Felicia picked up a fist-sized chunk of concrete. She planted her feet and threw, nailing the gorger from fifty feet away. It staggered backwards into the sunlight and swung around, as if trying to figure out what had attacked it.

"Nice," David muttered.

Over on the slope, Sierra was halfway up, putting more and more distance between her and the monsters, which bunched together in the shadows below.

"Steady ascent," he said.

"Steady ascent," Cameron repeated. They touched the controls and the carriage rose higher, but they wobbled, poorly synched, and Carol tumbled into David from behind. He jerked his hands from the controls to keep from accidentally triggering anything.

"Kevin's in trouble," Barry shouted.

David glanced down. "Where?"

Barry pointed to one of the closest pods. "He's in that one." A gorger ran right up to the pod. One of its forelimbs reached into the narrowing gap. Its neck pulsed. The pod closed, snapping off the end of its limb. The gorger wailed and vomited, waving its head around, spraying the smooth white surface.

"He's okay," David said.

"Felicia isn't," Priya said. "Look."

Farther back, Felicia climbed into a pod as a huge gorger charged straight for her. The pod was still wide open.

David glanced over at Sierra, who was near the top of the rubble pile. A mass of gorgers crowded the base on one side, still in the shadows. She held a chunk of concrete overhead with both hands and hurled it at the closest monster, knocking it into the creatures behind it.

Sierra retreated a few steps higher and picked up another piece of rubble. Full sunlight covered the cavernous hollow in the building behind her. She was in the clear, as long as the light held.

She'd taken a chance so the others could get away. He couldn't abandon her. But she'd also insisted they leave no one behind. There was still time.

"Left twenty degrees," David said, guiding them toward Felicia. "Down three feet." He and Cameron synced up better than before.

The giant gorger reached Felicia's pod right as the top half started moving downward. The creature placed two limbs on the edge of the opening. Its mouth aimed into the gap and it spewed ocher bile inside.

"*No.*" David flinched at the thought of lying in a pool of burning acid.

"Look," Cameron pointed.

Felicia rolled out the far side and fell to the ground. She scrambled to the next pod, which was still closed, and pounded on it.

The gorger sidestepped around the first pod, searching for her.

"Open faster," Carol chanted from the back of the carriage. "Open faster."

The top half of the new pod floated slowly into the air.

The gorger ran at Felicia. She darted around the pod, keeping it between them.

"Full speed," David said. "Hit it." They activated the controls in perfect unison and the carriage lurched forward, slamming into the monster.

Carol squealed.

Barry screamed in David's ear, "*Yeah!*"

Several of the gorger's limbs crumpled and bent over the front of the carriage.

"She's in," Priya said. "She's okay."

David glanced back, and for a split second, he saw Felicia, inside a pod. She looked terrified, but unharmed.

"Get to the slope," David said. "Circle one eighty." Cameron matched his movement, turning them back toward the center of the courtyard.

Two of the monster's feet were still hooked over the front of the carriage. Two more appeared, reaching, grabbing. Each limb ended in a curved black claw that clung like a grappling hook.

Cameron leaned back and kicked the closest claw with her heel. It didn't budge.

The pincers on the creature's mouth rose above the front of the carriage as it pulled itself up.

"Down, down," David said. They descended immediately. The nose of the craft dropped as they scraped the gorger across the ground below them. The limbs fell away with a wretched screech.

The carriage's nose stabilized, though David's stomach continued to tumble. He glanced over his shoulder, past Barry. Kelly had her arms and legs wrapped around Nick like a body pillow, keeping him stable. Priya was holding onto Carol, who looked blue. At least they were all still onboard.

He turned back to the slope. "Forward ascent." Now they just needed to grab Sierra and get the hell out of here.

"Oh shit," Cameron said.

The sunlight disappeared.

"Where is she?" David snapped. He looked up and down the pile of rubble.

Streaks of rain spattered the invisible dome covering them. Clouds blanketed the sky above them.

"Full forward," David cried. "Where the hell is she?"

Gorgers swarmed up the rubble slope.

Lightning flashed. Beyond the slope, the cavernous hole in the building was hairy with gorgers.

Sierra was gone.

Chapter Sixty-Four

Randall stood outside his cabin as everyone gathered in a wide half-circle, all of them keeping their distance. He shook his head. "I tried to warn y'all, but look what happened." He pointed at Mitchell's lifeless body on the ground, where he'd dropped like a two-flush turd. The fat bastard wouldn't be chatting with little Kimmie about anything now.

Wanda swayed on her feet. "I don't want to be here," she cried. At least she'd stopped whining about Judith.

"What do we need to do?" Jerry asked. He moved close to Wanda and put his arm around her. Randall licked his lips. Jerry would be in her pants by nightfall if he worked it right.

"You need to stay safe," Randall said. "That's what you need to do. You need to keep clear of this cabin."

"What happened to him?" asked Jordan. Christ, she even sounded like a cop.

"It looks to me like he came too close," Randall said with a shrug. "The aliens must have zapped him."

"Is he dead?" Dean asked.

Randall shook his head. "It's more like hibernation."

Dean started forward. "We have to help him."

Tyrell grabbed Dean by the arm and held firm. "Don't," Tyrell said. "It isn't safe."

Good boy, Randall thought. He'd been smart to keep the negro around after all.

Dean shook free. "Give me a break. There aren't any aliens."

Jordan stood with her arms crossed, which made her shoulders poke through the holes in her sweater even more. "Why did he come up here, Randall?"

"We'll never know." He kept his face blank, but anger swarmed in his chest. Her tone wasn't just suspicious, it was accusatory. She'd seen him go off by the outhouses with Mitchell.

Dean pointed at Randall and turned to face the others. "I think *he* killed Mitchell."

Randall's sphincter clenched. His demonstration had gone off perfectly, but this asshole was still challenging him. He forced himself to be patient. The show wasn't over yet.

"Why would he lie to us?" Gale asked. "Everything he's said turned out to be true." Randall swelled. *Thank you.* Miss Yoga Pants was gonna go places.

"Hang on," Tyrell said. "I think maybe Randall is an alien."

Randall had thought through a shit-ton of different scenarios about what his new villagers might say, but this was not on the list. He couldn't wait to hear more.

Tyrell pointed to the camping area. "I was over in the trees, watching Mitchell from a distance."

"You let him get killed," Dean said.

Tyrell looked genuinely hurt. "I was too far away to stop him. Honestly, I was too far away to be seen, and I was standing on the other side of a tree." He thrust his finger at Randall. "But he saw me. Somehow, he saw me, right through the tree."

Randall tensed his face so he wouldn't smirk. He loved this.

"That's why he doesn't want us near his cabin," said the frizzy-haired bracelet hippy. "It's where he changes his form."

Randall snorted. He couldn't help it.

Dean waved his hand. "Give me a break."

"Show us the aliens," Jordan demanded. "If they're real, if this really is an alien world, give us some proof."

Randall noticed movement in the sky behind her. Proof was on its way.

"Screw that," Dean spat. "There are seven of us and only one of him. Why are we putting up with this?" His chest rose and fell. He took a step closer.

Randall shrugged. "Come at me, bro."

The harvester drone flew in over the crowd. Its timing couldn't have been better.

"Look, look, look," The hippy pointed up, bracelets clanging. "Watch out, it's an alien."

Dean froze as the harvester descended.

Jordan stepped out in front of the group, her arms wide. "Nobody make any sudden moves."

Randall rolled his eyes. Detective Shoulder Holes actually thought she could protect them.

Gale pointed up. "Here comes another one."

"No, that's just a pod," Tyrell said.

The pod landed next to the cabin, more or less where Randall had sent it.

The harvester lowered two segmented arms toward Mitchell's body.

"We gotta stop that thing," Dean said, but he no longer seemed quite so eager.

"Why are you doing this?" Jordan called out.

Randall started to formulate a response until he realized she was shouting at the drone.

"We don't mean any harm," she continued. When the harvester didn't respond, she finally turned his way. "Can you make it talk to us?"

Randall shook his head. "I can't make it do anything." The lie came out smooth as butter. He'd ordered the drone to come pick up Mitchell right after zapping him. He couldn't quite figure out how long these things took. Sometimes they came right away, but sometimes they took fifteen or twenty minutes.

Everyone watched as the telescoping arms snaked under Mitchell and hefted him from the ground. Judging from the murmurs, most of them were sufficiently frightened.

Randall's plan had gone off perfectly, even with the last-minute swap from Tyrell to Mitchell.

He'd done it. The only thing missing was Kim. She was supposed to be here, but she wasn't in the crowd. No matter. He'd dole out her punishment later. He wondered what dog tasted like.

The harvester turned and floated to the pod, now open, where it placed Mitchell inside. Within seconds, they both rose into the sky and disappeared over the treetops.

"Anybody else want to come over here?" Randall asked, cool as a cucumber.

Dean still looked angry, but he didn't meet Randall's gaze. He looked sorta like Kona when she tucked her tail. Randall swelled.

"We're good," Jordan said, glancing at the others. "We don't want to cause any trouble and we don't want anyone else to get hurt."

"Thank you, Jordan. That's what I want, too." Randall took a step toward them. He'd done it. He'd gotten them under control. "Tell you what. Let's walk up to the canyon. I'll show you the giant rhinos." It would be their reward for obeying him.

"*No.*"

Randall froze, unsure who had spoken.

Kim pushed forward between two women. "We aren't going anywhere, you liar."

Chapter Sixty-Five

Sierra climbed down the back side of the rubble pile, heading into the cratered ruins of the building. When the clouds had returned, the wall of gorgers tracking her from the shadows surged up the slope. The monsters were going to reach the top before the carriage could get to her.

She'd gone deeper into the ruins, the only direction she could go, but it felt wrong, a descent into hell.

The caved-in building curved around the pile of rubble like the balconies of the Dolby Theater on Hollywood Boulevard. Each floor ended in a jagged edge, and most of the floors were crowded with gorgers.

Fortunately, the bottom looked clear.

She hopped down from one chunk of concrete to the next, fighting to keep her balance each time the rubble shifted. One bad slip would be a death sentence.

Back in the courtyard, the rubble pile sloped all the way to the ground floor, but on this side, it ended between the second and third floors. If she could get through the building, she could find her way to the street.

She dropped to her butt and slid down a twenty-foot slab of marble.

Three gorgers emerged from the darkness below on the right, their pale wormy bodies twisting upward, sensing her somehow. The bottom of the pit was no longer clear.

"Shit."

So much for getting to the street that way. She scanned the left side. Another gorger, one she hadn't noticed, had already started up from that direction and was even closer than the three on the right, maybe thirty or forty feet away.

You're in trouble. There wasn't anywhere to go. She glanced back up the slope, hoping to spot David and Cameron. *Right now would be great.* Instead, she saw the first gorgers cresting the peak from the courtyard.

Serious trouble.

All around her, each floor of the building ended abruptly where it had collapsed, and on each floor, gorgers stood watching.

Except one.

On her right, part of the fifth floor stuck out close to the rubble pile, just above her. Jagged iron twisted at the edge, and she thought she could use it to pull herself up to the room above, the only empty room in sight.

She climbed across the slope, working her way closer.

The fifth floor had once held a large dining hall. The metal frames of a hundred chairs lay scattered about. If she got up there, she might be able to use a chair to keep the creatures off her, like an old-fashioned lion tamer.

She only had to survive until David and Cameron got here. Hope spurred her faster, and she slipped on a wet chunk of concrete, skinning her palm when she caught herself.

Slow down. Keep your footing. She climbed up until she was even with the fourth-floor ceiling.

Twisted rebar protruded from the end of the rubble. She grabbed the closest piece, testing it, and reached for a second handhold.

A gorger appeared on the floor above, knocking a chair over the edge. Its worm-like head twisted toward her, three feet from her face. The chair clattered down the slope.

Sierra flinched away, trying to find some other place to go. The gorgers crawling up from the bottom would reach her in half a minute. A gurgling hiss came from behind. The ones coming down from the top sounded just as close.

Images of Dee getting torn apart flashed through her mind. She should have saved one last bullet. She looked for the closest gorger below her. She would jump onto it and tear it apart with her hands. She would go down fighting.

No.

She couldn't give up. She wouldn't. The ceiling of the room in front of her was damaged, and she spotted a few potential handholds. If she could crawl across the ceiling, she'd be out of reach. She unzipped her motorcycle jacket, freeing up full movement in her arms.

The gorger in the dining room above lowered its head, pincers wide. Acidic bile dripped from its mouth, just missing her.

Sierra jumped, grabbing the rebar directly below the monster. She swung forward and caught the sides of an I-beam with her bootheels, then shimmied further across the ceiling.

Gorger vomit pattered somewhere behind her, and the foul stench of ammonia wafted up.

On the slope, the gorgers crawling down from above converged with the gorgers climbing up from below. They jostled for position at the closest point, but they couldn't reach her. As long as she clung to the ceiling, she was safe.

How long can I hang here? Two minutes? Three? Her fingers were already trembling.

Rows of black metal shelves filled the room below her, most of them leaning against their neighbors like toppled dominoes. It had been a computer room, a server farm or something like that.

She looked for a rack that was still standing upright. If she could drop onto it, she could rest her arms and search for a way out.

Gorgers streamed in from the rubble, crawling over the server racks like crabs on an old jetty.

So much for dropping down.

She inched forward, gripping the beam with her fingers and heels, hanging over the server room the way she'd hung in the alien storage chamber. Her shoulders burned and her fingers throbbed. This was a hell of a lot harder in full gravity.

She made it another four or five feet before hanging debris blocked her path.

"Shit."

She turned her head back and forth, studying the space beneath her. She was out over the center of the server room. An eight-foot-wide crack split the floor right under her, with a dark maw below. On the far side of the crevice, the room looked empty. *Yes.* There weren't any gorgers on that side, and the ones that had followed her from the rubble might not be able to cross the chasm.

On the empty side of the room, a doorway led to a hall. Somewhere beyond, there had to be a stairwell to the ground floor, a way out to the street.

She lowered her feet from the beam. If she swung her legs enough, she thought she could drop and land on the far side of the chasm.

The gorgers behind her crowded each other to get close. One climbed up onto a desk and blew bile at Sierra's feet. She tensed and pulled her legs up. She tried to pull herself higher, but her arms wouldn't obey. Drops of acid sizzled on her boots.

Her fingers burned and her arms shook. Sierra roared. Terror and rage spilled out.

The sound of footsteps came from outside the server room. Shadows moved in the hall.

Please be the cavalry. Sierra pictured a squadron of soldiers blasting their way in.

The biggest gorger yet squeezed through the doorway.

Fuck. Her fingers were numb and rubbery. She couldn't hold on much longer.

Another dozen gorgers crowded into the room behind the seven-foot giant, hissing and clicking.

Sierra looked up. Maybe she could pull herself into the ceiling somehow. She could hide there until the gorgers cleared out. Until she got her strength back. Until the cavalry arrived.

She spotted an opening in the ceiling that she might be able to climb into, if she could somehow find the strength to pull herself up.

Below her, the big gorger rose, reaching for her with its front claws.

Sierra swung her legs until she got her heels back up to the I-beam, taking some of the weight from her hands. She inched toward the opening in the ceiling.

A shiny black talon broke through from the dining hall above.

No.

No. No. No.

She'd had a good run. She'd gotten everyone out of the zoo. She'd gotten close to Waldmire.

Tears blurred her vision. She looked down at the crack in the floor. If she could drop into the chasm, the fall would kill her, which had to be better than getting eaten alive.

"You're okay. We got you." The voice sounded like David's.

She craned her neck. No one was there. It was her imagination. A dozen gorgers swarmed below her in a blurry mess.

Blurry.

Sierra released her grip and dropped.

She landed on the invisible sled five feet down. It plunged from her impact. Hands caught her, holding onto her.

"Punch it," David shouted.

Sierra slid backwards, toward the edge of the sled, but Priya, Kelly, Carol, and Barry all held her tight.

They shot forward, knocking into one of the gorgers on the slope, sending it flying as they rocketed up over the rubble pile, out across the courtyard, and into open air.

Chapter Sixty-Six

Kim didn't know who to focus on. Dean was standing up to Randall and Jordan kinda seemed like she was taking charge of the situation, but Tyrell was the one she trusted. She wanted someone to help her, to keep her safe. She tried to stop shaking. She hadn't been this scared since Joe pointed a gun at her face.

Randall took a step back toward his cabin. His hand fidgeted inside his jacket pocket. He wouldn't shoot her in front of all these people, would he? He couldn't.

"What's going on here?" Dean demanded. Everything he said came out like a demand.

Kim took a deep breath. "He isn't an alien and he doesn't have any powers." She stood tall, which wasn't easy considering she was only fifty-two inches. She wanted to run back to her tree and climb to the highest branch. She pointed at the cabin. "He's got a device in there that can stun you if you get close. That's all." She exhaled. The words were out and there was no bringing them back.

Randall looked like he wanted to kill her. His hand shifted inside his jacket pocket, and something pressed against the fabric. It had to be a gun.

Dizziness crept up Kim's neck. She unlocked her knees. Before the schools shut down, one of the boys in her class had fainted during a comet assembly because his knees locked up. She was not about to let that happen to her.

The woman with all the bracelets crossed her arms. "A device? You're such a fake, Randall."

"Shut the fuck up, hippy."

"Harmony," she said, drawing out each syllable. She turned back to Kim. "What about the alien that picked up Mitchell? What was that?"

"It was a robot. He controlled it with the device," Kim said. "Make him move away from there, and you can go in and see for yourself. It can't hurt you unless he's operating it." She wasn't positive this was true, but she was pretty sure.

Randall took another step backwards. "She's a lying little bitch."

"What kind of man calls a twelve-year-old a bitch?" Kim asked. She felt powerful saying a curse word in front of all these adults. "He's a monster. He beat up a boy named Josh and tied him up so a dinosaur could eat him."

"Oh, come on, give me a break," Dean said.

A few people murmured agreement.

Kim's heart pounded in her chest. She shouldn't have mentioned the dinosaurs. She tried a different tactic. "Randall said he would kill Kona if I told you guys about this stuff."

"I've heard enough," Tyrell said. "This guy can't be trusted.

Jordan moved forward. "Randall, why don't you step away and let us have a look inside."

"It isn't safe," Randall spat. "I'm trying to protect you."

"Jordan," Kim whispered. She had to warn her about the gun.

Jordan made a little wave of her hand down by her hip. Kim knew what that meant. *Don't bother me, kid. Let the adults handle it.* She clamped her mouth shut, hoping Jordan knew what she was doing.

A hand fell on her shoulder. She looked up. It was Tyrell.

"Hey, you get away from her," Dean said, wagging his finger at Tyrell. He looked down at Kim. "You can't trust him, either."

She reached up and clasped Tyrell's hand. "Yes I can. He's one of the good guys. You can take that to the bank."

Tyrell tilted his head.

Kim gave him a small smile.

Jordan took another step toward Randall. She raised her left hand and patted the air. "It's okay. Everything's okay." The motion caused her sweater to rise up slightly, revealing a gun holstered at her side. Jordan's right hand remained down by her hip, just inches from the gun. "If you're telling the truth, Randall, step away from there and prove it."

Kim held her breath.

"I saved you," Randall said. He sounded desperate and small, which made Kim feel big.

"Yeah, you saved us," Jordan said, still creeping forward. "We all appreciate that. We aren't out to get you. We just want to understand what's going on." She'd covered more than half the distance to his cabin.

Harmony moved near the other two women and the skinny guy. The four of them stood off to the side, like maybe they didn't want to be all that close to Kim, in case Randall started shooting. The thought made her cold.

Jordan took another step toward the cabin. In one perfect motion, she drew the gun and began to raise her arm.

Something popped. Wet mist sprayed Kim's face, like someone had sneezed on her.

Way over in the trees, Kona barked.

A red blossom appeared on the back of Jordan's sweater. She crumpled to her knees, clawed the ground, and collapsed onto her face. Her gun tumbled from her hand.

Randall was gone. The mat hanging in the doorway to his cabin swung back and forth.

Wanda screamed. Kim screamed, too, but she was sobbing at the same time. All she could think was, *He shot her, he shot her, he shot her.*

Tyrell shoved past Kim and slid to the ground next to Jordan. "Oh my God, she's dead."

Dean ran up next to him and grabbed the gun.

Kim couldn't stop sobbing. It was her fault. She should have warned her about Randall's gun. She should have made her listen. No, she should have stayed in her tree. Jordan was dead and it was all her fault. He'd shot her, right in front of everyone, and now he was back inside, where the device—

The device.

"Get away!" Kim cried, flapping her arms. "Get away, quick."

Dean looked at her. "What? Why?" He waved his hand, just like Jordan had. *Don't bother me, kid. Let the adults handle it.*

Tyrell grabbed Dean by the wrist and jerked him back.

BBBBZZZZZZZZZRRRTTT!

The zipping sound came just as Tyrell and Dean scrambled away.

"Look out." Harmony pointed at the doorway, where a gun barrel nudged past the hanging mat. She turned and fled, leaving the other two women and the skinny guy behind.

Dean pointed Jordan's gun at the doorway and fired four times. Bursts exploded across the front wall of Randall's cabin. One shot punched a hole in the woven curtain. Randall's gun barrel disappeared.

Tyrell pulled Kim away. "Let's get you out of here." He got her moving, which was good, because she didn't think she could do it on her own. Even as they went, her eyes remained fixed on everything that happened.

Wanda dropped to the ground, sobbing.

"Randall, come out with your hands up," Dean shouted, like he thought he was a sheriff or something. "This is your last chance."

"Or what?" said the woman in the yoga outfit. "You gonna charge in there?" She shook her head and took a tiny step toward the cabin. "Randall, it's Gale. Let me in. We can work this out."

"Are you crazy?" Dean growled. "He just murdered her."

Gale gave him a side-eyed glare and hissed at him. "He shot her in self-defense."

While they argued, Tyrell maneuvered Kim to the closest empty cabin, at least sixty feet away. "Get inside," he said.

The cabin was almost halfway to her tree, where Kona was tied up. Kim wanted to run to her, but a pair of bracelet-covered arms grabbed her and pulled her in the doorway.

She shook free from Harmony's grip and looked back out. Dean still pointed the gun at Randall's cabin. Jordan's crumpled body lay in front of him. Beyond them, Gale was creeping forward and the skinny guy was trying to get Wanda to stand up.

"Throw burning logs in his windows," Kim said. Every cabin had two little square windows, high up on the side walls. "If the smoke gets bad enough, he'll come out and Dean can shoot him."

Tyrell straightened. "Damn, girl."

"If we don't do something, he'll kill us all."

"Okay, okay. You stay here."

Kim nodded, curling a lock of hair. The moment Tyrell left, she was going to run to Kona, but he didn't need to know that.

Gale stopped creeping toward Randall's door. She looked up. "Oh my God." A pod at least three times as big as the others floated down from the sky. "That one's big enough for all of us."

Wanda shook free from the skinny guy. "Yes, yes, yes," she said. "Let's all get in." She got to her feet. "We need to leave this place."

From the trees, Kona started barking.

The pod touched down off to the right of Randall's cabin, in the same spot as the one that had come for Mr. Vaughn.

Gale marched over to the pod and began slapping the side. "Open up."

"Is that the aliens?" Tyrell whispered.

"No," Kim said, trembling. "They don't ride in pods." She gripped his arm. It was the only thing to hold onto.

A line appeared around the equator and the top half started to rise. Something moved inside. Something big, like, dinosaur big.

Gale stumbled backwards.

A row of four-inch long jagged black claws appeared in the crack.

Chapter Sixty-Seven

Cameron co-piloted the carriage eighty feet in the air over the sandy desert that had once been the National Mall. Rain pelted the invisible bubble covering them. She reached back with one hand. "Sierra, you still got my gun?" A comforting weight landed in her palm.

"It's empty," Sierra said. "Sorry."

Cameron had expected as much. "Fair enough, I guess. You did save everyone." She thumbed on the safety and placed the gun in her lap. She still had four rounds in her other magazine, plus the firestarter round. After that, she was out. Using one hand, she ejected the magazine and swapped in the backup.

"Everyone?" Sierra asked.

"Every last one," Priya said. "They all got in the pods. Your plan worked. You did it."

Sierra exhaled. "Thanks for finding me. That was ... close."

Cameron glanced over her shoulder. Sierra looked wiped out. "Hey now, no emotional shit or we'll fly you right back there."

Sierra's mouth twisted into something that was half-smirk, half-grimace.

Cameron turned forward. It really had been close.

"Bless your heart," Carol said. "Everyone's safe because of you."

"Not everyone," David muttered.

Cameron placed her hand on his forearm. "We'll get Kim back. And I'll take care of Randall. You can be sure of that."

He squared his jaw.

"Is that really a spaceship?" Carol asked. The bulbous metallic teardrop floated above the sand a quarter mile ahead. Behind its tail, the pods landed in a grid, spaced out equidistant from one another.

"Yeah," Barry said. "It's cool inside. There's low gravity."

"We need to get everyone onboard right away," David said. "Twenty degrees down. Slow descent."

Cameron matched his moves. Working together, they landed in the sand halfway between the shuttle and the pods.

"Just a sec," Priya said. "I'll uncloak us."

Cameron didn't wait. She stood. Her belly and legs disappeared below the invisibility shield. Rain pattered her head. The water felt strange on the scar running through her hair.

Priya turned off the cloaking device and her legs reappeared, along with the carriage and everyone on it.

Carol held a liver-spotted hand over her mouth. Cameron chuckled. From below, she must have had a great view into her guts.

"David, we have to get the implants out of everyone before we go back," Sierra said.

"There's no time for that," he growled. "And I don't have any equipment."

"She's right," Cameron said. "Their whole security strategy is built around their ability to stun us. If we leave them in, we're helpless."

"We need to find something to use for anesthesia," Sierra said, helping Carol step down.

Kelly remained in the carriage with Nick, who was still unconscious. "Ice," Kelly said. "I'd give anything for some ice." Cloudy pus oozed from the acid burns on her leg.

Cameron surveyed their surroundings. The dense cloud cover would keep it dark for the rest of the day. They needed to leave before gorgers ventured onto the Mall. Fortunately, they had a clear view for a quarter mile across the sand in every direction. "Let's get everyone out of the pods and into the shuttle," she said. "Then we can figure out next steps."

"Are they all here?" Sierra asked.

"Yes," Barry said. "I counted. Thirteen."

That's all of them," Cameron said. "Most will be empty."

"I wanna open them," Barry shouted. He ran to the first pod, slapped it with both hands, and bent to peer through the gap as the top half rose. No one was inside.

Barry ran to the next one. Kevin peeked out. "It worked," he said, holding the amputated gorger leg. "The plan worked."

Barry took off for the next one. He slapped it and kept running, hitting two more.

Jasmine peeked out from one of the pods.

"Barry," David called out. "Get back over here."

Cameron scanned the horizon. There still weren't any gorgers approaching, but the sooner they got airborne, the better.

"I got him, Shug," Jasmine said, climbing out. "Barry, come here, Sweetie."

Barry kept running, almost to the farthest pod.

Back in the middle of the group, four spiny legs emerged from the pod next to Jasmine.

"Look out," Cameron shouted, but her voice was drowned by Elizabeth's scream.

Barry froze as a gorger slithered from the pod. Cameron raised the Beretta, but Barry was on the other side of the monster. She swung the barrel skyward. She couldn't take the shot.

Cameron raced toward them, moving diagonally, trying to get a clean line of fire. Each step felt weighed down, slowed by the sand.

The moment the gorger's last foot hit the ground, the creature sprang forward, knocking Jasmine onto her back.

The gorger's face inched toward her head, pincers stretched wide, like hedge shears. It lunged. Jasmine brought her hands up. The pincers sliced into her arms.

Cameron stopped, lined up her shot, and pulled the trigger twice, aiming high to avoid hitting Jasmine.

She was about to fire again when Reggie stepped in, reaching. He wrapped his arms around the creature's tail in a bear-hug and yanked it back. Cameron jerked her Beretta up again and ran closer.

Felicia appeared next to Reggie. She grabbed one of the creature's legs with two hands and pulled, dragging it sideways.

David circled around to the far side of the pods, putting himself between Barry and the gorger. He marched forward and kicked with his heel, snapping one of the animal's legs like a stick of firewood.

Sierra and Priya both grabbed legs. They pulled the creature away from Jasmine, who rolled clear, holding her arm against her chest. Grace and Elizabeth helped her to her feet.

Cameron ran up next to the gorger and placed her gun on the top of its head. She fired a single shot straight down.

The gorger slumped. Jasmine marched toward it, blood pouring from her sliced arm. She stomped the end of the creature's mouth, crushing it beneath her foot. "Don't you mess with us, you ugly maggot!"

Chapter Sixty-Eight

Tyrell's pulse pounded in his ears. On the far side of Randall's cabin, the top of the giant pod continued to rise, now two feet above the bottom. A snout appeared in the gap, thin nostrils flaring at the end.

"What is that?" he whispered. "Is it … a dinosaur?" He hadn't believed it before, but now he wondered if all that talk about dinosaurs might actually be true.

"Yeah," Kim answered. "I think so." Her eyebrows rose toward each other.

Over by the pod, Gale backed away slowly, as if she thought running might draw its attention.

The snout pushed through the gap and opened wide. The creature's jaws were as long as Tyrell's arm and filled with teeth the size of steak knives.

Wanda screamed.

Jerry bolted for Randall's cabin, leaving her behind.

Wanda started running too, but instead of following Jerry, she headed for the other cabins.

"That's right," Tyrell whispered. "Come on, this way."

Dean backed up right as Wanda passed behind him, crashing into her. They both fell in a heap.

Tyrell's legs felt like stone. He knew he should go help them, but a primal instinct kept him frozen in place. There was a goddamn dinosaur out there.

Jerry disappeared into Randall's cabin without being shot or stunned.

Gale gave up on moving slowly. She turned and ran.

The creature burst from the pod. It looked more like a crocodile than a dinosaur, but it wasn't low and flat like a croc. It carried its twenty-foot body up off the ground, like a wild dog.

The monster turned its jaws sideways and charged at Gale, grabbing her.

In one quick motion, the dog-croc thing jerked its head and Gale disappeared down its gullet. She was gone, nothing left. There wasn't even any blood.

Air spilled from Tyrell's lungs, gasping, groaning. *God, no.*

Dean pulled Wanda to her feet.

Tyrell's chest prickled, deep inside. He had to do something. He'd only been in the Air Force a few weeks, but he'd sworn an oath on the first day. He'd promised Dodge.

He ran forward across the open ground, grabbed Wanda by the hands, and pulled her back toward the other cabin.

Dean raised the gun and fired, emptying eight shots into the creature.

Tyrell shouted, "Come on, Dean!" A handgun wouldn't hurt anything that big. It had to weigh a ton.

The creature plowed into Dean like a truck. He flew, screaming, and landed in a tumbling heap.

Tyrell shoved Wanda into the cabin with Harmony and Kim. "Keep quiet."

He turned back for Dean, who was dragging himself across the ground. His legs weren't moving. *Jesus.* It looked like his spine was broken.

The monster pounced on him. Six-inch teeth punctured his leather jacket, crushing him. The creature shook its boxy head, flinging blood everywhere. It bent and ate, grabbing with the side of its mouth like a crocodile.

Tyrell held onto the doorframe and dry-heaved.

The dog-croc looked around and cackled. The goddamn thing sounded like it was laughing.

Hoarse barks came from Tyrell's left. *Kona.* She'd been barking this whole time, but the sound hadn't registered. He peered around the wall. Kona was still tied to the tree where he'd petted her. She pulled desperately at her leash, all four legs straining.

"Hush, girl," Tyrell begged.

The crocodile-dinosaur-dog-monster looked up from the wet mess of Dean's remains. Tyrell sank back through the doorway, praying it hadn't seen him. It started off toward Kona, but then got distracted when it stumbled onto Jordan's body.

Kona continued barking.

"Quiet, girl," Tyrell whispered. "Please be quiet."

Kim clenched his shirt. "You have to do something. You have to help her."

The horrible braying laugh came from the creature again, then the sound of wet smacks and crunches.

Tyrell knew he should stay inside and keep quiet, but he couldn't shake the image of Kona, tied to that tree, helpless. If the monster went after her, there was nothing she could do, and if she kept barking, it was sure to go after her.

"You three, keep quiet," he said. They'd be safe in the cabin, as long as that beast didn't come this way.

He took a deep breath and sprinted toward the tree.

Kona grabbed her leash in her mouth and jerked her head back and forth, whimpering.

Tyrell leaped over the tiny creek without slowing.

Kona dropped the leash and squealed, high-pitched and terrified.

He didn't need to look back to know why. The monster was coming for him. He ran faster.

The leash wasn't tied, thank God. The end was merely looped over a stubby knob three feet up the trunk. He slapped it loose as he ran past the tree. *You're on your own, girl.* It was all he could do. The dog howled and ran to beat the devil.

A second later, the tree shook as the dinosaur crashed into the trunk. Leaves rained down all around.

Tyrell ran back across the creek, toward Randall's hut. If he could get the thing to attack Randall, maybe the asshole would stun it, the way he'd stunned Mitchell.

No.

He knew better. Randall would stun *him.*

He swerved left. If he got too close to the hut, Randall would knock him out and the dog-croc would eat him right where he fell.

Bursts of light flashed in the high window, along with pops of gunfire.

"Fuck." The shithead was shooting at him. Shots whizzed by. Tyrell swerved farther left, past the back wall of the hut, where there weren't any windows.

The dinosaur's big pod sat on the other side of the small building, its top half still floating in the air.

The dog-croc splashed across the creek behind him.

Was there some way to send the creature back where it came from? Tyrell reached the pod, which seemed even bigger up close. The bottom half was as high as his shoulder. He glanced back.

The creature was right there. It lurched toward him, mouth open. Tyrell raced around the pod, keeping it between him and the dinosaur. The monster's jaws chomped, spraying him with spit.

He circled to the opposite side of the pod. The creature rose up, peering through the gap between the two halves.

"Yeah," Tyrell shouted. "Come and get me." If it crawled inside, the pod might close and carry it away.

BANG!

A gunshot pinged off the pod next to Tyrell's hand. Randall was shooting out the window on this side now.

Hot anger boiled in his chest. And fear. He was going to die here.

He grabbed the edge of the pod, pulled himself up, and crawled inside. It was the only place to go. He slid down into the concave bowl, shielded from Randall's gunfire. Bitter odors filled his sinuses, like in the reptile house at a zoo.

The creature grasped the far edge of the pod, blood and saliva dripping from its jaws.

"Come on, fucker. Climb in."

Once it was inside, he would tumble out and sprint toward the village wall. If he kept the pod between him and Randall's cabin, the asshole couldn't shoot him.

The creature's jaws pushed into the pod. Its breath stank of fetid decay.

Tyrell scrambled back on his elbows as the mouth reached for him. The dark ceiling above felt close, tight.

It's lowering. The top half was descending toward him.

An ember of hope flared. He remembered the shirtless bigot in Colorado Springs who got his legs sliced off. "Come on, close faster," Tyrell shouted.

Another gunshot hissed by. *Fuck you, Randall.*

The creature reached in. A talon landed on Tyrell's leg. He kicked with his other foot and screamed through clenched teeth as the claw dug into his flesh.

Everything grew darker as the top half of the pod lowered. The dinosaur's head pushed closer. The claw dragged Tyrell toward its jaws.

Wet snapping sounds came from the monster's throat. The top of the pod bit into its neck and kept descending. It thrashed, tons of scaly flesh jerking violently, but the pod continued to close.

The talon dug deeper into his calf. He screamed and jerked, which made the pain worse.

Crunching sounds came from the monster's neck.

The gap was now less than two feet.

The dinosaur's grip relaxed. Tyrell pulled his leg free, gasping at sharp pain, and crawled to the closest edge. He had to get out. He just needed the dinosaur's thick neck to hold the pod open a few seconds more.

But the top half kept lowering. When Tyrell reached the edge, the gap was too tight to fit through. He pushed back so he wouldn't be crushed. The light faded.

Pops and splashes came from the dinosaur's neck. Sticky wet fluid pooled at the bottom of the pod. As the two halves connected, the monster's severed head rolled against Tyrell's legs.

All light vanished, sealing him in darkness.

Chapter Sixty-Nine

The knife shook between Sierra's thumb and forefinger. The snow around her was red with blood. Frigid air stung her nostrils, but rays of bright sunshine warmed the back of her hand.

Greenland's ice sheet was a perfect gorger-free waystation, with glaring sunlight and nowhere for the creatures to hide. Plus, they'd found some supplies in the beached remains of a fishing boat a hundred miles from the nearest shore, where it must have been washed up by a tsunami.

Sierra steadied her hand. She'd watched David perform the surgery six times now, including on his own son. Now it was his turn.

She could do this. She had to.

David lay on the carriage in front of her, his head hanging over the edge. Priya had used the control device to stun him. The cloaking bubble bisected his neck, so that from outside the sled, only his head was visible, floating in the air.

From the inside, Sierra could see David's body, along with the top of his head on the outside, but right where it passed through the bubble, a two-inch cross section was rendered invisible. It created a gap in David's neck, revealing skull, tendons, and muscle.

She nudged his head until the implant was visible, took a deep breath, and pressed the knife blade forward. Blood dripped onto the edge of the sled as she sliced into David's flesh. She pressed further, and the tip of her blade appeared next to the implant.

The cloaking device allowed them to perform the surgery without exploratory cutting, because they could see the implants beneath the skin.

She wished someone else was doing this, but David said he trusted her. He told her she'd done a good job helping him with Charlie. Neither of them mentioned the fact that Charlie didn't survive.

"You're doing great," Felicia said, handing her another knife.

Sweat rolled down Sierra's back under her clothes, and for the first time since they'd landed here, she wasn't cold. She slid the flat end of the second blade alongside the first and widened the edge of the cut. The throbbing in her own neck grew worse, as if in sympathy. "There," she whispered.

Felicia reached in with a pair of needle-nose-pliers and grabbed the implant on her first try. The moment she pulled it free, David moaned, no longer stunned.

Cameron was ready with a handful of snow, pressing it against the back of his neck.

"Jesus, that hurts," David hissed.

"Lie still, Ace," Cameron said. "We've all been through it."

Felicia handed Sierra a modified fishhook that had been threaded with old nylon string, both of which had been scavenged from the boat.

"This is the worst part," Kevin said.

Sierra glared at him.

Cameron removed the bloody snow and Sierra fed the fishhook through David's skin. He hissed. She pulled the brittle nylon fibers through until the knot caught, then made a second loop and a third.

"Ice," Sierra said, sliding the fishhook off the line.

Cameron held snow against the stitches for a few seconds, then pulled it away so Sierra could tie the remaining string into a knot. Felicia snipped off the excess.

Sierra exhaled. "That's it."

She climbed out of the carriage and walked to an untouched patch of snow, where she scooped up a handful and placed it against the stitches on the back of her own neck. It helped, a little.

"Is he good?" Reggie asked, his face pale.

Reggie had endured his own procedure with barely a grunt, but couldn't handle watching anyone else's. After the second operation, he'd wandered off to puke on the far side of the shuttle.

Sierra started to nod, which sent a spike of pain through her head, then gave Reggie a thumbs-up instead. A blast of cold air gusted across the ice, wicking sweat from her skin. She shivered and zipped up the front of her leather jacket. Priya claimed it was warmer here than it used to be because of the Ender, but it was still plenty cold.

The thirteen pods glistened in the glaring sunlight. Five were closed. Their group was down by six people.

Nick and Kelly had been sealed in a pod together, where hibernation would hopefully preserve them until David could figure out some way to treat their injuries.

The moment Jasmine had realized that was an option, she gave Reggie a half hug and climbed into a pod herself. David had done his best to bandage her, but Jasmine's arm had been sliced to the bone in two places and she was in miserable pain.

Sierra ached at the thought of losing her. Reggie seemed even more distraught. He'd stood watching with clenched fists and a trembling chin as Jasmine's pod closed.

When David began removing implants, Elizabeth, Grace, and Carol had declined the procedure and opted to be put in pods, too. Sierra tried to change their minds. They couldn't afford to lose anyone else.

Cameron had ended the discussion with a harsh yet undeniable comment. "They wouldn't be much help anyway."

Only eight people remained, which hardly felt like enough. Priya, Cameron, Reggie, Felicia, and Kevin were all that were left from the village. From the first island, it was just Sierra, David, and Barry.

Kim would bring the total to nine.

Barry lay curled up beside Priya under some tattered blankets they'd found in the wreckage of the fishing boat. Somehow, the boy had managed to fall asleep. Sierra was jealous.

She nodded toward the device in Priya's lap, then winced in pain. *Ugh.* She had to remember not to nod or shake her head. "Any luck finding Kim?"

"No." Priya's shoulders sagged. "I can connect to the ship for some things, like storage, but I can't see anything on the islands."

David's face tightened. "What if she isn't there?"

"We'll find her," Cameron said.

The others gathered around. "Do we have a plan?" Felicia asked.

"Yeah," David said. "We need to leave. Now. We'll figure out the rest on the way." He looked pale, and Sierra didn't think it was just from the slice in his neck.

Cameron placed her hand on his shoulder.

"That's assuming we can even get back onboard," Reggie said.

"I believe we can get back," Priya said. "They haven't shut off access to this device. They haven't done anything to deactivate the shuttle." She pointed at the cluster of bloody implants lying in the snow like tiny robot tadpoles. "They really are dependent on those things to control us."

"You sure?" Kevin asked.

Priya glowered.

"She doesn't like that question," Sierra said. She turned to David. "We'll find Kim. We won't give up. If she isn't in the village, we'll keep looking until we find her."

They stood quietly for a moment.

Reggie broke the silence "Let's get moving, then. Gotta do as we can."

"What do we do after that?" Felicia asked. "Are we going to stay on the islands?"

"No," Sierra said, looking around. "We take back Earth."

She was met with dubious faces.

"You got a plan for that?" Felicia asked.

"Gorgers can be killed," Cameron said. "We killed several already."

"Yeah," Sierra said. "They're jackals and vultures, nothing more."

"There's an awful lot of them," Kevin said.

Sierra took a deep breath. "We need answers. The caretakers must know more than they've told us. They said the gorgers sent the Ender. How can that be possible? They're mindless bugs. How did they even get to Earth?"

Felicia nodded, then winced at the motion.

"What makes you think the caretakers will help us?" Reggie asked.

Sierra sighed. She'd lost hope that she could convince the aliens to work with her. "The gorgers are their enemies," she said. "They must have some idea how to defeat them. We'll make them help."

Reggie held her gaze. "Okay."

Sierra turned to Priya. "Can you send these pods to storage?" They had decided the people in them would be safer in storage than here on Earth, at least for now.

"I'm on it," Priya said.

Sierra turned to David. "Let's go get your daughter."

Chapter Seventy

The giant pod lifted into the sky, leaving behind the headless croc-monster. Randall stood on his tiptoes so he could see out the window. He licked his lips. Fresh meat for supper.

"What happened?" Jerry asked from the opposite corner of the cabin, where he'd been ordered to sit. He hadn't moved an inch and he'd barely said a word.

Smart kid.

"The pod decapitated that fuckin' thing," Randall said.

The croc-monster's spine was a white knob in a circle of glistening meat.

"Tyrell?"

Randall grinned. "He got stuck inside. He's gone. Jordan and Dean are both dead, too. Everybody who tried to make trouble is gone."

Well, almost everybody.

Jerry exhaled. "Who's all left?" Nervous uncertainty danced across his face. "Did Wanda make it?"

Randall leaned over his device, allowing the light beams to fill his eyes. "Yeah. She's in the next cabin with Kim and Harmony." He zoomed out. He couldn't find Gale, which sucked. She'd been his favorite.

"What do we do now?" Jerry asked.

"I don't know," Randall snapped, annoyed at being rushed. "Let me think."

Jerry shushed.

What he wanted to do was slap the living shit out of Kim. The little bitch had ruined everything. But he couldn't lose his cool like that in front of Jerry.

Nevertheless, Kim had to go. Randall tapped the device and ordered an empty pod, human-sized this time. Then he returned to the map and navigated to the island where he'd sent the saber-tooth tiger. He checked dot after dot, searching for Dave and Cameron, but couldn't find them. He couldn't find the saber-tooth either. Just a whole mess of those finback dinosaurs.

He didn't need Kim for insurance anymore. Dave was dead. He had to be.

Randall zoomed back to his island and made sure the three females were still in the other cabin. They hadn't moved. They were probably waiting until dark to sneak away. It's what he would have done. He sighed. He needed to put all three of them in the pod together and start over. They couldn't be trusted.

It was all about trust.

Randall turned to Jerry. "Can I trust you?"

Jerry nodded, with a little too much enthusiasm.

He wanted to trust Jerry. He *thought* he could trust Jerry. Sometimes you could just tell about people, but he wasn't quite there yet.

He had to be sure. He couldn't spend the rest of his life jittery and nervous that Jerry would turn on him, the way he himself had turned against The Piper.

In the movies, the boss always made his men prove their loyalty by killing someone.

Randall walked over to his little armory, in the opposite corner from where he'd made Jerry sit. He picked up a semi-automatic handgun and the AR-15. He extended the pistol to Jerry. "Get up. We need to go deal with our problems. Are you with me?"

Jerry stared at the gun, then Randall. He nodded and took it.

"Be careful. The safety's off." Randall gestured toward the exit with his rifle. "Let's go."

He let Jerry lead the way. The ground outside the cabin was muddy with blood. It was still light out, but nighttime had to be coming soon.

The pod he'd ordered for Kim floated in and landed over near the dead croc-monster. He glanced to make sure it was empty, then followed

Jerry to the other cabin. They stopped twenty feet from the entrance.

"Everyone out of there," Randall shouted at the doorway.

"What are you going to do?" came one of the voices. It sounded like the hippy.

"I'm sending you away," Randall shouted. "I can't trust none of you."

Muffled arguing came from inside the hut, which meant they were talking about it.

Jerry looked at him. "Even Wanda?"

"Maybe," Randall snorted. "If so, we'll find you someone else."

Harmony came out and stood in front of the opening. Randall licked his lips. Perfect.

"Let us go," she demanded.

"You can go," Randall said. "Go get in that pod."

"No." Harmony actually wagged her finger at him, which made those annoying bracelets jangle and clack. "We'll leave and you can have the village," she said.

"Is that a fact?" Randall raised the AR-15, but instead of aiming it at her, he slung it on his back, leaving his hands empty.

It was obvious from Jerry's darting eyes that he was wondering what he should do. Randall couldn't wait to find out himself.

He took a long, deep breath and then spoke quietly. "Jerry, shoot that hippy bitch."

"Are you insane?" Harmony's hands dropped to her side, like she was trying to make herself small. It worked. She seemed tiny. Insignificant.

Jerry studied his gun, clearly unaware that it was unloaded. This was the perfect test. If he pulled the trigger, Randall would know he could be trusted. If Jerry tried to shoot him instead, well, that's why he'd brought the AR-15.

"I never killed anyone," Jerry stammered. His gun trembled, but he kept it pointed more or less at Harmony.

"Listen, Jerry, she's refusing my order," Randall said. "That can't be permitted." He stared at Jerry. "Are *you* refusing my order?"

Jerry frowned.

Harmony's mouth dropped open. Her eyes grew huge.

"On three," Randall said. He counted fast, eager to get it over with. "One, two, three."

An empty metallic click echoed through the village as Jerry pulled the trigger.

The dark stain of piss spread across Harmony's hippy paints. An angry scowl grew on her face. Her hands tightened into fists.

Randall grinned and brought the AR-15 off his shoulder. "You passed the test, Jerry."

Jerry raised the gun in front of his face, breathing hard. "It's empty?"

Randall tilted his head. "I just had to make sure I could trust you, that's all."

He raised the long gun to his shoulder and aimed it straight at Harmony. "Everyone out, right now, or I really will shoot her. This one's loaded."

He must have been convincing, because Wanda and Kim both came out, with Kona leashed at Kim's side. The dog let out a low growl.

Randall licked his lips. He finally had control, and a loyal lieutenant to help him keep it. "Here's how it's going to go," he said. "Kim and Miss Piss-Hippy are gonna get in that pod over by my cabin. Wanda, you can stay, but only so long as Jerry wants to keep you."

"No." Kim shook her head. "You're done."

Randall laughed. The defiant little bitch still hadn't learned her lesson.

"How you gonna stop me?"

Kim smiled. "I'm not. My dad will."

"Your daddy ain't—"

Kim's eyes danced up, just a hair, to the air behind him.

A loud zipping noise surrounded Randall. He tried to turn, but his legs stopped working. The ground rushed up and everything went dark.

Chapter Seventy-One

David jumped down from the carriage and ran to Kim, shaking. He'd flown up behind a goddamn firing squad. He and Cameron had gotten just close enough to stun Randall and the guy beside him without also zapping Kim and the two other women.

It had been close. Too close.

He dropped to his knees and pulled Kim into his arms, tears in his eyes, hugging her as tightly as he could without hurting her. "Kimmie, Kimmie."

Kona barked and bounded into them, licking David's face and wagging like mad.

"Is Barry okay?" she asked.

"Yes, he's fine, he's fine." Fresh tears flowed.

The two women bombarded him with questions.

"Who the hell are you?"

"What's going on?"

"Are you with the aliens?"

David pushed Kim out to arm's length. "Who are these new people? Can we trust them?"

She nodded, then pointed to the guy on the ground next to Randall. "Not him, though." The words came out dark and angry. Kim's cheeks flushed and her nostrils flared.

Cameron stood over Randall. She drew her gun and pointed it at his skull.

"Wait," David said. He wanted her to shoot him. He almost told her to do it. But he didn't want Kim to watch Randall's brain explode across the ground. "Just get some vines and tie them up for now," he said finally.

Cameron's eyes narrowed. After a moment, she stepped away.

"Search them, too," Sierra said as she climbed down from the carriage. "Get everything out of their pockets."

"Cinch them tight," David added through gritted teeth. He leaned close to his daughter, whispering. "Did he hurt you? Did he ..."

She shook her head. "No. He said awful things, but he never touched me." Her jaw worked silently. Her face looked hard, like she was steeling herself for something. She didn't look like Kim.

A cold ache filled David. He pulled her close again.

When he finally let her go, she looked at her arm, which was wet with a thin smear of blood. She'd been hugging his neck.

"What happened?"

"My implant was removed. It's okay. I'm okay."

Kim turned toward Priya, sitting alone up on the carriage, and her eyes lit up. For a moment, she looked like herself. "You got a device."

Priya peeked over the top of her orange half-sphere. "You've seen one of these?"

"Yes. Randall has one in his cabin. We need to get it." Kim gasped. "We need to get Tyrell back."

"Who's Tyrell?" Cameron asked. A thick knot of vines covered Randall's wrists and she was winding rope around the arms of the other man.

"Tyrell is one of the good guys. He saved me and Kona." Kim pointed to the headless body of a dinosaur on the far side of Randall's cabin. "He killed that thing."

"What's the deal with that pod beside it?" Cameron asked.

"He was going to send us away," Kim said. She pulled on David's arm. "We need to find Tyrell."

"Let's get your brother first," he said. He wanted all three of them together. The situation seemed more or less under control now. Sierra was speaking with the two new women, who looked terrified and overwhelmed.

"Where is he?" Kim asked.

David realized what seemed different about her. She seemed older. She even sounded more adult.

"He's on the beach with the others." He turned to Priya, who was monitoring them with her device. "Are they still okay?"

She gave him a thumbs-up. "The shuttle is still on the beach, and nothing has come near them." She couldn't actually track Barry or the four people with him, because their implants had been removed, but she was watching the area for carriages or any other creatures.

Cameron joined David and Kim, holding an assault rifle she'd taken from Randall. "I'll go with you." She winked. "Just in case."

David nodded and took Kim's hand. "Come on. I'll show you our new spaceship." He stopped and looked at her. There was so much he needed to share. "We've been to Earth."

Kim's eyes narrowed. "Is everyone ... Is anyone ... left?"

She was asking about her mom. David paused to make sure he could control his voice. "No. It's overrun. There are aliens there, except they aren't like the aliens here. They're like giant bugs." He didn't tell her about Dee or Lauren, or the people who had chosen to stay in pods. There'd be time for that later.

They started down the path through the fields, with Kona bounding along next to them. The dog's tail hadn't stopped wagging.

"Daddy?" Kim stood motionless.

"What is it?"

Her face let go. Everything she was holding in suddenly melted, and she was Kimmie again. "Thank you for—" Her voice cracked. "For coming back, Daddy."

David pulled her into his arms and held her. "Of course, baby. I'm so sorry I left you." He shook, crying. "I'm so, so sorry."

They stood holding one another until finally their sobs trailed off. David wiped the tears from Kim's face, took her hand, and together they followed Cameron and Kona to the beach.

Chapter Seventy-Two

Sierra leaned against the rock wall of the fire pit and held Josh's knife out in front of her, admiring the eight-inch blade. The grip felt like it was made for her hand, with a groove for each finger. They'd found the knife in Randall's hut, along with a cache of guns and an alien device. Sierra claimed the knife for herself. It was good to have something that belonged to Josh. He'd been so proud of it. He said his father had given it to him.

They'd taken care of everything for the night, except one final issue, and Sierra was steeling herself for that last task.

The two new people were caught up, more or less. Felicia had described everything that happened on Earth, along with most of what had gone down in the village before Randall took over.

Harmony and Wanda seemed dubious about some of the details, but that was okay for now. Soon enough, they would see that it was all true.

Everyone had gotten plenty to eat. They'd sliced hunks of meat from the decapitated dinosaur and seared them over the fire. It was rubbery and bland, like overcooked lobster tail, but there was more than they'd ever be able to finish.

David and Kevin were laying thin strips of extra meat on smoking racks to make jerky they could take with them. Barry helped with the fires.

All of Randall's guns were disassembled and lying on a blanket in front of Cameron. Reggie and Felicia were watching her put them back together, along with Harmony, the one with the frizzy hair and bracelets.

Cameron had agreed to give guns to everyone who wanted one after she cleaned them and inspected them. The onlookers were getting an impromptu lesson in firearms maintenance. Sierra had retrieved Joe's big revolver from the raft, where Priya had hidden it, back before they dove into the sea.

Priya and Kim sat side-by-side on the sled, with the two alien devices in front of them. Priya alternated between keeping watch of the area surrounding the village and trying to learn what she could about the mothership. She'd taught Kim how to use the interface, and the girl was searching through the pods in storage, looking for her mom and a guy named Tyrell who had apparently killed the big dinosaur. Wanda, the tall one with red hair, leaned in next to Kim so that several of the lights shone into her eyes. She was hoping to find her daughter.

Kim described the occupants of each pod. "Four from Minnesota. Six from South Dakota, or maybe Nebraska. Two, Minnesota again." Wanda marked a piece of wood with charcoal as Kim spoke, documenting their findings.

Every time Kim selected a new pod, her eyes sparkled with hope, and every time she saw strangers inside, that hope was crushed. Sierra wanted to tell her to save herself the heartache, but she knew nothing would stop the girl from going through the exercise. Maybe there was even something cathartic about it.

The majority of the pods had landed in a three-hundred-mile cluster centered more or less over southern Minnesota, with a long tail that thinned out as it spread southwest across the country. They didn't know why that location had been chosen, but Priya speculated the tail was due to some of the pods arriving after the initial group, and hitting the Earth as it rotated.

Sierra herself had been damn lucky. So far, Kim had only reported two other pods from California.

The good news was that the average occupancy was four, with some pods containing as many as eight people. That meant they'd have a larger group to help take back Earth, and eventually, a larger gene pool to draw from.

Felicia had organized a watch rotation for the night, so that everyone could get some sleep, in shifts.

Sierra couldn't think of anything else that needed to be done, except that one final task. Once it was completed, she would do her best to sleep. After they were rested, they would storm the ship and get answers. She walked over to the alien sled, which hovered a foot off the ground beside the large fire pit. "Have you found any more caretakers?"

"Just four," Priya said.

Reggie squinted at her "You're telling me this whole operation is run by only four aliens?"

"That's all I've been able to find," Priya said.

"I can handle four," Cameron said, snapping a metal piece into place on one of the guns.

"Wait," Harmony said. "Are we going to attack them? Are they friends or enemies? I'm so confused."

"They aren't friends," Sierra said. "They helped Randall murder people."

"Then why do we have to confront them?" Harmony asked. "Why don't we just go straight to Earth?"

"She's got a point," Felicia said. "Maybe we should get while the gettin's good."

"We need answers," Sierra said. "We need the caretakers to tell us everything they know about the gorgers if we want any chance of surviving on Earth."

David, Barry, and Kevin came over and sat down with the others.

"Why don't we just stay here?" Wanda asked. "You said this village was made for us."

"No," Cameron said. "It's a prison."

"Exactly." Sierra had been saying that all along. Hearing someone else say it felt affirming. "Earth is our home."

Wanda nodded slowly. "Okay."

"And the implants are really their only security measure?" Harmony asked.

David shrugged. "They never needed anything else. They never captured a species that could perform surgery or figure out technology."

"They did hide the exit to this place at the bottom of the sea," Kevin added.

Harmony rubbed the back of her neck, making her bracelets clink. "Can you remove my implant?"

"Be careful what you wish for," Kevin said. "It hurts like hell."

"Eventually," Sierra said. "For now, you'll stay in the rear guard. If you get stunned, we'll revive you."

"Don't worry. We got this," Cameron said, snapping two more pieces of metal together. She'd been in a splendid mood ever since finding Randall's arsenal.

"Is there anything else to do tonight?" David asked.

"Just one last thing," Sierra said. "I'll take care of it." She took a deep breath. It was time.

She walked to the bodies lying in front of the storage sheds, right at the edge of the firelight. Randall and Jerry lay side-by-side, hands bound, still in suspended animation. She knelt and pressed the knife to Randall's throat. Aching pain filled her as she remembered the bullet striking Waldmire's forehead, snuffing his life. She grimaced, trying to turn the pain into rage, so she could do what had to be done.

"What are you doing?" David asked.

"I'm taking care of our last problem," Sierra said.

Several people murmured. They sounded generally supportive.

The knife shook, scratching the stubbled skin on Randall's neck. Thin beads of blood glistened in the firelight. She remembered slicing into David's neck to remove his implant. Her stomach roiled. She would need to cut much deeper. She pulled the blade away and tightened her grip, mustering the courage to accomplish her task.

"Hold on," David said. "You can't do this."

"Watch me," she hissed, breathing hard. "He deserves it."

"I know," David said. "I'm not talking about him. I'm talking about you."

Sierra looked back at the others. Most of their faces were shrouded in black because of the glowing bonfire behind them.

"We have to deal with them," she said. "He killed people. Good people."

"I'm not disagreeing," David said. "I'm simply suggesting that we do this right." He lowered his voice. "We don't want to give our new friends the wrong impression about us."

Wanda reached across her chest and rubbed her arms.

The image of Joe executing Thad by the waterfall flashed in Sierra's mind. It had been her introduction to the villagers and had fouled her impression of them.

"We need to hold a trial," David said.

Waldmire's words came back to her, along with the hollow ache in her gut. *You don't execute people in public. You hold a trial.* Sierra glanced at Randall. "We can't wake them up. I'm not willing to take that risk."

"That's fine," David said. "The important thing is that we go through the motions. We all need to be a part of this, not just one person."

She slid the knife into its scabbard. "Okay. I testify that Randall killed Waldmire Bock, an innocent man." She swallowed and added. "He murdered my father."

Priya looked up. Prismatic colors from the device splashed the side of her face. "Wait, I thought you didn't know for sure that Waldmire was your father?"

"I don't know," Sierra said. "I believe."

Waldmire had goaded Randall into killing him. He'd done it to protect her. Who would do something like that? A father.

She shrugged. "If I'm wrong, what difference does it make? I believe because believing helps me." She looked down. "That's something Waldmire taught me about faith."

For a long, cold moment, no one said anything.

Harmony broke the silence. "I testify that Jerry tried to shoot me. He pulled the trigger. His gun was empty, but he didn't know it. He meant to murder me."

"He did," Wanda said. "And Randall killed Jordan, too."

Kim nodded, her face dark.

"Randall also killed Morrie," Felicia said. They'd found two sets of charred remains outside the village. "Kill that motherfucker," she whispered.

Sierra's eyes grew moist. How many lives could have been saved if they had dealt with Randall earlier?

"Will anyone speak in their defense?" David asked.

Silence.

"I suggest that we find Randall and Jerry guilty," David said. "All in favor?"

Everyone said, "Aye."

The village grew still.

It had been a simple exercise, but somehow it took a weight off Sierra. She wasn't alone. "All that's left is sentencing," she said.

"Why don't we just leave them to rot?" Kevin said, looking around at the others.

"I like it," Reggie said. "Execution, without the executioner."

"That's no good," Sierra said. "We don't know what would happen if we left them like that, or how long it would take. Plus, the caretakers could revive them after we leave."

Priya called over. "Hey Sierra."

"We need some sort of prison," David said.

"We could use a pod," Kevin said. "Wouldn't that be like prison?"

Sierra shook her head. "We can't risk it. Again, the aliens might revive them." Nothing would change her mind on this subject.

"Sierra," Priya repeated.

"Just kill 'em both," Felicia said. "Be done with it."

Reggie grunted his approval.

"*Sierra*." Priya stood on the sled.

"What?" she snapped.

"We're about to have a visitor." Priya pointed into the darkness over the fields. "There's a caretaker flying this way."

Sierra drew the big revolver. "Bring 'em on. It's time to get some answers."

The story concludes in

PART III

BEASTS OF PREY

PREHISTORIC SPECIES

Tyrannosaurus rex (Tyrannosaurus carcass)

Entelodont daedon (Entelodont/ Wolf-Pig)

Coelodonta antiquaitatis (Woolly Rhinoceros)

Dimetrodon angelensis (Sailback)

Arthropleura armata (Giant Centipede)

Titanosaurus indicus (Titanosaur)

Homo neanderthalensis (Paleolithic Hunter)

Mammoth primigenius (Mammoth)

Megatherium americanum (Giant Ground Sloth)

Allosaurus fragilis (Allosaurus)

Stegosaurus ungulatus (Stegosaurus carcass)

Smilodon populator (Saber-Toothed Cat)

Razanandrongobe sakalavae (Dog-Croc)

THE PRESERVATION OF SPECIES

PART I

RULE OF EXTINCTION

PART II

STRUGGLE FOR EXISTENCE

PART III

BEASTS OF PREY

ACKNOWLEDGEMENTS

I couldn't have written this book without my family. Thank you Erin, Shannon, and Sydney for your patience, encouragement, and support. And also to River, who often lay curled at my feet.

My editor, Jacquelyn Ben-Zekry, really helped tighten this story. Her work made the book better.

Jim Stigall's excellent cover design sets the mood and entices the reader, all while balancing a tremendous load of words.

If you ever want to revisit this story, I recommend the audiobook. Stacy Carolan's narration truly brings these characters to life.

Special thanks go to Andrew Caldwell and Michael Smith for providing astronomical information. Their knowledge made the book stronger, though any inaccuracies should be attributed to the author.

Additional thanks go to my critique groups for help polishing the story: Heather Caspi, Dani Coleman, Heidi Farmer, C. R. Hodges, Steven Johnson, Laura Lauda, Katheryn Lumsden, Kyle Massa, Nathan Pipelow, Margot Romary, Jason Rush, and Neal Williams. Look them up and read their work.

I'm indebted to several devoted beta readers who offered valuable feedback: Greg Chiarella, Mike Giese, Jordan Itkowitz, Bill Jones, Christopher Jones, David Jones, Erin Jones, Shannon Jones, Sydney Jones, Nathan Stormzand, and Danny Talavera.

Thank you all so much for your time and your insights.

Finally, thank you, the reader, for coming along on this adventure. If you enjoyed *Struggle For Existence*, please take a moment to leave a review and share your thoughts on social media.

Every single review helps a book find its audience.

Now, steel yourself for excitement, heartbreak, and maybe even a glimmer of hope. *The Preservation of Species* comes to an epic conclusion in *Beasts of Prey*. David, Sierra, and all the rest discover the true nature of the gorgers and fight to bring humanity back from the brink.

Geoff Jones
Broomfield, Colorado